TRISTAN

PIRATE LORDS SERIES BOOK 1

ELIZABETH ROSE

D1519630

ROSESCRIBE MEDIA INC.

Cover created by Elizabeth Rose Krejcik
Edited by Scott Moreland

ISBN: 9798673829332

TO MY READERS

Tristan, my hero, and his brothers, Mardon and Aaron, are first mentioned in **Pirate in the Mist**, Book 1 of my **Second in Command Series** as the brothers of my heroine, Gwen. My hero, Brody, of that series was once the first mate of Rowen, the hero of *Restless Sea Lord* from my *Legendary Bastards of the Crown Series*.

Nairnie, Tristan's grandmother, was first seen in my *Seasons of Fortitude Series* and her backstory is first revealed in *Autumn's Touch – Book 3*.

Each of the books mentioned are stand-alone reads and you don't need to have knowledge of the previous books to enjoy *Tristan*. That said, if you want to know more in-depth information about these characters, it is always a good idea to read each of the series mentioned.

For your convenience, here is a list of the series that are related to my *Pirate Lords Series.*

The books in the Legendary Bastards of the Crown series are:

Destiny's Kiss – Series Prequel
Restless Sea Lord – Book 1
Ruthless Knight – Book 2
Reckless Highlander – Book 3

This is followed by the Seasons of Fortitude Series:
Highland Spring – Book 1
Summer's Reign – Book 2
Autumn's Touch – Book 3
Winter's Flame – Book 4

And this is followed by the Second in Command Series:
Pirate in the Mist – Book 1

Enjoy!

Elizabeth Rose

PROLOGUE

A woman on board was considered bad luck, but two women traveling as passengers on the *Desperado* were more than enough to drive Brody Banks mad. The squall that brewed up quickly on the North Sea only added to his anxiety.

Brody did his best to hold the ship on a steady course, but they were being tossed around in the waves as if they were naught more than a toy of the powerful sea. Why the hell had he ever agreed to let his wife and the old woman come along on the journey? This was just too dangerous. What had he been thinking?

His ship, the *Desperado,* wasn't built for the deep sea. It was a fishing vessel meant to be used near the coast. It had been given to him by his wife's late father on his deathbed. Brody spent years fixing up the vessel after it was nearly destroyed in the same storm that claimed Gwen's father's life. It was a much better vessel now, but it still couldn't compare to the *Sea Mirage* that Brody had once captained.

Brody was a reformed pirate so he knew how fickle the sea

could become, and also how quickly situations could change for the worse. This ship was no place for a woman, let alone two of them.

"Shorten the sails!" Brody shouted to his crew, trying to be heard over the high winds. "If we don't do something fast, we're going to capsize. Dammit, shorten the sails, I said! What in the bloody hell are you waiting for?"

"We're tryin', Cap'n, but the winds are too strong!" Lucky Dog, or Lucky, as his first mate was called, had trouble being heard at times because of his gravelly voice. His throat had been slit while he was a crewmember of Rowen the Restless. The man was lucky to be alive, let alone still able to talk. He and Brody were both pirates and crewmates aboard the *Sea Mirage*, serving under their captain, Rowen the Restless, who was one of the *Legendary Bastards of the Crown*. When Rowen stepped down from piracy, the ship was given to Brody. Brody moved up from first mate to captain, and then his crew turned mutinous and it was all over for him until Gwen found him during his darkest hour.

That was all in Brody's past now. He was no longer a pirate and had turned a new leaf. A married man with four children, his youngest one was only six months old. Brody was hopelessly in love with Gwen. If not, he never would have agreed to help her find her three brothers in the first place. Tristan, Mardon, and Aaron, had turned to piracy and left Gwen and her father years ago. All she wanted now was to find the men and bring them back home where they belonged.

Rain pelted down mixed with hail. Hitting the deck hard, the small pellets bounced back up, looking as if they had a life of their own. The beastly black waters of the North Sea rose up angrily, threatening to consume them all at any moment.

Once more gust of wind and they might capsize, bringing about the demise of every person there. This was only a squall and should end quickly, but not fast enough for Brody. He'd been giving this trip much consideration, thinking he'd made a wrong choice. He was sure of it now. This storm was the sign he looked for to call an end to this expedition. Much to his regret, Brody would have to disappoint Gwen and her grandmother, Nairnie. Still, as a husband and father, he felt his main job and commitment was to protect his family.

The crew frantically ran back and forth, trying to batten down the cargo and keep it from sliding into the sea. A barrel of wine as well as a trunk slid across the wet deck one way and then back the other, each time the ship listed. Everyone jumped out of the way. If the women weren't careful, they were going to get hit, or possibly pushed overboard.

"The ropes are tangled at the top of the mast," called out the old woman, Nairnie, shielding her eyes from the rain, trying to keep her balance by gripping on to a line. She pointed one boney, crooked finger upward at the massive square sail as she spoke. Nairnie was a tough old woman and the long-lost grandmother of Brody's wife, Gwen. Nairnie was also a Scottish Highlander. She had raised the man known as the Beast of Ravenscar, after her English lover abducted her only son, Cato, many years ago. It was only recently that Gwen and Nairnie met, never even knowing each other existed. Rowen, one of the bastard triplets of King Edward III, was the one who had brought them together.

This journey was naught but a mission of mercy, but turning sour very quickly. If only Brody hadn't made his wife a foolish promise, then none of them would be in this dangerous situation right now. Gwen's brothers were at one time simple fishermen as well as her father, but turned to piracy. They wanted more out of life than just an occasional net of fish. They longed for riches . . . gold . . . treasure, just like any other pirate. Gwen thought she could find them and turn them straight. Brody knew it was going to be damned well impossible after this long. The only thing he knew of that could turn a man away from piracy was falling in love with a good woman. Just like what happened to him.

As a child, Brody had been abducted and raised by pirates. Because of it, he knew only too well the dangers involved in purposely seeking out the scupper class of the sea. But love makes even the toughest man vulnerable to the wishes of the woman he adores. As much as he'd wanted to deny her request from the start, Brody hadn't been able to tell Gwen no.

For nearly seven years now, Brody managed to stall the trip, hoping his wife would change her mind. When Gwen never stopped asking, Brody eventually gave in. They'd left from Cornwall on their journey nearly a fortnight ago. Even after making many stops at ports along the way, and asking lots of questions, they hadn't had much luck in finding out the whereabouts of Gwen's brothers.

The last fisherman they'd spoken to told them the pirates they sought normally raided the area up near the North Sea. So that's where they'd headed. This trip was turning into a suicide mission quickly instead of a rescue mission, and it was time to call it quits.

"I'll do it. I'll untangle the lines," called out Gwen eagerly, holding on to whatever she could to keep from falling as the ship veered back and forth. At one time, she was deathly afraid of storms but, through the years, Brody had helped her to overcome that. Her long, blond hair whipped around her in the cold breeze. Quickly tucking it back under her hat, she continued toward the main mast, trying not to slip on the rain-covered slick deck. Through the years of being on the fishing boat with her father, she'd mastered crossing the deck of a rocking ship with ease. Still, she hadn't been out on the water much in years now and her sea legs weren't as reliable as they used to be.

The ship listed again, the waves crashing over the sidewall even harder now, soaking them all. This damned storm threatened to dump every one of them overboard.

"The hell you will, Gwen!" Brody growled, scolding his wife from atop the sterncastle as he tried to steer the ship. He couldn't let the mother of his four children risk her life like this. He had to stop her! Gripping the helm tightly, he desperately tried to keep things under control. It was the middle of the day, but the dark, foreboding clouds made it seem like midnight. Thunder boomed overhead and lightning streaked across the turbulent sky. The smell of the sea rose up and filled his senses, reminding him of the unyielding power of nature.

"Lucky, get up here and take the helm," Brody yelled, ready to strangle his wife for even offering to climb the rigging in this weather. Gwen had given birth to their fourth child, Katlyn, only six months ago. She didn't let the birth of her babies slow her down but, still, she shouldn't be climbing up a mast right now, especially in this kind of weather. Their other children, Breckon, Geneveve, and Eric were all under the age of six. These past years of their marriage had been very busy indeed.

Brody wasn't about to let his children end up as orphans –

the way he grew up. They needed their parents. His good friends, Edwin and Marta, were watching their children right now, and he wanted nothing more than to keep his promise of returning home soon. This insanity had to stop and he was the only one who could put an end to it.

"Aye, I'm comin' Cap'n," called out Lucky, scaling the stairs of the sterncastle quickly, taking the helm from Brody.

The rest of the crew rushed around the deck, doing all they could to secure the ship and help them make it through the squall without capsizing. Canvas coverings flapped wildly in the wind, and loose items spilled over the rail into the sea with each wave that crashed upon the deck.

Nairnie's voice could be heard over the wind as she shouted orders to the men, commanding his crew as if she had the right to do so. The scrappy old woman could put the fear of God in anyone, even a pirate. Brody decided he never wanted to be on her bad side. In a way, he almost pitied Gwen's brothers if they ever really found them. A storm at sea was nothing compared to the storm that was brewing within Nairnie. He could only imagine what she'd do to her grandsons for turning to piracy once she found them.

"Gwen, Nairnie, get below deck. Fast!" Brody commanded, taking hold of the ratlines and climbing as quickly as possible to untangle the main mast.

"Be careful, Brody," shouted his wife, peering up at him through the rain, doing nothing to heed his warning. Her concerned, blue eyes watched him like a hawk, making him feel the same way he did the day she and her father first fished him out of the sea. God, he hoped he wasn't about to die today, the way he almost had when his crew committed mutiny and threw him overboard. All he wanted was to hold

Gwen and his children in his arms once again. He wanted to forget all about his past – and all about this blasted mission. Brody no longer wanted anything to do with goddamned pirates!

Quickly and nimbly untangling the lines, his fingers stiffened in the cold air. Any man with a lick of sense knew not to purposely travel on the North Sea unless he had to. The weather was too unstable and the sea too unforgiving. This storm only reminded him that no matter how comfortable he was on the water, in the blink of an eye, everything could change. That is, he could lose the woman he loved forever.

"I've got it," he called out, fixing the lines and starting his descent. That's when something caught his eye in the distance. He saw lanterns of another ship out on the water. He'd been a pirate long enough to know that it wasn't a trade ship or a fishing vessel this far out. Then he saw the black sails that were the markings of a pirate ship, and this one looked familiar. He immediately got a sick feeling in the pit of his stomach. They were sailing right into the eye of a storm and it had to do with more than just the weather.

He'd seen this vessel many years ago, he was sure of it. It was the *Falcon*, and also the ship that carried Gwen's brothers.

"Damn it!" he spat under his breath. This was the last thing he wanted to see right now. He'd just made up his mind to turn around and take the women, his crew, and his ship safely back to Cornwall. If his wife discovered that her brothers were this close, she'd never let him leave. Suddenly, he wondered if it was all worth it. Even if they did find her brothers, what was to say they wouldn't all end up dead by the hands of the cutthroats? After all, they were pirates.

"B-Brody? W-what is it?" cried Gwen, holding on to a rope

and peering upward to see through the pouring rain. "D-did you spot s-something? A s-ship perhaps?" Her teeth chattered together as she spoke. She looked so cold and tired that all he could think about was taking her home and tucking her into a nice warm bed. Yet everything she'd been hoping for was finally right here within her grasp, and Brody was the only one keeping her from finding her brothers now.

Struggling with his conscience, he remained silent. He just couldn't tell her. If he did, Gwen would want to sail further into the storm to approach the pirate ship to find her brothers. Right now, that was the last place he wanted to go. They didn't know what to expect. Could they reason with pirates, or would her brothers only want to pillage and plunder his ship? It had been years since she saw them. While she swore they wouldn't give them trouble, people changed over time. When fishermen turned to piracy, there were no longer morals involved. Only one thing was for certain. Whatever was about to transpire, it wasn't going to be good.

"Get yer skinny arse down here before ye fall into the drink," shouted Nairnie. "I dinna want my granddaughter bein' a widow at such a young age."

Before he could move or even reply, lightning struck the bow of the ship. Brody felt the bolt of energy go right through him. His stiff fingers could no longer hold the lines and he fell face first, landing on the deck right at Gwen's feet.

Gwen screamed and hunkered down next to him. Brody lifted his head. His eyes shot upward, half-expecting to see the mast falling next, like it had in the past. This certainly seemed like history repeating itself, and that worried him. Thankfully, the lightning had only hit the bowsprit. There was a small fire, but nothing that couldn't easily be extinguished, especially in the rain.

"Fire on the bow!" Brody pushed up to his hands and knees, feeling as if his shoulder were broken. "Put out the flames and turn this godforsaken ship around anon!" he commanded his crew.

"Turn around?" asked Gwen, confused and sounding shocked. "But we haven't found my brothers yet."

"And we're not going to," he told her. "Not now. My only concern is for your safety. These are bad omens, Gwen. It's a sign and I will not ignore it. We're turning around and going home, and I won't hear another word about it."

He thought he heard a muffled scream just as the ship listed in the opposite direction. A wave washed over them. Brody reached out, holding on to Gwen with one hand and the lines with the other as his wife's feet slipped out from under her. When the ship rolled back the other way, Gwen coughed up water and looked behind her.

"Nairnie?" she cried. "Grandmother, where are you?"

She jumped to her feet, slipping, running to the sidewall.

"Gwen, get back here before you fall overboard!" Brody's shoulder felt on fire as he hurried after his wife.

"Nairnie!" Gwen screamed with tears streaming down her face. She looked over the side of the ship, searching for the old woman. "Brody, I think she fell overboard. We have to save her."

"Gwen, we don't know that for certain."

"Look!" Gwen pointed to a piece of clothing floating on the surface of the water. "There's her wimple. She fell in, I know she did."

Quickly scanning the water, Brody searched the area, but

didn't see the old woman anywhere. "Sweetheart, I'm sorry. It's too late. She's an old woman and cannot survive a fall from the ship. If she fell overboard, the sea has already claimed her. Now get below deck before the same thing happens to you!"

He pulled her with him toward the door of the hold, having a hard time keeping his grip on her since the squall was not yet over.

"Nay! Let go of me," cried Gwen, fighting him, accidentally hitting his injured shoulder. He bit back the pain. "We can't let her drown. We need to go after Nairnie."

Brody spoke through gritted teeth now, having no more patience this day. "Gwen, that's enough! She's gone, and we have to move on without her."

"Nay, Brody! She can't be dead." Tears mixed with rain washed down her face.

"Get below deck and stay there," he commanded. "I'll not lose you, too." Yanking the door open to the hold, he shoved her inside, closing and locking the door behind her.

"Let me out!" came her muffled scream as she banged with both fists upon the wood.

"I'm sorry, Gwen, but it's for your own good. I can't focus on anything else unless I know you are safe."

"Cap'n, is everythin' all right?" asked Big Garth who had once been the cook on the *Sea Mirage*.

"Aye, what is it?" Odo, another of his old crew, limped over the deck, making his way toward them.

"We're turning the ship around and heading for home," Brody instructed.

"Are the women in the hold?" asked Big Garth, looking at the door as Gwen continued to pound on it from inside.

"Just my wife," he told them. "I think the old woman fell overboard."

"Overboard? Shall I go up the lines and see if I can spot her?" asked Odo.

Brody hesitated a moment, weighing out the consequences. If they stayed there to look for the old woman, there was no telling how many more of them would die in the storm. And if Odo climbed the lines, he was sure to see the pirate ship and announce it. Brody couldn't allow either of those things to happen.

"Nay, don't climb the lines, it's too dangerous right now. Just scan the water for the old woman over the sidewalls. I'm sure it's too late since she could never endure the fall at her age." It hurt him to answer this way, but they all knew what he said was true. Plus, it was his duty to see to the safety of the entire crew. He couldn't endanger them all just to look for one old woman. It could be no other way. "Tell Lucky to turn this ship around and get us the hell out of here."

"So there's no chance of savin' Nairnie?" asked Big Garth, challenging his decision. The entire crew had become fond of the old woman since she acted like a mother to all of them. He couldn't blame the man for trying. Brody would miss her, too.

"If you see her, let me know, but don't get your hopes up. I'm telling you, there is no chance she could survive the fall," said Brody. "Now put out that fire because we are heading home."

"Aye, Cap'n," said Odo, and the two men turned to go.

Barely able to tolerate the pain, Brody was sure his shoulder was broken. Even if he wanted to continue this mission, he couldn't. He'd be of no use to anyone now. In his condition, he'd never be able to swing a sword if Gwen's brothers decided to board the *Desperado* and attack. Nay, Brody would not be able to defend his wife, and this didn't sit right with him at all.

Gritting his teeth to bear the pain, he headed to the side-wall and looked down into the water once more. Nairnie was nowhere to be found.

"I'm sorry, Nairnie, but I have to get Gwen to safety," he said under his breath. "I'm sorry you'll never be able to meet your grandsons even though I know how much it meant to you. But at least now you'll be with your son, Cato, in the afterworld."

While he didn't see Nairnie, he did see the pirate ship in the distance and it was getting closer. Hopefully, his crew would be too distracted with turning the ship around to notice.

However, if he could see the *Falcon*, then that meant their captain could see the *Desperado*, too. This was his last chance to get Gwen home safely. Bid the devil, he would do it, even if it meant breaking his promise to her. It was for her, and also for their children. Aye, this was the right thing to do.

"Do ye see Nairnie, Cap'n?" called Odo from the deck.

"Nay. She's gone," he called back, knowing they had to leave right now. His head told him to acknowledge the other ship, since this was the goal of their mission, but his heart told him otherwise. If Gwen hadn't been along, he might reconsider. But now, after already losing Nairnie, he realized there was no decision to be made. It could be no other way. He had to protect the mother of his children.

"Take us home, Lucky," he called out from the deck, climbing the stairs to the sterncastle. "Get us the hell out of here because we're aborting the mission."

"Are ye sure ye want to do this?" Lucky asked in confusion.

"That's right, I do." Brody sighed and nodded slightly, once more looking out to the angry sea. "I'm taking my wife away from this godforsaken place. She's going home where she belongs. If her brothers are never found, I no longer care. All I'm concerned about is my wife's safety."

CHAPTER 1

*T*ristan Fisher, Pirate Captain of the *Falcon,* held his ship steady in the high waves. The squall had come out of nowhere, and they hadn't even had time to prepare for it. Still, it didn't matter. Having spent a lifetime on the water, Tristan felt at home in any type of weather conditions.

Peering out to the sea, he thought at first his eyes were playing tricks on him. Blinking twice and looking again, he realized he really did see something in the distance. That is, something that he never thought he'd see again in this lifetime and certainly didn't expect to find here and now. It was his father's fishing ship, the *Desperado,* and it was coming right toward them.

"Ramble, get over here," he called out to his cabin boy who was the messenger of the ship and tended to his needs as well as the needs of his two brothers.

A young man with movements as quick as a rabbit and an overabundance of untethered energy, Ramble bounded up the stairs of the sterncastle, coming to an abrupt halt at Tristan's side.

"What is it, Cap'n? Did ye see somethin'?" asked Ramble. He looked quickly at Tristan, and then his eyes darted out to sea and back again. "Is there somethin' botherin' ye? Because if there is, I can help ye out. Just tell me what I can do no matter what it is and I'll do it."

Ramble was a lad of ten and five years. Tristan wasn't even sure what the boy's real name was. He'd just called him Ramble since the day he'd met him because of the fact he was always rambling on about one thing or another. He'd been brought aboard after one of their raids in Scotland about six years ago. Actually, Ramble, being an orphan, had been trying to rob them at the time. Instead of cutting off his hand since he was so young, Tristan took a liking to him and ended up keeping him as part of his crew. He found that orphans, especially the younger ones, always made the most loyal crewmembers. Ramble might be pesky at times, but he'd never caused half the amount of trouble as Tristan's brothers, Mardon and Aaron.

"Cap'n? Did ye hear me?" asked Ramble, waving a hand in front of Tristan's face.

Tristan gripped him by the wrist, slamming his hand down upon a wooden box. His dagger followed, the tip sticking into the wood between Ramble's fingers.

"Never do that again," he warned the boy in a low and even voice. "You do, and you'll find your hand severed from your body next time. Savvy?" Rain pelted down, soaking Tristan's long, brown hair. Water dripped from the end of his nose, dribbling onto the boy's hand.

Ramble's eyes opened wide and he swallowed forcefully. Daringly, he checked to see that his fingers were still all intact.

"So sorry, Cap'n," he squeaked out. "Ye just seemed . . . distracted today, that's all."

"Contemplative, Ramble. Never distracted," Tristan corrected him, always priding himself on the fact that he was the only one out of his siblings with stable emotions and a clear head. However, listening to Ramble all day long sometimes tended to wear on him. Today was one of those days.

Tristan learned to ignore the boy's talking most of the time, only putting up with him because he was one of the best thieves he had. Ramble could disappear in a crowd of people and reappear on the ship, having picked the pockets of every man in town before they even noticed. Sometimes one had to put up with irritations to get what one wanted. It was just one of those things.

"Find my brothers and tell them to join me." Tristan's wet hair clung to his shoulders as the wind bit at his exposed flesh. However, he was accustomed to days like this. He could also tell the squall was letting up, and would be over soon.

"Aye, Cap'n," said Ramble, hurrying back down the stairs.

It was late spring and the last few months had been sparse when it came to pillaging and plundering. Not many ships had traveled the North Sea since last fall. Tristan's crew was hungry and ornery and their supplies were running low. If they hadn't made an agreement to stick to the North Sea, he would have raided the channel by now. Well, they would just have to dock again soon and raid on land, not that he liked to do that. Tristan was more of a sea pirate, and tried to keep his raids to the water. In cases like this though, he didn't have much of a choice.

He steered the *Falcon* toward the ship he saw in the distance.

Sure it was the *Desperado*, he couldn't imagine why his father would take his fishing ship on the North Sea, especially this far from home. It was a dangerous time of year and the weather was unpredictable. His father's ship was small compared to the *Falcon*. It could easily be smashed to pieces from high, turbulent waves. The *Desperado* was a good ship, but not nearly as large and sturdy as the one that Tristan now commanded. Neither was it made to endure bad weather and rough waters like this. To even risk himself and his crew, his father must have good reason. Aye, it must be something of great importance for him to come after them this far away from home.

The storm started to recede, but it continued to rain. Still, it didn't bother Tristan. His home was on the sea. On his ship and in the water is where he belonged. The rougher the sea became, the more he liked it because it made him feel alive. Tristan loved a challenge and had never backed down from one in his life. His biggest accomplishment was that he stole the *Falcon* from his father and convinced his brothers to join him. Tristan had been a pirate captain since the age of seventeen. If it meant sailing right into the midst of trouble to get what he wanted or go where he planned, he'd do it without even batting an eye.

Pushing a long strand of hair from his face, he watched his father's ship get tossed about in the waves. It was obvious his father's crew was struggling. If they weren't careful, they'd end up capsizing and going down.

Almost as if his father could hear his thoughts, the *Desperado* suddenly turned direction and headed away from him. Still, this made no sense to Tristan. His father, Cato Fisher, was once a pirate and feared nothing. If he came this far to find his sons, why the hell was he turning around now when he'd obviously seen the *Falcon*? Something wasn't right here and Tristan was determined to find out what.

"Batten down the rest of that cargo quickly before we lose it in the storm," yelled his brother, Mardon, hurrying up the stairs to join him. Mardon was quartermaster, or second in command on the *Falcon*, also serving as Tristan's first mate.

At eight and twenty years of age, Mardon was just a year younger than Tristan. Their youngest brother, Aaron, was six and twenty. Each with a personality of his own, the brothers were nothing alike. Sometimes that was a good thing, but they also disagreed often and had their share of quarrels.

Mardon's white shirt was open in the front, exposing his broad chest and dark ringlets of hair. The men had become used to any weather and, in the summer months, often walked around with very little clothing at all.

Mardon's bright blue eyes sought out Tristan's green ones. Concern shown within them. "Ramble said you called for me. Do you need me to bring the *Falcon* through the storm safely?" The ship tossed about, but the men stayed solid, having their sea legs about them.

"Nay, I've got it."

"You know that I can handle the wrath of an angry sea and bring us out alive and unscathed." Mardon held great pride in his skill of being able to sail a ship through storms and rough waters. It was guided by his inborn ability to always be able to get out of any harrowing situation. Especially if the situation involved a beautiful woman. He was cunning and wise, and seemed to be able to sniff out trouble before it reached them, guiding the crew to safety before they were ever caught.

"It's not the sea that takes my concern tonight," Tristan

told him as the wind whipped at the sails, filling them with air. The ship moved quickly over the water.

Since Tristan was the eldest of the three brothers, he'd claimed the title of captain for himself. Mardon often challenged him since he'd always thought he should be captain and didn't like being told what to do. Aaron, on the other hand, didn't care which of them was captain as long as it wasn't him. He was the wild one of the bunch and liked his freedom. He didn't want to be saddled down with having to reprimand a drunken crew or make any decisions that involved the destiny of others.

"Where's our brother?" asked Tristan, following the path the *Desperado* had taken. He took a deep breath, inhaling the scent of spring. He could see the clouds breaking in the distance and a small stream of sunlight starting to shine through. It was like new life was budding and something mysterious was about to develop. Aye, he felt anxious and, at the same time, cautious because he was sure it all had something to do with his father but he didn't know what.

"Aaron, get down here," Mardon called out, using the flat of his hand to shelter his eyes from the rain as he peered upward. "He's up in the lookout again. Can't keep him out of there even in a damned storm."

As the ship's boatswain, or bosun, Aaron's responsibility was to make sure that everything was in good shape and the vessel was safe for travel. He was in charge of the crew, setting the sails, dropping the anchor, and making sure the deck got swabbed.

"I'm on my way," Aaron shouted from up above. Instead of climbing down the ratlines carefully in the storm, like anyone would, Aaron took hold of a loose line and swung down like a monkey. He dropped to the deck right between his brothers with a loud thump, almost knocking into them. The ship listed just then, and he stumbled, hitting up against Mardon.

"Dammit, Aaron, climb down instead of jumping." Mardon pushed him away.

Aaron righted himself and his ochre eyes glared at his brother. He resented being the youngest of the three and often felt as if they were taking advantage of him at times. Tristan had to admit that it was probably true. It was just something that older siblings did.

"Stop it, both of you," said Tristan with a sigh. Sometimes he felt like he'd taken on the role of a parent ever since the three of them left the fishing industry to turn to piracy once again. Their father stayed behind with their twelve-year-old sister, Gwendolen, after the death of their mother. Actually, Tristan and his brothers blamed their father for their mother's death and had never really forgiven him. "Aaron, if you'd wear shoes once in a while, mayhap you'd be able to stand upright in a storm."

"That's right," agreed Mardon. "Wear shoes."

"And Mardon, if you'd stop telling Aaron what to do, mayhap he'd stop resenting you so much." Tristan shook his head, keeping his eyes on the churning sea.

"That's right," agreed Aaron, a long blond strand of hair covering one eye. "I don't like being a third wheel."

"Listen up, both of you. I've been trying to tell you something," Tristan continued.

"Oh, Tristan, I saw another ship from up in the lookout basket," Aaron told him anxiously. "I couldn't see the flags clearly in the rain, but somehow the ship seemed familiar."

The three men stood in the pouring rain, acting like it

didn't matter. And it didn't. Living on a ship, they were always exposed to the elements and learned to live with it.

"Another ship? Is that why we've changed course?" asked Mardon, hard to fool even in the midst of a storm. He always knew when the ship changed directions without having to be told. "Let's go faster and mayhap we can catch it and raid it. It's been a long time since we've seen another ship out here. Mayhap our luck is changing."

"Nay, we can't raid this one." Tristan glanced up at the sky. The rain suddenly let up and the clouds parted. It looked like the storm was just about over. This was common out here on the sea. Storms and squalls blew up out of nowhere and were gone just as fast as they started.

"Why can't we raid it?" asked Mardon. "I'm the quarter-master and decide which ships we board. I say we do it."

"Nay, I told you we can't. Not this one."

"Why not?" asked Mardon again. "Is it a Cinque Ports ship? If so, even more reason to raid them since the bounty will be in abundance."

"Nay, it's because it is the *Desperado*," said Tristan in a calm voice. "It was headed right toward us, but now it's changed course and is headed away from us."

"The *Desperado*?" asked Mardon and Aaron together.

"Father's here?" Aaron stretched his neck, looking over the side of the ship. He wasn't as tall as his brothers, but he was lithe and twice as fast. He wore a red head cloth covering his hair, and had two gold hoop earrings, both in the same ear. "So that's why it looked familiar to me."

"It's his ship all right," said Tristan. "I'd know it anywhere. However, I'm not convinced he's on it."

"Why not?" asked Mardon, gripping on to the railing as the ship rocked again.

"Because they changed course, and I know they saw us, that's why."

"Mayhap it's because of the storm," said Aaron. "At least it's almost over now. We should be able to catch the *Desperado* easily. It's not nearly as sturdy or as fast as the *Falcon*."

"My point is that Father wouldn't run from us," Tristan told them.

"Well, mayhap they didn't see us." Mardon gave the excuse, but he didn't seem as if he believed it.

"They saw us, all right," Aaron assured them. "I spotted someone up in their rigging when I was in the lookout basket. I can't believe I didn't realize it was the *Desperado*."

"It's been a long time since any of us have seen it," said Mardon in his brother's defense.

"Or seen Father." Aaron frowned.

"Aye, twelve years now." While Tristan had missed their father and sister, he'd never doubted their choice of turning to piracy. Living life as a poor fisherman, relying on food from the sea to make a living, never suited him. Now, they shaped their own future by the plunder they attained from ships out at sea, or during their raids on land as well. They'd always had more than they needed as pirates. That is, until lately.

"Let's see if we can catch the *Desperado*." Mardon urged his brothers.

Tristan directed their ship to follow their father's but the *Desperado* was already blown far from them because of the storm.

"Look, I see some of their cargo in the water." Mardon pointed over the side of the ship.

"Flotsam!" shouted Aaron excitedly. "It's just what we need."

"Get some ropes and grappling hooks and a shuttle boat to collect it." Tristan started to turn the ship, having already passed up some of the flotsam. Thank goodness, the waves were starting to calm down. It should be easy to pick up all the bounty.

Mardon bounded down the stairs with Aaron at his heels.

"Goldtooth, drop the sail," shouted Tristan. "Stitch, come take the helm, and try to hold her steady so my brothers and I can collect the flotsam."

Stitch was an older man, and the most fatherly one of the lot. He was also the crew's navigator and could chart their course and get to their destination just by using the stars. He'd been a seafaring man for longer than most and was wiser than any of them when it came to matters involving the sea. His body was covered in scars from the many stitches he'd endured in his lifetime from his many battles. Goldtooth, on the other hand, was a big, burly man with arms the size of tree trunks and a look that was frightening enough to turn a man to stone. He didn't move fast, but followed directions without question and was very strong. He was also one of Tristan's best warriors when it came to fighting. He'd covered one of his front teeth with gold after one of their raids, gaining him his name.

"Slow down as we approach the cargo, and keep an eye on the waves," Tristan said, handing over the helm. He started after his brothers. "If we can, we'll try dropping a shuttle, but we'll have to play it by ear."

"Aye, Cap'n." With Stitch at the helm, Tristan had no worries.

By the time Tristan made it over to his brothers, they were already lowering the shuttle boat into the water. Aaron and Ramble were inside while Mardon stayed above to point out the booty.

"Wait! The water might be too choppy to use the shuttle boats," explained Tristan, looking over the side.

"It's a chance we've got to take," Mardon told him. "If not, we'll never get those barrels and trunks on board. It'll be hell trying to haul them up with just nets."

"Fine, we'll risk it," agreed Tristan seeing more of the *Desperado's* cargo floating their way. They needed this booty and he wasn't about to lose it. They'd do whatever it took to bring it on board. "Get it all," Tristan instructed. "And hurry. Mayhap when we're done we can still catch Cato's ship." Tristan referred to their father by his Christian name. Cato was the man who first introduced the brothers to piracy when they were just young boys. It was because their father was struggling to put food on the table for his family. They'd kept this a secret from their sister and mother. The women never even knew Cato had the *Falcon* hidden in a cove.

"Look, what's that?" asked Ramble, pointing at something in the water.

Tristan glanced over the side to see what looked like a person clinging to two floating vats of wine that were tied together.

"We've got ourselves a man overboard from their ship," announced Mardon. "Loot him and then kill him quickly. He's of no use to us."

Once the shuttle boat hit the water, Ramble rowed it over toward the survivor. Aaron drew his sword with one hand and pulled the vats of wine closer with the other, reaching over the side of the small boat. "Bid the devil, it's an old crone!" gasped Aaron.

Tristan realized now that an old woman hung on to the rope connecting the barrels, clinging to it for her life. She looked up at them, and her feeble voice cried out. "Help me, please." Long silver, unbound hair floated on the water around her shoulders.

"Well, I'll be. It really is a lass," said Ramble.

"She's old," Aaron remarked, surveying the woman. "What should we do with her?"

"Bring the vats of wine on board and leave the old hag to the sea," commanded Tristan.

"Ye're goin' to leave her to die?" asked Ramble. "Mayhap we should help her."

"Nay. Tristan's right," agreed Mardon. "We have no need for a woman of that age. Besides, it's bad luck to have a wench on board. You know that."

"All right, whatever ye say." Ramble reached out to try to pry the woman's fingers from the rope, but she turned her head and bit his hand, causing him to cry out.

"Ow. She bit me!" he shouted, rubbing his hand. "What am I supposed to do?"

"I don't give a damned, just bring that wine aboard. I'm thirsty," said Mardon, his only interest being in the bounty they'd just procured.

"Aye. Hit her over the head with the hilt of your sword if you need to, but just put her out of her misery," suggested Tristan. "Now get that wine aboard the ship because there is also a trunk I don't want to lose." Tristan and his brothers embraced their pirate ways, having learned from their father to be ruthless, heartless and cold. Cato Fisher had told them if they started feeling sorry for people, it would be their ticket to doom. He was right. The last thing they needed was on old woman on board. Their ways had worked well for them all this time, so there was no need to change now. They were considered pirate lords of the sea.

"I'm not goin' to touch her again. Ye do it, Aaron," said Ramble, still rubbing his hand, seeming leery of the woman.

"Did ye say Aaron?" The old woman's head lifted and she looked first at Aaron and then back up to the others on the ship. She coughed and sputtered, her bony fingers turning white as they clung tightly to the rope while the barrels kept her afloat. "If he's Aaron, are ye two Mardon and Tristan?" she asked, her tired eyes looking up to Tristan and his brother.

Her question surprised Tristan. How did the wench know their names? Mayhap she'd heard them from their father.

"Don't worry who we are, because you're not going to live long enough to remember our names anyway," Tristan assured her.

"Nay, wait a minute," said Mardon with a raised hand. "How do you know who we are?" he asked the old woman.

"Do you know our father?" asked Aaron curiously. "After all, you were on his ship, the *Desperado*, weren't you?"

"Aye, I was, and of course I ken yer faither," she answered, glaring at them now.

"Well, where is he?" asked Tristan. "Why did he sail away when I know he saw us? And why didn't he come after you?"

"Why were you even on the ship to begin with?" asked Mardon. "Who are you to someone like our father? It doesn't seem likely he'd be traveling with an old woman."

"Bring me aboard and I'll tell ye lads everythin' ye want to ken."

Tristan and Mardon exchanged glances, but both of them shook their heads.

"Nay, it's bad luck," said Mardon, crossing his arms over his chest. "No wenches on board."

"Plus, it goes against the code," added Tristan with a shrug.

"I dinna give two hoots about any pirate code! Now bring me aboard," demanded the old woman."

"Why should we?" asked Aaron.

"Because I've got some valuable information for ye," she told them, her fingers starting to slip. "Plus, I can cook and also heal."

"I don't know," said Tristan, not liking this idea at all.

"God's toes, help me already and stop talkin' about killin' me, ye fools," commanded the old woman, not seeming afraid of them at all. Odd, since they were pirates. Most people were frightened out of their minds and rightly so.

"Who are you?" asked Aaron, scrutinizing the woman.

"My name is Nairnie," she spat, looking madder than hell. "Yer sister, Gwen, tells me she sailed with ye lads on yer faither's boat. She said ye were guid fishermen, but she failed to tell me ye were all stupid fools."

"Hush up, old woman." Mardon didn't care about his old life and neither did Tristan.

"Don't call us fishermen because that's an insult," said Tristan, taking more offense at that part then her calling them stupid fools. "We're pirates now if you haven't noticed."

"Oh, I noticed, and it disgusts me," she ground out. "Bring me aboard the ship and I'll make ye a guid meal."

"I could go for something to eat besides hardtack," said Aaron, looking up at his brothers, always hungry.

"You said you know our sister, Gwen," said Mardon suspiciously. "So, tell me. How is she?"

"Get me out of this bluidy cold water at once and I'll tell ye everythin' ye want to ken, I swear."

"Let's bring her aboard," suggested Aaron, looking up at his brothers from the shuttle boat licking his lips. He was obviously thinking about food again. They all were. Another wave slapped over them and the old woman went under and came up sputtering and spitting out water, nearly losing her grip. She wouldn't be able to hold on for long.

"Nay," said Tristan. "And that's final. Now push her off the barrel and get the wine aboard. We need to go. We've already wasted too much time with this."

"I could go for some wine, too," said Aaron, reaching out for her.

"Nay!" cried the old woman. "Ye dinna want to hurt me."

"Really?" Tristan raised a brow. "Why not? You give us a better reason to spare your life than cooking a meal and mayhap we'll consider it."

"If ye leave me to die, ye'll never find out about yer faither."

"Sure we will. We'll track down the ship and find him for ourselves," said Mardon.

"God's eyes, ye mischant lads, ye're twice as troublesome as yer faither was as a lad. Now, get me out of this water before my muscles freeze up."

"You sound like you knew our father when he was young," said Aaron.

"Well, I should hope so," spat the old woman. "After all, Cato was my son."

"Your . . . son?" asked Mardon, looking over to Tristan once again.

"Then that makes us . . ." started Aaron, but he was cut off by the boisterous woman.

"Aye, ye lousy scuppers of the sea, that's right. Whether I like it or no', ye're my grandsons! And I can tell ye that ye're already a huge let down from what I hoped ye'd be. Yer faither didna live with me long, but I'm sure he's turnin' over in his grave right now because his sons are plannin' on lettin' their own grandmathair drown!"

"Our father's dead?" asked Mardon in surprise.

"As dead as ye three are goin' to be as soon as I get my hands around yer necks for the way ye're treatin' an auld woman. Now help me up."

"How do we know you're telling us the truth?" asked Tristan. He wasn't sure he trusted the old woman's story.

"Well, if ye ever catch up to the *Desperado*, ye can ask yer sister about it yerself."

"Gwen? Does she know we're out here?" asked Aaron.

"Aye, she does! It was her idea to look for ye lads. Now, get me onto the ship and I'll tell ye all about her and Brody and their four children."

"Brody? As in the pirate that sailed with Rowen the Restless?" asked Tristan, surprised to hear this name springing from her lips."

"He's no' a pirate anymore and neither is Rowen. I wish I could say the same for ye three." She coughed up a little water and blew air from her mouth, making a face as another wave hit her.

"Gwen's got four children? Really?" asked Aaron with a smile. "Our little sister is a mother."

"Two lads and two lassies," she answered.

"Did she name any of them after me?" asked Mardon curiously. Tristan wasn't surprised by this since Mardon seemed to think everyone wanted to be him.

"I'll no' tell ye another thing before ye help me aboard yer ship."

"What do you think?" Mardon asked Tristan.

"Let's go." Tristan looked up to the sky and squinted, trying to make sense of why the *Desperado* turned around. "If Father's really dead, then mayhap that's why they turned around. But if Nairnie is really our grandmother, then why would Gwen not do something to save her when she fell overboard? I don't believe the old wench's story."

"They probably dinna even ken I'm gone," Nairnie cried out, overhearing their conversation.

"Nay. Carry on," Tristan called out to his crew, not knowing what to make of the old woman but realizing bringing her aboard would only mean trouble.

"Wait!" she cried out. "I didna want to have to tell ye, but I found a treasure map on yer faither's ship."

"Treasure map?" That gained Tristan's interest. "What are you talking about? What treasure?"

"I believe Cato hid it from ye lads because he'd given up his pirate ways and didna want ye louses to find it."

"Do you think that's the map to the king's treasure that Father used to tell us about?" asked Aaron, looking up the side of the ship at his brothers.

"It must be," said Mardon. "I knew he had the map and hid it somewhere, but I never thought he'd leave it on his ship."

"Give Aaron the map," commanded Tristan, pointing to the shuttle boat. "If it's real, we'll bring you aboard."

"I canna do that," she said. "Besides, ye'd probably kill me once ye have it."

"Search her for the map," Tristan ordered.

"Dinna bother. It's no' on me," she told him. "It was stolen on the way here."

"Like I said, she's no use to us." Tristan waved his hand through the air.

"However, since it was just stolen, I'm sure if ye kent where I lost it and who took it, ye'd be able to get it back easily."

"Perhaps we should bring her aboard and find out about the map," suggested Aaron. "Plus, I wouldn't mind hearing about Gwen."

"Mayhap he's right," agreed Mardon, looking over at Tristan. "We could always get the information and then dump her back into the sea afterwards."

"I heard that!" she shouted. "Ye do that and ye'll never have a guid hot meal again."

"Hot meal," repeated Aaron, his eyes lighting up. "We'd better not let her drown." He looked up the side of the ship at his brothers. "Just in case she's really our grandmother."

"I am yer grandmathair!" snapped the old woman. "And once I'm out of this cold water, I swear I'm goin' to box in yer ears for treatin' me this way."

"More trouble than it's worth?" Mardon asked Tristan.

"Probably," said Tristan, looking back out to sea. It didn't seem that the *Desperado* was coming back at all. He had no need for the old woman, but now after everything he'd heard, he couldn't just let her drown. She'd piqued his interest and thrown down a challenge. If she really knew where to find the king's treasure, it could solve all his problems. Besides, the thought of eating hot food again did sound enticing. They hadn't had a good meal ever since their cook died over the winter. The old wench was spunky and something about her called out to him. After all, what woman of that age could survive a fall from a ship in a storm and still have the nerve to talk to pirates in this manner? She sounded just as ruthless as them. It was too good to pass up. He needed to know more. Especially if she truly was their grandmother.

"All right. Get her aboard," he finally agreed, hoping to hell she wasn't going to bring them any more bad luck. Lately, that was all they seemed to have. "All I can say is, by God, she'd better really know where to find that treasure map and also how to cook."

As soon as they hauled the old woman onto their ship, Nairnie stomped over to Tristan with her heavy, wet plaid leaking all over the deck. Before Tristan knew what hit him, her hand shot out and she slapped him across the cheek. The sound of skin against skin got everyone's undivided attention.

"Did she just . . . slap you?" asked Mardon with a chuckle.

"Aye, ye bet yer arse I did." Nairnie's hand shot out and she slapped Mardon next. When she turned to Aaron he just closed his eyes and lifted his chin, taking his beating like a man.

The crew laughed and made a few rude comments.

"Keep that up and the rest of ye will be next!" she retorted. The crew immediately stopped laughing and went about their chores.

"Well, take me to my quarters and find me some dry clothes," she commanded. "Then show me to the galley so I can cook up some food like I promised. Although, no' a one of ye deserves anythin' to eat after even thinkin' of lettin' yer

33

own grandmathair drown!" She stormed off across the deck with every man there giving her a wide berth.

"Still wonder if she's really our grandmother?" asked Mardon, gently touching his stinging cheek.

"Nay, I've no doubt in my mind that she is," said Tristan. "No other woman would be so bold to say and do the things she just did." He smiled and shook his head and the three of them started laughing. The only thing Tristan wondered now was how long it would take for bad luck to hit them since he'd just brought not only a woman aboard, but a woman who wouldn't think twice of putting each and every one of them in their place.

CHAPTER 2

PIRATE LORDS

*G*avina Drummond followed her father to the tavern, staying hidden in the shadows so she wouldn't be seen. He'd told her to stay back by the horse and cart, but she feared for his safety and didn't listen. Ill luck had befallen her family over the past few years, taking each member from her in one way or another. Now her father was all she had left. His bad habits of drinking and gambling had left them with nothing besides the clothes on their back, their old horse, and a wagon that was falling apart.

"Finn," she heard a man call her father by name as she neared the Crooked Crow Tavern. She dove behind an empty barrel, trying to listen to their conversation.

"Birk, I came as soon as I could," said her father, sounding extremely nervous.

"Were ye followed?" asked the man.

"Nay, of course no."

"Did ye bring what I asked for?"

"I did. Now let's get on with the game."

"Game?" Gavina whispered to herself and pursed her

mouth in aggravation. After they'd lost their house in a card game, she'd made her father promise that he would never gamble again. Why was she surprised that he'd already reverted back to his old ways?

"Step inside," said the man, scanning the area quickly. They disappeared into the back door of the Crooked Crow located on the docks of Stonehaven. It was a dangerous place since the area was inhabited with sailors, fisherman, tradesmen, and sometimes even pirates of the North Sea.

Gavina had never been inside this establishment, but heard about the fights that broke out here constantly, and all about the ruffians that inhabited the place. It wasn't far from the remains of their little town of Steeple Glen that had been raided and burned by the English a few years ago.

Her hand went to her wooden flute hanging from her side as she wondered what to do. Her brother, Liam, had carved this flute for her years ago and she'd learned to play it. Her mother had always loved her music. She missed them both dearly. Her father, on the other hand, just thought her music was naught but a hindrance.

Gavina's flute comforted her in troubled times and she only wished she could play it now without being discovered. Letting out a sigh, she stood up, meaning to go back and wait for her father by their horse. Before she could, a hand covered her mouth and an arm wrapped around her waist.

"Looks to me like I found myself a whore for the night," laughed the man. "Now, hold still while I enter ye from behind," came his hot whisper in her ear.

Gavina stomped on his toe, biting the man on the hand at the same time causing him to yell out.

"Leave me alone," she warned him, pulling her dagger from her belt and holding it steady, aimed at his heart.

"Get back here, ye bitch," spat the man. His lip curled up and she could see his blackened, rotten teeth. She was planning on stabbing him, until two of his friends stepped out of the shadows to join him.

"Blethers!" she gasped, knowing she couldn't outfight three men. She'd also never be able to outrun them, trying to get back to the horse. There was only one thing she could do and she didn't hesitate to do it. Turning on her heel, she ran as fast as she could to the tavern. Yanking open the door to the Crooked Crow, she stumbled inside. It was dark in there and her eyes needed to adjust from being out in the bright sun.

"Well, well, what have we got here?" asked a drunken patron, meeting her at the door.

Gavina sidestepped him, eyeing the place filled with ruffians and sailors. They were laughing and talking loudly, all drinking and playing dice. The stench of alcohol and sweat filled the air, assaulting her senses. She looked to the floor only to find it covered with dirty rushes. Picking up one foot, the rushes stuck to her shoe, black from mold and wet from spit or mayhap urine.

Several scantily-dressed whores straddled the laps of the patrons as they kissed the men and let themselves be fondled. One whore and man seemed to be coupling right there in front of everyone atop the chair but no one seemed to notice, or perhaps they just didn't care. Not able to move forward and not able to turn back, she realized her mistake. She was trapped in this hellhole and wished now that she had stayed outside.

"She's mine," said the man from behind her, reaching out

to take her arm. Gavina turned and slashed him across his wrist, drawing blood.

"Ye'll die for that!" spat the man, his wrinkled face turning red with anger.

She turned and pushed her way through the crowd, only stopping when a man opened a door to a back room and she crashed right into him.

"What's all the ruckus about?" he spat.

She looked up to see the man named Birk that her father had gone inside with earlier.

"The wench cut me," whined the man from behind her, holding his bloody arm.

"Gavina?" Her father poked his head out from behind Birk.

"Ye ken her?" asked Birk.

"Aye, she's my daughter," he answered. "Birk, please dinna hurt her."

"Hmmm, she's a bonnie lass." The man named Birk reached out and grabbed her chin, looking her over as if he were inspecting a workhorse before he bought it. She wanted to slap his hand away and yell obscenities at him, but decided against it. If she did that, it would put her father in an awkward position because of her.

"Please, leave her be," begged her father. "Let's just get back to the game."

"Of course," said Birk, smiling, still looking her over. "However, I do believe that the stakes have just gotten a little higher."

"What do ye mean?" asked Finn.

"I want *her*," he said, yanking Gavina into the room and slamming the door behind them.

"Ye want my daughter? Nay. Ye canna have her," spat Finn.

"I already wagered my horse and cart. Besides, that wouldna be a fair trade."

"Ye wagered our horse and cart on a card game?" she gasped. "Papa, how could ye? It is all we have left! Ye promised ye wouldna gamble anymore."

"This will be the last time, Gavina, I promise," he tried to console her. "I'm goin' to win and then I'll be able to fix my past mistakes. Just look at the pile of coins on the table." He nodded down to the card game in progress, his eyes lighting up with greed.

"Hrmph," she sniffed, not impressed at all. "That pile of coins might be worth a horse and cart, but certainly no' a person! Papa, dinna wager me away, too."

"Of course, no', Daughter. Dinna worry." He reached out and patted her on the arm. "I would never do such a thing."

"No' even for this?" Birk pulled out a rolled-up parchment from under his tunic and held it up for both of them to see.

"What's that?" asked Finn curiously, never able to resist temptation.

"It's a map that shows where the king's treasure is buried."

"The king's treasure?" Finn's eyes widened. "I thought that was stolen by pirates years ago."

"I guess the pirates decided to bury it for safe keepin'," said Birk.

"How did ye get the map?" asked Gavina, being suspicious of the man.

"I stole it just this mornin' from an old woman who was travelin' with an ex-pirate named Brody. They never even kent I took it," he laughed. "It was so easy. I swear it was like takin' sweetmeats from a child."

"Who is Brody?" asked Gavina.

"Daughter, he was Rowen the Restless' first mate," her father answered for Birk. "Ye ken . . . he was one of the *Legendary Bastards of the Crown*."

"Oh, aye, I've heard of him. He and his brathairs once raided their own faither and were kent as the Demon Thief."

"That's right," said Birk. "So ye ken if Brody had this map aboard his ship, it's real. He was probably goin' after the treasure himself. The bounty buried where this map leads is more than a fair exchange for yer daughter." Birk raked his eyes down Gavina's body, making her feel ravished.

"I wonder how much treasure there is," said Finn excitedly.

"I'm sure it's a treasure of gold coins and expensive jewelry," Birk answered. "A treasure fit for a king since it once belonged to the English King Edward III himself."

"I suppose ye're right," said Finn. "That treasure could change my life forever."

"Faither! Ye canna really be considerin' this outrageous offer," snapped Gavina.

Her father leaned over and whispered in her ear. "With this treasure, we'll finally have what we need to buy back yer brathair's freedom as well as free all the orphans from Ravenscar."

"Aye," she answered, feeling hopeful yet anxious. Her father's idea was risky, but if he could pull this off, they'd end up as heroes. His debt to the black-hearted Beast of Ravenscar was more than they'd ever be able to earn in a lifetime. When the English lord showed up in their little Scottish town on the border, he'd demanded the money her father owed him. It was money her father was supposed to be collecting from the area, giving it to Ravenscar to keep the small villages safe from attack. However, her father had already gambled away all the funds. In rage, Ravenscar raided their town, killed her mother and brother, and took several children captive. Her little brother, Rab, was among them. Ravenscar had killed men, women, and children, too, as if their lives didn't matter. Then he had the nerve to demand a ransom if the children were ever to be returned.

Gavina's family didn't belong to a clan, having left on their own to live with those who were in the village. Therefore, they didn't have the protection from the Scots they needed. After the attack and deaths of her mother and brother, Gavina and her father left, traveling up to the Highlands. Since her father was responsible for all the death and destruction, they couldn't even ask the rest of the Scots for help.

Their only hope now was to take that money to Ravenscar before the children ended up dead as well. Raising that kind of money took a long time, and it had already been years. All of this was a horrific happening and, sadly, money was the only thing that could fix it. Mayhap, Gavina decided, this was what they'd been waiting for to pay for her father's mistakes. He seemed sure of himself, but Gavina wouldn't play this risky game unless she knew for certain her father would win the bet.

"How do I ken it's really a treasure map?" asked Finn, expressing Gavina's sentiments exactly. "Let me see it." He held out his hand to Birk.

"Now, if I do that, ye'd have no need for the map," said Birk with a chuckle. "If ye memorized it, where would that leave me? However, to be fair, I'll give yer daughter a sneak peek." He unrolled the map and flashed it at her. It looked to be a map of Scotland leading all the way down the east coast to England. He rolled it up again so fast that she couldn't be sure of anything. She wasn't even able to get good look at the area marked by the X, depicting the spot to find the buried treasure.

"Is it a treasure map, Gavina?" her father asked excitedly.

"I – I guess so," she said. "It was really too fast to tell much, but it looked like one."

"That's all ye're gettin'," snarled Birk. "Now, Drummond, are ye in or no'?"

"Why would ye want to even gamble it away if it is worth so much?" she asked the man suspiciously. None of this made any sense to her.

"Yer beauty has me mesmerized," said Birk, waggling his eyebrows, making her want to retch. "I think ye're worth the risk. Besides," he added with a chuckle, "I've heard from more than one source that ol' Finn here has a habit of losin'. I'm goin' on the fact that he'll lose this bet, too. Now, once again Finn, are ye in or no'?"

Gavina suddenly started to become very nervous. If her father lost the bet, she'd belong to Birk. Anger filled her. She wasn't a possession to be bartered away like a horse and cart. Nay, this idea was preposterous. "He's no' takin' yer bluidy bet," Gavina answered for him, wanting to save her brother but not wanting to put her life in her father's hands. He did have a bad habit of making the wrong choices, just like Birk said. He wasn't good at winning card games, and their loss of almost everything they owned proved it. Still, her father sounded confident, or mayhap it was the alcohol talking. She wasn't sure why he thought this time would be different. "My faither would never wager his own daughter in a doitit card game," she sniffed. "After all, I'm his flesh and blood. Nay, Birk, there is no deal."

"Aye. I'll do it!" her father blurted out, making her head jerk up so fast that a pain shot through her neck. He smiled and smoothed down his wrinkled tunic, sitting back down at the gaming table.

"What did ye say?" she asked, not believing her ears. Was her father really going to do it? "Papa, think about what ye are sayin'. I'm the only child ye have left in this life right now. Please, dinna do it. This is no' a guid idea." Gavina understood her father's desperation to get that treasure to trade for her little brother and the other children of their village. Part of her felt like it really could work. That is, if anyone but her father was the one playing the game. Bad luck seemed to follow him wherever he went. Gavina hated being in this position. Because of her father's bad decision, once again, her future was about to be determined by a blasted game of chance. The worst part was that she wasn't feeling all that lucky today either.

"Daughter, we'll be rich when I win, so dinna fash yerself about it. This is the answer to all our problems. I'll be able to redeem myself for all my mistakes." Her father smiled as Birk shuffled and dealt the cards.

"No' all of them," she ground out, since nothing they could do would bring back her mother or older brother. "Ye say this is the answer to all our problems, but mayhap it's only the beginnin' of them instead," she mumbled. "Papa, what if ye lose?" She tried to reason with him, not even able to imagine herself being bedded by the awful Birk. Men like him were not to be trusted. Just by looking at him, Gavina could tell he was naught but a thieving wharf rat, stealing from the seafarers in one form or another. She was sure card games were one of his better business deals.

"I willna lose, Gavina. I assure ye." Her father tried to convince her as he waved his hand through the air. It was almost as if he really believed he could win this time.

"One hand is all we get," said Birk, picking up his cards to take a look. When he did, Gavina saw him slip a card into his pile and remove another.

"Wait!" she cried, quickly looking over at her father to tell him. To her horror, her father was cheating, too! This is why he was so confident that he would not lose the bet.

"What's the matter, Daughter?" asked Finn, slipping a card atop his pile and palming another under the table.

"Aye, is somethin' wrong?" asked Birk.

With both men staring at her, she felt tongue-tied and wasn't sure what to do. Should she expose Birk? Would Birk know her father was cheating, too? This could end up being a very bad situation.

"I – I . . ." Her eyes flashed over to Birk and then back to her father. What was she supposed to do at a time like this? Whatever she said here could make or break the deal. Or could it? She was so confused and flustered that she became tongue-tied, not knowing what to say.

"Turn over yer cards, Birk," said her father anxiously.

"Ye first," snarled Birk.

"Nay. We'll do it at the same time," suggested her father.

Birk thought about it for a second and then just shrugged. "Have it yer way," he agreed, both of them turning over their cards at once.

Gavina's jaw dropped when she saw duplicates of the ace of spades – one in each of their spreads. Both of the players' cards also added up to the exact amount as the other.

"Och, nay," she said under her breath, knowing there was about to be trouble.

"Ye cheated!" spat Birk, pulling a dagger out of his belt.

"Nay! Ye cheated. I saw ye," screamed Gavina, running to her father's side. "Faither, let's get out of here, now."

"No' before I collect my winnin's." Finn chuckled when he said it, his speech already slurring from too much drink. He was ruled by greed and making bad choices once again.

"Over my dead body, ye will!" growled Birk. Before her father even had a chance to defend himself, Birk stood up and plunged his blade into her father's heart.

"Naaaaay!" screamed Gavina, crying, bending over her father, cradling his head in her arms. His eyes bugged out and blood dripped from the corner of his mouth.

"I-I'm so s-sorry, Gavina," Finn said with his dying breath. "Get the map . . . find the treasure. Use it to set free . . ." The life drained from his body as Gavina held him and he drew his final breath. Then fury filled her and she slowly got up, watching as Birk collected his winnings, scooping the coins into a pouch.

"Ye will die for this!" she said with revenge in her heart. Her fingers gripped the hilt of her dagger and she lunged for him, wanting to make him pay for what had just happened.

Birk looked up quickly, his hand shooting out and clasping around her wrist. He pressed hard until she could no longer hold on to the blade. It released from her fingers, clattering to the floor.

"That's no' a very nice thing to do, lass," he hissed. "Especially since ye belong to me now."

"Nay! I dinna belong to anyone, especially ye. Ye are a cheat and a murderer and I'll never be yers."

"Birk!" A red-haired man rushed into the room, out of breath. He stopped abruptly when he saw Finn lying dead on the floor.

"What is it, ye fool? Canna ye see I'm busy?" snapped Birk.

"Pirates have arrived. They've just docked and are askin' a lot of questions about the map. They will be headed this way soon. Ye'd better hide that map because ye ken they'll take it."

"Damn!" he spat, sounding concerned. "Stall them. Dinna let them in here if ye can help it." He released Gavina's wrist and started to pace the room, his hand to his chin in thought.

"What are ye goin' to do?" she asked him, wanting to run, but also not wanting to leave her father behind.

Birk stopped in his tracks and looked over at Gavina. "I'm goin' to hide this map somewhere where they'll never find it."

Once the red-haired man left, Birk grabbed the map and pulled Gavina into an adjoining room. She struggled against his hold, but he was too strong for her.

"Take off yer clothes!" he commanded.

"Nay! I'll never give myself to ye."

"I dinna want yer body. Or at least no' yet." He pulled out some kind of metal writing tool and a bottle of ink out of a chest on the table.

"What are ye doin'?"

"I'm savin' the map as well as yer life." He stormed across the room, coming toward her with the map in his hand. "If those pirates get ahold of ye, ye'll be naught but the ship's whore when they're done with ye. Now hold still and dinna move."

He reached out and threw her down on the floor, ripping open the back of her gown.

"Nay! Leave me alone!" she cried, kicking and screaming, fighting to keep her virginity intact.

"Blethers! Ye give me no choice, Wench," he ground out. She felt something hit her on the back of her head. It caused her to see stars and then she passed out.

Not sure how long she'd been unconscious, Gavina was awakened by Birk shaking her hard.

"Get up!" he commanded.

She pushed up to her knees, feeling pain in her back as well as her head. Rubbing one blurry eye, she saw Birk lighting the map on fire and throwing it into the hearth.

"Ye're burnin' the map?" she asked in astonishment.

"Aye. I'm burnin' the map so those cutthroat pirates will never find it. I've copied it and put it somewhere where it will be safe. Somewhere that they will never look." He chuckled, as if he were proud of himself for fooling pirates.

She sat up rubbing the bump at the back of her head. Then her hand went to her aching back. Why did it hurt so much? "Where did ye hide the map?" she asked.

"I've copied the map in ink upon yer back," he told her.

"What?" Her eyes and mouth both opened wide. "It's on my back? Nay!" This shocked her and scared her all at the same time. She jumped up to discover he'd taken her clothes and dressed her in the attire meant for a lad while she was unconscious. "What did ye do to me? What am I wearin'?" She looked down at her body, holding the baggy clothes out from her body.

"Ye're Gavin, my servant boy now," he told her, brushing his hands together. "Gavina is no more."

Before she could respond, he picked up some shears and

reached out, yanking her to him by grabbing her long, black hair in one hand.

"Ow!" she cried. "Ye're hurtin' me. Let me go."

"This willna hurt half as much as what those pirates will do to ye if they discover ye're really a lassie." He cut off her hair, even shorter than men usually wore it. Then he walked back and threw it into the fire as well. "I'm savin' yer life, Wench."

"Savin' my life?" Her hand went to her head, feeling the skin at the back of her neck that was now exposed. A cool breeze bit at her flesh, making her shiver. Her long, black hair that she prided herself on was now chopped off so short that she felt naked. She now looked like a boy. Tears fell from her eyes. "Ye've killed my faither and then abducted me and had yer way with me!"

"Nay. I didna ravish ye. No' yet, lassie. However, there will be time for that later. Now, hush up about yer faither because I killed him in self-defense."

"That's no' the way I saw it," she spat through gritted teeth. "My faither never even had a chance to defend himself."

"Och, get over there and haud yer wheesht, ye troublesome wench." He pushed her into the corner, causing her to fall in a heap in the shadows of the room. The door to the room burst open and a tall pirate with brown hair hanging almost down to his waist entered the room with two other pirates right behind him.

"Ahoy, Matey," said the man with a sarcastic tone. "I figured your men were distracting us and thought we'd find you here cowering in the corner."

"Ye'd best be on yer way, Tristan," said Birk. "I've got nothin' here ye'd want."

"Really? Well, that's funny." The man named Tristan coolly and calmly strolled into the room, while the other two pirates entered and started picking up items and sticking them into canvas bags. "You see, word on the dock is that you've got something that I definitely want. It seems you stole a treasure map from an old woman named Nairnie. Now give it back." He moved further into the room.

"I had it, but it's gone. Ye're too late," Birk told him.

"Don't try my patience, Birk. Hand it over." Tristan walked right up to him and held out his empty palm.

"I dinna ken what ye mean." Birk smiled and shrugged.

"Give me the damned map," demanded the man in a low voice. "I won't ask again."

"I told ye, I dinna have it. It's gone for guid."

The blond man who looked to be the youngest of the three rushed over to the hearth. "I see it, Tristan. It's in the fire. He's burning the map!"

"Pull it out!" yelled the third man with black hair, coming to join him. "Hurry, before it's gone."

"It's too late. I told ye that," sneered Birk. "The map is gone and now ye'll never get yer hands on the treasure and neither will Nereus."

"Nereus?" asked the pirate named Tristan. "What does my nemesis have to do with the map?"

"I sent word to him as soon as I obtained it," explained Birk proudly. "I was goin' to sell it to him, but my plans changed."

"That map once belonged to my father." Tristan put his hands on the table and leaned in closer to the man, talking right up in Birk's face. "So, the way I see it, the treasure now belongs to me and my brothers. I want that map."

"There is nothin' I can do." Birk raised his palms in surrender. "As ye see . . . ye're too late." He nodded at the fire and the remnants of the blackened parchment.

"Nay!" Tristan slammed his hand down atop the table, causing Gavina's heart to jump. She cowered in the corner, barely able to breathe. She'd never seen pirates before, and now there were three of them right here in the same room with her. It was a terrifying sight.

"I don't believe for one minute you'd do such a foolish thing as to burn a treasure map. Why would you? What would possess you to do such a thing? What do you gain from that?"

"I burned it so ye wouldna get it," Birk answered with a cocky chuckle.

"Then, I guess you're even stupider than I thought." Tristan's tone sounded impatient and irritated now.

"I have the map memorized," said Birk, tapping the side of his head with his finger. "That's why ye need me alive and canna kill me. I'm the only one who kens where the treasure is."

"Nay," grumbled the pirate with black hair. "You wouldn't have burned it without making a copy."

"I agree, Mardon," said the blond, youngest pirate.

"Thanks, Aaron." Mardon smiled. "After all, it's not often you agree with me on anything."

"There is no copy, I tell ye," Birk tried to convince them. "It's all right here, just like I told ye." He once again tapped his temple, making a face.

"I'll kill him!" The pirate named Aaron drew his blade and rushed over to Birk.

"Aaron, wait," shouted Tristan, but Birk had already drawn his blade and was fighting with him. As their swords clashed together, several of Birk's men burst into the room. Gavina watched in horror as the pirates fought with Birk's men, ending up killing them all. She held her hand tightly over her mouth in order not to cry out when one dead man after another hit the floor. One of them landed right by her, his outstretched arm almost reaching her. She pushed back into the corner and closed her eyes, wishing for this to be over and for the pirates to leave.

When she heard a blade hit the floor, her eyes sprang back open. The pirate named Aaron had disarmed Birk and now held his sword to Birk's throat.

"Can I kill him now, Tristan?" asked Aaron. "Can I?"

"Not yet. Lower your sword and stand away." Tristan slowly walked over to Birk, his boot heels clicking against the wooden floor, the sound thundering in her ears as he walked right past her. He slowly bent down, picking up Birk's sword, placing it on the table. None of the men even noticed Gavina silently crouching in the corner and she prayed they never would. "Tell me something, Birk," said Tristan, resting his butt on the table next to the sword. "What's the name of my ship? Now, think real hard, because you're not going to want to get this wrong."

"I – I dinna remember," admitted the man.

"Give me an answer, because your life depends on it." Tristan stood up right in front of the man now, looking and sounding very threatening. He was tall with wide shoulders, his presence filling the small room. Next to him, Birk looked tiny. "I'm waiting, Birk."

"It's ... it's ..."

"Yes?" Tristan raised a brow.

"It's the *Sea Hawk*."

"Is it?" Tristan's eyes flashed over to his brothers and they all smiled.

"Nay, mayhap it's the . . . the . . . *Condor*," said Birk nervously. "Aye, that's yer ship's name."

"Are you sure?" Tristan's voice remained calm and steady as he used his sleeve to shine the flat end of his sword that lay across his lap. Gavina wondered what kind of game he played with Birk. Whatever it was, it seemed to make the man very nervous.

"Nay, wait a minute," squealed Birk, his voice raising an octave. "Just give me a minute to think. It's the . . . the . . . *Eagle*." He snapped his fingers in the air. "Aye, the name of yer ship is the *Eagle*."

"Wrong for the third time, and the odds are not looking to be in your favor." Tristan remained calm, slowly standing up with his sword clutched in his large fist. "Mayhap I should just tell you. It's the *Falcon*," said Tristan, leaning in closer when he revealed his ship's name.

"Aye, of course it is. The *Falcon*. I kent it was a bird," said Birk. "I promise ye I'll never forget it again."

"Don't worry, because you won't have to remember."

"I willna?" Birk's eyes flashed over to the brothers and back to Tristan. Then his attention was on his dead men lying sprawled across the floor. Slowly, he took a step backwards, looking very frightened. "Why no'?" he asked, his lips quivering as he forced a smile.

"Because, I'm going to kill you, that's why."

"B-but ye canna. I have the m-map memorized," stuttered Birk, his palms going up in the air as if he were trying to make an invisible wall between him and the pirate. "If ye kill me ye'll never find the treasure."

"Not true." Tristan smiled and Birk frowned. "You see, it's clear to me that if you cannot even remember the name of my damned ship, then you don't have the map memorized either. That means you've got a hidden copy of it somewhere. You stole what was supposed to be mine, and I cannot let you get away with it."

"Nay, ye've got it wrong." Birk seemed desperate now. "I didna ken it was yer map when I stole it from the old hag. And I dinna have a copy. Ye've got to believe me." Then he slowly lowered his hands and his spine stiffened. His chin lifted as he boldly continued. "Besides, even if I did have a copy of the map, I'd never tell ye where I hid it."

"I know that. So, I guess I'll just have to find it myself. Search the room, boys," Tristan told the two others that were with him.

"With pleasure, starting with Birk." Aaron reached out and ripped open Birk's shirt, searching him for a copy of the map.

"Get away. I told you I dinna have it." Birk pushed him, and Aaron stumbled.

"You'll die for that, Birk." With his sword drawn, Aaron lunged at Birk, but Tristan held him back.

"Wait, little brother."

"What for?" grumbled Aaron. "Let me kill the sneaky bastard."

"Let's find that copy of the map first. Search every corner. He couldn't have hidden it far. He'd never let it out of his sight."

Gavina whimpered, covering her mouth, but it was too late. They'd heard her.

"Who's there?" Tristan's head snapped around and he peered into the far corner. "Come out here into the light where I can see you." He lifted his blade, leading his way across the room.

Gavina shook with fear, unable to even move. These were the cutthroat pirates that Birk had told her about. Things had gone from bad to worse ever since she set foot in the tavern, and it looked as if her life were over now unless she could somehow escape.

"I said, get out here!" Tristan shouted, reaching out and yanking her to her feet. Her body crashed into his, her cheek momentarily resting up against his bare skin poking through his opened shirt. She pushed away, daring to look up into the eyes of the pirate devil.

"Who are you?" he growled, demanding an answer.

"Leave him alone," spat Birk from across the room. "He's naught more than a lad."

"I see," said Tristan, studying Gavina with a penetrating perusal. "What are you to Birk?"

"He's my servant boy," Birk answered, and she was thankful. The last thing she wanted to do was to talk to a pirate. "He kens nothin'. He walked into the room right before ye did, I swear."

"You look more like a milksop to me," said Tristan with a grunt. "Tell me, Boy, do you know where Birk hid the copy of the map?"

Gavina swallowed hard, her eyes glancing over to Birk who was slowly moving toward her. He gave her a small shake of his head, warning her silently not to tell them.

"N-nay," she said, barely able to say the one word. She cleared her throat, realizing she was supposed to be a boy and should probably try to lower her voice.

TRISTAN

"Search the boy," Tristan said over his shoulder. His brother, Mardon, headed in her direction. Gavina let out a small whimper and backed away from him, her back hitting up against the wall.

"Ye're scarin' the lad. Let me show ye that he doesna have it." Birk held his hands in the air to show he had no weapon, and slowly moved toward her.

"All right," agreed Tristan. "Then do it."

Birk patted her down, pulling up the legs of her trews and then pulling up the front of her tunic, quickly showing her stomach, but not going high enough to let them see her breasts.

"I don't see a map anywhere," said Mardon, throwing things through the air as he searched through a trunk.

"Damn. If only we were a few minutes earlier, I might have been able to save it." Aaron poked at the fire with the tip of his sword, trying to salvage the burned remnants of the map, but to no avail.

Gavina didn't say a word.

"What's this?" asked Tristan, looking down at Gavina's feet. He used the tip of his sword and picked up her flute by the string that was attached to it.

"That's mine! Dinna touch it." She reached out for it, but Birk held her back with his arm, making her feel as if she were pressing up against a stone wall.

"It's just a flute, lad, let him have it. It can be replaced," said Birk.

"That one canna," she said, trying to remember to make her voice sound lower. She wore a hat, and kept her face tilted downward, trying to hide beneath the brim.

"Can you play it?" asked Tristan, surprising her by the

55

question, running his hand along the length of the flute like he was stroking a lover.

"Of course, I can play it! I said it's mine." Her jaw clenched as she held back her emotions, watching him touch her flute. For some reason, she swore she could feel him touching her as well, though he wasn't. Gooseflesh rose on her arms and she rubbed her hands over them. That flute was sacred to her and the last remembrance she had of her older brother, Liam. She prayed the pirate wouldn't break it or take it.

"What's your name, lad?" Tristan asked her, looking up from the flute.

"His name is –" Birk started, but Tristan held up his hand to silence him.

"I'm talking to the boy," he growled.

"I'm Gavin- . . . Gavin," she answered, almost giving him her real name, but catching her mistake at the last minute.

"Gavin, Gavin?" he asked with a smile. "Either your parents had an odd sense of humor, or I'm frightening you."

"Ye dinna scare me," she said, not wanting the man to know how much he really did. Her eyes settled on her flute in his hand once more.

"Oh, then it's this that takes your concern." He held her flute up between them. "Take it," he said. "I don't know how to play it so it has no value to me."

"Thank ye," she whispered.

When she reached out for it, he snatched it away before she could even touch it. "On second thought, I think I'll hold on to it for now." He knotted the string from the flute around his belt. Her eyes focused on his thick waist belt carrying many weapons. He had a second belt over one shoulder with the sheath to his sword.

"You can see I dinna have the map, so leave us, and dinna return," Birk told the pirates.

"I will," said Tristan. When Gavina looked back up, he was staring right at her. His green eyes met hers and she noticed that they were the color of the sea. For some reason, she couldn't look away. "We'll be leaving, but I will be taking your servant boy with us."

"Nay!" both Birk and Gavina shouted at the same time.

"Ye canna have him," protested Birk.

"I find it odd that you're so protective over a mere servant," Tristan remarked, his eyes darting back to his brothers. "Why is this boy so important to you?"

"He's no'. It's just that I . . . I need him," stuttered Birk. "To do my biddin'."

"Well, so do I," Tristan met him in challenge with his words. "We've had some deaths aboard the *Falcon* over the winter. One of the men I lost happened to be my ship's musician. I think Gavin will fill that void nicely." He patted the flute at his side.

"Nay. Ye're no' takin' him!" Birk stepped in front of Gavina with his arms outstretched.

"You took my map, if I must remind you," Tristan told him. "So, until I find out where you hid the copy, I'm taking not only the boy with me, but you as well, Birk."

"Never!" Birk dove for his sword lying on the table. When he grabbed it and spun around, his blade met with Tristan's. The sound of clashing metal filled the small room.

"I don't have time for this," Tristan grumbled. "Now put down the blade and come with me peacefully, or I'll be forced to kill you."

"Ye willna kill me because then ye'll never find the map."

Tristan managed to disarm him, but Birk picked up Gavina's dagger from the floor and lunged at him again. Once more, Tristan disarmed him.

"Uh oh. Trouble is coming," said Aaron, looking out the door. "I just saw one of Birk's men run out of the tavern and it looks like he's trying to round up more men to fight us."

"Then let's be done with this. Everyone, back on the ship," commanded Tristan. This time, Birk reached out and grabbed Aaron's sword since his attention was out the door.

"Bid the devil!" spat Aaron, racing after Birk as Birk thrust the sword at Tristan once again.

"I warned you, fool." Tristan plunged his sword into Birk's side, causing Gavina to gasp and cover her mouth when she witnessed all the blood. "Let's get the hell out of here." Tristan yanked his sword from the man's side as Birk clutched his wound and fell to the ground. "Here, Aaron," said Tristan, ripping the sword out of Birk's hand and tossing it to his brother. "How many times do I have to tell you, never take your eye off your weapon?"

Aaron mumbled something under his breath, snatching his sword from his brother.

A big, burly pirate with a gold front tooth stuck his head into the room. "Cap'n, we've looted the tavern but Birk's men are gatherin' and comin' for justice." He had a bag slung over his shoulder filled with what looked like pilfered items. In one hand, he held a shiny red apple, tossing it up and down. "Shall we go back to the ship?" He caught the apple, taking a huge bite as if he were doing naught but going about a day's business.

"Mardon, Aaron, help Goldtooth and the others bring the booty back to the ship," said Tristan.

"What about the map?" asked Mardon. "It's not in the room. Mayhap we should continue to check the rest of the tavern."

"Nay, if it was there, someone from our crew would have found it by now," Tristan told his brothers.

"So we're leaving without it? I don't understand," complained Aaron.

"We'll find it, just as soon as I get this boy to talk."

Tristan reached down and picked up the flute to look at it again. Gavina held her breath, waiting for him to give it back to her. "Let's go, Musician," he told her, dropping the flute back at his side and turning toward the door.

"I willna come with ye," she boldly answered, hoping he wouldn't run his sword through her like he did to Birk because she was resisting.

"What did you say?" He turned around with a scowl on his face. "Is there a reason you'd rather stay here?" He motioned with his head to Birk lying still on the floor in a puddle of blood. "Perhaps, you'd like to join Good Old Birk?"

"Nay," she answered, trying to hold back her tears. Seeing Birk in a puddle of blood only reminded her that the man had killed her father. She scanned the dead men littering the floor and wanted to scream in terror. Nay, she decided, she really didn't want to stay here, either.

"Now, you either get moving on your own, or I'll carry you out of here over my shoulder," Tristan gave her the ultimatum. "Either way, you're coming back to the ship and I'll not hear another word about it. Savvy?"

He reached out and grasped her arm before she could say a word. As he walked, he pulled her along with him.

"Please, dinna take me," she begged, trying to fight for her life. If she was taken aboard his ship, she may as well die because it wouldn't take the pirates long to figure out she was a lass. "I dinna ken anythin' about a map. I wouldna be help to ye at all."

"I said I don't want to hear another word about it," he reminded her. "Now still your tongue!"

As they walked past her father lying dead on the floor in the next room, she stopped in her tracks. "Are ye no' goin' to bury the dead first?" she asked him softly.

"Nay. They attacked us. Why should we? Let them rot for all I care."

"This man isna one of Birk's men," she told him trying to keep from crying. "Birk killed him over a silly card game."

"Really." He looked down, following her gaze. "Is that your father?" he asked, surprising her that he knew. Her head snapped up to look at him and her tongue shot out to wet her dry lips. She didn't answer. Instead, she looked down at the floor once more. Gavina could see that the pirates had already gone through her father's pockets and even taken his boots. She didn't want to admit that she knew him or they'd be ripping off her father's clothes next, looking for that stupid map.

"Nay," she said with a shake of her head. "I'm an orphan." She spoke to Tristan, but her eyes stayed locked on her father. This would be the last time she ever saw his face. In her mind, she asked him to forgive her for denying she knew him. Even with all her father's bad choices and vices, she still loved him. She was his daughter, and he had been the man who sired her, giving her life.

Her late mother's words rang out in her ears, telling her that there is good in everyone but sometimes one just has to look harder in order to find it. Her mother loved Finn even though he was a drunkard and a swindler. She used to tell Gavina that he was not always this way. She'd say that sometimes a man gets lost and just needs a good woman to help him find his way back. If only her mother hadn't died, Gavina was sure she would have been able to help Finn be the man he once was.

"Are you sure that's not your father?" Tristan asked her.

"Aye. I'm sure," she said, feeling a stab to her heart for denying this.

"Well, this man is nothing but a drunk and most likely gambled away everything he owned," remarked Tristan. "Just leave him, and let's get going."

She quickly bent over, using her hand to close her father's eyes. Anger and despair filled her, overtaking her intense sadness. She might have to leave with the pirates, but she would escape and find that treasure that her father died for. She'd find it and use it to buy back her brother's freedom from Lord Ravenscar if it was the last thing she ever did.

"Mardon, take the lad to the ship and make sure he doesn't escape," Tristan commanded, pushing Gavina forward as they joined the other pirates in the tavern. All of the drinking men and the whores had disappeared.

"Aye, let's go," said Mardon, taking her by the arm and guiding her out the door.

TRISTAN SIGHED, having had no other choice but to take the boy with them. Gavin knew something about the treasure map, he was sure of it. Mayhap with Birk dead now, Tristan could convince the lad to talk after all. This boy seemed valuable to Birk and he even risked his life to keep the lad with him. That told Tristan everything he needed to know. Gavin was the key to finding the treasure. That is why he couldn't leave him behind. It might take a while, but Tristan would get him to spill his secrets, no matter how frightened the boy was. He'd find out where Birk hid the copy of the map and then he'd come back and get it.

By the way that Gavin closed the dead man's eyes in the gambling room, he would bet anything it was the boy's father. The man looked to be a drunkard and a gambler and a man who always made wrong choices. Tristan could spot someone like this anywhere since he'd grown up with a father just like that. If he was correct, the boy was better off without him. It wasn't the first time that Tristan took an orphan aboard his ship, making them part of his crew . . . his family. Ever since Tristan and his brothers left their father and sister behind, his crew had become his new family, even if it wasn't the same.

Birk wasn't a pirate, but he was a conniving, no-good wharf rat. This tavern would be crawling with his friends in a few minutes. Tristan didn't really feel like killing anyone else today, so he decided the best thing to do was to leave before they arrived.

"You there. Show yourself," he said, stopping at the drink board, sure someone was hiding behind it. "Stand up, or I swear I'll take off your head."

"Nay, please dinna do that." An old man stood up, raising his hands over his head in surrender. "I have a wife and family. Please dinna kill me."

"I'm not in the habit of killing, unless I'm attacked first or someone's done me great wrong. Since you're guilty of neither at the moment, I'm not going to harm you." He pulled a few coins out of his pouch, tossing them onto the drink board.

"What is that for?" asked the man, shaking like a leaf.

"I want you to bury the dead man lying by the game table. That's your compensation for giving him a proper burial and a grave marker made of stone. Do you know his name?"

The man glanced over his shoulder into the open room. He kept his hands raised over his head and nodded.

"Aye, he's a common patron here, and always gamblin' away his money," the man relayed the information. "His name is Finn Drummond."

"That's the one. Bury him right away."

"What about the rest of the dead?"

"Do whatever the hell you want with them. They're not worth the time, so just let the crows peck out their eyes and the rats gnaw at their carcasses. I don't really care." He started to walk away, but stopped in his tracks when he had a thought. He looked back over his shoulder. "Did Finn have a son by any chance?"

"Aye," answered the man. "I believe he had two."

"Was his son here today?"

"Nay, Lord Pirate. His sons were both taken from him."

"By pirates?" He raised a brow.

"Nay. Killed by an English lord, I believe. However, I dinna really ken all the details."

"So he had no son that was here in the tavern today?"

"Nay," said the man, shaking his head.

"I see." Tristan was sure he was right, but perhaps he'd misjudged Gavin. He turned to go, but with the man's next words he froze in his tracks.

"Finn Drummond did have a daughter though."

"A daughter?" He turned around, his mind racing. That lad did sound and look a little feminine to him, but he wasn't sure. "Have you ever seen her?"

"Aye, of course I have. She came in here earlier today lookin' for Finn, bein' chased by some ruffians."

"What's her name?" he asked curiously, starting to wonder if he'd been had.

"I – I'm no' sure," said the man. "I think I heard him call her somethin' like . . . Davina?"

"Was it Gavina," he asked, everything now suddenly starting to fall into place.

"Aye, Gavina, that's it." The man's head bobbed up and down. "I saw her go into the back room with Birk and her father earlier."

"Did you see her come out?"

"Nay, Lord Pirate, I didna. But then again, I couldna see much from my hidin' place behind the drink board."

Tristan was sure that no girl came out of the back rooms, because if there had been one in there, Tristan would have seen her. Damn, that meant he'd been had after all.

"Don't forget to bury the man," grumbled Tristan, turning and heading for the door. Inwardly, he cursed himself for his bad luck. He never should have allowed Nairnie onto his ship. Tristan was superstitious, and rightly so. A woman aboard a ship – especially a pirate ship – was nothing but trouble. Nairnie was old and crusty and no man would want her in his bed, so he didn't really worry much about that. However, if Gavin was really Gavina, his troubles were just beginning. If her identity was discovered by the crew, he'd have a big problem. Every one of his men would most likely try to roger her at the rail. At this point, he didn't have much of a choice and had to take her with him. The girl had to know something about the map, and he needed that treasure.

"Will there be anythin' else, Lord Pirate?" asked the proprietor, still shaking like a leaf.

"Nay. You've been more helpful than you know."

Tristan headed out the door, wondering how in the hell he was going to command a ship with not one, but two wenches aboard now.

CHAPTER 3

Gavina was pushed along in a group of a dozen or so men as they hurried her away from the tavern and down to the dock toward their ship. Never would she have thought she'd be in the presence of wretched pirates, and as their captive nonetheless.

These men were rugged, ruthless thieves and killers. She didn't belong here. It was the last place she'd ever want to be. They smiled and laughed as they carried their bags full of booty flung over their shoulders, acting like this was nothing more than a trip to the market for them. Several of the pirates rolled barrels of stolen ale down the pier toward the ship, while others carried wooden boxes containing loaves of bread, vegetables, and even fresh fruit. What gave them the right to plunder a tavern and steal things that weren't theirs? What sort of beasts acted this way and got away with it? Her anger was growing stronger now, overtaking her fear of being their captive.

When she approached the pier, she looked up to see their ship. It was docked further out in deeper water. Their shuttle boats were all tied to the pier. The ship was large and fore-boding. It rose up majestically, its tall masts filling the sky, dwarfing the other ships in the harbor. The pirates didn't bother to hide their presence here, but rather boldly announced their arrival. Black sails half-unfurled told everyone on the dock exactly who they were.

She broke away from the pirate named Mardon and turned and ran, trying to escape. Unfortunately, she didn't get far. Tristan stepped out in front of her and blocked her way.

"What's the hurry, lad? We're going in the opposite direction if you haven't noticed."

For the second time that day, she found her face smashed up against his bare chest since his shirt was unlaced almost down to his navel. Oaken curls of chest hair tickled her nose, threatening to make her sneeze. She quickly stepped back, wiping her nose with the back of her hand. Daringly, she lifted her gaze to peruse him close up.

His long hair was loose and lifted in the wind, making him look like a bold Viking. Seeing that beautiful mane only made her miss her long tresses more than ever now. Her hand shot to the back of her neck, feeling the ends of her brutally chopped hair. It made her want to cry out in despair. She'd always prided herself on her lush, long, thick locks. Now it had all been taken away from her, and it felt as if her femininity had been stripped from her as well. Dressed in boys' clothes with short hair made her feel ugly.

Tristan wore a long, brown leather coat that touched the tops of his knee-high boots. The coat was held shut by a thick belt with a metal buckle that had a skull engraved upon it. His weapons consisted of not only a large broadsword, but a smaller curved sword, two daggers, and something that looked like a hook or a pick. She supposed this is how pirates dressed, armed to the hilt and always ready for a war.

Her eyes fastened to her flute next that he had hanging from his belt as if it were some kind of spoil of war. It swung slightly from the cord she'd previously used to carry it around her neck. Her prized possession had been ripped away from her and was now settled against his groin, causing her to notice the way he filled out his breeches.

He cleared his throat, causing her eyes to shoot up to meet his. Heat encompassed her cheeks, probably turning them red. The man was very tall with wide shoulders. The top of her head only came up to his armpit. The intensity of his green eyes made her freeze. She suddenly felt as if she couldn't breathe. This man named Tristan was downright handsome . . . for a pirate, that is. It made no sense at all, but part of her was intrigued. Could it be some sort of attraction to the man? She shook her head, hoping to clear her terrible thought. No one would ever be attracted to their captor, and that is exactly what he was. This was all wrong and it made her feel disgusted that she had felt this way, even if it was only for a second.

Pirates were evil, no-good, bottom of the barrel scum feeders. Now, if only he would stop looking at her like he could see clear through to her very soul, it might stop her from feeling so anxious. His perusal of her made her feel vulnerable . . . almost as if she were naked.

Crossing her arms over her chest, she raised her chin and met his gaze of unspoken challenge. "I'll no' come with ye and be yer prisoner, so leave me be."

He chuckled, wrapping his long fingers around her shoulders and turning her around toward the shuttle boat. "I can't do that. Now get into the shuttle and stop causing trouble."

Her breath hitched at the feel of his touch and a strange surge of excitement ran through her. She expected him to treat her roughly, but he didn't. A pirate shouldn't have such a gentle touch, should he? It angered her that her body was responding to him in this manner. This man named Tristan confused her mind. What was the matter with her?

"Dinna touch me!" she spat, pushing his hand away, having to break the connection. The two men that were his brothers looked in their direction curiously.

"Just leave the boy here," grumbled Mardon, tossing his bag of pilfered goods into the small boat and climbing in after it. "We don't need troublemakers aboard the *Falcon*. It's already trying enough with Nairnie along."

"Aye," agreed the pirate named Aaron, following him. "Grandmother actually washed my clothes already and made me hang them from the ship's lines. She said I was dirty, but she's wrong. I washed them just last month!"

"Yer . . . grandmathair?" asked Gavina in confusion, sure she'd heard him wrong. After all, pirates didn't even have grandmothers. Did they?

"Aye. Her name is Nairnie," explained Aaron.

"Get in the boat," commanded Tristan, holding on to her arm and guiding her to board. He untied the shuttle from the pier, pushed it, and jumped inside, settling down on the seat next to her. His presence filled the small area. He was so close to her on the bench that his leg pressed up against hers. "Let's go, Ramble," he told the pirate that was rowing.

Anchored a short ways from the dock, she focused on the tall ship with three masts. The main sail was being raised in preparation of their departure. Her anxiety grew as the sail unfolded, becoming bigger . . . and blacker as they got closer to the ship. This was all getting way too real. The sight of the ship made her legs tremble.

"Stop shaking," whispered Tristan, his hand quickly resting on her knee. This only made her more uncomfortable. Why would he do that? Did he put his hands on the knees of other lads as well? After all, he thought she was a boy.

She shifted, moving her leg so that he'd retract his hand. Thankfully, it worked. She had to take her mind off all this, especially the fact that she was now a prisoner of pirates. A prisoner, that is, with a secret map that they were looking for inked on her back. The worst part was that she couldn't even see it. These pirates would do whatever it took to find that treasure map and, sadly, she didn't know how long she could keep it hidden. Anything she did or said was now a risk. It wouldn't be long before they discovered she was a girl and when they did, they'd find the map as well and probably kill her. She had to get their minds off of maps and treasure or they'd be asking her more questions or possibly searching her next.

"Ye keep yer grandmathair a prisoner on yer ship?" she asked, trying to direct the conversation. The thought of this made Gavina wonder just what kind of men they really were.

"Oh, nay, she's not a prisoner," explained Aaron with a swish of his hand through the air. The sun shone down on his blond hair and reflected off one of his earrings. She noticed he had tattoos – lots of them up and down his arms and even one peeking out from under his shirt. Her back ached as she thought of how much pain he'd probably had to endure just acquiring them. She'd only been inked on the surface but it hurt like hell for some reason. "Nairnie is only with us because she fell overboard, and we needed a cook," Aaron continued.

"What?" she gasped in shock. "I suppose ye were the ones who pushed her overboard to begin with."

"Nay, but her story of being our grandmother did keep us from killing her." Mardon repositioned himself on the wooden seat of the boat and started digging through the bag of goods they'd pilfered. The shuttle boat continued to head for their ship along with three others right behind them.

"Ye were goin' to kill yer own grandmathair?" Her eyes opened wide. These were cutthroat pirates just like Birk had told her. She frantically looked back to shore, hoping there would be someone who could help her. Unfortunately, everyone was afraid of the pirates and was in hiding. In a way, she couldn't really blame them. Pirates had a bad reputation, and rightly so, because their actions had earned it.

"Nay, that's not true. We were only going to let her drown, not kill her. And that was before we knew who she was," explained Mardon.

"I dinna see how killin' someone or lettin' them drown is any different," she retorted, trying to remember to keep her voice sounding low.

"Enough!" Tristan bellowed. "I don't want to hear anything more about this for now. Gavin will be my personal cabin boy so I don't want any of you giving him trouble. He takes orders only from me. Is that clear?"

"Personal cabin boy?" asked Gavina, surprised to hear this. "I thought ye said I'm to be yer ship's musician."

"That, too," said Tristan, glancing out over the water.

"That's an odd thing to say, Brother," commented

71

Mardon, looking at him in confusion. "What did you do? Take a fancy to boys now since you've been so long without a wench?"

All the men in the boat started laughing and making crude comments about bedding women.

"Stop it," growled Tristan.

"Why don't we stay in port a while?" suggested Aaron. "What's our hurry? I noticed a few lightskirts in the tavern when we walked in that were enticing. I'd like to have a little taste before we go."

"Aye, I know what you mean, Brother." Mardon looked up with interest. "Did you see the one with the red hair, rounded hips, and big breasts?" He waggled his eyebrows and made wavy motions with his hands like the figure eight. "I'd like to get her under me and plow into her until she cries out for mercy."

"Aye," said one of the other men. All of them suddenly sounded like randy, lust-filled curs.

"You can have her only after me," said Aaron, laughing. "She'll scream louder when I take her bent over a table, than she ever will with you lying atop her."

"Oh!" exclaimed Gavina, covering her mouth with her hand and squeezing her legs together. She couldn't help picturing every one of these lust-filled pirates bending her over the rail and having their way with her until she cried out for mercy. Filled with fear, she couldn't let them know she was really a girl. If so, just like Birk said, she'd end up as nothing but the ship's whore.

"What's the matter, lad?" asked Mardon, one side of his mouth turning up slightly. His bright blue eyes were filled with amusement that she didn't understand. "You act so squeamish hearing us talk like this. Haven't you ever bedded a wench before?"

"I should say no'!" she retorted.

"That's a pity," Aaron broke in. "You don't know what you're missing out on. You've got to try it, and stop walking around feeling as hard as a rock." He grabbed his groin and all the men started hooting and hollering. "Brothers, mayhap when we go back we should give Gavin a turn with the redhead, too," suggested Aaron.

"Stop the talk, now!" said Tristan.

"What's gotten into you, Brother?" Mardon narrowed his eyes and shook his head. He continued to dig into the bag and pulled out a metal tankard, holding it up to the light to inspect it. He tapped it with his nail, and it made a clinking noise. "You're usually the one suggesting we get ourselves a good bedding every time we get to port."

"Well, not today," Tristan answered. "Now, I don't want to hear another word about it."

Mardon and Aaron exchanged glances and shrugged, not seeming to give it another thought. Instead, they started talking about their newfound treasures.

"Everyone out and make it quick," ordered Tristan as soon as the shuttle boats got to the ship. "I see some of Birk's men at the dock starting to follow. I think it's time we pull up the anchor and be on our way."

"On our way? Where?" Gavina looked back to shore, but Tristan blocked her view once again as he stood up and pulled her along with him. He pushed her toward the rope ladder that was hanging over the side of the ship. "Climb up, and whatever you do, don't tarry," he told her.

She looked up the high side of the ship, trying to keep her

balance as the shuttle rocked beneath her. She was afraid of heights and already her stomach was roiling. "I canna."

"Sure, you can. Now, up you go." Before she knew what was happening, Tristan's large hands closed around her waist. Her feet left the shuttle boat as he lifted her effortlessly and placed her on the ladder. "Make it fast," he instructed.

"I-I've never climbed a rope ladder before," she protested, hanging on to it for her life. Glancing back down to the water, she became dizzy. She quickly squeezed her eyes shut and didn't move. "I canna do it." Her fear of heights scared her right now even more than the pirates.

"Get moving!" She felt Tristan's hand on her bottom end as he pushed her upward. Her eyes sprang open. She moved so quickly that she carelessly caught her foot in the rope ladder. When she tried to untangle it, her shoe fell off and dropped into the water far below.

"My shoe!" When she reached for it, her hand slipped and she lost her balance.

"God's eyes, you're already too much trouble." Tristan caught her, putting her back on the ladder, sheltering her body with his as they continued to climb.

"I need my shoe."

"You don't need shoes. I never wear them," Aaron called out from the top of the ladder. She looked up at him, realizing for the first time that he was barefoot.

"I'll find you a pair of shoes on board," Tristan half-whispered into her ear. She could feel his breath against her bare neck as well as the heat of his body pressed up against her back. They climbed the side of the ship with his arms on both sides of her, holding the ladder and keeping her from falling.

"I'll also find you some clothes that fit you properly," he continued. "I'm surprised you haven't already tripped on those trews that are too big for you." With his body pressed up against hers and his strong arms cradling her on the ladder, she felt safe and protected for the first time in a long time. Odd, that it took a pirate to make her feel this way. As soon as Gavina was hoisted over the sidewall and landed on the deck, she noticed a plump woman hurrying toward them from the bow of the ship.

"Where have ye boys been?" griped the old woman, putting her hands on her ample hips. She didn't seem frightened of the pirates at all.

"Don't worry about it, Nairnie. We had some business to tend to," Tristan told her as he flipped over the sidewall and landed on the deck next to Gavina. "Get those shuttle boats hoisted up and raise the anchor anon," he called out to his crew.

"Aye Cap'n," said a man with a peg leg, hobbling over to help. Men filled the deck of the ship, going about their chores, not even paying any attention to her.

"I hope ye were no' out pillagin' the commoners," scolded the old woman. "Mardon, what have ye got in that bag?"

"It's nothing," said Mardon, tucking the bag under his arm and pushing past Nairnie. He didn't get far before the brave woman grabbed the bag from him and threw it down on the deck. Goblets and bowls, coins and playing cards, spilled out at her feet.

"I kent it! Ye stole these things, didna ye?" snapped the old woman.

"We're pirates, Grandmother," explained Aaron with sigh, walking over with a bag of booty as well. "It's what we do."

Gavina wondered what the old woman would say if she knew they'd killed men on shore as well.

"God's eyes, stop calling her Grandmother," complained Tristan. "Start acting like a pirate, not a milksop, little brother. Now everyone, leave your bags here and don't try to palm any items or you'll pay for it, I warn you. Mardon will divvy up the plunder when we get out to sea. I'm going to get us the hell away from here."

"Fine, but I'll take this as part of my share right now." Aaron held up a neck chain with a ring attached to it. The ring twirled around, sparkling in the bright sun. Gavina's eyes fell upon it and it was all she could do not to cry out when she recognized her mother's wedding ring dangling from the chain. It was an amethyst stone that her father had bought with money he'd earned as a fisherman when they'd first married and times weren't as trying. That was before they had three children to feed and before he let his vices ruin him. Aye, it was a time when Finn Drummond made his living as an honest man. She thought her father had buried the ring in the grave along with her mother. Now, she realized his love for her was what made him keep it after all. It had to have meant a lot to him since he'd never gambled it away like he did with the rest of their belongings – even her!

As Gavina focused on the ring, she realized these thieving men must have stolen it right off her dead father's body.

"Can I see that?" she asked boldly, holding out her hand.

"Huh? I guess so," said Aaron with a shrug. "It's not like you're getting any of the booty nor are you going anywhere with it since you can't leave the ship." He held it out, but before she could even touch it, Tristan's hand shot out and he snatched the chain and ring away from her.

"I said, we'll divvy up the goods later," he spat through gritted teeth. "Now get to work, all of you."

"All right," grumbled Aaron. "Come on, Gavin. If you're going to be part of this crew, you need to learn to climb the rigging, raise the sails, swab the deck, and a lot of other chores as well. I'm the ship's bosun and in charge of keeping things in top condition. You'll be taking orders from me now. I'll put you to work right away."

Gavina's eyes shot over to Tristan in a silent plea of desperation. She couldn't do all these things Aaron was talking about. Especially not climb the rigging. Her eyes swept upward and her stomach turned as the ship rocked back and forth in the waves. She wasn't strong enough to do all these chores, and neither had she any idea what swabbing a deck even meant. Her eyes drifted upward to the rigging and she watched a couple pirates holding on with only their legs as they untangled the lines. She could never go way up there. The thought terrified her. What was she going to do? Should she go with Aaron or stay by Tristan? Right now, neither seemed to be a good choice.

"Wait just a minute," said Nairnie, stepping closer to her. "Who are ye?" The old woman squinted one eye and cocked her head, perusing Gavina.

"This is Gavin. He's my new cabin boy and the replacement for our ship's musician," Tristan answered before Gavina even had a chance to speak.

When Gavina glanced back at Tristan, he was putting the chain with her mother's wedding ring attached around his neck. The thought of the symbol of her parent's love being displayed like a war trophy by a thieving cutthroat seemed like blasphemy to her. She wanted to rip it right off of him, but that would only bring her trouble. Her hand went to her aching back and her mind raced. She needed to find a way off this ship and fast. She also needed to find that treasure. The only problem was, she couldn't see the blasted map, and now she had no one she trusted to read it for her. No matter what happened or what decision she made, she was already doomed.

"Cabin boy?" Nairnie asked Tristan. "Ye mean servant boy, dinna ye? And I'll bet the lad is here against his will. So, now it seems my grandsons have stooped so low as to take prisoners. Well, I dinna like it in the least."

"Nay, it's not like that," Tristan told her. "Gavin is an orphan, and will be part of our crew and family from now on." He hurriedly removed the flute from his belt and handed it to Gavina. "Here, play something for Nairnie. After all, you're the ship's musician since our last one died over the winter. As musician, you'll also get a small portion of the booty."

Gavina snatched her flute from his hand, but did not play it. "If I get part of the booty, then I'll take that ring and chain ye just put around yer neck."

He laughed. "I said small part of the booty. This ring is mine now since I'm captain." He ran his hand over the ring and smiled.

"Tristan, as long as I'm aboard this ship, there will be no prisoners," snapped Nairnie. "I willna have my own grandsons stoopin' to that level. Do ye hear me?"

"Listen, old woman." Tristan clenched his jaw and he looked out to sea when he spoke. He seemed to be trying to keep from exploding with anger. "Unless you want us to throw you back where we found you, you're going to have to stop trying to tell us what to do. It's getting annoying." He looked over to Aaron's clothes blowing in the breeze. "And take down that damned laundry from the stays. No pirate ship is going to be hanging clothes from the rigging!"

Gavina turned to see clothes flapping in the breeze, attached to the lines near the bow of the ship. It almost made her laugh aloud. Any woman who did this was someone that Gavina wanted to get to know.

"Hrmph!" Nairnie busied herself with wiping invisible lint from her skirt. "Well, someone's got to do it." Her mouth was pursed in aggravation. "I swear, if I'd kent my own grandsons were goin' to end up as pirates, I would have . . ."

"You didn't even know you had grandsons until recently, so just stop with all the idle threats," Tristan warned her. "Now, take the boy with you for now, and don't let him out of your sight. Mayhap he can help you in preparing the meals. I'm still waiting for that hot food you promised."

"Well, it isna exactly easy to make a hot meal when I only have hardtack, dried fruit and salted meat to work with," snapped Nairnie. "Let me go to shore and get the proper ingredients, and ye'll have yer guid meal, I promise."

"Nay. You're not going to shore, so forget it," Tristan told her. "We've brought some food from the tavern, so see what you can whip up with that."

"The food isna what needs to be whipped here," mumbled Nairnie under her breath.

"What did you say?" Tristan had all he could do not to reach out and hit his own grandmother because of the way she was acting. But Tristan had never hit a woman in his life and wasn't about to start now.

"Let's go," said Gavina, taking a hold of Nairnie's arm, starting to walk away. She did this to keep a fight from

79

breaking out between a feeble old woman and big, brawny men. She was sure Nairnie would take on all her grandsons in a verbal or even physical confrontation if she had to. Gavina admired the old woman's courage, but this ship was no place for an old woman or any female at all. Walking away from this conversation was the best thing they could do right now.

"I'm goin' but this isna over," Nairnie told her grandsons over her shoulder as she waddled over the wooden deck. "Gavin, I'm warnin' ye right now. Once ye're off this ship, dinna ever have anythin' to do with pirates again if ye ken what's guid for ye. I ken they're my grandsons, but I wouldna wish them on anyone the way they are right now. God help any lassie they get near, because they'll never respect one as long as they live. They'll just take what they can get from her and leave her hung out to dry like one of their headscarves blowin' in the wind." She nodded to Aaron's clothes hanging on the line. Sure enough, a red headscarf fluttered in the breeze.

Gavina couldn't help but smile. The old woman painted a dark picture of her grandsons, and Gavina knew she should heed the old woman's warning. Nairnie was right. Gavina needed to stay away from these men, especially after the way she'd felt being so close to the pirate named Tristan.

TRISTAN GRINNED as he watched Nairnie hauling the girl to the galley that was really just a small enclosure at the bow of the ship where his cook prepared the meals. He wasn't sure what he was going to do with Gavina. The wisest thing would be to let her go, but he couldn't do that. Something told him she knew more about Birk's treasure map than she was letting on. Resting his hand on her pear-shaped bottom earlier as he'd helped her climb the ladder had almost been his undoing. Even dressed like a boy and with that chopped off hair, she didn't fool him . . . not anymore. He was sure she was the daughter of the dead gambler. Her name was Gavina Drummond. The only thing he couldn't figure out is why she was disguised as a boy. He also wondered how long it would be before his crew figured out she was a woman. He'd have to keep a close eye on her for her own safety.

"Why'd you let the boy go with Nairnie?" griped Aaron. "I have work for him to do."

"Aye, he needs to pitch in if he's going to be a part of this crew," complained Mardon.

"Oh, I'm not worried about him being part of the crew." Tristan's eyes stayed fastened to Gavina's back end as she and Nairnie entered the galley. How could he have missed that slight sway of her hips or the way she walked with her legs close together? Her features were dainty, and her bone structure thin. Her shoulders were narrow, too. When he'd seen her bare foot, he'd almost thought it looked regal. He let out a frustrated breath because she was getting him aroused and she was still disguised as a blasted boy. That didn't make him feel good at all. He needed to maintain control of his emotions. It had never been a problem before, so what was it with this girl that was rattling his nerves?

"What do you mean, you're not worried about him being a part of the crew?" asked Aaron.

"Aye, that doesn't make any sense," said Mardon. "Tell us, why did you even bring him here at all? You've got Ramble to fill the position of cabin boy. You don't need another servant," Mardon pointed out. "Not to mention, we've done fine without that obnoxious music of our last drunken musician. I just don't see the point. Especially since you've already offered him part of our booty."

"I think he knows more about the treasure map than he's letting on," Tristan revealed his thoughts to his brothers.

"Birk burned the map," Aaron reminded him. "I saw it with my own eyes, smoldering on the hearth."

The wind picked up, blowing Tristan's hair. He pulled it back in a queue, tying it with a small strip of leather he wore around his wrist. "Mayhap he did burn it, but we all know Birk couldn't remember his name if someone didn't call him by it once in a while. The man was a swindler, and not the sharpest blade in the weapon belt."

"True, but he did manage to find Father's hidden treasure map," Mardon pointed out. "That is something that even we couldn't do."

"Aye, I thought that map was gone forever," agreed Aaron.

"He didn't find the map, he stole it," Tristan said. "That's different."

"Do you really think Birk made a copy of the map and was trying to trick us?" Aaron walked over to the laundry, testing his headscarf with his fingers, seeing it was no longer wet. He ripped it down from the line and wrapped it around his head.

"That's exactly what I think." Tristan turned and headed up the stairs to the sterncastle, leaving his brothers standing there contemplating the thought.

"Come on, Mardon, let's go rough up the boy and shake him down until we find the copy of that map," he heard Aaron say from behind him.

"Aye, he must have it," Mardon answered.

"Nay!" Tristan shouted from the top of the stairs, turning

and taking them two at a time, making his way back to his brothers. "He's already been searched. The boy doesn't have it. Leave him alone."

"Then we'll get him to tell us where it is if we have to keelhaul him to do it." Aaron put his hand around his throat and made a drowning noise, laughing. To keelhaul someone meant to tie a rope around a person for punishment. They were dropped over one side of the ship and pulled under the keel, brought up on the other side. It was a horrific experience, since the man usually got cut on the barnacles on the hull, and sometimes they even drowned before they got to the surface.

"Aye, we haven't had a good keelhaul in a while now," agreed Mardon with a nod.

"If either of you so much as touch Gavin, I'll have your heads," Tristan ground out. "I told you I will find out what we need to know. Now, leave it to me. Savvy?"

"Why the hell are you acting so strange?" groaned Mardon. "What's gotten into you, Tristan?"

"My only concern is that we find that treasure." Tristan tried to calm down. It wasn't usually like him to lose control of his emotions. But talk about keelhauling Gavina was more than he could take. "Our hold is half-empty and the crew is getting restless. We need coins and gold and clothes and food. Enough to last us for months in case we don't get the opportunity to board another ship for a while."

"Bring the boy along on our next raid," stated Mardon. "That will break him in quickly."

"Aye. I'll work with him, showing him how to pick a pocket." Aaron smiled and plucked the rest of his clean clothes from the line. "Gavin can accompany Ramble using sleight of hand. The boy's small so should be good at it."

"Nay, I said." Tristan angrily yanked the clean clothes out of Aaron's hands and threw them down on the deck.

"Nairnie's not going to like that," said Aaron, making a face at his clothes now lying on the dirty deck.

"Forget about it," snapped Tristan. "The lad is not like most men. I don't want you two scaring him off. If so, we'll never find out the whereabouts of that treasure."

"I sure hope you're right about this," said Mardon, scratching behind his ear. "With that treasure, we'll be rich and will rule the sea."

"I'm taking us south," announced Tristan.

"South?" Aaron made a face. "Are we leaving the North Sea and sailing through the channel? I don't understand."

"That's the direction the *Desperado* headed," said Mardon. "We're going after our sister, aren't we?"

"Nay," said Tristan. "I don't care about that. It's better if Gwen never finds us. After all, you see how Nairnie is acting. You know Gwen will never accept us being pirates either. Hearing one woman complain about it is already more than I want to listen to. We need to focus on finding that treasure."

"Well I, for one, wouldn't mind seeing Gwen again," remarked Aaron. "It's been such a long time and I kind of miss our little sister."

"I suppose we could take Nairnie home and get her off the ship. That should make you happy, Tristan." Mardon crossed his arms over his chest and waited for Tristan's answer.

"It might be nice to see Cornwall again," mumbled Tristan, starting to feel a little homesick as well. "Not to mention, I could go for an ale and a bucket of clams at the Three Gulls right now."

"Then it's settled. We're going to Cornwall!" Aaron smiled, as if he thought he'd won the argument but he hadn't.

Tristan held his hand up to get his brothers' attention. "I'm not finished. While I said that I'll think about returning to Cornwall, we can't. Or have you two forgot our agreement?"

"We promised to stay on this side of Britain, but it no longer matters," said Mardon. "That agreement was made with Rowen the Restless. And unless you haven't been listening, Nairnie said Rowen is no longer a pirate. Therefore, there is no longer an agreement to honor."

"What is the matter with you two?" asked Tristan, thinking that Nairnie had shaken them up and they were making bad decisions. "Did you forget when we left the fishing boat, we made a life choice that can't be reversed? We're pirates now, and that is what we'll always be. No one in Cornwall who knew us as fishermen will accept us. Neither will Gwen. There is no point in going back after the things we've done."

"Mayhap you're right," said Aaron, his smile disappearing quickly.

"I know it hasn't always been easy, but we are richer and have so much more than we ever had as fishermen," Tristan reminded them. "The opportunities now are boundless where, before, we struggled just to survive another day. Do you two want to go back to that way of life?"

"Nay," said Mardon, hanging his head.

"Me, either," agreed Aaron, bending down and picking up his clothes.

Tristan continued. "If Father would have stayed a pirate the first time, instead of going back to being a fisherman, we'd be unstoppable and rule the seas by now. All we need is this treasure and we'll be set, able to live like kings. After all, the treasure once belonged to a king."

"You're right," said Mardon, sounding much more confidant now. "Gwen is no longer our concern. Nairnie tells us she's married with a family and that she is happy. All we'll do is make her miserable if we return. Like you said, she'll only want to change us."

"Right," agreed Aaron, shaking the dirt off of one of his tunics. "Our sister saw our ship and turned around so she must not want to find us after all. Besides, now we've got Grandmother, so it's not like we've lost our entire family."

Tristan shook his head, hating it when Aaron called the old woman Grandmother. It made them look weak in front of the rest of the men. "Put those clothes down," complained Tristan, taking them from Aaron's hands and tossing them back down to the deck. "Aaron, you need to stop calling the old wench Grandmother. Call her Nairnie if you want, but never Grandmother. It'll only make you weak in the crews' eyes. Both of you, stand firm with who we are and what we do. Don't ever let anyone convince you otherwise. And for God's sake, whatever you do, don't ever let a wench try to change you. There is no coming back from a tragedy like that!"

CHAPTER 4

"*Did* my grandsons hurt ye?" asked the old woman named Nairnie as soon as Gavina entered the small enclosure and closed the hanging curtain that served as a door.

"Nay, I'm fine," she said, looking around. "So, is this where ye cook the meals for the pirates?"

"It is," she said, clearing off a board that served as a counter. "But I'd prefer if ye didna call them pirates."

"Well, that's what they are." She sat down on a wooden box, inspecting a silver spoon that was resting on a gold-plated platter filled with crumbs that looked to be left over from a meal. "After all, these men would never have dishes and utensils like this unless they stole them from a wealthy noble." She held up the spoon to prove her point.

"Harumph," said Nairnie with a puff of air from her mouth. She snatched the spoon away from her. "Mayhap so, but Tristan, Mardon and Aaron are still my grandsons. I swear I will reform them if it's the last thing I do – even if I have to die tryin'."

"I see," said Gavina, noticing the pain on Nairnie's face. "This must be hard for ye. Were yer grandsons always so . . . troublesome? Even when they were just boys?"

"I dinna ken." She became suddenly quiet as she reached into a barrel and pulled out a few apples, laying them atop the cutting board. "I didna even ken they existed until a few years ago." She picked up a knife and started to sharpen it against a stone.

"Why no'?" asked Gavina. "Did somethin' happen that took them away from ye?"

"Ye could say that." She slammed down the stone and furiously started slicing the apples. "I had a son named Cato. He was taken from me when he was just a lad by the man who sired him. I never saw him again."

"Och, I'm sorry," said Gavina, realizing how hard that must be for the old woman to bear that pain.

"Then, no' long ago, it was brought to my attention that Cato had died and left behind a daughter named Gwendolen, and I was able to meet her. When I saw my son's grave, I cried. Then I became angry when I found out he was once a pirate and that I had three grandsons that turned to piracy as well. Gwen wanted to find her brathairs, and so we convinced her husband, Brody, to take us along to look for them. Then I fell overboard in a storm. Thankfully, my grandsons didna leave me to die, but fished me out of the sea instead. Now, I'm here." She scooped up the apples and dropped them into a wooden bowl and handed it to Gavina. "Here, ye must be hungry. Eat."

"Thank ye," she said, eagerly taking a slice of apple since lately she was always hungry. She and her father didn't have enough money to buy much food. "Was their sister, Gwen, really tryin' to find them?"

"She was." Nairnie put down the knife and slowly sat down on a stool. "Gwen wanted more than anythin' to be reunited with her brathairs. And I wanted to see my grandsons before I died."

"Did Gwen and Brody try to save ye when ye fell overboard?" Gavina shoved another piece of apple into her mouth.

"I'm no' sure," she said. She tried to hide it but Gavina saw her quickly wipe a tear from her eye. "They probably thought the sea claimed me and that's why they turned around. I canna blame them. Brody has Gwen and his four children to think of, and they are more important than an auld woman like me."

Gavina's heart went out to her. "Well, at least yer grandsons saved ye."

"Aye." She let out another sigh and stood up. Since she was short, her head didn't hit the underside of the forecastle. "At least there is that, even though I'm no' sure they shouldna have left me to be claimed by the sea." She fished another apple out of a barrel and inspected it closely, holding it up to let Gavina see she found a worm in it. "It's such a disappointment that my grandsons are all rotten to the core." She tossed the wormy apple to the side. "I'm afraid they'll never be anythin' but bad."

"Dinna say that." Gavina slowly put down the slice of apple. "My mathair used to say that there is guid in everyone, but sometimes ye just need to look deeper to find it."

"Really." Nairnie looked at her as if she were mad. "How did yer mathair die?"

"She . . . she was killed in a raid by an evil English lord who ended up also killin' my older brathair."

"Need I say more? No' everyone has guid in them, I'm

afraid to say. I learned that a long time ago when my son was taken from me. The worst of the lot is pirates."

"Well . . . mayhap no' all pirates are . . . bad." She heard the words coming from her mouth but wasn't even sure why she was saying this. Mayhap it was just to comfort Nairnie.

"My grandsons took ye captive, so that should prove there is no' guid in them like ye seem to think."

"I suppose ye're right," she said sadly, wishing that Nairnie was wrong. But the evidence only proved that she wasn't. Gavina picked up her flute, running her hand over it in thought.

"Can ye really play that thing?" Nairnie looked over her shoulder as she cleaned off the piece of wood that served as her counter.

"Aye," she answered. "My brathair, Liam, made this for me when I was just a child. We were always close. I treasured it and learned to play it. The music has always been able to calm my weary mind."

"Then mayhap ye'd better play it for me, lass. After all, my mind could use some calmin' about now."

"Of course. I'd be glad to." She lifted the flute to her mouth but stopped when she noticed Nairnie smiling at her. Suddenly, she realized that the old woman had called her lass, and she hadn't corrected her. Gavina had been so caught up in her thoughts that she made a crucial mistake. "How did ye ken?" she asked softly.

"How could I no' ken? I'm a woman and it's as plain to me as the nose on yer face that ye are no laddie, but a lassie."

"Yer grandsons think I am a lad. So do the other pirates."

"Well, dinna expect that to last. They'll sniff ye out sooner or later as if ye were a bitch in heat. Mark my words, ye willna be able to fool them long."

"I hope ye're wrong," she told her.

Nairnie reached out and touched Gavina's chopped hair. "Who did this to ye, lass? Tell me, why are ye pretendin' to be a lad?"

"It was Birk – a swindler from the tavern who did this to me. He – he told me it would save my life. From bein' ravished by pirates. He and his men kent that yer grandsons and their crew would be upon them and – and he did it to protect me. He said if they kent I was a lass, I'd end up as the ship's whore."

"He did, did he? How odd," she said in a tone that said she didn't quite believe her. "Was this Birk a friend of yers?"

"Friend?" she gasped. "Nay! I hate the man. He killed my faither."

"Yet, ye let him do this to ye because he . . . just wanted to protect ye?"

"Aye," she said, looking down and playing with her flute, realizing how silly this must all sound. If she told Nairnie about the map it would all make perfect sense to her. But Gavina couldn't bring herself to do that. Not yet. Nairnie was the grandmother of the pirates that abducted her, and she wasn't really sure if she could trust her or not.

"Did Birk rape ye, lass?"

"What?" Her head snapped upward. "Nay! He didna touch me . . . no' like that. I'm still a virgin."

"I see." She started cleaning up some dirty plates, putting them into a big bucket of water. "I've never kent a man to go to such extremes to protect a woman who hates him. That is, unless there was somethin' in it for him. So, what was it?"

"I – I dinna ken what ye mean." Gavina's hand went to the back of her short hair and she nervously stroked the ends.

"I suppose it doesna matter. When ye're ready to tell me the whole truth, ye will." She wiped her hands on a rag. "In the meantime, ye'd best stay close to me and far away from the men, in case they catch on to who ye really are. If so, Birk will have been right in sayin' they'll use ye as naught but the ship's whore."

Gavina's heart lodged in her throat. This thought frightened her more than anything. "Tristan told the others to leave me alone," she blurted out, not wanting to admit to the old woman that she thought the man was handsome and that she somehow felt protected when she was near him. That was something that even Gavina thought sounded ridiculous. "He said he was the only one who would give me commands."

"Did he now?" she said with a chuckle. "Well, if so, then Tristan is the one ye need to stay away from the most, because that means there is somethin' he wants from ye. And if he finds out ye're a lass, I guarantee what he'll be wantin' is somethin' ye willna be willin' to give. With these boys, an action like that is nothin' but a way to be admired by the others. I've heard so much talk from these men about what they do with women that my head is spinnin', and I've only been on board a day."

"What do ye mean, Nairnie? Do ye really think I need to fear Tristan? Yer grandson has been nothin' but nice to me so far. He even seemed to go out of his way to protect me from the others."

"That is exactly what I mean, lass. Ye must be some sort of prize to him. He must have plans for ye or he would never have brought ye on board to begin with. Pray he doesna find out ye're a lass because that is the worst thing that can happen at this point."

"Worst thing? Why? What do ye mean?"

Nairnie looked at her and pursed her mouth the way she had done when she talked with her grandsons earlier. "What is yer name, lassie? Yer real name?"

"I'm Gavina. Gavina Drummond. The men just think I'm Gavin.

"Well, Gavina Drummond, one thing ye need to learn quickly about Tristan is that he is very superstitious. These men believe havin' a woman on board is bad luck."

"But ye're a woman and they took ye on board."

"Aye, but they almost didna."

"Still, they did once they found out ye were their grand-mathair."

"Is that what they told ye?" She laughed. "They were still goin' to let me drown even when they kent who I was."

"They were?"

"Aye," she answered with a nod. "It was only when I told them I could tell them where to find a treasure map that they took me aboard."

"A treasure map?" Gavina's heart jumped.

"Aye, I found it on my late son's ship, the *Desperado*. I was bringing it along in case I needed to use it to lure my grand-sons to me. However, it was stolen from me at the Crooked Crow Tavern by a man named Birk. The same Birk ye are tellin' me about, I'm sure." She moved the hanging blanket aside and peered out to the deck, narrowing her eyes. "In all the excitement, I didna even get the chance to ask them if they found the map."

"They didna," she told them, not even able to look at Nairnie when she spoke.

"That's a shame. I was hopin' they'd find that treasure. Are ye sure about this, lassie?"

"Oh, I'm sure. Nairnie, if ye dinna like yer grandsons bein' pirates, why did ye hope they'd find the treasure?"

"I suppose I hoped they'd find it just so they'd have enough to live on and leave piracy forever. It doesna matter. Just remember, lass, that all men are the same. They are pigheaded stubborn, and make stupid decisions. They will never listen to the reasonin' of a woman. Therefore, there are only two things that entice them into doin' what ye want."

"What are they?" she asked, curious to know.

"Well, temptin' them with food is the only one that would work for me, so that is what I'm doin'." She pulled down a mortar and pestle and started grinding fresh herbs that were probably stolen from the tavern.

"I dinna ken how to cook. No' really," said Gavina, feeling her hope diminishing quickly. "What is the second thing that will get a man to do what a woman wants?"

Nairnie stopped grinding herbs and turned to look at Gavina. "It's somethin' that I ken ye would never use to yer advantage since ye seem to be a guid lass. The second way to control a man is to use yer body."

"Ye mean – couple with him?"

"Missy, ye're on a ship full of men who have lustful thoughts of wenches day and night. Of course that's what I mean! Now, I wouldna advise ye to use this method. Hopefully, ye'll be off this ship and far away from here before any of them discover that ye are no' who ye pretend to be."

"Of course, I will," said Gavina in deep thought. She

wanted nothing more than to escape this pirate ship but, unfortunately, she couldn't leave and it wasn't just because she was being held prisoner. She couldn't leave because she needed Tristan and his crew's help in finding the treasure so she could use it in trade for her brother's life. Now, she just had to figure out a way to convince him to do her bidding – without using either of the ways Nairnie suggested.

"TAKE THE HELM, STITCH." Tristan handed over the ship to his navigator while he headed down to the deck where his men were patiently waiting for their share of the booty they'd collected from the Crooked Crow. When he got to the bottom stair, it squeaked as always, about driving him mad.

"I told you, I'll divvy up the plunder as soon as Tristan gets his ass down here," Mardon was telling the others, using the tip of his sword to push back the anxious men from the loot.

"My ass?" Tristan repeated, walking into the center of the circle of men. They moved aside, letting him pass.

"Sorry, Brother. It's just an expression," mumbled Mardon.

"Where's Aaron?" Tristan's eyes scanned the crowd but he didn't see his youngest brother amongst the men.

"He's still up in the lookout," Ramble relayed the information.

"Aaron, get down here," Tristan bellowed, looking up to see his brother climbing down the rigging. "Peg Leg Pate, where are you?" Tristan called out.

"I'm here, Cap'n." The round-bellied man walked over from next to the yardarm, his peg leg thumping on the wooden deck along the way.

"How many times have I told you to fix that bottom stair? It's still squeaking," Tristan complained.

"Aye, Cap'n I'll fix it." The man said the words but didn't move. He was the ship's carpenter and in charge of the ship's structural integrity. He fixed anything from damages incurred after a storm, to holes, to even keeping the yardarm and masts sound. In trying times, he even acted as a surgeon if the need arose to cut off a limb.

Pate always had a peg leg in the time that Tristan knew him, but word was that the man cut off his own leg rather than to let someone else do it. Tristan didn't know if it was really true, and neither did he care. As long as his men were loyal and did their jobs, that is all that took his concern. "I'll get to it right after Mardon divvies up the booty, if that's all right with ye," the man explained. "Ye understand, Cap'n, don't ye? I don't want to miss out on my share."

"Fine," said Tristan, thinking this crew was like a pack of wild dogs when it came to getting their share of booty. Then again, it had been a long winter and the plunder had been scarce. Spring wasn't proving to be much better. His men needed something to look forward to and he couldn't blame them. He'd been getting restless himself lately.

"I'm here," said Aaron, pushing his way to the front of the crowd to join them, walking surefooted in his bare feet.

"All right then," said Tristan. "Mardon, get to it."

Mardon dumped all the bags out, and the crew moved in closer.

"I'll take that knife," said Coop, the barrel maker. "I could really use it."

"I want that sword," said Pate, moving toward the pile.

"Ye always get the swords. I want it," complained Noll,

sticking out his foot and tripping Pate. The man stumbled and Tristan reached out to keep him from falling.

"Watch where ye're goin', ye clumsy fool," complained Wybert, another pirate, pushing his way to the front of the crowd. There were about two dozen men on the ship, and this booty was extremely small. Tristan knew it was going to cause problems.

The men started arguing, so Tristan put his fingers to his mouth, whistling loudly to get their attention. "Quiet down," he warned them. "Everyone, wait your turn."

Tristan looked up to see Gavina emerge from the galley with Nairnie. She held on to her flute as they watched. Why did he feel as if he didn't want the girl or his grandmother there? Something about the women watching seemed . . . wrong. He needed to finish this up quickly.

"Go on, Mardon," commanded Tristan. "And make it fast. I don't have all day."

"What about that ring on the chain around yer neck?" one of the men called out. "That was part of the booty, too, wasn't it?"

"I want the ring," complained another man. "I never get anythin' good."

"Ye get more than me," shouted another. "How about if I get my share before him this time?"

Tristan's hand covered the ring in thought. He knew without even looking that Gavina was staring a hole through him. He'd seen one of his men take it from the neck of the dead man that he was certain was Gavina's father.

"This ring will be my share of the booty," he told the men.

More gripes went up from the crowd.

"If I must remind you all, as captain, I get double share and have the right to choose first. Mardon is my quartermaster and also gets double share, choosing second. Then my brother, Aaron, who is bosun gets his share and a half. All the food and drink is shared evenly, and Mardon determines the order in which the rest of you will choose, or decides if you get anything at all. I know the booty is small, but there will be a huge bounty soon."

"If not, I think I'll join Nereus' crew," Tristan heard one of the men mumble. "At least they aren't starvin' and poor."

"Who said that?" Tristan's head snapped up. "Talk like that will not be tolerated aboard my ship. It'll only get you strung up from the yardarm. Now who was it? Answer me."

"It was Noll," said Goldtooth with a nod of his head.

"Bring him here," commanded Tristan.

Goldtooth grabbed the man by his tunic and hauled him over to Tristan.

"What is the matter with you that you'd say a thing like that?" growled Tristan.

"Well, it's no secret that we've been hungry these past few months," complained Noll. "What about the treasure map? Ye let a man burn it in front of ye? We could have used that booty."

"You think I don't know that?" shouted Tristan, losing his patience with this man. "Don't worry, I'm going to get a hold of that map and we're going to be rich soon."

"How do ye plan on doin' that?" asked the man boldly. "It seems to me that lately ye're not half the pirate ye used to be."

Tristan had no choice at that point but to punch Noll in the face. "I'll teach you not to talk to your captain like that again."

Noll jumped up and reached for his sword. With a nod

from Tristan, Aaron and Mardon disarmed him and held his arms.

"Take him to the main mast," commanded Tristan. "Ramble, fetch me my whip."

"Aye, Cap'n," said Ramble, running to where the whip was hanging and hurrying back with it. "He really shouldna be talkin' that way to ye, Captain. I'm surprised ye're no' makin' him walk the plank or that ye're no' keelhaulin' him instead."

"You need to stop talking, Ramble," said Tristan, taking off his coat and handing it to the boy, retrieving the whip from him.

"Aye, of course, Cap'n, I'll stop talkin' at once. I ken I tend to talk a lot at times, especially when I get excited."

Tristan picked up the whip and moved toward the post where Aaron and Mardon had stripped Noll of his tunic, exposing his back. They tied the man's hands around the post. Something made Tristan look over to Nairnie and Gavina. Nairnie was glaring at him with her hands on her hips. Gavina stared at him with wide eyes, her face turning very pale. He lowered the whip slightly and spoke to Ramble.

"Ramble, take Gavin to my quarters and leave him there."

"To yer quarters?" asked Ramble in question. "Ye usually make the new men watch as ye punish someone."

"Just do it," he ground out.

"Aye, Cap'n. I'll take the lad to yer cabin right away." Ramble ran off and collected Gavin, doing as ordered. Nairnie still stood there with her hands on her hips. Why did Tristan feel like naught but a child right now who was about to get scolded? He hated having the women on the ship because it made him vulnerable in more ways than one.

He turned back to Noll, but spoke to Nairnie over his

shoulder. "Nairnie, take the food from the tavern and go to the galley and start making us something to eat."

"It's no' time to eat again."

"Do it!" he bellowed, not able to look at her when he spoke. "I want two men to help her with the food. There will be extra rations involved for those who do it."

Suddenly, everyone wanted to help Nairnie.

"Get back," he heard the old woman telling them. "Ye all stink and I dinna want yer filthy bodies so close to me."

"Coop and Goldtooth will help Nairnie," he called out. "The rest of you stay far away from that food as well as the rest of the booty or I'll slice off your fingers as soon as I'm finished with Noll."

He glanced over to see Gavina turn and look over her shoulder as Ramble opened the cabin door. She stared at Tristan as if she thought he were some sort of monster. He hadn't even done anything yet, but the way she looked at him, it cut him to the bone. Why the hell should it matter what she or Nairnie thought? It didn't. This was his ship and he was the captain. He needed to maintain control and not let anyone speak out against him. If he didn't do something about this right away, there could be a mutiny on his hands next. He had no choice. Tristan raised the whip and, in one motion, brought it down hard across Noll's back.

CHAPTER 5

*G*avina flinched when she saw Tristan bring the whip down across the pirate's back. The cracking noise made her twitch. Pain shot through her own back from Birk inking the map onto her skin. How could anyone endure the sting of the whip? It must be so painful.

"In here, Gavin." Ramble grabbed her arm and pulled her into the room. "I know it's hard the first time to see a whippin', but just be glad it isn't ye." They entered the room, leaving the door open behind them.

"Does he do that often?" she asked, feeling dazed as she stepped into the small cabin.

"Not as often as he uses his fist against their faces, but more often than he keelhauls a man."

"Keelhaul? What's that?" she asked.

Ramble chuckled. "Ye've sure got a lot to learn. Don't worry, Tristan will teach ye everythin' ye need to know."

"I'm no' sure I want him to teach me anythin'. No' after what I just saw him doin'." Her eyes scanned the room. It was small and the ceiling barely high enough for a tall man to stand. Two hanging beds, one made of canvas with shallow sides, and the other made of netting, swung back and forth from the ceiling as the ship swayed. There was a pillow and a bunched-up blanket thrown haphazardly atop the canvas bed. On the bed made of netting was a blanket that was folded up neatly with the pillow placed precisely on top of it.

On the floor beneath the messy bed was a pile of clothes and a pair of boots. There was also an open trunk filled with things spilling out onto the floor. The neat bed had two closed humpback trunks at the foot on the floor. Directly under it was what looked like a pallet stuffed with straw.

"Do ye sleep here, too?" she asked Ramble.

"Nay."

"Why are there three beds?"

"Well, Tristan's brother, Mardon, uses that bed," he said, pointing to the neat one.

"Is Tristan's bed the messy one, then?" she asked.

"Aye, it is. The two of them are nothin' alike. Mardon's things are always impeccably neat and clean. On the other hand, our captain doesn't seem to care as much about things like that at all."

"Who sleeps on the pallet?" she asked curiously, pointing to the one stuffed with straw on the floor.

"Oh, that pallet and one of the trunks belongs to their youngest brother, Aaron. Aaron doesn't use it much. Most of the time, he just sleeps on the deck with the rest of the crew, or up in the lookout basket."

"In the lookout basket? How could anyone want to sleep there or even go up there at all?" Just the thought of climbing that high made her dizzy and queasy.

"Aaron is like a monkey," he explained. "He loves it up

there. Plus, he knows it's a place to go where he won't be bothered."

"I see." She continued to study the room that was being lit only by the light coming through the door and one small window by Tristan's bed.

Across the room, a horizontal board hung from the ceiling by ropes, serving as a table. Several items were atop it. A barrel was to one side, used for sitting on. A wooden bench was on the other. Next to the table were stone busts of naked mermaids emerging from the wall. And in the center of the mermaids hung a painting of a naked woman sprawled out across a blanket in a most provocative pose.

"Och!" she gasped, shocked and a little embarrassed to see this.

"Aye, isn't that entiein'?" asked Ramble smiling from ear to ear. "The crew keeps sneakin' in here to look at it, and to . . . relieve themselves on occasion. It infuriates the captain and he has to threaten them to stay out. We picked that up from a French ship of very wealthy nobles."

"Stolen," she muttered, not at all surprised. Everything owned by pirates seemed to be things they'd pilfered. Her eyes scanned the wooden slats on the wall that held plates made of silver. Several golden goblets as well as strings of pearls filled a basket nailed to the wall. She walked over to a smaller trunk and curiously lifted the lid. "What's in here?"

To her surprise, she found a blue silk gown with a velvet black bodice that laced up the front. "I suppose yer captain stole this as well since there doesna seem to be any lassies on the ship but Nairnie." She held it up to get a better look. "This certainly isna Nairnie's size."

"I'm not sure about it. I've never seen it before," said

Ramble, walking up closer behind her to inspect it. "I suppose it came from a raid, but I don't even know why the captain keeps it. He should let me rip it up and use the cloth to make some new tunics for the crew."

"Ye ken how to sew?" she asked, talking to Ramble without looking at him. Her eyes were fastened on the beautiful gown.

"Aye. Cap'n taught me to sew when I first came aboard the ship as part of his crew."

"Tristan did? He kens how to sew?" She laughed aloud since the idea amused her.

"Aye. He does," said Ramble, suddenly seeming lost for words. He cleared his throat from behind her.

"I canna imagine a big, brawny, ruthless pirate like Tristan doin' such a dainty chore." She continued to inspect the gown, picturing herself wearing it. Her fingertips glided across the smooth silk and settled on the fuzzy velvet. It was the most beautiful gown she'd ever seen. Just the feel of it in her hands made her feel royal.

"He's . . . very good at it," stated Ramble, clearing his throat again, this time a bit louder.

Gavina held the gown up higher, turning it to see both sides. "Well, losh me! I thought all yer captain kent how to do was whip, torture, and murder men. That is, besides steal everythin' he can get his hands on. I figured he'd be guid at tearin' apart things or people and slittin' throats, but certainly not sewin' things together and doin' the work of a lady! "

"And, I didn't figure you to be someone who would judge another so easily before you even knew anything about them," came a low voice from behind her.

Gripping the gown, she spun on her heel, almost falling when the ship listed again since she only wore one shoe.

There stood Tristan, outside the small doorway, holding his coat in one hand and the whip in the other. She could see the deck and the men behind him through the open door. Noll was being released from the whipping pole, and she saw the lashes on his back. The men laughed and talked loudly, as if nothing bad had just happened at all. Then they followed Mardon back to the pile of booty, eager to get their share.

"Tristan!" she gasped. "I didna ken ye were there."

"Obviously not." He ducked and entered the room, his tall body bent over slightly since his head was already scraping the low ceiling. "Leave us, Ramble."

"Aye, Cap'n," said Ramble, hurrying to the door.

"Wait." Tristan handed the whip to the boy. "I don't want to be disturbed," he told him. "I'm going to rest now."

"Aye, Cap'n," said Ramble stepping over the threshold. He turned back and continued talking. "I'll make sure to tell all the men that they are not to –"

Tristan slammed the door in his face. There was a small, round window in the room that overlooked the sea. Light spilled into the cabin, but it was still partially dark and musty inside.

"I – I suppose I'll go help Nairnie with the food then," she said, putting the gown back into the trunk. She turned and headed for the door. As she approached the door, he stepped in front of her and she found herself staring at the small beads of sweat dripping down his bare chest. "Excuse me, Cap'n," she said, calling him by his title the way Ramble had.

"Nay, you're staying here."

"Here? Alone with ye?" she blurted out, wanting to kick herself for voicing her thoughts aloud. She was supposed to be a boy but was sure she was coming across sounding like a scared wench about now.

"Aye. With me," he said, throwing his coat down atop the messy pile of clothes under the hanging bed by the window. He then unbuckled and removed his weapon belts and laid them on the table. "I thought we could get to know each other better, now that you're part of my crew." He reached over to the trunk with the gown in it and slammed it shut. "The first thing you need to learn is that you never touch my things. Since you're new here, I'll let you off with just a warning this time. But don't let it happen again. Savvy?"

"Savvy?" she asked tritely. "I'm sorry, but I dinna talk pirate."

"Well, then you'd better learn."

"If I dinna start talkin' and actin' like a pirate, what will ye do?" She blinked twice. "Will ye tie me to the mast next and whip me the way ye did to poor Noll? Or will ye do that heel kaul thing to me?"

"It's keelhaul," he corrected her, "and I'm more than sure you don't even know what it is since you can't even say it right. Don't worry about poor Noll. The man was going to start a mutiny against me with talk like that." He kicked off his boots and started to undress. "I am captain of the *Falcon*, and need to maintain control of my crew. I'll do whatever it takes to do it."

"W-what are ye doin'?" she asked in surprise when he pulled off his shirt and threw it to the floor next. His broad chest was now naked. The man looked strong and fit by the amount of muscles she saw in his arms. There was no question about it. Dark hair trailed down the front of his chest and disappeared under the waistband of his breeches, making him look very masculine. When he started to reach for the top of his breeches, she quickly turned around.

"I like to take time to think and rest in the middle of the day," he explained. "So, I'm going to take a nap."

"Takin' a nap?" She spun back around to see him removing his breeches and almost cried out. Once again, she turned around. "I didna think pirates did that."

"Only on days when I'm not out raiding, pillaging, plundering, and torturing people," he remarked sarcastically, obviously having overheard what she had said to Ramble. "However, I've already done all that for the day so now it's time to rest."

She heard the creak of the ropes and realized he was getting into the bed. Slowly, she turned around, thankful the canvas sides came high enough that she couldn't see if he was totally naked or not.

"Well, what am I supposed to do in here while ye're so busy thinkin' and restin' from all that hard work of whippin', pillagin' and plunderin'?"

"How about you tell me where Birk hid the copy of the map." He put his arms behind his head and closed his eyes.

"I told ye . . . I dinna ken anythin' about a map."

"Well, I don't believe you. Birk was willing to risk his life to protect you, so you obviously were of great value to him. You must know something."

"I'm only a simple servant lad. I dinna ken."

"Ha! If you're a boy, I'm the king of England," he answered with a chuckle.

"What do ye mean?" she asked softly, hoping he didn't know her secret.

"What do you think I mean . . . Gavina?" He opened his

mesmerizing eyes and stared a hole right through her. He knew! It was too late. She was alone with him in his cabin and now she'd be at his mercy.

"Ye ken," she said softly, feeling doomed. There was no reason to go on with the charade since he'd already discovered her secret. She considered running for the door, but what good would that do? As a prisoner on his ship, there was nowhere to escape to and no place to hide. "Did Nairnie tell ye?" she asked, feeling as if the woman were a traitor.

"Nay, and she didn't need to. I knew you were a wench before we even left the tavern. What I don't know is why the hell you're pretending to be a boy."

"Birk did this to me," she explained, nervously reaching back to smooth down the tufts of her short, dark hair.

"Birk did what?" Tristan looked over at her, rolling onto his side. "Did he . . . have you?"

"Nay! Birk was a swindler and a thief. No' a pirate!"

"I've got news for you. Swindlers and thieves often act worse than pirates."

"Hmmph," she said, not wanting to infuriate him, but not believing this one bit.

"Well, then were you his lover?"

"Nay! Of course no'." She gripped the top of her tunic closely to her neck. "I would never give myself to a man like Birk. He told me if the pirates found out I was a lass, I would be abducted and taken back to the ship and used as –" her eyes shot over to the naked girl in the picture and she couldn't finish her sentence. "Used as . . . " She tried again, but the thought was so horrific that she just couldn't say the words aloud.

"The ship's whore?" he finished her sentence for her.

Closing her eyes, she bit her lip and nodded slightly. The sound of the creaking bed ropes filled the air. Then she felt his hand on her cheek, and her eyes shot open.

"Stay away from me!" she warned him, jumping back and reaching for her dagger at her waist. However, she'd forgotten that Birk took her dagger and that she no longer had a weapon. Instead, her hand brought forth her flute.

"What do you plan on doing with that? Stabbing me with your flute?" he asked with a chuckle, grabbing his breeches and pulling them on. He was naked after all, and she'd just glimpsed his family jewels surrounded by a nest of curly, dark hair.

"Och!" she cried aloud, holding her hand over her mouth. She dropped the flute and it swung from the cord attached to her waist. "Please, dinna hurt me!"

"Take it easy, love. And stop shouting, because the rest of the crew will hear you."

Love? Did he just call her, love? Aye, he did, and it made her heart flutter. No one had ever called her "love" before. "So, what if they do hear me?" she asked. "I really dinna care."

"Nay?" His eyes darted over to the painting of the naked lady and then back to her. Suddenly, it was more than she could bear.

Sinking to her knees, she started crying. Losing her father and being abducted by pirates all in one day was proving to be the worst time of her life. However, even as bad as that was, if she were going to end up as the ship's whore, she would rather die.

"Stop the crying," he said in a low voice, dragging her to her feet. "I knew having a wench on board was only going to be a problem when I let Nairnie join us. Having two wenches on board now is only going to bring me horrible luck. I've already lost the treasure map. I don't want the damned ship to sink next. Tomorrow, we'll head for shore and I'm going to leave both you and Nairnie there on land. A pirate ship is no place for any wench, young or old."

"Do ye mean it?" she asked with a sniff, his words starting to calm her.

"Aye."

"Oh, thank ye!" Feeling so happy, she threw her arms around his neck and gave him a big kiss on the cheek.

As if his luck couldn't get any worse, Tristan's blood froze in his veins when the door opened just as Gavina was hugging and kissing him.

"Well, well. It looks like our brother really did take a liking to boys after all," Mardon said to Aaron, who was standing next to him. Ramble, unfortunately, was with them, too. With the way Ramble liked to talk, Tristan was never going to be able to keep this a secret.

"Gavin? What the hell are you doing to our brother?" Aaron shot across the room and pulled Gavina away from Tristan, throwing her to the ground.

"Dammit, Aaron, stop it!" shouted Tristan. "She's been through enough today and doesn't need you throwing her around." Tristan reached down, taking Gavina's hand and helping her to her feet.

"She?" asked Mardon and Aaron together.

"Her?" said Ramble.

"Bloody hell," mumbled Tristan, releasing Gavina and dragging his hand through his hair. He hadn't meant to say that. He wasn't going to tell them about Gavina. Or at least not yet, and certainly not like this. His brothers had taken him by surprise, and he'd made a mistake. "All right, so she's a wench," he admitted. "So now you see I am not interested in boys."

"Gavin is a – a lass?" asked Ramble, peeking out from between Mardon and Aaron.

"It's Gavina," she told them, wiping away a tear.

"Why?" asked Mardon. "How?"

"What?" said Aaron, making a face and shaking his head in disbelief.

"Just get in here and keep your voices down." Tristan hurried over and looked out to the deck before quickly closing the door. When he turned back, his brothers and Ramble were all standing there with their mouths hanging open, just staring at Gavina.

"What's . . . going on?" Mardon finally asked. "What the hell are you up to, Tristan?"

"Sit down," commanded Tristan.

Aaron started to sit on the barrel, but Tristan stopped him. "Nay! Let Gavina sit there. You take the bench."

"The barrel is my chair," complained Aaron.

"Just do it!" snapped Tristan.

Aaron begrudgingly went to the bench, but Ramble and Mardon were already sitting there and it was only big enough for two.

"Move, Ramble," commanded Aaron.

Ramble got up and walked over to sit on a trunk, his eyes fastened to Gavina all the while.

"I had no idea at first that Gavin – Gavina, was a girl," Tristan explained, pacing the floor.

"Why are ye dressed like a lad?" asked Ramble.

"Birk did this to me," Gavina told them. "He did it to protect me from men like ye. From pirates."

No one said a word. The men just kept staring at her, looking stunned. Finally, Mardon spoke up. "How the hell didn't I notice?"

"Aye," agreed Aaron. "Mardon can sniff out a wench over an entire sea and three towns away. He likes women even more than whisky!"

"I see." Gavina glanced over at the naked woman painting and then back at them.

"Taking that painting might have been my idea," admitted Mardon. "But Tristan is the one who wanted to hang it up between the mermaids."

"Only to keep my crew from having more lustful thoughts day and night than they already have," said Tristan. "Now, enough about the painting or the mermaids. I need to figure out what to do about this situation."

"I thought ye were goin' to drop me off at shore tomorrow along with Nairnie," said Gavina. She looked up at Tristan with wide, blue eyes filled with hope.

"Let you go?" Mardon's eyes flashed over to Tristan. "Please don't tell me you really promised her that."

"He wouldn't have done such a daft thing," said Aaron. "After all, she's the only one who possibly knows where Birk hid the copy of the map."

"Well, I might have said that," admitted Tristan. "Only because I didn't want any more bad luck having two wenches aboard my damned ship."

"What?" Gavina stood up. "So, what are ye sayin'? Are ye goin' to go back on yer word? Where is yer sense of honor?"

"Honor?" Ramble laughed at that. "Pirates always lie and have no honor. That's just the way they are. After all, if a pirate –"

"Shut up before I cut out your damned tongue, Ramble," warned Tristan.

"Aye, Cap'n." Ramble repositioned himself on top of the trunk, pressing his lips together tightly.

"Well, which is it, Brother?" asked Mardon, slowly standing up. "Are you letting her go or not?"

"She said she doesn't know about any copy of a map," explained Tristan.

"You don't honestly believe that! Are you too much of a simpleton to see that wenches always lie just to get what they want?" asked Aaron, standing up as well.

Tristan paced faster. His brothers did have a point. Gavina could be lying about the map. He'd only told her he'd take her back to shore because he wanted her to stop crying. Damn it, why did she have to cry? He supposed he'd also told her that to protect her since he didn't want his men rogering her at the rail. Ever since he discovered she was a girl, all he wanted to do was to protect her.

"Gavina, I need to know the truth," said Tristan. "Do you or don't you know anything about the map?"

"I ken that my faither was willin' to gamble away every-thin'" in a card game against Birk to get some kind of treasure map," she answered.

"Your father? The dead man on the floor?" asked Tristan.

"Aye." She nodded slightly.

"I thought so."

"Did ye see it? Did ye get a look at the map?" asked Ramble.

"Aye, Birk showed it to me, but only for a second," she told him.

"Then you can remember what the map looked like," said Aaron excitedly. "Tell us about it."

"Nay, I canna because it was all too fast. I barely saw it at all and dinna remember a thing."

"Well, why did Birk burn it?" asked Mardon.

"He and my faither were both cheatin' at the game. They got into an argument and Birk killed my faither. Then Birk heard ye pirates were on shore and burned the map." She sniffled and wiped away another tear.

God, was she going to cry again? Tristan certainly hoped not. If so, it was going to be his undoing. His little sister used to cry in storms when she was young, and Tristan was the one who had always comforted her. This only made him want to comfort Gavina now in the same manner.

"Why was Birk willing to risk his life to protect you?" asked Tristan.

"Aye, and even take the time to dress you up like a boy?" added Aaron.

"I – I'm no' sure. I think it was because he wanted to claim me, and he didna want ye pirates to have me."

"So, you never saw him make a copy of the map?" asked Tristan.

"Nay. I can honestly say I didna see Birk make a copy of the map."

"All right then," said Tristan. "Ramble, take Gavina to the galley to stay with Nairnie for now, and be sure to keep her away from the men. Tell Nairnie that Gavina is a girl."

"She already kens that," said Gavina, surprising Tristan even more.

"What? Nairnie knows and she didn't say anything to me?" he asked, thinking the one person he should be able to trust over anyone else would be his grandmother. Now he realized it wasn't true.

"Why would Nairnie tell ye?" asked Gavina.

"Why wouldn't she?" rallied Tristan. "After all, I'm her grandson and also captain of this ship."

"I told you, wenches always lie," mumbled Aaron, crossing his arms over his chest, sounding so sure of himself.

"Come on, Gavina," said Ramble, taking her by the arm.

"God's eyes, Ramble!" spat Tristan. "Don't call her Gavina out loud. We all need to keep it a secret for now from the rest of the crew that she's a girl."

"Of course, Cap'n. Sorry about that. Let's go . . . *Gavin*." Ramble led her out of the cabin and closed the door behind them.

"Well, what are we going to do about this?" asked Mardon once they'd left.

"We can't just drop her off at shore when she's probably lying and knows exactly where the map is," said Aaron.

"Leave it to me, Brothers." Mardon smoothed back his hair. "I've got a way with women. I'll woo the wench and while we're making love, she'll spill all her precious secrets to me."

"Nay, you won't," growled Tristan, not wanting his brothers near Gavina.

"Then I'll shake her down and make sure she's not hiding the map under her clothes," suggested Aaron. "If she is, I'll steal it from her before she even knows what happened."

"Nay, you won't," said Tristan once again. "Birk already showed us that she didn't have the map. Neither of you will touch her or give her trouble of any kind or you'll have to deal with me."

"So, you're just going to do nothing about finding the map then?" asked Mardon in confusion.

"She told us her story," answered Tristan. "She doesn't have it."

"If you believe her, you're a fool." Aaron waved a hand through the air and released a puff of air from his mouth.

"I told you both, I'll handle this," Tristan repeated. "Now, once again, leave her alone and don't tell a single man aboard this ship that she's a girl."

"You really think Ramble is going to keep his mouth shut?" asked Mardon.

"Bid the devil," said Tristan, pacing and running his hand through his hair once again. Ramble couldn't keep a secret if his life depended on it. Tristan was in trouble. "I just need to think. Now leave me alone so I can figure out what to do."

"We need that map to find the treasure," said Mardon, heading to the door.

"Aye. The crew is getting restless lately," Aaron joined in. "We've had a dry spell lately where booty is concerned. If we don't give the crew something worthwhile soon, they're all going to be threatening to jump ship and go join Nereus' crew."

"Nereus," Tristan ground out, speaking of his nemesis who was also a pirate. "He always seems to be one step ahead of us."

"Then this time, let's get to the treasure before he does," said Mardon. "Tristan, our only hope to keep our crew and keep our reign of the sea is to do away with Nereus."

"In order to do that, we need to find that treasure," said

Aaron. "Once the crew is motivated, we'll be able to overtake Nereus and we'll gain another ship and crew along the way."

"Don't worry. I'll find that damned map and we'll get to the treasure before Nereus does, no matter what I have to do to make it happen." Tristan made the promise, hoping he could keep it. However, things were starting to look grim.

"Bed the girl and find out where it is," suggested Mardon.

"Nay, strip her and check inside the lining of her clothes," Aaron gave his opinion next.

"Leave me be," Tristan grumbled, walking back to his hanging bed and plopping down in it as his brothers left the cabin. He closed his eyes, feeling his emotions calming as he rocked back and forth in his bed as the ship swayed. Trying to forget about Gavina, he listened to the melodic rhythm of the waves hitting against the sides of the ship, bringing him back to his normally controlled state.

He needed to find out the truth about what Gavina knew about the map before she left the ship. She claimed to know nothing, but he couldn't ignore the fact that it was a lie. His brothers were right. Gavina knew something, or Birk never would have given his life trying to protect her. He knew that, too, but just didn't want to believe it. Part of him wanted Gavina far away from this ship and also far away from him. He'd taken an odd liking to the girl, and this was only going to cause him trouble.

He considered both Mardon and Aaron's suggestions but, unfortunately, neither of them felt right. The girl had been through so much lately that he didn't want to hurt her. Instead of taking her and using her for his own needs, something inside him made him want to protect her from the rest of his lusty crew. Mayhap it was because Gavina was about his sister's age and reminded him a little of Gwen. Or mayhap it was because since he'd seen his father's ship and found Nairnie, it was bothering him more than he wanted to admit that he'd chosen piracy over staying with his sister after all.

That was all a long time ago, he told himself. He needed to push this from his thoughts. He and his brothers made a choice, and there was no going back after the things they'd done. They were pirates now. They could never be mere fishermen ever again and neither did he want to. He liked his life and decided he was never going back to working so hard for a living and still ending up so poor.

Tristan swung his feet over the side of the bed and got up. He knew what he had to do now. He needed to get that information out of Gavina, no matter what it took. Tonight, he decided, he would convince the girl to tell him everything he wanted to know, and then mayhap even more. He would do whatever it took to get this information, even if he had to act like the pirate he truly was, in order to get his answers.

CHAPTER 6

PIRATE LORDS

"J told ye it wouldna be long before Tristan figured out ye were a lass." Nairnie stirred the contents of a large iron pot hanging on a tripod over a small fire outside on the deck. The fire was contained in a metal box filled with sand. The smoke rose up into the air with the scent of root vegetables, fish and spices, as well as some kind of meat.

"Shhh, dinna say that so loud, Nairnie." Gavina glanced over her shoulder but thankfully none of the pirates seemed to have heard. "Besides ye, only Tristan, his brathairs, and Ramble ken my secret. I dinna want the rest of the men to find out."

"Ye are no' safe on this ship, lass. Ye need to get off of it as soon as possible. Mayhap since Tristan kens yer secret, he'll take ye to shore now."

"I dinna believe so. He thinks I ken somethin' about that map that Birk stole."

Nairnie stopped stirring the pot and cocked her head. "Do ye?"

"Can I tell ye somethin' that is for yer ears only?" She

glanced around, hoping that if she told Nairnie about the map on her back, the old woman would help her to read it. If Gavina had a copy of it that she could see, then mayhap she could convince Tristan to drop her off at shore and she could hire someone to take her to find the treasure.

"Aye, of course, lass. Ye can tell me anythin'. What is it?"

"Well, ye see, Birk burned the original map," she started.

"Burned it? Nay! That isna guid. That map was supposed to be for my grandsons. Now they'll never find the treasure."

"Nairnie, ye mentioned the map once belonged to yer son. Who was he?"

"His name was Cato."

"He was a pirate, then?"

"He was. However, I didna ken it. I never even kent him, really. He was taken away from me as a child by the bastard that spawned him. I never saw Cato again."

"Oh, I'm sorry."

"I dinna agree with piracy, but it is a shame the map is gone," said Nairnie, waddling over and picking up a stack of wooden bowls, placing them down atop a wooden board that made up a table. "That map was supposed to bring my grandsons the ultimate treasure. I wish they would have found it."

"Ultimate treasure?" Gavina blinked, not believing her ears. She started to see Nairnie in a whole new light. She was going to tell her about the map on her back, but now she wasn't sure she could trust her. "Nairnie, ye almost sound like a pirate yerself. I'm surprised ye are no' happy the map was stolen and that yer grandsons canna go after it."

"I just want them to be happy, that's all." She picked up a stack of spoons and placed them down next to the bowls. Then she picked up her ladle and the lid from a pot and started banging them together, making a loud clanking noise. "Come get yer food," she called out to the pirates, and then looked back over to Gavina. "So, what was it ye wanted to tell me?"

"Nothin' that canna wait," said Gavina, stepping aside as the men stampeded over to the food table. Nairnie held up a big, oversized ladle and stood behind the pot.

"No pushin'," she called out. "There's enough for all of ye."

The men pushed anyway, scrambling to grab a bowl and a spoon. Nairnie reached back and grabbed a sack, pulling it up next to her. "Gavin, come here and break off pieces of bread for the men or they'll kill each other tryin' to get some."

"Of course," she said, hurrying over to Nairnie and peeking into the bag. There were at least a dozen loaves of freshly baked bread. "Nairnie, how did ye bake this on a ship?"

"I didna," she said as the men lined up in front of her. "My grandsons stole that from the tavern today. Usually they eat hardtack."

"Hardtack?" she asked, not knowing what that was.

"Aye, it's a hard, flat biscuit that keeps a long time. That is, as long as it's stored in a covered container and kept away from maggots."

"Fill it up to the top, Nairnie, I'm starved," said Goldtooth, holding out his bowl. He'd out-muscled the rest of the men to get to the front of the line.

"Ye ken if I serve ye before my grandsons and the higher rankin' men, they'll have my head," scoffed Nairnie, not doing a thing to serve them.

Goldtooth leaned over and whispered. "Just a little taste until they get here? I'll give ye a nice, big, juicy kiss if ye do." He leaned in closer and puckered up his lips.

Nairnie reached out with the large, heavy ladle and smacked Goldtooth across the knuckles.

"Argh, what was that for?" griped the man.

"Ye ever try to kiss me and next it'll be my foot kickin' ye in yer blasted doup," she warned him. It was amusing to see how courageous Nairnie was against these cutthroat men of the sea. She didn't allow them to intimidate her. Instead, she ended up making them feel insecure. Gavina held back a chuckle, but Goldtooth noticed.

"What are ye laughin' at, Boy?" he sneered.

"I-I'm no' laughin'," she stuttered.

"That scallywag was laughin'. I heard him, too," shouted another of the crew.

"Why is that landlubber up here by the food?"

"He must have hornswaggled the old hag to be at the front of the line," called out another man. "Let's show him where newcomers are supposed to be."

They all started laughing, making Gavina very nervous. She wasn't sure she wanted to find out where newcomers were supposed to be.

Suddenly, all the pirates started closing in around Gavina and grabbing for her. She dropped the bag and stepped behind Nairnie who was now hitting all of them with the ladle, trying to keep them away.

"Back! Get back, all of ye!" shouted Nairnie.

"What the hell is going on here?" Tristan's voice raged as he and his brothers came forward, followed by Peg Leg Pate and Stitch.

"That scurvy dog needs to go to the back of the line," shouted one of the pirates.

"He's such a milksop that I think we need to toughen him up a little," said another.

"I say we do it now," yelled someone else.

Gavina was starting to worry until Tristan stepped to the front of the line and held up his hand. "No one gives that sort of command on my ship but me or my brothers. Goldtooth, I'm surprised you are a part of this. I thought I could count on you."

"I'm sorry, Cap'n," apologized Goldtooth. "It just seems that some of the crew think ye're givin' that new runt special treatment."

"Gavin is not a runt and I don't want to hear anyone refer to him in that manner again. However I treat a crewmember is not for you, or any of you to judge," Tristan told them. "I warn you all, if any of you so much as touches Gavin, I'll have your heads."

Grumbles came from the crew who were all glaring at Gavina now, making her feel like she wanted to jump overboard just to get away from them.

"Did you hear me?" Tristan bellowed.

"Aye, Cap'n."

"We heard ye."

"We understand, Cap'n," came the answers from Tristan's crew.

"Goldtooth, you and the dozen men around you will go to the back of the line," instructed Mardon.

"What? Nay, I'm hungry," complained Goldtooth.

"We all are," said Aaron. "Now, you heard him – move!"

"All right, we're goin'," said Goldtooth sluggishly moving to the back of the line, followed by the dozen others.

Tristan picked up a bowl and came over and looked into the pot. "What's that, Nairnie?"

"It's pottage I made up. I used some of the food from the tavern and added some spices."

"It's hot!" said Aaron, looking over Tristan's shoulder, grasping his bowl and spoon.

"We haven't had a hot meal in months now," remarked Mardon pushing his way in front of Aaron.

"It smells good," said Ramble, looking on. "A lot better than any of the food Blade ever made for us."

"Was Blade yer cook who died?" asked Gavina.

"Aye," said Tristan. "He died over the winter. From food poisoning."

"Och!" said Gavina, wondering how a man could die from eating food he cooked.

"Nairnie, it's not safe to start a fire aboard the ship," Tristan told her. "You need to be careful and keep the flames low and contained. And no fires if the sea is not calm."

"Ye dinna have to worry, Tristan. I promised ye hot food and that is what ye're goin' to get." Nairnie held out her hand. "Now give me yer bowl. These men are wantin' to eat and ye are holdin' up the line."

Tristan handed her his bowl. "Well, just don't make a habit of it," Tristan told her. "I don't fancy the thought of my ship going up in flames just because you were trying to give us a hot meal, although I appreciate it."

"I'll leave the sailin' to ye and ye just leave the cookin' to me." Nairnie handed back the bowl, half-filled with pottage.

"Fill the bowl to the rim," he told her with a nod.

"To the rim?" she asked. "Tristan, I ken ye're the captain, but this pot of food has to feed the entire crew."

"Do it," he said still holding out the bowl.

"Aye, Cap'n," said Nairnie, begrudgingly doing as told.

"Ramble, get up here," Tristan called out.

"Me?" Ramble pushed his way through the crowd, snatched up an empty bowl and ran over, holding it out to Nairnie. "Thanks, Cap'n. I've never been at the front of the food line before."

"Put the bowl down, Ramble," Tristan told him.

"Put it down? I don't understand." Ramble's look of hope started to fade. He still held on to the bowl tightly, holding it out to Nairnie.

"You're taking Gavin's place handing out bread."

"Oh," said Ramble, his smile fading as he dragged his feet, walking over to take Gavina's place.

"I dinna mind doin' this," said Gavina. She reached back into the bag and Tristan's fingers closed around her arm.

"Don't even think of disobeying me, or you'll wish you hadn't," he said in a low voice. "Now grab a loaf of bread and come with me."

Gavina looked over to Nairnie for guidance. Nairnie slowly nodded. Taking a loaf out of the bag, she snuck around Ramble and followed Tristan as he headed toward his cabin. Still not being used to the way the ship rolled on the water, and finding it hard to walk with just one shoe, she had to stop several times to gain her footing.

"I'll take that," said Tristan, snatching a bottle of whisky away from Noll who was about to take a swig.

Noll didn't dare protest, probably because he was afraid he'd be whipped again.

"Where are we goin'?" she asked, as Tristan tucked the bottle under his arm and opened the door to the cabin.

"Where no one can see you," he said, walking inside. She followed. "Out of sight, out of mind. Hopefully," he mumbled, setting the bowl down on the table and raising the bottle to his lips.

GAVINA WATCHED TRISTAN SWALLOW, her eyes fastened to his sun-kissed throat. He licked his lips and let out a satisfied sigh. The scent of alcohol filled the air. Her eyes traveled up to his mouth next and she found herself wondering what it would feel like to kiss his lips.

"Quit looking at me like that, or you're going to end up under me."

She jerked back, afraid he had somehow read her thoughts. Thoughts that she had no business thinking and no idea from where they'd come. "Under ye?" she asked in confusion, then noticed his eyes dart over to his bed.

"Oh," she said, her eyes fastening to the loaf of bread in her hands instead. It was a dark loaf that looked to be made from rye rather than oats like she normally ate in Scotland. Dark bread was for peasants, whereas white bread was only eaten by the nobles.

"Sit down," he commanded, crossing the room and slamming the door, leaving them once again alone in his quarters.

She slowly sat at the table and put the bread down in front of her, running her hand over the smooth surface of it, trying to use it like a worry stone to ease her mind. Without meaning to do it, her eyes once more traveled upward to his face. Dark stubble that covered his face, and his long hair that almost reached to his waist made him look more rugged than either of his brothers.

"Like it?" he asked.

"Like what?" she asked, continuing to run her hand over the top of the loaf of bread in thought.

His hand slammed down on the table right in front of her, causing her to jump. Then he leaned over and spoke to her through gritted teeth, his face almost touching hers.

"You keep fondling that loaf of bread like you're stroking a man's shaft, and I'm not going to be able to stop myself from ripping off your clothes and having my way with you right here on this table. After all, I've been at sea for a long time without the comforts of a woman. I can't hold back like a saint forever."

"I'm doin' no such thing!" she gasped, her eyes looking directly into his now. This close up, she could see the small dark speckles peppering the rich green hue. He truly did have beautiful eyes. And when the tip of his tongue shot out and he slowly licked his lips, her eyes followed his motions down to his mouth. An inner heat stirred within her. It surprised her and frightened her at the same time that she was reacting this way to a pirate.

"You're a horrible liar." He pulled away and straddled the barrel, sitting across the table from her. "I brought you here to eat, and that was my only intention. Or at least for now."

He picked up the spoon and scooped up some of the pottage, shoving it into his mouth. Then he picked up another spoonful and held it up to her mouth, surprising her once again. She moved her head back, not sure what to do.

"It's the only spoon I have. I don't have fleas, so take a bite before you starve to death."

"Why do ye even care what happens to me?" she asked, hesitantly reaching for the spoon. She thought he'd give it to her, but he held on to it instead. She had no choice but to cover his hand with hers.

"I don't want anything happening to you before you tell me where Birk hid the copy of the map." She opened her mouth, but before she could speak, his free hand shot up in front of her face. "Don't even think of denying it, because I know he made one."

"What makes ye so sure he did?" she asked.

"Just answer my question."

"As soon as ye answer mine." She blew on the spoon to cool the food. "After all, ye keep insistin' I ken about this map when I told ye I didna see Birk make a copy, or hide it." She blew on the food again. This time, her breath must have hit his hand because she heard his sharp intake of breath. When she glanced up at him, his eyes were closed. She opened her mouth and took in the food. It was good and her tongue darted out to lick a drop of liquid from her lips. His eyes opened just then and his gaze fastened on her mouth. Dropping the spoon to the table, Tristan jumped to his feet.

"I KNOW YOU'RE LYING," said Tristan, turning away from the girl and pacing the floor. Feeling lusty and distracted, he ran a hand through his long hair, trying to maintain his composure before he lost control of his emotions. Egads, why did the wench have to blow on his skin and then lick her lips afterwards? It was driving him mad. Even dressed like a boy and with that godawful cropped hair, her actions were like those of a siren luring him to do something he was trying hard not to do. This woman excited him for some reason. He figured he just needed to bed a few more whores more often and he wouldn't be attracted to girls who looked like boys. When he was around Gavina, he couldn't seem to think straight.

"Nairnie is a guid cook. It's amazin' she can whip up somethin' so tasty on a pirate ship. And hot, too." She continued to blow on the food to cool it and, of course, lick her lips. He already felt himself growing hard beneath his breeches. How much more teasing could he take before he bent the wench over the rail and plunged his hardened length into her up to the hilt? "Here, have some more," she said, picking up the bowl and walking over to him. She scooped up a spoonful of food, blew on it and held it up to his lips. "Open up," she said with a playful smile. Her straight, white teeth made her look like a princess, rather than a commoner. "I swear I dinna have fleas either," she toyed with him, repeating his words back to him.

Open up is exactly what he wanted to say to her, but meaning it in a much different way. Bid the devil, he needed to get away from her fast. Even though a part of him said there was nothing wrong with taking her quick and hard for his own needs, another part of him felt as if this girl deserved better than to be ravished by a black-hearted pirate.

"Nay," he said, pushing her hand away so hard that she dropped the spoon. It went flying from her hand and clattered to the floor.

She looked down and took a deep breath, only causing his eyes to roam to her chest as he searched for those two bumps that she hid so expertly beneath those baggy clothes.

"Ye could have just said no instead of bein' so forceful with me," she pouted.

He couldn't stop himself from wanting her, and that bothered him. He'd never felt such intense desire for a wench in his life. She was like the forbidden fruit, and he the serpent. His want was eating him up from the inside out.

"If you think that is forceful, then you've not been around a pirate long enough to know."

"Long enough to ken what?" she asked innocently, her eyelids flickering as she waited for his answer.

Needing to taste her lush, ruby lips, he reached out, grabbing her shoulders and pulling her up hard against him. He heard the bowl drop from her hand and land on the floor alongside the spoon. Always taking what he wanted in life without asking, he bent over and pressed his mouth against hers, claiming her with a passionate kiss.

Her arms hung limply at her sides and her head fell back. As he deepened the kiss, he swore he heard a small moan of pleasure come from the back of her throat. And when he broke the kiss and pulled back to look at her, he noticed her eyes were closed. This meant she liked it as much as he did. It gave him the sign that it was all right to continue.

She tasted like honeyed mead. It was alluring and only made him crave her more. Tristan was a man used to taking what he wanted. And right now, he wanted Gavina.

He went back for a second helping. This time, he let his tongue slip in between her tantalizing lips, filling her mouth completely with his presence. His hands slid down her back, past her small waist, stopping to rest on her curved bottom. Wanting to know how her womanly buttocks felt in his hands, he cupped her cheeks in his palms and squeezed her pear-shaped doup. Pulling her up tight against his erection, he felt like he was going to burst. God's teeth, this felt good! Their bodies being pressed up against each other almost seemed to cause steam between them.

Tristan was expecting to hear another moan of desire coming from her but, instead, he felt sharp pain in his mouth. Shocked, he realized that she had the audacity to bite his tongue! At the same time, she stomped on his foot with the one shoe she wore, and then her knee came up and connected with his hardened groin. Her fingers dug into his arms next, the sharpness of her nails scraping against his skin.

"Devil take you, you landlubber wench!" he spat, pushing her away from him. His hand automatically went to his mouth. The tangy flavor of copper slid down his throat from his own blood. "What the hell did you do that for?"

"I dinna appreciate bein' ravished by a stinkin' pirate!"

"What do you mean? You enjoyed the kiss, I know you did! I heard you moan. And I'm not a – a stinking pirate." When he rubbed his arm, his head turned toward his armpit and he tried to sneak a sniff, just to see if he really stank. The scent of the sea mixed with sweat filled his senses, making him realize she was right. He was nothing but a stinking pirate and about to ravish her just because she was a woman.

Tristan turned away from her, snatching up the bottle of whisky as he headed for the door. "Stay inside the cabin and don't dare show your face on deck before morning. Even then, you're not to go anywhere unless I'm with you."

"Stay here?" The idea didn't seem to please her at all. "Nay, I canna do that. I have to relieve myself," she said, making him stop in his tracks. It only brought to mind he was trying to relieve his lustful needs by pushing himself on her. But what she was talking about had nothing to do with lust. "Where does one do something like that on a pirate ship?"

"The men piss over the side of the ship," he explained. "If

it's more than just pissing you need to do, take a walk to the head."

"The head?" Her eyelids flicked in confusion.

He looked down to see the bulge below his belt and only wished he would have chosen his words more carefully.

"At the bow, or head of the ship, there is a board with a hole in it that extends out over the water," he told her. "Savvy?"

"Aye, I savvy," she said, sounding snide. "And do you savvy that all I have to do is pull down my trews to use it, and I'll have no' just ye, but dozens of lustful men tryin' to poke me?"

"Then use the damned pot in the corner," he said, pointing to it on the floor. It looked to her like one of Nairnie's cooking pots, but much smaller. "Gavina, don't expect me to protect you from any of my crew again." He turned and looked over his shoulder, gripping tightly to the bottle of whisky. "Let me make myself clear. When I say my crew, that also means me." He turned and walked out the door, wondering just how long he could refrain from rogering her at the rail after all.

CHAPTER 7

"Where have you been, Brother?" asked Mardon, as he and Aaron joined Tristan at the bow of the ship right after nightfall set in. It was a calm night and they weren't far from shore. They'd already dropped anchor. It wouldn't take long to make it to shore in the morning.

"Aye, we've been looking for you," said Aaron, climbing up on to the sidewall, resting one leg on the bowsprit. "You and . . . *Gavin* disappeared at mealtime and we haven't been able to find you for hours."

"It's not that big of a ship, you fools." Tristan half-smiled and shook his head, leaning on the wooden rail, looking out to sea in thought. "If you two couldn't find me, it's only because you weren't really looking."

"All right, so we knew you were on the bow but figured since you missed your nap, you needed time to think," said Mardon.

"That's right," agreed their younger brother. "You get irritable and ornery when you don't get your time to rest, so we didn't want to bother you for fear you'd bite off our heads."

"I'm not that bad," said Tristan, even though he knew his brothers were right. He'd flogged men for nothing more than bothering him when he wanted to be alone.

"Tristan, is there anything you want to tell us?" One side of Mardon's mouth rose into a half-grin.

"I didn't take the wench to my cabin so I could bed her, if that's what you're hinting at." Lifting the bottle, Tristan brought it to his mouth, taking a deep draw of whisky.

"We know," said Aaron with a chuckle. "If you had, you wouldn't be nursing that bottle so desperately."

"Aye, you would have used the wench as a wetnurse instead. That's what I would have done as soon as we found out she was a girl." Mardon leaned on the rail and looked out to sea, still grinning as if he were picturing it in his head. He was the randiest of the three of them, and never stopped thinking about women. He also prided himself on the fact that with his looks, he could always get any woman he wanted to lift her skirt for him quite willingly. Tristan wasn't as lucky. Then again, it was probably because he didn't want to waste time trying to woo women when he could pay for what he wanted and have more time to spend looking for treasure instead.

"Believe me, the thought went through my mind to play wetnurse with her," he told his brothers, looking down at the bottle and swirling around the remaining contents in deep thought.

"You almost bedded her? Really?" asked Aaron excitedly, leaning forward so as not to miss a word. He moved so quickly that he almost lost his balance when the ship listed hard. Aaron reached out and grabbed on to the lines to keep from being dumped into the sea.

"Well, why the hell didn't you?" asked Mardon. "God knows you need it. We all need a little female company about now. It's been too long."

"I don't know." Tristan shrugged. "Something about bedding Gavina just didn't feel right."

"Mayhap because she looks like a boy," said Aaron through a fake cough.

Mardon laughed. "Nay, that's not it. She rejected you, didn't she? Just admit it."

Tristan was in no mood to deal with his brothers and all their questions. "It doesn't matter because that's not why I brought her on the ship to begin with."

"Give her to me. I'll take her to my bed, and I assure you she won't push me away." Mardon bragged, turning to go. Tristan's hand clamped around his brother's arm to stop him.

"Leave her be," he warned him in a low voice. "She doesn't want you, or any of the men here. She's young and innocent and most likely still a virgin."

"A virgin? Damn, that makes the wench even more desirable," said Mardon with a wide smile.

"You know how long it's been since I've had any wench with that kind of innocence?" asked Aaron. "She must be truly pure . . . and tight as well."

Mardon and Aaron chuckled.

"Stop it," ordered Tristan, not liking that his brothers were talking about Gavina this way. "She's staying a virgin so don't even think of touching her, or you'll have to answer to me."

"Bid the devil, what the hell's the matter with you, Tristan?" Mardon shook off Tristan's hold and scowled. "You almost sound as if you care about the damned wench. This is so unlike you."

"Aye," agreed Aaron. "She's a stranger to us, not to mention, she's just a girl! A girl that the rest of us would enjoy getting to know."

"No one but me is going to be getting to know Gavina, so forget about it, little brother," snapped Tristan.

"You're letting her get into her head." Mardon brushed off his shirt, always liking his clothes clean and neat. Tristan had wrinkled Mardon's sleeve when he'd grabbed his arm. Mardon's disapproval showed in his expression. It would probably bother him now for the rest of the day.

"She's more than just a wench," Tristan told them, not able to push the vision of Gavina's clear blue eyes from his mind.

"What does that mean?" asked Aaron.

Tristan stood up straight, turning so he could see both of his brothers at the same time. It was a quiet night, the only sounds being the snoring crew, the creaking of the vessel, the slight flapping of the sails, and the sound of waves lapping against the side of the ship. "It means that I'm sure she somehow holds the key to finding the king's treasure. I don't want anyone scaring her off before she tells me where to find the copy of that map."

"If you think Birk made a map, shouldn't we be searching the Crooked Crow or its surroundings again instead of sailing south?" asked Aaron, throwing his leg back over the side of the ship and hopping down to the deck – with bare feet as usual.

"Birk would never have let the copy of the map out of his sight," Mardon told them. "I think we need to turn around and go back to shore."

"Mayhap you're right," said Tristan, swirling the last of the whisky in the bottle, lost in his thoughts. "It wouldn't hurt to go back and take another look." His brothers did have a point. Tristan's only concern was that treasure. Ever since Nairnie told him about finding the map, he should have made that his priority. Instead, he'd let Gavina distract him. Now, they were most likely sailing away from the treasure instead of toward it. They'd already dropped anchor for the night but, tomorrow, they'd turn around and head back toward the Crooked Crow. He never should have left the tavern in the first place without that map. It had to be there, or at least nearby. "Tell the crew that we sail back to the Crooked Crow to look for the map at first light."

"Then you admit you made a mistake by telling us to follow the path of the *Desperado?*" asked Aaron.

"Aye, and you admit that I was right and you should have listened to me?" Mardon broke in. "After all, I'm quartermaster. I decide when and where we pillage a ship and when we turn around."

"Don't break your arms patting yourselves on the back, Brothers," grumbled Tristan. "I never said we were following the *Desperado*. I just said we were heading south."

"But we're right," said Aaron.

"Every once in a while, you two seem to come up with a good idea, whether it is purposely or merely by accident," said Tristan. "The only thing we need to be chasing after is that treasure."

"The treasure will make a good future for us," said Mardon.

"If Father would have let us go after it years ago, mayhap we wouldn't have had to go back to piracy," said Aaron.

"I know it's been a long time, but do I have to remind you

two that one of the reasons we left was because it was our father's fault that Mother died?"

"Mayhap we should have stayed," said Aaron, sounding like he was having second thoughts. "If nothing else, perhaps we should have been there for Gwen."

"Stop it," said Tristan, becoming irritated by this conversation. "We made a choice and we live by it. No regrets, remember? Besides, according to Nairnie, Gwen is happily married with a family, so it sounds like she isn't hurting any by our leaving."

"Tristan's right," agreed Mardon. "That is all behind us now. Once we find the king's gold, we'll be set for life. The crew has been restless for a long time now and for more than just food. Sailing the North Sea isn't half as productive as the channel where we'd have ships to plunder every day if it wasn't for Nereus. Making an agreement with Rowen was one thing, but we never should have done so with Nereus, too."

"I agree. We're pirates. We don't need to stick to our word," said Aaron.

"Never say that!" Tristan shook his head. "We stick to the code."

Mardon laughed. "Well, in that case, I guess you'll need to be put to death, dear brother. Or did you forget number six of the code says that anyone found seducing a woman aboard the ship, or bringing her to sea in disguise is subject to death?"

"In my defense, I thought she was a boy when I decided to bring her on board," said Tristan. "However, I admit I had a good suspicion she was a girl before she set foot on the ship, and could have left her on shore after all. But the map was at stake and she was our only hope of finding it. She still is. So, don't mention it again. After all, we're all guilty of breaking the code because we brought Nairnie on board."

"Oh," said Aaron, looking down to his hand. "Well, we couldn't leave our own grandmother to die."

"He's got a point," said Mardon. "I suppose sometimes the code needs to be broken."

"Do you think the crew is going to agree with us?" asked Aaron. "We could have a mutiny on our hands because of the wench."

"The wenches," Mardon corrected him.

Tristan raised his hand. "Both of you, stop worrying about it. The crew is not going to find out about Gavina. I told her to stay in the cabin. Her secret is safe."

"Oh, really?" Mardon looked down to the main deck where the men were relaxing and drinking and getting ready to sleep for the night. "Well, I don't think she heard you."

"What are you talking about?" Tristan turned around to see Gavina sneaking out of the cabin, almost tripping on her trews since they were so long. She walked awkwardly, only wearing one shoe. She was heading toward the galley and probably going to talk to Nairnie. However, before she could make it that far, she was stopped by some of the crew.

"Damn it, why can't she listen?" growled Tristan, knowing there was about to be trouble. The men were well in their cups. They started surrounding her in a circle. He heard raucous laughter and words that weren't fit for a lady's ears as they tried to provoke her. Even if they didn't know she was a girl, he didn't like them treating another crewmember in this manner. Only he, as the captain, was allowed to discipline others in ways that he felt were needed. "We'd better get down there quickly. The fool wench is going to get herself killed coming out on the deck at this time of night," said Tristan, taking off at a near run.

* * *

Having been bored just staying in the cabin, not to mention feeling a little seasick, Gavina snuck out and headed over to Nairnie's quarters in the galley meaning to visit with her. Right now, she felt like she needed to be around another woman. However, the crew saw her and now she wished she had stayed put. As they closed in around her, she noticed their angry faces in the light of the lanterns hanging from the railings. She could also smell the strong stench of alcohol and knew they'd been drinking heavily.

"I dinna want any trouble," she told them, holding up her hands and backing away. "I'm just on my way to the . . . to the head," she said, remembering what Tristan had told her.

"The head is over there," said Noll, stepping forward with his sidekick, Wybert, at his side. He pointed across the ship, on the opposite side of the galley. These two men seemed more frightening than the rest, most likely because they were filthier. Noll had already shown no respect to Tristan so she expected trouble.

"There's no need to use the head. Just pull out your snake and do it over the side like the rest of us," said Wybert, motioning to the side of the ship.

"What? Nay, I'd rather no'," she said, backing away from them as they continued to come closer.

"Blimey, I think the lad needs a little help gettin' it out," said Noll, laughing. "Boys, shall we give him a hand?"

"What the hell is all the noise out here?" complained

Nairnie, walking out from her small enclosure with a lit lantern in one hand and the oversized ladle in the other. She wore what looked like one of the men's oversized shirts, using it as a nightrail. Around her shoulders was wrapped a coarse woolen blanket. She waddled up next to Gavina.

Gavina moved closer to Nairnie for protection, hoping that the men would back off now and not try to rip off her trews. Nairnie was a crusty old woman and, hopefully, these men wouldn't want to make her angry.

"Get out of the way, old woman," said Wybert, proving Gavina wrong. "The lad needs a little initiation as a welcome to our crew."

They continued to move closer, all of them staggering as if they were very drunk. Gavina eyed several barrels of wine on the deck as well as some empty bottles.

Aaron swung over on a line and dropped down from the rigging next to her, facing the men. "What's going on?" he asked the crew.

"We're just givin' the boy a little welcome to the ship," said one of the men, sniggering. "Want to help us?"

"I don't think so." Aaron looked over at her, and then at Nairnie, trying to decide what to do.

"Clear the way for our captain and quartermaster," shouted Ramble, pushing the men aside, making a path for Tristan and Mardon.

"What's the trouble?" asked Tristan.

"Yer puppet has come out of hidin' and we're just givin' him a little welcome to the ship, that's all," said Noll, holding his hand out as if to keep Tristan away. "Or are ye goin' to protect the milksop again and hide him in yer cabin?"

"Aye, if he's part of the crew now, quit treatin' him like a wench," said Wybert.

"Mayhap he's really a wench in disguise," said one of the men, laughing. "Let's get his trews off and find out for ourselves."

"We always strip the new members and throw them in the sea," Goldtooth agreed. "Cap'n, ye're usually the one to do it. Why don't ye take the honors?" Goldtooth stepped aside, holding out his arm.

That suggestion only wound the men up more. Gavina could see that she'd put Tristan in a very bad position. She had to do something fast before Tristan's crew turned against him and she was the one to blame.

"Yer captain said he wanted me to play some music for ye," said Gavina, lifting her flute and bringing it to her mouth. Before anyone could object, she started playing a lively tune.

"That's not bad," said Mardon with a nod.

"Good enough to dance to," agreed Aaron, holding his hands out to Nairnie. "Dance with me, Grandmother."

"Nay, get away," scoffed Nairnie, putting down the lantern, trying to shoo him away with her ladle.

"I'd like to see this," said Mardon, snatching the ladle away from Nairnie. "Go on, dance."

"Now, boys, I'm an auld woman and can barely stand on the deck without fallin', let alone dance," Nairnie protested.

"Go on, Nairnie. Dance with Aaron," said Tristan. "That's an order."

Nairnie sighed and took Aaron's hands. "Och, I had hoped to someday dance at my grandchildren's weddin's, but no' with drunkards on a pirate ship."

"So consider this practice," said Aaron, taking her by the

hands and spinning her around as he danced in his bare feet. Nairnie's blanket fell from her shoulders and landed on the deck. All the men laughed and more alcohol was brought out for the occasion. To Gavina's relief, they forgot all about stripping her, and instead all started dancing with Nairnie and laughing and falling down drunk.

Tristan walked over to Gavina, standing behind her as she continued to play her flute. He leaned over and whispered in her ear.

"If you want to stay a virgin, you'd better not stop playing that damned flute until every last one of them falls down and passes out."

She started to play the flute even faster, her heart beating so rapidly that she thought it would burst right out of her chest. It was a close call tonight and now she realized it was crucial she get off the ship as soon as possible. How many more times would Tristan be able to save her?

Hours later, when all the men seemed to finally fall down and sleep, Gavina lowered her flute, feeling ready to pass out herself.

Nairnie sat down on a wooden box and rubbed her feet, trying to catch her breath. "They're tryin' to kill off the auld woman, that's what they're tryin' to do," she scoffed.

Gavina's hands lowered. She felt as if she could not play another note. It was an effort just to keep her eyes open. The only reason she hadn't already fallen asleep was because Tristan had told her to play for her life and so she had.

. . .

TRISTAN FINALLY RELAXED when all of his crew was sleeping. The only ones still awake were Aaron and Stitch who were on the first night watch.

"Nairnie," said Tristan, picking up the blanket and wrapping it around her shoulders. "It's time for bed. I hope the men didn't wear you out dancing tonight."

"I only did it to save Gavina and ye ken it," she told him in a low voice. "Now, ye'd better come up with a plan to protect her from these bluidy curs, because I canna go through this again. If I have to, I swear I'll beat every one of them with my ladle." She scooped up the ladle from the ground and held it high in the air to prove her point.

"There will be no need for that, Nairnie," Tristan told her, helping her to stand. "Now, keep the ladle for cooking instead of hitting, and get some shut eye. Morning comes quickly around here." He handed her the lantern and directed her toward her quarters.

She had a pallet in the corner of the small galley to sleep on. The enclosed space was deemed Nairnie's room so she wouldn't have to sleep on the deck with the men.

Nairnie stopped and turned around. "Gavina's comin' with me." She put down the lantern and reached out to take the girl's arm, still clutching on to her ladle with the other.

"Nay," said Tristan with a quick shake of his head. "The *boy* will sleep in my quarters where there is more room and I can keep an eye on him."

"Oh. The boy," she repeated, yawning, now realizing her mistake. "All right," said Nairnie, stifling yet a second yawn. "Guidnight then." She disappeared into the galley, holding the blanket tightly around her.

"Let's go," said Tristan, grabbing Nairnie's lantern, the only light that was still lit this late on deck. The rules were that they had to save their resources, therefore the lights were usually put out an hour after nightfall set in.

"Am I really sleepin' in yer cabin tonight?" asked Gavina, yawning as well.

"You are, unless you'd rather sleep out here on the deck with the men."

Her hand shot out and covered his that was atop her arm. "Nay, I'll go with ye," she answered quickly.

"Smart decision – not that you had a choice." Tristan led the way to the room, pushing open the door and stopping in his tracks when he heard the guttural roar.

"What's that awful noise?" asked Gavina, peeking out from around him into the darkened room.

Tristan knew exactly what it was, but held the lantern higher so she could see. "It's my brother, Mardon. He drank too much as usual and, once again, has passed out in my bed instead of his." Tristan put the lantern down on the table and walked over to his hanging bed by the window. "Mardon, get up," he said, shaking his brother by the shoulder.

"Mmphf," mumbled Mardon. "Is it two o'clock already?"

"Nay, not yet. But you're in my bed."

"Why did he ask if it's two in the mornin'?" she whispered from behind him.

"That's when his shift starts for night watch."

"When is yer shift?" she wondered.

"I take the morning shift, starting at five o'clock. Dammit, Mardon, get out of my bed." He shook him again, but Mardon just rolled over and started snoring.

"Why dinna ye just sleep in his bed?" she asked, pointing to the net bed hanging across the room. Tristan hated the

145

netting since he could never get comfortable inside it, and usually ended tangled up by morning. That's why his bed was made of canvas.

"You take Mardon's bed," he told her.

"Me? Where will ye sleep?" she asked, muffling a yawn with her hand.

"I'll sleep on the pallet below it. It's Aaron's bed, but he won't mind. It's a nice night and he'll most likely sleep in the lookout after his shift anyway."

"If ye say so." She walked over to the hanging bed, putting her hands on the sides. She started to lift her foot but the ship swayed and knocked her off balance. She almost fell over, having to grab on to the nettings, being pulled back and forth with the ship. It almost made him laugh. She looked so help-less. The bed was too high for her to get into without his help.

"Take off your shoes and I'll help you up," he offered.

"Ye mean shoe. I only have one unless ye've forgotten. Ye promised me shoes and a change of clothes."

"Tomorrow," was all he said, putting his hands around her small waist and lifting her up.

She giggled, and flopped down into the hanging bed, making it swing back and forth. "I'm sure glad I didna drink too much or I think I'd retch right now."

"Close your eyes," he told her, reaching over and taking off her shoe and throwing it to the floor. "Let the rocking lull you to sleep like a babe does in its mother's arms."

"Mother's arms," she repeated softly, as her eyes drifted closed. In a matter of minutes, she was sound asleep. If only he could fall asleep as easily as these two. Having to sleep with one eye open, he wasn't sure he'd get any rest at all.

Tristan blew out the lantern and got undressed, settling

himself atop Aaron's pallet beneath Gavina's bed. The creaking of the ropes above him as the bed swung back and forth only reminded him that a woman he desired was sleeping right above him and in arm's reach.

He tossed and turned and realized this was never going to work. Map or no map, he couldn't keep Gavina on the ship any longer. It was too distracting. He had a crew to manage as well as duties, being captain of the ship. He'd already stuck out his neck for her more than once. If he continued to do so much longer, he swore his crew was going to know something was not right.

"She goes back tomorrow," he told himself softly. When they returned to the Crooked Crow to continue looking for a copy of the map, he decided Gavina was going to stay there and not return with them to the ship. He'd pay someone to look after her, and get her somewhere safe. It pained him to even think of leaving her behind, but he had no choice. It was for her own good.

No matter what, he couldn't bring her back aboard the *Falcon* because it was getting much too dangerous for her to stay here. And unfortunately, the one she should fear the most, whether she realized it or not, was not Noll or Gold-tooth or any of the rest of the crew. The one she should fear over all the others was none other than him!

CHAPTER 8

$\mathcal{T}$ristan finished his shift on night watch and headed back to his cabin while Stitch took his place on the sterncastle. Tired, and worried since he'd left Gavina alone in his cabin with Mardon, he wasn't sure what he'd find when he returned. Only Mardon's sincere promise not to touch Gavina put his mind at ease. His brother had never lied to him yet, and Tristan trusted him completely.

Slowly opening the door to his quarters, he could hear Mardon snoring again from his bed. Gavina occupied Mardon's bed, sleeping on her back with her arm thrown over her face. Hoping for a few more minutes of sleep, Tristan settled down atop the straw pallet directly under Gavina.

Lying on his back, he looked up at her, barely able to see something odd in the scant light streaming in from the small window from the rising sun. "What the hell is that?" he said to himself, looking harder and realizing just what he was looking at. Gavina's large tunic had ridden up and exposed her back while she slept. Tristan could see the slight curvature of her spine and also her milky white smooth skin. As much as that took his interest, there was something else that caught his eye even more. It was a big black X just above her buttocks.

"The map!" he exclaimed, bolting up to a sitting position, bringing his face closer to her. Sure enough, through the holes in the netting of the hanging bed, he was staring at some kind of treasure map inked right on to Gavina's back. He reached up and poked his finger through the netting to touch it, making her jump up in surprise.

"Dinna touch me!" she cried out, still half-asleep. "Leave me alone!" The bed swung back and forth as the ship listed and Gavina fell out of the hanging net bed, landing right on top of him. She was face down against his chest.

"Oomph!" The weight of her body slamming against his knocked the breath right from him.

"Tristan!" she gasped. With his arms around her, she looked up with those sparkling, magical eyes. Her face was so close to him that all he wanted to do was reach up and kiss her again. "Why did ye poke me?" she demanded to know. "What were ye tryin' to do?" She pushed away from him and hurriedly stood up. He got to his feet as well.

"What was *I* trying to do?" he asked, his anger growing. "Mayhap you should be the one answering that question, not me."

"I have no idea what ye're talkin' about." Her bare shoulder was exposed since the tunic was twisted from sleeping in it. When she noticed Tristan looking at her bare skin, she yanked her tunic back into place.

"I think you know exactly what I'm talking about. Take off your tunic. Now!"

"What? Nay, I willna do that." She gripped the neck of her

top tighter. "Ye want me to undress with ye and yer brathair in the room? What kind of a lass do ye think I am?"

"A dishonest one. There's no doubt about that."

"What's all the yelling about?" grumbled Mardon, sitting up in bed and rubbing one sleepy eye. "Can't a man get a little shut eye around here? All this noise is hurting my head."

"Mardon, leave. Now," growled Tristan.

"What? Why? Egads, Tristan, are you still sore that I slept in your bed again?" He swung his feet over the side and hopped out of bed in one quick motion. Raising his arms over his head, he stretched and yawned. He wore naught but a small pair of braies.

"Och!" gasped Gavina, her eyes fastening to his bare chest.

"You like that?" asked Mardon with a devilish smile. His hair was tussled and he scratched at his chest when he spoke.

"Get the hell out of here!" shouted Tristan, picking up Mardon's neatly folded clothes and shoving them into his hands.

"All right, take it easy, Brother," said Mardon with a nod. "If you want to be alone with the girl, all you had to do was ask." His bare feet shuffled across the floor as he slowly headed for the door.

Tristan had enough of this. He needed to take a good look at that map and his brother was only slowing things down. In two long strides, he was across the floor and ripping open the door. "Go," he told him.

"Go where?" asked Mardon with another yawn.

"Anywhere that isn't here." He pushed his brother out the door and slammed it behind him. Then he turned back to Gavina. "I'm not going to tell you again. Take off the tunic."

. . .

GAVINA FROZE. She hadn't felt frightened of Tristan as much as the rest of the crew until now. He looked angry and demanding, and very dangerous. Although the last thing she wanted to do was to undress in front of him, she felt that if she didn't, he might tie her to the mast and have her flogged next.

He moved toward her slowly, like a predator stalking its prey. It made her want to run, but there was nowhere to go. She was his prisoner on this ship and trapped in this room with his large body blocking the path to the door.

"All right," she told him, seeing she had no choice. "I'll take off my tunic, just please dinna hurt me." She figured he was feeling lusty again and probably wanted a look at her womanly form. Unfortunately, she wore nothing beneath the tunic. Shyly, she started to turn around to remove it. Then, remembering about the map, she decided that was the last thing she wanted him to see. So, seeming like the only choice right now, she faced him and quickly brought the tunic up and over her head, exposing her bare breasts.

"There, I did it," she said, clinging to the tunic, daring to look at him. His eyes were fastened to her chest like she knew they'd be. Quickly, she hid her nakedness by holding the tunic in front of her.

"Turn around," he said in a low, sultry voice.

"Why?" she asked. "Did ye want to see my bum next? I'm still wearin' the trews ye realize. It'll be hard for ye to force yerself on me while I'm still half-dressed."

"You're in no position to be talking to me in that manner. I advise you to stop with your little game because it's only making me angrier than I already am. Now, do what I say." He reached out and ripped the tunic from her hands and threw it to the ground. The tension between them hung thick in the air. She wanted to close her eyes and block all this out, but she wouldn't give him the satisfaction. If he was going to ravish her, she would stare him in the eyes when he did it. Afterward, hopefully, he'd never forget the vengeance he saw there.

He spun her around and bent her over the table. The boat listed and the hanging table moved. She grabbed on to the rope to keep from falling, feeling the rough wood scraping her stomach.

"Bloody hell, I've wanted this for such a long time," she heard from behind her, making her very frightened now.

She could barely breathe as she waited for what was to come. She hoped he'd be quick about it and that it wouldn't hurt too much when he thrust himself into her. Life only seemed to get harder every day, and she didn't have anything to look forward to anymore. Worst of all, never had she thought she'd be losing her virginity in this manner and to, of all people, a pirate.

Just when she thought he'd be ripping off her trews next, he surprised her. Instead of feeling him forcing himself on her, she felt the tip of his finger gently grazing down her spine. It caused a tingling sensation to flit through her. She wondered just why he did this.

"I knew you were lying when you said you knew nothing about Birk making a copy of this map."

The map! She tensed and also breathed a sigh of relief at the same time. In her worry, she'd almost forgotten that a pirate would choose treasure over a woman any day. She'd cursed the fact she'd been saddled with this map, but now she was grateful because it was the only thing saving her from being taken by the pirate right now.

"I didna lie, no' really," she told him, her cheek smashed down against the table. "I told ye I didna see Birk copy the map and that is the truth. He knocked me unconscious before he did it, puttin' it where even I couldna see it."

"Either way, you had it all along and kept that fact from me. Why? Were you going to go back to Birk's men now that he's dead and find the treasure with them?"

"Nay!" she answered, standing up straight, crossing her hands over her chest in modesty. "Birk killed my faither," she blurted out. "Why would I want to go back to that awful place?"

"Aye, that dead man in the game room," he said with a nod, fingering the ring hanging from the chain around his neck, in thought.

"Aye, he was my faither, and ye stole my mathair's weddin' ring right off his dead body. How black-hearted of a man are ye?"

"Do you really want to know?" His dark eyes bored into her as he raised his thick brows. Plucking up the ring in two fingers, he inspected it closely while he talked. "For your information, I wasn't the one who took this off your father, it was one of my men."

"Give it to me," she demanded, still trying to hide her breasts with one arm as she reached for the ring with the other.

"Nay," he said, pushing her hand away. "This amethyst ring is mine now. Besides, your father is dead and has no need for it."

"Well, I have a need for it," she said. "Now give it to me. It's mine, no' yers." She reached for it again and he grabbed her hand, still looking at the ring.

"How does a peasant such as you come to possess something of such value to begin with?"

"That's none of yer concern. I need that ring, now give it to me."

He dropped the ring and it swung from the chain, settling against his chest. "I have a need for something that you have as well. So why don't you be a good wench and give me what I want without giving me any trouble?"

"I – I nay," she said, daringly looking into his eyes. His gaze settled on her lips. Her eyes settled on his mouth as well.

"I'm not used to being denied what I desire. Especially from a woman." His voice sounded dangerous and sexy. He leaned over and kissed her before she could object. Gavina's eyes closed when his lips touched hers. She thought the kiss would be hard and forceful but, instead, it was soft, gentle, and almost caring.

Their lips slowly parted and his hands closed around her waist, cradling her protectively.

"Did you think I was going to hurt you?" he asked.

"I – I wasna sure." The tip of her tongue shot out and touched her top lip. His raw essence still clung to her and she savored the flavor of this man's pure power. "I've always heard that pirates are thieves, liars, and cutthroats. They take innocent women against their wills just to satisfy their carnal urges."

He laughed. "Don't believe everything you hear about pirates. Although . . . I suppose most of it is true."

Just then, the door burst open and Ramble walked in.

"Cap'n, time to get up," said Ramble, stopping in his tracks when he saw what was going on. His eyes opened wide and his jaw dropped. "Oh, sorry, Cap'n, I didn't know ye were couplin' with the wench. I can come back later."

Tristan pulled Gavina to him, so she wouldn't be exposed.

"Ramble, have you ever heard of knocking?"

"Mardon said you were actin' odd this mornin' and I just wanted to make sure ye weren't feelin' ill. Sorry to disturb ye and the wench."

"Did I hear somethin' about a wench? Is there a wench in there?" Several of the men overheard Ramble and hurried over to the open door. Tristan wrapped his arms around Gavina and pulled her closer. The men pushed each other to get into the room, Noll being the first among them.

"The Cap'n's got a wench in here, all right," shouted Noll. "That's breakin' the code!"

"It's that lad, Gavin," said Goldtooth. "He's really a she!"

"We've got a wench on board disguised as a boy," shouted Coop.

"Aye, that's breakin' the code twice," Wybert pointed out.

"Get out! All of you," yelled Tristan.

"I want my turn with her when ye're done," said one of the men.

"Nay, I get her before ye. I don't want her worn out," said another.

"No one will touch Gavina," said Tristan through gritted teeth. "And I warn you, whoever tries to do so will be strung up from the yardarm and left there until the crows peck out their eyes."

"What's that on her back?" asked Wybert, peeking out from around Noll, pointing to Gavina.

"It looks like some sort of a map," said Goldtooth.

"It is a map! It's the copy of the treasure map we've been

lookin' for." Noll pushed Ramble aside and shot forward. "The Cap'n knew she had it all along and wasn't goin' to tell us about it."

"Aye, he wanted the wench and the treasure all for himself," said Wybert, joining Noll in riling up the men.

"Mardon! Aaron, get in here," Tristan called out, reaching over to his weapon belt on the table to draw his sword.

Gavina could tell a fight was about to break out and it was all because of her. Tristan would never be able to fend off the men if he had one arm around her. She broke free from his hold and dove for the tunic on the floor. But as she picked it up, Noll's foot came down atop it.

"Let's see that map, Wench," he sneered. But before he could touch her, Tristan's sword was at Noll's throat.

"What did I just say?" asked Tristan.

"I didn't touch her," said Noll, holding his hands out to the sides. "I only asked to see that map on her back."

"Out of the way. Get out of my way, ye fools," came Nairnie's voice from the door. She held her soup ladle in one hand and a cast iron skillet in the other, swinging them both at one man after another, hitting them and pushing her way into the room. The men held up their arms to block her blows and quickly cleared a path for her. Mardon and Aaron ran in right behind her.

"Nairnie, get over here and help the girl dress," Tristan commanded, the tip of his sword still pushing against Noll's throat. "The rest of you, out!"

"Tell us what's goin' on, Cap'n," said Stitch, stretching his neck, trying to see over the crowd.

"The captain's been hiding a girl on the ship in disguise.

That's breakin' the code and punishable by death," spat Noll, even with the sword to his throat.

"And what do you think the punishment is for mutiny?" growled Tristan. "I know that's what you're trying to do by getting everyone worked up into a frenzy. I should just push this blade through your throat right now and be done with the likes of you."

"Nay, Cap'n, I was only jestin' about goin' to work for Nereus," Noll pleaded, slowly raising his palms.

"Cap'n, why were you keepin' it from us that ye had a wench on board?" Peg Leg Pate's wooden leg thumped against the floor as he hobbled over to Tristan.

"I'll explain everything, but not here," Tristan answered. "Everyone meet me on the deck below the main sail," he told his men. Slowly, he moved the blade away from Noll's throat. "Remember, I don't want any trouble."

The men, talking to each other in low voices, headed out the door.

"What are you going to tell them?" asked Aaron as he and Mardon approached Tristan. Ramble stood waiting at the door.

"There has been a change in plans," Tristan explained. "We've got the map now so there's no need to go back to the Crooked Crow. We'll set a course to find the treasure anon."

"The map? Where is it?" asked Mardon, looking around. "Did I miss something?"

"It's inked onto the girl's back," Ramble called out from over by the door.

Nairnie was tying the neck of Gavina's tunic tighter than it needed to be, as if that would stop a pirate from touching her if he so wanted.

"I'm confused," said Aaron. "So, she had the map on her back all along and we didn't know about it?"

"Aye, it seems so." Tristan put his sword down on the table and donned his weapon belt. "However, I don't think she was working with Birk."

"I'm no' workin' with that horrible man. I already told ye that," said Gavina. "Birk and my da were bettin' me against the map."

"What?" Tristan spun around, his sword in his hand. "Your own father put you up as part of the winnings in a game of chance?"

"He did," she admitted, the thought making her extremely sad. "But he only did it because he wanted the treasure map and was sure to win. Ye see, he was cheatin'."

"I saw him lying dead on the floor so I guess his plan failed," remarked Tristan, sliding his sword into his scabbard.

"It did fail," she agreed, feeling ill at the thought of what had transpired. "They were both cheatin' and my faither paid the price."

"All right, let's go," said Tristan. "I have to calm the men down before I have a mutiny on my hands."

"Wait," said Mardon, stopping in his tracks. "Shouldn't we copy down the map on a piece of parchment first?"

"Aye," agreed Ramble. "That way, if anythin' happens to Gavina, we'll still have the map."

Gavina's head snapped up at hearing that remark. Fear coursed through her. "What's goin' to happen to me?"

"Nothing is going to happen to you as long as you listen to me," said Tristan. "Ramble, go get a few bottles of whisky for the men to help them relax. I'll be there in a minute."

"Whisky? Don't ye mean ale?" asked Ramble. "After all, ye

always stress that the good stuff should be saved for nighttime or even special occasions. Ye always say –"

"Forget what I said in the past and listen to me now," snapped Tristan. "The men are pretty upset and I can't say I blame them."

"Aye, Cap'n. I'll do it right away," said Ramble, rushing out the door.

"I'll head the ship for the Crooked Crow so we can drop off the girl before she's . . . enjoyed . . . by the men," Mardon told him.

"Aye, even the three of us aren't going to be able to hold them off now that they know there's a wench on board," said Aaron.

"Ye're takin' me back to the Crooked Crow?" asked Gavina. The thought of being left there all alone was just as frightening as staying around all these lusty men. Visions of her father lying dead in a pool of blood filled her thoughts and made her shiver. Birk's men were still there and could not be trusted. She might be the one to end up dead in a puddle of blood next.

"Nay, we're not taking her back after all," Tristan told his brothers, opening up a trunk and digging through it as if he were looking for something important.

"Well, we can't bring her with us when we search for the treasure," said Mardon. "That would be absurd."

"Why no'?" she asked. "I want to come with ye to find the treasure."

"Och, lass, what are ye sayin'?" asked Nairnie. "If ye ken what's guid for ye, ye'll go home and get away from these men as fast as ye can."

"Nay! I have no home, Nairnie. I'm goin' with ye all to find the treasure, and ye canna stop me."

"Don't be ridiculous, of course we can stop you." Tristan spoke with his head down in the trunk.

"If ye dinna take me along, then I . . . then I . . . I willna give ye the map." She spied a jug of water sitting in a basin atop a box. Hurrying over, she picked it up.

"Gavina, do you know how silly you sound right now?" mumbled Tristan, not seeming at all concerned. "Oh, good, here it is." Tristan stood up with a book in his hand.

"I mean it," she threatened, pulling her tunic off one shoulder and exposing part of her back. "If ye dinna let me come with ye to find the treasure, I swear I'll dump this water over me and wash the map away before ye can ever use it."

"Nay, you won't." Aaron laughed. "You can't do that."

"Nay?" she asked in challenge.

The smile disappeared from Aaron's face. "Can she, Tristan? The map is tattooed on to her back and can't come off. Right?"

"Are ye willin' to bet on that?" Some of the water dribbled from the spout of the jug, landing on Gavina's shoulder.

"Tristan?" Mardon looked his way.

"I'm afraid she might not be bluffing," said Tristan. "It didn't look like the ink was etched into her skin, but was just on the surface. However, I've already seen the map. She hasn't. Gavina, are you sure to want to wash it away when this treasure seems to be so important to you for some reason?"

"Are ye sure ye got a guid enough look at the map to remember the details?" she asked in return, still holding up the water, ready to throw it over her back.

"Damn," spat Mardon, clenching his fists. "Tristan do something about this wench, or I will."

"I guess there's only one thing to do. We're taking her with us," answered Tristan.

"Guid." Gavina smiled and handed the jug to Nairnie.

"Ye canna think ye can protect her against this ship full of bluidy curs," spat Nairnie, shaking her head in disgust. "The lass isna safe here, Tristan, and ye ken it."

"Nay, she's not. I agree," Tristan told her. "However, I have a plan to make her safe. After it's carried out, I promise, not a single man here will try to touch her again."

"What plan?" asked Gavina, wondering what he could possibly do to keep the men away from her.

"Mardon, as my quartermaster, I give you the honors." Tristan handed Mardon the book.

"What's this?" Mardon blew dust off the top of a small, black leather-bound book. He surveyed the cover and his eyes opened wide. "God's eyes, you can't be serious, Brother!"

"Dead serious," said Tristan.

"What are ye two talkin' about?" asked Nairnie. "Share it with the rest of us before I have to beat it out of ye."

"I'll let Tristan tell you." Mardon turned on his heel and hightailed it out the door with Aaron right behind him.

"Tristan? What are ye goin' to do?" Nairnie cocked her head and squinted one eye as she glared at her grandson.

"I'm going to do the only thing I can that will hopefully protect Gavina from the rest of the men while we look for the treasure."

"Are ye goin' to lock me away in a cage?" asked Gavina, not liking the idea. Even so, it was better than being abducted by every man there.

"Nay." Tristan's eyes met with hers and Gavina suddenly felt a shudder of desire go up her spine. He had that look in his eyes again like before when he'd kissed her. Why did he make her feel desirable in this way? Certainly, looking like a boy, she wasn't attractive to anyone. "When I'm finished, no man will even think of getting near you, because they will know that you're mine and mine alone. You will be off limits and none of them will dare touch you."

"I'll be yers?" Gavina glanced over to Nairnie and that back to Tristan. "What does that mean?"

"Tristan," said Nairnie. "What can ye possibly do that's goin' to put the fear of God in these men and keep them away from Gavina?"

"They won't dare touch her or get near her again, because if they do, they will know I'll kill them on the spot."

"I still dinna understand," said Gavina.

"It's easy, my dear," he said, holding out his arm for her to take it. "The last thing any of them would ever attempt is going after their captain's wife."

CHAPTER 9

"Captain's wife?" asked Gavina, suddenly understanding exactly what he meant. "Blethers, I am no' yer wife and neither do I plan on ever bein' married to a pirate."

"It's either that, or I drop you off on land while we search for the treasure without you," Tristan told her. "Gavina, you are not staying on this ship unless we are married. It's the only thing that will keep the other men away from you."

"Nay. I willna marry ye," she refused.

"Then you'll be dropped off at the Crooked Crow." Tristan headed to the door.

"Wait!" she called out after him. He stopped in his tracks and looked over his shoulder. "I want to go with ye to find the treasure."

"So you've said." He turned around to face her. "Tell me. Why are you so adamant about this?"

"I – I just want to find treasure."

"You're not needed. I've already seen the map and it's

engraved in my memory. I'll take one more look at it before washing it from your body and then you are free to go."

"Free to go?" She narrowed her eyes, angry that he forced her to come onto the ship to begin with and now he was discarding her like spoiled food. She was more valuable than this! Tristan would not treat her this way and get away with it. She didn't care if he was just a pirate, he needed to show her some respect. "How can ye say ye're goin' to marry me one minute and set me free the next? For that matter, why do ye even want to marry me at all? Ye could just copy down the map and throw me overboard."

"Don't tempt me." By the way his jaw clenched, she could tell he was becoming bothered.

"I – I need that treasure," she told him.

"*You* need it?" Tristan crossed his arms over his chest. "Why would you need treasure? And what would make you be willing to steal it in the first place? You're sounding more like a pirate every minute."

"I just need it, that's all. My faither gambled away everythin' we own. I have no place to live and no money at all. I need to survive," she told him, trying to say as little as possible. If he knew the entire truth, he would surely not take her along.

"Don't be daft! Even if you come along on the search, you're not getting any of my treasure," he snapped. "It'll be split up amongst my crew." The words felt like the sharp tip of a dagger twisting in her heart.

"Dinna ye mean *my* treasure? After all, I'm the one with the map."

"Hah!" He smiled and looked the other way. "Are you talking about a map you can't even read unless I do it for you?

It seems to me that you need me, even though I no longer need you."

"Well, I thought ye told yer men that since I'm part of the crew, I'd get a portion of the treasure as well."

"That was before they knew you were a girl. If I give part of the booty to a wench, I'll have a mutiny on my hands for sure. Nay, Gavina, I'm sorry but that offer no longer holds true. Now, if you're marrying me, be out on the deck in two minutes. If not, I'll have Mardon set a course for the Crooked Crow and you'll be left on land." With that, he turned and headed out the door, his actions only reminding her of what kind of man he really was.

"Oh, Nairnie, I canna marry him," cried Gavina, wiping a tear from her eye.

"Why no'?" asked the old woman, cleaning up the mess on the floor from when Tristan emptied the trunk looking for the book with the wedding vows in it. "It seems to me he's taken a fancy to ye. After all, pirates dinna usually marry. Ye should feel lucky that he wants to keep ye around."

"Lucky? Hah! Tristan is naught but a murderer, a liar, a blackheart and a thief. He's nothin' but a no-guid, bluidy, bottom of the barrel, scupper class of the sea pirate!"

Nairnie slowly stood up and glared at Gavina as she continued to fold clothes. "He's also my grandson unless ye've forgotten. I dinna let anyone talk about my family in such a disrespectful manner."

"Och, I'm sorry, Nairnie," apologized Gavina, suddenly feeling no better than a pirate for what she'd just said. "I didna mean it like that."

"Aye, ye did lass and we both ken it. Somethin' ye might want to remember is that Tristan has been nothin' but nice to ye ever since ye've set foot aboard the *Falcon*. He's stuck out his neck more than once and even broken the pirate's code just to keep ye safe."

"Well, I suppose that's true but –"

"No buts," said Nairnie, shaking a finger in Gavina's face now. "Ye should be grateful he's protected yer innocence and also kept ye from gettin' yer throat slit while ye've been here."

"I am. I'm thankful," she told her, truly meaning it this time, and trying not to anger the old woman.

"Ye call my grandson all those nasty things, yet ye, yerself are no' much better."

"Wait a minute," said Gavina, not liking to hear this. "Ye were the one that said they were rotten to the core."

"I may have said it, but I'm their grandmathair, so that is different. Ye, on the other hand, have no right to say those things when ye are no' much different than them."

"What do ye mean by that?"

"Well, ye're a liar, for one."

"I am no'."

"Tell me the truth then. Why is findin' that treasure so important to ye?"

"Like I told Tristan, I need it to survive."

"I said the truth, lass." Nairnie gave her the evil eye.

"Oh, all right, I'll tell ye." Gavina let out a deep sigh and sat down on the bench, fussing with the long sleeve of her tunic, trying to roll it up. "I lost my faither and most of my family and I'm all alone. That part is true. However, I do still have a younger brathair. Somewhere. He was taken by the same English lord who raided my village and killed Mother and Liam."

"I'm sorry to hear that, lass. Did ye tell this to Tristan?"

"Nay."

"Why no'?"

"Because, the reason I want that treasure is to give it to that lord to buy back my brathair's freedom."

"Are ye daft? Ye're goin' to give treasure to a man who killed yer family?"

"I dinna like the idea, but I have no choice. Ye see, my faither stole lots of money from the lord and then gambled it all away. I want to at least clear my faither's name by payin' it back."

"Ye should have told this to Tristan. Ye should have also told him right away that ye had the map on yer back. Ye lied!"

Gavina looked down at the ground rather than at Nairnie's scolding face. "I suppose I am a liar, and no' much better than Tristan after all," she said softly. It didn't feel good to be compared to a pirate. "Now, because of it, I will be alone the rest of my life."

Nairnie's hand covered hers. "I'm so sorry, lass, about yer family. I ken yer heartache of losin' loved ones. My son, Cato, was taken from me as a boy. He died before I could ever see him again."

"Tristan's faither?" she asked.

"Aye. I lived in grief most of my life until I recently found out I had grandchildren. I swore I wouldna die before meetin' them, and spendin' time with them, too. I never really got that chance with Cato."

"Well, ye've found yer grandchildren now, so ye've fulfilled that wish," said Gavina.

Nairnie smiled and stood up. "I suppose I have. Thank ye for pointin' that out, Gavina. I'm sure when Tristan hears yer story of why ye want the treasure, he'll understand ye more. Things will be better between ye."

"Nay!" Gavina jumped to her feet. "I dinna want him to ken."

"Why no'?"

"Without soundin' disrespectful, Nairnie, yer grandsons are pirates. Tristan has already informed me I willna get one piece of gold. My only hope to save my brathair is to pay back my faither's debt to the evil lord. In order to do that, I am goin' to have to have a good portion of that treasure. If no', I will never see my little brathair again."

"Are ye plannin' on stealin' from Tristan and the crew to get it?" asked Nairnie. "Because if so, ye're actin' like a pirate."

"Nay, I could never manage to steal from pirates and live afterwards, I ken that. My only hope is if I can find the treasure on my own, before they do. Then, all my troubles will be over."

"Why are ye even tellin' me this, lass?"

"I'm tellin' ye my plans because I need ye to help me. I canna find the treasure unless I can see the map. I need ye to look at my back and copy down the map for me."

"Ye're askin' me to keep secrets from my own family and to help ye steal their treasure?"

"It's no' their treasure, Nairnie. It belongs to King Edward."

"It does. So, it's no' yers then, either."

"Please, Nairnie. Ye have to help me copy down the map."

"And then what? Ye're still aboard a pirate ship if I must remind ye."

"I am for now, but I'm goin' to take a shuttle boat and

sneak away durin' the night. I'll head back to land and pay a fisherman to take me to the treasure."

"Nay," spat Nairnie, her fists resting on her rounded hips.

"Nairnie, please. We are the only women here. I canna trust any of the men to do it because as soon as I bare my skin, they'll have somethin' else on their minds."

"I'm sorry, lass, but I canna help ye. I'll keep yer secret for now, but I willna enable ye to take away my grandsons' treasure. I canna do it."

"Now ye're soundin' like a pirate again, Nairnie. You seem to want yer grandsons to find that treasure, when it really belongs to the king."

"I'm the one who found the map," said Nairnie, poking her finger against her own chest. "If it wasna for me, no one would be goin' after a treasure right now. Nay, I'm sorry, but I willna help ye to deceive my family. Pirates or no', the boys are still my grandsons. I need to watch out for them in whatever way I can."

Gavina was frustrated to hear this, but it was no use trying to convince the old woman once she'd made up her mind. "Fine, then," said Gavina. "Then the way I see it, I truly have no other choice. There is only one thing I can do." She got up and headed for the door.

"Where are ye goin', lass?"

"I'm goin' to do this the hard way, but I swear to ye, I will get that treasure and save my brathair one way or another."

"Are ye goin' to leave the ship?"

"Nay. No' yet. I'm goin' to do whatever it takes to get what I want. If I have to act like a bluidy pirate to do it, so be it."

"Gavina, what are ye sayin'?" asked the old woman.

"I'm goin' to marry yer grandson, Tristan. If I have to use

my body to control him like ye suggested, then so be it. I will do whatever it takes to get him to do my biddin' without him even realizin' it at all."

* * *

"Are you sure you want to do this, Brother?" whispered Mardon, holding the book in his hand, glancing over to the angry crew. "Mayhap you should think it over."

"I have thought it over. I've already told the crew all about the map," said Tristan. "We can't keep it a secret from them since they've already seen it. The treasure will be split between us and the crew."

"That's not what I mean. I'm talking about marrying the wench," said Mardon.

"Oh, that. Aye, I have thought about that, too," said Tristan. "Marrying Gavina is the best way to protect her, not to mention strengthen the respect of my crew. We all know a wench is fair game, but not a one of my men would try to seduce her if she's my wife. If they even tried, they know they'd end up dead."

"You said *your* crew, but you mean *our* crew," Mardon corrected him, since the two of them were in charge together. The next in line was their brother, Aaron.

"Tristan, the men are getting restless." Aaron walked over, stepping on something and jumping back, rubbing his foot. "Ow, what the hell did I just step on?"

"Wear shoes and you wouldn't have that problem," grumbled Tristan, looking down to see something sparkling on the deck. He realized it was the ring he'd been wearing that Gavina said was once her mother's. The chain had broken and it was lying on the deck at his feet. He bent down and picked up the amethyst ring, inspecting it to make sure it hadn't been damaged.

"Is that the ring you took as your share of the booty?" Aaron rubbed his bare foot as he spoke.

"Aye, and I think I will use this as a wedding ring when I marry Gavina. Here," said Tristan, handing it to Aaron.

"What do you want me to do with it?" Aaron was hesitant to take it.

"You're going to be my best man while Mardon will officiate the wedding."

"God's bones, you're not really marrying the wench, are you?" asked Aaron. "That is insane. I want no part of this." He pushed his brother's hand away.

"He's determined to go through with this, although for the life of me I don't understand why." Mardon agreed with Aaron.

"I told you. It's the best way I can protect her," explained Tristan, not admitting to his brothers that he'd become smitten with the girl and really didn't want her to leave the ship after all. He hadn't even had time to get to know her.

"Just drop her off on land and you won't have to worry about protecting her," Mardon offered the suggestion.

"Nay. I can't do that." Just the thought of leaving the poor girl in the hands of people like Birk made Tristan sick. How could any man deface a woman's skin by inking a map on it and then chopping off her hair? And how could he dress her up and tell her to pretend she was a boy, just to protect his own hide? This disgusted Tristan.

"I thought you gave her a choice about getting married, and she said no," Aaron reminded him.

"She said no, but she'll change her mind," said Tristan, hoping to hell she would. Otherwise, he might have to make her stay, and that is something he didn't really want to have to do.

"Give me one reason why we can't leave her on shore," Mardon challenged him.

"Because the only map we have is on her back," Tristan answered. "I'm not all that sure it'll be easy to wash off. Someone else might find it before it fades completely. We need to protect the map because that is the inheritance our father should have given us." He handed the ring back to Aaron.

"I think the wench has muddled your mind." Aaron snatched up the ring, holding it high in the sun to inspect the amethyst stone, letting out a low whistle. "You know how much we can get from this if we sell it?"

"We're not selling it," said Tristan in a firm voice. "It was Gavina's mother's ring and all she has left of her family. It's important that I give it back to her."

"I don't understand how a peasant could have a nice ring like this," said Aaron, pushing the ring on to the tip of his little finger, moving his hand one way and then the other.

"Her father was a thief. He most likely stole it from a noble." Tristan looked out at the crew, making sure none of them were causing trouble.

"Tristan, since when do you care about family?" asked Mardon. "We left our family years ago, and not once have you ever even batted an eye about it or held regret."

"Aye, it was all your idea to become pirates again and steal father's ship," said Aaron.

"True, but that's different," said Tristan, not really sure it was. "We have each other. Gavina has no one. She's all alone now since both of her parents are dead." Tristan put one of his arms around each of his brothers' shoulders. "Certainly, you boys don't want the poor girl to be lonely for the rest of her life?"

"Let's get this over with," grumbled Mardon, pushing Tristan's hand off of him and climbing the raised platform surrounding the mast.

"I agree. Let's do this fast because I need a drink," said Aaron, reaching out to grab a line, pulling himself up next to his brother.

Tristan was about to climb up to join them when he spied Gavina coming out of his cabin with Nairnie right behind her. Nairnie still held on to her ladle and swiped at any of the pirates who got too close to Gavina.

"Get back! Make room," commanded Nairnie, herding the men back, giving Gavina room to walk. Tristan chuckled inwardly. Mayhap he didn't need to protect the girl after all. None of his men wanted to raise Nairnie's hackles. Even if they did, she wouldn't think twice about putting them in their place.

The girl looked pitiful in those baggy, dirty clothes and with that cropped hair that stuck out in all directions. Still only having one shoe, she waddled much the same way as Nairnie. If he hadn't seen into her soul through her translucent eyes, he wasn't sure he'd be attracted to her at all. After all, she wasn't his normal type.

Tristan liked his women voluptuous, with breasts spilling out and long, bare legs showing when they walked. He liked them dressed to the hilt in velvet and lace and sometimes even feathers. Lots of sparkly jewelry that twinkled in the sun is something that he liked to see on his girls. Aye, he wanted his women to parade around like peacocks. This girl was no peacock. She was more of a hen crossed with a duck. Nay, he never thought he'd be marrying a girl who looked like this! Then again, he never thought he'd ever marry at all, so what did it matter?"

"All right, I'm here," said Gavina with a raised chin, facing this challenge bravely as if Tristan had dropped a gauntlet at her feet. "What do I have to do?"

"So, you've decided to marry me instead of being dropped off on shore?" He'd hoped this would work, and it had. He'd seen the lust in her eyes for that treasure and it looked just as potent as that of his crew.

"I'm here, am I no'?" she asked. "So let's get married. What are we waitin' for?"

"Well, we're going to need to get higher so everyone can see us," he told her, reaching over to take her arm to join his brothers standing high on the platform beneath the main mast.

"Higher?" Her face turned pale as her eyes slowly traveled up the tall mast.

"It's not the lookout basket," he said with a chuckle. "What's the matter? Are you afraid of heights?" He knew the look of fear and she had it. However, this fear wasn't because of him or his crew. This girl was truly afraid of heights.

"I'd just rather have both my feet on the ground, and my hands on a railin', that's all." The ship swayed and she stumbled, waving her arms wildly to try to right herself. Tristan caught her and helped her gain her balance.

"Mardon, Aaron," he called out to his brothers. "Up on the sterncastle instead." He and his brothers walked up the steps with Gavina and Nairnie with them. "Pate, that stair is still squeaking," he called out to the man.

"I'm workin' on it, Cap'n," Peg Leg Pate called back to him.

Once atop the sterncastle, Tristan turned and addressed his crew down below on the deck. "Today, I've seen disrespect from most of you, especially regarding the girl," he spoke loudly.

"The girl?" Gavina looked up at him and scowled.

"Regarding Gavina," he corrected himself.

"Two wenches on board are only goin' to bring us bad luck," one of his men shouted.

"Dump her into the sea," yelled another.

"Stop it," yelled Tristan with an upraised hand. "No bad luck has come to us, but rather good luck since Gavina came aboard the *Falcon*."

"Good luck? Cap'n mayhap ye bedded her but the rest of us haven't been so lucky," called Coop, causing the rest to join in with loud complaints.

"We now have the map to the English king's lost treasure, thanks to her." Tristan looked over and smiled at Gavina. She didn't smile back.

"Cap'n, are we goin' to drop her off at the Crooked Crow?" asked Goldtooth. "We have the map now, so we don't need her."

"She'll only slow us down," called out another man.

"Nay," Tristan answered. "Gavina is not going anywhere."

"Then make her walk the plank instead," shouted Wybert.

Once again, the men made a ruckus.

"I know you're not happy about having women aboard, but neither am I happy that some of you have been questioning my word, and also getting too close to my wife."

"Wife?" asked Stitch. "Cap'n, I didn't know ye were married."

"I'm not," Tristan told him. "Not yet, but I will be as soon as Mardon has us repeat our vows." He reached out and took Gavina's hand in his.

This time, the men were left speechless.

"Once we're married, any man who so much as comes close to my wife will be killed with no questions asked. Savvy?"

No one said a word.

"I said . . . savvy?" Tristan ground out.

"Aye, Cap'n."

"Savvy."

"We hear ye," came some of the responses from the crew.

"All right, then. I'm glad that's settled." Tristan looked up and nodded at Mardon. "Go ahead."

Mardon thumbed through the captain's book, not able to find what he was looking for.

"What's the problem?" mumbled Tristan, becoming impatient. He wanted to get this over with before the crew protested or possibly Gavina changed her mind.

"Well, we've never used the wedding ceremony before and I'm not even sure where to find it in here," explained Mardon. "Oh, I found it. Here it is." He cleared his throat and started saying a few words about a man and woman becoming husband and wife. Hearing the words husband and wife got Tristan wondering if he'd reacted too quickly now. Looking over at Gavina, he almost cringed when she sniffed and wiped her nose with the back of her hand, leaving a big dirt streak across her face.

"Tristan? Did you hear me?" asked Mardon. "Do you take Gavina . . . what's her surname?" he whispered.

"Hell if I know." Tristan looked over to the girl. "What's your surname?"

"Drummond," she told him.

"Oh, that's right," he answered, suddenly remembering that the proprietor at the tavern had told him that. "Drummond," Tristan repeated to Mardon.

"I'm not deaf," Mardon grumbled, throwing his brother a daggered look. "Do you take Gavina Drummond as your wife?"

"I . . . do," he said, almost unable to spit out the words. His stomach felt all queasy. "All right, your turn," he told Gavina before she had a chance to bolt.

"Are ye sure this is real?" she asked, sounding suspicious. "Can Mardon really marry us?"

"The captain of a ship can perform the ceremony if the ship is at sea," he told her. "Aye, I assure you this is legitimate."

"Well, I thought ye're the captain, no' him." Her eyes flashed over to Mardon.

"Now, Gavina, darling," said Tristan, trying to keep from exploding. "I can't very well officiate the ceremony and be the groom at the same time now, can I? Mardon acts as captain when I'm not on the ship, so I assure you it is fine."

"All right, then. I do," she said, before Mardon had even asked her to say her vow.

"Well, wait a second –" started Mardon.

"Never mind," Tristan told him. "Give me the ring, Aaron." Tristan held out his hand.

Mardon scoffed at him. "If you aren't going to do it correctly, then why did you ask me at all?" He always had to be so precise. Tristan hated that about his brother. Tristan more or less winged things, and didn't care how they were supposed to be done. He was into shortcuts.

The men below were starting to get restless. Tristan wanted this over with as quickly as possible. "I said, give me the ring." He held out his open palm in front of Aaron's face.

"I've got it right here, but I can't seem to get it off." Aaron had jammed it onto his little finger and now it wouldn't budge. "Ugh, it's really stuck." He tried again.

"Is that my mathair's ring?" asked Gavina, sounding concerned.

"Aye, it is." Tristan looked over at his brother. "Why the hell did you have to put it on your finger?"

"I didn't want to lose it. Sorry, but it's really stuck." Aaron yanked at it, but it wouldn't slide.

"Then I'll cut off your damned finger if I have to, but I'm getting that ring one way or another." Tristan reached for his dagger, just as the ring gave way. Aaron's elbow jabbed into Tristan's ribs with a jerk. "Argh," he ground out, doubling over. "Watch it."

"Here's the ring." Aaron held it up proudly.

"Ye're givin' the wench a gemstone?" asked Noll, moving closer to get a better look at it.

"It's my share of the booty and I can do what I want with it," Tristan ground out. "Gavina, give me your hand."

GAVINA'S HAND shook as she lifted it up, and held it out to her new husband. Tristan slipped her late mother's ring onto her finger, sealing their wedding vows. This was all wrong, she decided. A man and woman were supposed to marry for the sake of alliances, and sometimes even for love. Neither of these reasons held true for her. She'd just married a pirate over nothing but a stupid treasure! This was supposed to be sacred, but it wasn't anything more than a stepping stone to getting what she wanted. Mayhap Nairnie was right. She wasn't any better than the black-hearted pirates after all.

"Well, that's it," said Mardon snapping the book closed. "Go ahead and kiss the bride."

Gavina nervously glanced over to the crew down below. Some of them watched eagerly, as if they were hoping to experience this themselves. Others had looks of disgust or anger on their faces. All of them were staring right at her! She felt so vulnerable . . . and ugly.

"You heard my brother," came Tristan's low voice dragging her attention away from the crew. She turned to find her new husband staring at her mouth. She felt her stomach flutter. Tristan was a devilish, dangerous pirate, yet he was dashing and downright handsome. This excited her. She'd never bedded a man before. Now she was married and could only guess what it was like to couple. Then again, Tristan wasn't just a man . . . he was a pirate!

Tristan slipped his arms around her waist and bent her backwards, leaning over and kissing her passionately in front of all the men. One of her feet left the ground, but his strong arms held her and kept her from falling. Her arms went around his neck. There were whoops and yells and some of the men shouted out some crude remarks not fit for the ears of a lady. She liked the feel of Tristan's lips against hers. Her eyes drifted closed as she started to relax and allow herself to enjoy this. Then, before she knew it, he put her back on her feet and he was done.

"Mardon, set sail for the channel," he commanded, taking her by the hand. "Crew, man your positions. Trim those sails. Full speed ahead to the king's treasure!"

The crew cheered and hurried to do Tristan's bidding. The mood had changed drastically aboard the *Falcon*, because now the men were in pursuit of something they wanted badly. The promise of the king's treasure.

"What's our final destination?" asked Mardon, taking the helm.

"Head south for now. I'll let you know more in a few minutes," said Tristan. He pulled Gavina along with him, heading to his cabin at a fast pace.

"A few minutes, Cap'n?" asked Ramble as he passed by. "Is that all the time it takes to consummate a marriage?"

"I guess you'll never find out, Ramble. Now stop talking and get back to work."

"Wait. What?" Gavina looked back at Ramble as Tristan hurried over the deck, pulling her into his cabin behind him and closing the door.

"All right, let's get this over with, I don't have all day," he told her, nodding toward his hanging bed.

"I ken ye're a pirate, but ye're also my husband now," she told him, feeling anxious and at the same time let down. "Ye can at least try to have some manners around me."

Tristan sighed and shrugged his shoulders. "All right, then. Will you please remove your clothing and lay down in my bed?"

"I most certainly will no'!" she spat. "If ye are goin' to bed me, the least ye can do is try to make it pleasurable for me as well. I am no' one of yer crewmen and ye canna order me to do yer biddin'."

"Bed you?" He looked at her and laughed. "Is that what you thought we were doing in here?"

"Well . . . aye," she said, looking down at the ring on her hand, feeling as if she might have been too presumptuous. Still, it felt good to have her mother's ring on her finger. It was almost as if her mother were there in spirit with her. "Tristan, we were just married and I thought that . . . I mean we're supposed to . . ."

"I brought you in here only to keep the crew from seeing your bare breasts when you disrobe so I can make a copy of the map." He hurried over to a chest on a small table in the corner and pulled out a piece of parchment, a quill and some ink, bringing them over to the hanging table.

"Ye mean to tell me that ye only brought me in here because ye wanted to see the map again?" Her heart sank in her chest. This made her feel even more undesirable. If her own husband didn't want to consummate their marriage after he'd made a point of telling her that he hadn't bedded a woman in a while, then what did that mean? He must not really want to be married to her after all. Nay. He didn't want her in the least.

"Aye, that's right," he said, reaching out and starting to pull up the bottom of her tunic. "Take this off. I need to tell Mardon the fastest route to get to the treasure, but I need another look at the map first."

"Dinna touch me!" she slapped his hand away.

"Gavina," he said in a low, warning voice, his disapproval raining down like hellfire from the sky. "Stop it."

"I'll do it myself." Slowly, she turned around and brought the tunic up and over her head. Then she used the trunk and jumped up into the hanging canvas bed. Laying on her stomach, she hid her face. "Let me know when it's over," she said into the pillow.

When Tristan saw Gavina lying there as if she were waiting for him to ravish her, it didn't make him feel good. He had never forced himself on a woman in his life and he wasn't about to start now. No matter what she thought about pirates, she didn't know him at all. He decided he needed her to know this, now that she was his wife.

"Gavina, mayhap we should talk." He picked up the ink and uncorked it, dipping the quill inside the bottle.

"I have nothin' to say," her muffled voice came from the pillow. "Ye got what ye want, now take it and just leave me alone."

This wasn't the way a husband and wife should be acting right after they married. He wasn't exactly sure what to do . . . except for consummating the marriage, which is obviously what she thought they were about to do. Picking up the parchment, he took that and the quill over to the side of the bed. "I don't know why you're so angry at me."

"Ye wanted yer damned map, now take it," she spat, lifting her face off the pillow to talk to him. "And when ye're done copyin' it down, just roll my body out of this bed and throw me into the sea." She slammed her face back down into the pillow.

Tristan rolled his eyes, thinking she was being overly dramatic. "Now, wait a minute, Gavina. You know I'd never do a thing like that."

"Do I?" Her head came back up and her eyes fell on the parchment in his hand. "Yer precious treasure map is all ye care about. Now make yer copy so ye can go find yerself somethin' to plunder." A tear dripped down her cheek and it was all he could do to stop himself from brushing it away. She turned her face away from him. By the way her body jerked slightly, he knew that she was crying.

"God's eyes, why me?" he mumbled, wondering now why he hadn't listened to his brothers. They should have just brought her back to the Crooked Crow and forgotten all about her. Nay, he couldn't do that, he realized. She meant more to him than that. He had feelings for her, and he would miss her if she left.

"Are ye done yet?" came her muffled voice from the pillow.

Tristan's eyes fell to the map on her back. Putting the inked quill and parchment in one hand, he reached up and gently touched her. She flinched, making him feel even worse. He didn't want his wife flinching at his touch. Nay, he wanted her to crave it.

Slowly, he took one finger and traced the squiggly line on her back, leading down the coast from Aberdeen, past Stonehaven, and around the tip of St. Andrews. The map curved around toward Kirkcaldy in the cove near Edinburgh. Then it continued past Alnwick and toward Hartlepool, out into the water, but that was all he could see. The X that marked the actual resting place of the treasure disappeared under her waistband. Since it was hidden, he couldn't tell which of the islands was marked as the destination of the treasure. In order to see which island it was, and where on the island to dig, he needed to remove the rest of her clothing.

His hand wavered above her bottom end and, all of a sudden, the damned treasure wasn't the only thing on his mind. This was his wife! The reality of it hit him hard. It had all happened so fast that his head was spinning. He was a married man now, he reminded himself. Instead of copying treasure maps, he should be making love to his new wife. What the hell was the matter with him?

"Well? Have ye finished yet?" She looked back over her shoulder, looking like she wanted to kill him. He quickly pulled his hand away. Those innocent blue eyes were filled with tears as she lay there, waiting for him to take what he wanted without her consent, as if she were some kind of virginal sacrificial offering to a pagan god. His stomach clenched and his head throbbed. He couldn't continue looking at the map now. If he did, it would only make him seem uncaring, ruthless, and disinterested in her, which was the furthest thing from the truth.

"Aye," he said, turning away from her, his heart feeling heavy in his chest. He cleared his throat, hoping he'd say the right words at a time like this. "I believe I'm finished here." God's teeth, that wasn't what he meant to say. That only made him sound more like a . . . like a black-hearted pirate.

He hurried over and shoved the quill and parchment back into the chest, not able to copy down the map after all. Neither could he bring himself to consummate the marriage, because this all seemed like nothing but a farce. He saw the key to the door in the chest and picked it up in his hand, staring at it in thought. He'd never had to use it before, but had a feeling he should now. "Gavina, I'm locking the cabin door, but I want you to know I'm only doing it for your own safety."

"What?" Her head popped up above the side of the bed. "Ye're keepin' me a prisoner in here? I'm yer wife now! How could ye?"

"It's just for now," he told her, not sure yet that he could trust that none of the crew would bother her. With that map on her back, it might be too damned tempting for men like Noll to try to get a copy of it so he could somehow find the treasure for himself. "Stay here. I'll be back later." He hurried out the door, locking it behind him.

When he heard her soft sobbing from inside the room, he realized that he'd made a big mistake. In marrying her, he had just ruined the poor girl's life forever. It was his own selfishness of wanting to keep her here that made him do it. He liked having her around, and didn't want her to leave because he'd miss her. Now, instead of things getter better between them, it was his fault that they were only getting worse. What did he expect? He was a pirate, and getting married was the last thing he should have ever done!

CHAPTER 10

"Cap'n, ye're done already?" asked Ramble as soon as
Tristan stepped out of his cabin and locked the
door.

"Get out of my way, Ramble." Tristan headed over to the
galley, noticing every man's eyes on him.

"Well, I must say, that's got to be the fastest beddin' ye've
ever given a wench." Ramble hurried to keep up with Tristan's
long stride.

"What I do is none of your concern." Tristan walked
around a man carrying a skein of rope, and picked up a cleat,
tossing it to another crewmember.

"I didn't mean anythin' by that, of course," Ramble continued. "Not that there's anythin' wrong with a fast beddin', mind
ye. After, all ye're our captain and a very busy man. Ye don't
have much time for things like this. I just know how ye
usually like to take yer time with the lassies. Except, of course,
when it's one of those classy whores, the kind that Mardon
likes, who charge twice as much for their time than ye want to
pay. Then, ye're usually in a big hurry."

Tristan stopped, turning around to face Ramble. "Are you comparing my wife to a whore?"

Ramble's eyes opened wide. "Nay, of course not, Cap'n. I'd never suggest anythin' like that. Gavina is a fine lass. A fine lass, indeed. She is kind and smart and witty, and talented. She can play the flute like none other. I didn't mean that she was a whore in the least. Honest, I didn't, Cap'n."

"Go swab the deck or something," he spat, leaving Ramble as he opened the curtain hanging in the doorway of the galley and ducked to step inside the darkened area. The aroma of spices and fresh herbs filled his senses bringing back memories of his childhood when his mother used to cook with these. It was something he hadn't had much of since living on the sea. "Nairnie?" he asked, his eyes still trying to get accustomed to the dark after being out in the bright sun.

"Tristan, what brings ye here?" asked Nairnie, humming as she chopped up some cooked chicken that he figured his men must have stolen from the Crooked Crow. She seemed to be in a good mood, which wasn't normal as far as he knew. Of course, then again, he'd only known his grandmother for a few days. Still, the entire time he knew her she was usually threatening someone, slapping them, or chasing a man down with her ladle.

"I wanted to talk to you about Gavina."

"Ah, Gavina, that angel. Yer new wife." She giggled. "My first grandson is married, and I canna tell ye how happy that makes me," she said proudly, sounding much too chipper. "I only wanted to live long enough to dance at one of yer weddin's. Now I need to dance with ye the way I danced with Aaron. We need to have a special celebration and a weddin' feast."

"Nay, that's not necessary," he told her, not feeling like celebrating after what had just happened between him and his new wife.

"Well, now that the marriage is consummated, I might even live long enough to see a great-grandchild or two in my lifetime, and it's all because of ye. Ye have no idea how happy that makes me. It's all because of ye, Tristan." She pushed the cubed chicken aside and started chopping onions next, wiping a tear from her eye. He wasn't sure if the onions were making her eyes water or if those were tears of joy. God's teeth, he hoped it was only from the onions. Because if she was shedding tears of joy, they were soon going to turn to tears of sadness, and that would be because of him as well.

"Nairnie, I need to ask you something."

"If ye are wonderin' if I'll watch yer bairns someday, ye needna worry. I've spent so much time with yer little nieces and nephews, that even though it's been a long time since I cared for a bairn of my own, I dinna think I've lost the touch. So, aye, I'll be happy to do it."

"Nairnie!" he shouted to get her attention. Why was everyone rambling on today about things that were none of their concern?

"Ye dinna need to shout, Tristan," she told him, slamming down the cleaver. "I might be an auld woman, but I'm no' deaf."

"I'm trying to ask you if you'll check in on Gavina to see if . . . to see if she's all right."

"What?" She wrinkled her brow. "Why wouldna she be? Och, Tristan, were ye too rough with yer love makin'? I hope ye didna hurt her. The lass was a virgin and ye should have been gentle."

"She is still a virgin, and don't worry because I didn't hurt here. Or at least not in that way," he mumbled, running a hand through his hair and looking in the other direction.

"Are ye sayin' that ye didna consummate the marriage?"

He peeked back at Nairnie to see the shocked look on her face. Tristan didn't want to admit it to anyone, and he certainly didn't want his brothers or the crew to know he hadn't even consummated his marriage. Still, he needed to tell Nairnie, because he was concerned about Gavina. He needed Nairnie's help. Tristan had a feeling he'd made a mess of things and wasn't sure how to fix it.

"Nay, Nairnie, we didn't . . . make love."

"Well, why the hell no'?" Her voice was hard and stern. Tristan could look a man in the eyes as he slit his throat and never flinch. But when Nairnie talked to him in this tone, he wanted to look anywhere but directly at her. "We all saw ye drag her into the cabin in an all fire hurry. If ye werena beddin' her then what in the devil's name were ye doin' in there?"

"I – I was in a hurry to copy the map that's on her back," he admitted, feeling very small about right now.

"Ye did what?" Nairnie's hands flew to her hips again, and that was never a good sign. The first thing he learned about having his grandmother on board was that when her hands were on her hips, you didn't want to be anywhere near her because something bad was about to happen.

"Never mind. It doesn't matter. I don't have time for this right now. Just please check on her for me because I think . . . I think she might be crying." He placed the key to his cabin down on the table and turned to leave.

"*Might* be cryin'?"

Tristan made a face but didn't turn around. "Aye, I think so."

"What's this key?" he heard her say. "Please dinna tell me ye locked her in there."

"It's for her own good. I am trying to protect her," he said, still not turning around to face her.

"Tristan Fisher, if ye broke that lass's heart on her weddin' day, I am goin' to break yer neck."

Tristan's hand went to his neck, not doubting that the old woman could do it. Without responding, he hurried out of the galley and up to the sterncastle, avoiding eye contact with any of his men. Taking the steps two at the time, he stopped beside Mardon who was at the helm.

"Well, Brother, how was it?" asked Mardon, a ruddy tone coloring his cheeks as he waited for the details.

"You're back already?" Tristan heard from above him, looking up to see Aaron untangling a line to a twisted sail. "Wybert, you and Noll finish up here," said Aaron, dropping down right next to Tristan. "Well, Brother, how is it being married? I didn't hear any moaning or screaming at all. Is Gavina one of those quiet girls or did you muffle her cries of passion so the men wouldn't hear and get too excited?"

"Aye, I'm dying to know what she looks like under those baggy clothes," said Mardon. "Actually, I'm surprised you even wanted to marry the wench since she doesn't seem to be your normal type at all."

"That's true," said Aaron with a nod and a chuckle. "Usually you like the loud ones in more ways than one."

"Why don't you two just shut up?" Tristan ground out. "I'm not up here to talk about what happened between me and my wife. That is nobody's business. I'm here to discuss finding this bloody treasure."

Mardon and Aaron looked at each other from the sides of their eyes and shrugged.

"All right," said Mardon. "So, tell us. Where is this treasure buried?"

"Go south," Tristan answered, looking out to sea.

"I am going south," said Mardon. "How far?"

"You've got a ways to go yet." Tristan waved his hand through the air. "Just head toward Hartlepool, but stay clear of the mainland. It's buried on an island."

"An island? Which one?" asked Aaron. "There are quite a few islands in that area."

"Just head south," he told them, honestly not knowing which island it was. He needed to get another look at Gavina's back.

"Aaron's right. Which one is it?" asked Mardon. "Give me a name, will you?"

"It doesn't matter. Just keep sailing in that direction." Tristan needed to get away before they asked him anything else.

"Is this some kind of addled guessing game?" Aaron sounded very disgusted. "Why don't you just give us the copy of the damned map and let us see it for ourselves?"

"Aye. Where is the copy of the map?" asked Mardon. "I don't see it on you. Is it back in the cabin?"

"Nay, dammit, I don't have a copy!" he blurted out. "I intended to make one, but when she started crying, I just couldn't bring myself to do it." Suddenly, he was feeling very vulnerable and as if he were losing control of his emotions. This had never happened to Tristan before Gavina came aboard. He was always the one who was able to maintain control, not letting anyone or anything rattle his nerves. Lately, it seemed like he was rattled all the time.

Mardon and Aaron both became quiet, making Tristan realize he'd already said too much. He grimaced, waiting for the barrage of questions from his brothers that were sure to come.

"You made her cry?" asked Aaron in surprise.

"Mayhap, I did. I'm not sure." Tristan started pacing back and forth.

"So . . . you really don't have a copy of the map?" asked Mardon, as if he couldn't believe it. Tristan couldn't blame him, because he couldn't believe it either. This treasure was the most important thing in his life and yet the final destination of their future was still unknown. Tristan thought about that. It wasn't only the resting place of the treasure that was unknown, but also his future with Gavina. Hell, he didn't know anything anymore.

"Nay, I don't have it," Tristan admitted, his hands waving in the air. "I did see it, though, even if I didn't have a chance to write it down."

"Good," said Mardon. "Then tell us . . . on which island is the treasure buried?"

Tristan stopped pacing. "I . . . I'm not exactly sure. The bottom of the map was . . . it was . . . well, what I mean is . . ."

"It was what?" asked Aaron. "God's eyes, it didn't wash off, did it?"

"Not exactly."

"Then tell us what you saw," said Mardon. "Why are you acting so odd?"

"I didn't see the whole map because the bottom of it with the island and the X was hidden beneath under her trews."

Mardon and Aaron looked at each other and smiled.

"Interesting," said Mardon. "Tell us, Brother. How did you couple with your new wife without removing her trews?" Mardon's tone was snide and Tristan didn't like that.

"You didn't do it!" Aaron looked as if he were going to burst out laughing. His face became bright red. "You couldn't do it!" said Aaron.

"Nay, that's not it. Of course, I could. I'm quite capable of bedding a woman any time day or night."

"Then why didn't you?" asked Mardon.

"Enough! I'm tired of this conversation. Now, I'm going to my cabin to rest," said Tristan, starting down the stairs. He stopped when he saw Nairnie knocking on his cabin door. Deciding being with Gavina wasn't the best idea right now, he turned around and headed back up the stairs. "On second thought, I'm going up to sit in the lookout basket for a while and keep watch," he told his brothers.

"The lookout?" Mardon chuckled. "That's Aaron's hideaway. I can't remember the last time you were up there. You never go up there."

"Well, I am today. So, what of it?"

"It's all right, calm down," said Aaron with a smile. "You can use it, Tristan. If you're hiding from your new wife, you know she'll never go up there since she's afraid of heights."

"I'm not hiding from anyone, and certainly not my wife," Tristan protested, even though it was true. "I just want to see if there are any ships on the horizon to pillage. Now, handle things down here, and I don't want to be disturbed. Savvy?"

As Tristan took a hold of the lines and started to climb, he could hear his brothers talking about him from down below.

"I can't blame him for not wanting to bed her," said Aaron. "After all, she's not much to look at."

"Aye," agreed Mardon. "I'm still puzzled why he even wanted to wed her in the first place since it will be like being married to a boy."

They both got a good laugh out of that, only upsetting Tristan even more. What the hell was happening here? Tristan never let anything bother him. He's the one the rest of crew came to when they were upset or having problems with someone. Tristan could always set things straight because he never let emotions take the best of him. That is, not until he brought two women aboard and all hell broke loose. Now he could see why lassies on the ship were forbidden in the pirate's code.

Having his brothers say these things about Gavina really upset him. The poor girl lost everything, and she sounded as if she had no future to look forward to either. She was made to look like a boy against her will, and didn't choose that.

He flipped his body into the lookout basket, letting the breeze lift his hair and blow away his worries. Still thinking about his conversation with his brothers, he started wondering what Gavina would look like in a gown.

Then he started thinking about when he'd kissed her. It was nice. Even though she looked like a boy, with his eyes closed, she was very alluring indeed. That only made him feeling randy, causing him to feel more uncomfortable than ever. He needed to do something to remedy this situation, and he needed to do it quickly. If he couldn't push these wretched emotions aside and take control of his life, soon everyone on board the *Falcon* would know that he'd never consummated his marriage. That, he decided, would be the worst thing that could ever happen, because then he would lose the respect of his entire crew forever.

* * *

GAVINA STOOD on Tristan's bed, trying to push her shoulders through the small opening of the cabin window, realizing that she was stuck. Not able to go out, nor able to get back into the room, she found herself in a very harrowing situation. If she didn't break free before Tristan returned, he would be furious about this. Plus, she never wanted to see him again.

The sound of someone knocking on the door made her freeze. Her heart sped up, and she didn't know what to do.

"Gavina?" she heard Nairnie's muffled voice from outside, and then more knocking. "Can I come in, lass?"

"Nairnie!" she called out, thankful it was the old woman and not one of the men. "Tristan locked me up like a prisoner and took the key."

"Dinna worry, lass, I have the key."

Gavina heard the sound of the lock turning, and Nairnie poked her head into the room, looking around.

"Where are ye?" asked Nairnie.

"I'm up here." With her shoulders stuck, she could barely look back to see the old woman behind her. The hanging canvas bed beneath her feet moved every time the ship rocked back and forth

"Losh me! What are ye doin', child?" Nairnie's mouth fell open.

"Nairnie, help me," said Gavina. The old woman started to

run to her, but Gavina stopped her. "Nay! First close the door."

"Och, of course," she muttered, closing the door and waddling quickly over to the window. "What were ye thinkin', lass?"

"I was tryin' to escape, but I got stuck. Can ye grab a hold of me and pull me back in?"

"This is preposterous," she grumbled, pushing aside Tristan's hanging bed to get closer to the window. When she did, Gavina's feet moved beneath her, and the weight of her hanging body caused her to slip out of the window and fall to the ground.

"Oomph," she said as she hit the floor hard.

"Are ye all right?" asked Nairnie, reaching down to help her to her feet.

"I think so." She stood up, brushing off her clothes.

"My grandson never should have locked ye in here, and ye shouldna be tryin' to escape. Ye're married now."

"I ken. That's the problem. I dinna ever want to see Tristan again."

"Stop it." Nairnie's hands went to her waist. "Now sit down at the table and I'll help ye clean up and ye can tell me what is goin' on."

"I dinna like bein' married," she said with a pout, plopping down on the bench.

"Tristan said ye were cryin'. He asked me to check on ye." Nairnie picked up a piece of clothing from the floor, wetting the end of it, using the jug of water.

"He did?" she asked, surprised that Tristan would even care.

"Aye, that's the truth."

"Well, it doesna matter. I never want to see him again."

"Ye're married, lass," Nairnie reminded her, using the wet end of the tunic to wipe a smudge off Gavina's face. "This is supposed to be a happy time, but both of ye seem miserable. What is goin' on?"

"Tristan doesna want me, Nairnie. All he cares about is this stupid map." She slapped the back of her shoulder. "I never should have been daft enough to marry a pirate. I should have figured it was goin' to be a horrible thing."

"Then why did ye?" Nairnie bluntly asked her.

"I had no choice."

"Of course ye did. Tristan told ye that ye could stay on the ship and marry him, or he'd drop ye off on land and ye were free to go."

"Ye dinna understand, Nairnie. I need at least part of that treasure to buy back my brathair's freedom."

"Oh, I understand more than ye think. Ye both only married each other out of yer own selfish needs."

"I'm no' the one bein' selfish," spat Gavina. "I'm only tryin' to fix my faither's mistake and be reunited with my little brathair once again. My family."

"Tristan is only tryin' to find the treasure to take care of his crew. *His* family."

"I'm his family now, too, but yet he doesna care about my needs."

"I'm sure that's no' true."

"He is a pirate, Nairnie. He already took back his offer of givin' me part of the booty. The treasure will be split with his crew and I canna see them willingly handin' their share over to me since now they ken I am a lass."

"Then ye must find another way to save yer brathair."

"There is no other way. I need to find that treasure and use it for my own needs. I have to look out for myself, since no one else will."

"I will think of a way to help ye, Gavina." Nairnie seemed confident that she could. "However, in the meantime, ye need to get along with yer new husband. This is no way to start out a marriage."

"This isna a marriage, Nairnie. No' a real one. I dinna belong livin' on the sea. I feel this ship is naught more than my prison."

"Then ye two are goin' to need to change all that," she said, getting up and brushing off the apron tied around her skirt.

"I am one woman aboard a ship of men. How can I change things between me and Tristan?"

"Give him somethin' else to think about other than that blasted treasure."

"Like what?"

"Well, for starters, ye can try lookin' more like his wife instead of his servant boy." Nairnie made a face and smoothed down a stray tuft of hair on Gavina's head, surveying her from head to toe. "Blethers, lass, I really have my work cut out for me. I only hope I'm no' too late."

CHAPTER 11

*T*ristan had finally fallen asleep inside the lookout basket letting the swaying and rocking of the ship calm him down. When he awoke it was already late in the day. Golden hues lit up a silver lining of clouds, and reflected off the water. The sea was calm right now, unlike the recent storm. Up here, Tristan was able to control his emotions once again, because his troubles seemed to be far away. He understood now why his brother, Aaron, took such a liking to being up here, away from the crew and the rest of the world. It was peaceful and private, too. Sometimes while living on a ship of men, a little time away from everyone was exactly what was needed. He stretched and yawned, never having meant to take a nap for most of the day. Not having slept after his shift, he was glad he had this time, because it was definitely needed.

He heard whistles coming from down below and knew it sounded like trouble. Whistling wasn't allowed on board because it brought about bad luck. Those fools knew it, so what the hell were they thinking?

He poked his head over the top of the basket and peered

down to the deck. In the rays of the setting sun, he saw the most interesting sight.

A woman in a gown with a wimple covering her hair was strolling across the deck. Nairnie was at her side like a guard dog, equipped with an iron pan and her almighty ladle gripped tightly in her hands. They stopped at the sidewall of the ship and the girl looked over the rail at the sea.

Still half-asleep, it took Tristan a second to make sense of this. Since there were only two females aboard his ship, the woman with Nairnie had to be his wife. "What the hell is she doing?" he spoke aloud, knowing that parading around dressed like that was only going to cause trouble. His men were already drooling at the mouth.

He grabbed a hold of the lines and climbed down to the deck as quickly as he could while all the men encircled the women.

"What's everyone looking at?" asked Tristan, jumping down to the deck, surveying his crew. He groaned when he noticed his brothers at the front of the group, motioning him over.

"Tristan, come look at this. You're never going to believe it," said Aaron.

"Aye, it's amazing," said Mardon with a wide smile. "I wouldn't believe it myself if I hadn't seen it with my own two eyes."

"Move aside," said Tristan to his men, resting his hand atop the hilt of his sword as he made his way toward the women. When he approached, Gavina turned around.

"Well, hello, Husband. I wondered where ye'd disappeared to." She removed the wimple, letting it fall to her shoulders, enabling Tristan to see her face.

"Gavina?" he asked softly, gazing upon one of the most beautiful women he'd ever seen. Her face was clean, her cheeks rosy, and her lips red. Her short, cropped hair that had previously stuck out in all directions was now encircled with a headpiece that was entwined with colorful ribbons of yellow, pink, and blue. She wore the blue silk gown with the black velvet bodice that Tristan had made for his sister, Gwen. The gown was too big in the bodice for her but, still, she looked beautiful. The breeze blew her wimple from around her shoulders and it landed at her feet. She quickly reached down to pick it up, causing Tristan's heart to beat faster. He could see right down that gaping bodice. Her creamy white breasts and those pink little nipples were fully visible and making him grow hard beneath his trews. He would have taken a moment to enjoy the view if all his crew hadn't been looking, too.

"Everyone, get back," he commanded, turning around and waving them away. The men became restless. Tristan heard a few lustful remarks about the girl's breasts. Gavina didn't fill out the bodice like most of the women he'd been with, but neither did it matter. She had many beautiful attributes about her and looked stunning dressed like a woman instead of a boy. He glanced over his shoulder and caught Nairnie's eye, nodding toward Gavina. "I'll get that, sweetheart," he said, scooping up her wimple, and throwing it over her shoulders, holding it together in front.

"That's for my head," Gavina told him, as if he were being foolish. "I dinna want to cover up this beautiful gown." When she pulled the wimple off, the men suddenly got closer.

"The meal is ready," announced Nairnie, coming to his

rescue. "We're havin' chicken and vegetables with a garlic and herbal sauce today as well as biscuits with butter."

"We are?" asked Aaron. "Tristan only lets us eat that good on special occasions."

"Well, today is a special occasion. We are celebratin' the marriage of Tristan and Gavina. Besides, it's the food ye all brought back from the tavern so I thought we'd better eat it before it goes bad."

"Aye. Let's eat," called out one of the men.

"I want extra food. I'm starvin'," said another.

The men all started running toward the galley, more interested in food right now than Gavina.

"Wait! Dinna touch that food until I get there," warned Nairnie. "Anyone who does might be missin' a few fingers when I'm through with ye." She banged her ladle against the iron pan to get their attention. "Tristan, ye and Gavina will eat yer meal in yer quarters," said Nairnie. "I'll have Ramble bring ye yer food. Now go."

Tristan was so lost in thought that he almost didn't hear Nairnie. "What?" he asked, realizing she was giving him an order. "Nay, Nairnie. I'm captain and I'll eat with the crew. It's what's expected of me."

"Nay ye willna. Ye'll eat in yer cabin with yer wife. That is what's expected of newlyweds," said Nairnie, her hands going to her hips. "Remember, ye're no' just a captain but also a husband now. Spendin' time with yer new bride is important."

"Well I –"

"I'll no' hear another word about it. Now escort yer wife to yer quarters anon."

"Biscuits!" shouted Aaron from across the deck. "They're hot and covered in butter and herbs."

"Nay! Dinna touch those biscuits yet. Didna ye hear what I said, Aaron?" Nairnie hurried away, grumbling to herself.

GAVINA STOOD there looking into Tristan's eyes, barely breathing. Dressed like a woman, she saw the way he looked at her now and she couldn't deny that she liked it. Nairnie had helped her to fix her appearance and, for that, she was ever so thankful. Even if Gavina had managed to escape the ship, she would have been all alone. That is one thing that really bothered her. She didn't want to be alone. What Gavina really wanted was to be around family.

"Are ye hungry?" she asked shyly.

"Aye, I'm hungry, but not for food." His eyes scanned down her body.

"Och!" She held a hand to her mouth, not expecting him to answer that way. Suddenly, she started to feel very nervous because she knew exactly what he meant. He was talking about consummating their marriage.

"Shall we go to my cabin?" He put his arm around her shoulders and escorted her to the back of the ship. Opening the cabin door, he let her enter first. When he closed the door behind him, his presence filled the small space making her feel as if she could barely breathe. "I'm . . . sorry about earlier, Gavina," he said, clearing his throat. The room was dark and he walked over and lit a candle.

"Me, too," she said in a half whisper.

"You look good in that gown."

"Thank ye." She looked down and smoothed out the skirt. "Nairnie suggested I wear it. I must say I like it better than wearin' the clothes of a boy."

"I do, too," he told her. "Unfortunately, I'm afraid my crew feels the same way."

"Well, that's guid," she said with a smile. "I want them all to like me."

"Oh, they like you. More than you know."

She wasn't sure what that meant, but figured it was a good thing. "This is the gown that Ramble said ye made, right?" Reaching out, she ran her hands over the velvet bodice, down to the silk skirt.

"Aye," he admitted, removing his weapon belts and hanging them on a hook.

"Who did ye make it for?"

"Why do you want to know?" He kicked off his boots and shoved them under the hanging bed.

"I guess I would rather no' wear it if it once belonged to a whore."

He chuckled, as if her words amused him. "Nay, I made it from pieces of other clothes we picked up on raids. I had hoped to someday give it to my sister."

"Yer sister? Do ye mean the girl named Gwen that Nairnie told me about?"

"Aye." He seemed choked up if she wasn't mistaken. "I've been meaning to send it to her, but somehow I never did."

"Why dinna ye bring it to her yerself?"

His eyes darted over to her in a panic. It was as if the idea frightened him for some reason. "Nay. I can't do that. I'm a pirate now, and wouldn't be accepted back in my hometown in Cornwall."

"I suppose no'. People might no' like the idea that ye are a pirate."

"Exactly."

"How did ye learn to sew like this?" She daringly walked closer to him, her gown swishing across the floor behind her.

"I served as sailmaker on my father's fishing boat."

"I see. Ye made sails. That makes sense. Then I suppose ye would ken how to sew."

"The gown is lovely on you, Gavina, but it doesn't fit you right. I need to fix it. It's too big."

"Too big?" she looked down and shook her head. "Nay, I dinna think so. I like it the way it is."

"Bend over," he told her, making her heart jump into her throat.

"Why?" She held her breath, waiting for his answer.

"I want you to see something." He looked around the room, spying something, and came back with a silver platter in his hands. "Bend over, and when you do, look at your reflection in this platter."

"What?" She giggled.

"Just do it."

"All right." Slowly, she bent forward a little, looking up at him. "Like this?"

"More. Do it like you did on the deck before. Pretend you are picking up your wimple."

"Oh, like this?" She bent over and touched the floor with her fingers.

"Now stay there, but look up at me."

"I dinna understand." She looked up and he held the silver platter in front of her. In it, she could see her reflection. Immediately, she noticed that the bodice bulged out and her bare breasts were clearly visible. "Losh me!" She jumped up and slapped her hand over her chest. "Do ye think the crew saw – saw me?"

"Oh, they saw all right," he said, tossing the platter aside. "So did I." He came closer, staring a hole right through her. "However, I feel like I didn't get to see enough." He stopped in front of her, so close to her that she swore she could feel his body heat. He reached out, his fingers grazing her cheek and lightly trailing down her neck to the front of her bodice. "You are beautiful, Gavina," he said in a mere whisper. "I'm ashamed that I didn't notice this sooner."

"Mayhap it was because my hair was chopped and I looked like a lad?"

He chuckled deeply. "I suppose that's why. Well, you certainly don't look like a boy now." He gently lifted her chin and her eyes closed as he brought his mouth to touch hers in a tender kiss. "We never consummated our marriage," he reminded her.

"I ken," she said, her chest heaving since her body warmed under his touch.

"Since we're married, we need to stick to the code." His lips touched hers again while his hand settled atop her chest and then slowly dipped down inside her bodice. She almost cried out in anticipation as his fingers moved down and around one breast, her body growing so hot that she felt as if she would be burned. Then his fingertip swept over one nipple and her back arched of its own accord. She felt a delicious shiver run from her nipple all the way down to between her legs.

"The pirate code?" she asked in a breathy whisper.

He chuckled again. "Nay, Gavina. I'm talking about the marriage code. The one that says we are not really man and wife until we consummate it. We need to couple." He kissed her again. His thumb and forefinger rolled her nipple at the same time his tongue slipped between her lips and filled her mouth. Then, to her surprise, he pulled back, looking at her like a lion getting ready to pounce upon its prey.

"What is it?" she asked him.

"Don't talk." Before she could ask him why, he reached out and ripped her bodice open. She gasped and looked down to see her bare breasts with her taut nipples pointing upward, exposed. But this time, it was for his eyes alone.

"Was that really necessary?" she spat. "Ye've ruined the gown."

"Then I'll fix it," he told her, not at all concerned. "I told you I had to alter it anyway."

"Still, I dinna think ye should have done that."

"Bid the devil, I'm a pirate, Gavina! I am used to taking what I want, when I want, and without having to ask. I'm sorry if I frightened you, I didn't mean to. I'm just afraid I'm not good with subtlety or patience."

"Nay, I suppose no'."

His fingers slid around her breasts as he cupped one in each hand and grunted.

"You are more of a woman than I thought. You managed to hide these well." His head dipped down and he took one nipple into his mouth, suckling her, making her squirm excitedly beneath his touch. "Mmmm," she heard him say in satisfaction as he continued with his foreplay.

"What are ye doin'?" she asked, since this was new to her. Her breathing deepened every time he mouthed her, making her want it more and more.

"I'm preparing you for what's to come. Now, just relax and enjoy it."

She felt him grip the bottom of her gown and yank it

upward. He continued his exploration as his hands slid up her bare legs, getting closer and closer to her womanhood, making her nervous, excited, and very randy.

"We're never going to be able to couple when you're wearing all these clothes," he said against her skin. He reached for her undergarments next and moaned loudly when his hands touched her bare skin. "You're not wearing under-garments."

"Well, I noticed ye dinna wear them either. Wait!" she said, when he pushed her gown higher, meaning to slip it off over her head. "I dinna want to take the gown off yet."

"Then have it your way," he said, grabbing her around the waist and lifting her up. She squealed, surprised by this and not expecting it at all. Then he plopped her down in a sitting position atop the hanging table. It swayed, and she jerked backward as it acted like a swing. Gavina grabbed on to the side rope so she wouldn't lose her balance.

"Why did ye put me on the table?" she asked. "I thought we were goin' to couple."

"We are. I put you here because I told you I was hungry. Now spread your legs for me, sweetheart. I want a taste."

"What?" she gasped. "Tristan, I – I dinna understand."

"Then let me show you." With that he pushed up her skirt and leaned forward, flipping her skirt over his head.

She laughed at first, thinking how silly he was being. Then when she felt his hands sliding up her inner thighs, she real-ized what he was doing. First she felt his hand fondling her womanhood, playing with her folds. She moaned, liking the way it felt. Then, to her surprise she felt his cheek between her legs, followed by a quick flick of his tongue as he tasted her most private spot.

"Oh!" she shouted, frightened by this action. Her legs clamped together around his head.

Immediately, his head popped up from under her skirt. "Just relax, Wife. You'll enjoy it, I promise."

"Nay. Ye're scarin' me, Tristan."

"There's nothing to be afraid of. I'm not going to hurt you."

"I think ye're movin' too fast."

"I see," he said, dropping her skirt back into place and standing up. "Then I guess we'll slow down, because the last thing I want is for you to be frightened of me."

A quick knock sounded at the door and Ramble walked in, carrying a tray of food and a bottle of wine. "Food's here, Cap'n. Are ye ready?" He stopped in his tracks when he saw Gavina sitting on the table. She quickly pulled her skirt down to cover her legs, and pulled her bodice together, hiding her bare breasts.

"Oh, I see ye're already at the table," he said, walking over and putting the tray down next to Gavina as if it were a normal thing to do, sitting atop a hanging table. "That's an odd way to eat yer meal, but whatever ye do it's none of my business. I'm just here to bring ye yer food."

"That's right, it's none of your business." Tristan reached out and helped Gavina off the table.

"Nairnie made the best chicken dish. Plus, these biscuits with warm butter and herbs are like a piece of heaven." Ramble lifted a lid off a square, wooden plate and held the plate up to Tristan. "Just smell that." He wafted air at him with the lid.

"Ramble," said Tristan in a low voice.

"I had to fight off Aaron just to get you a few of these delicious biscuits," Ramble continued talking. "I figured since this was yer weddin' celebration and all, ye deserved at least a few."

"Ramble," said Tristan again.

"Aaron grabbed a whole handful of these just for himself," Ramble told him, putting down the plate and lid and picking up a biscuit between two fingers, holding it out to show it to them. "Look at all the butter oozin' from it, and those little pieces of green that Nairnie said are fresh herbs." He stayed focused on the biscuit and licked his lips. "When Nairnie started swingin' her ladle at Aaron, he took off up the ratlines and hid in the lookout basket so she wasn't able to stop him. I'm sure he had at least four biscuits with him, when Nairnie said we were only allowed one each."

"Ramble," said Tristan.

"Just give this a taste, Cap'n. It's so delicious, ye're just goin' to die."

Tristan grabbed Ramble's hand with his, crushing the flaky biscuit between Ramble's fingers. Butter oozed out and ran down Ramble's arm.

"You're going to be the one to die if you don't get the hell out of here," growled Tristan.

"All right, I'll go," said Ramble, opening his hand to see the smashed biscuit. He held out his open palm to Tristan. "Where did you want me to put this?"

"I've got a few suggestions, but I won't say them aloud since my wife is present."

"Oh!" Ramble looked down at his hand and then over to Gavina. "I suppose ye'd like to be alone, being that ye're married now and all."

"What gave you that idea?" asked Tristan.

"I just thought since –"

"Thank ye, Ramble," said Gavina with a giggle. "Ye may keep that biscuit."

"Oh, thank ye," said Ramble, shoving the smashed biscuit into his mouth and licking the butter off his fingers as well as his arm as he headed out the door.

"I suppose I should thank you," Tristan told Gavina once Ramble had left the room. He picked up the wine, pulling the cork out of the bottle with his teeth, and spit it across the room.

"Thank me? For what?" Gavina watched him lift the bottle to his mouth and then stop.

"For keeping me from strangling that pesky Ramble."

"I think he's kind of cute," she said with a giggle.

Tristan took a swig of wine, drinking it down as if it were water. "Never call a pirate cute, no matter how young he happens to be. It's not a compliment, I assure you." Straddling the bench, he sat down and started to eat. It was only when she cleared her throat that he noticed she was still standing there.

"Have a seat," he said, nodding to the barrel. "This food is for both of us."

She sighed and sat down, somehow expecting him to act more like a gentleman since they were now married. Then again, she was only fooling herself if she really thought he would. He was a pirate and pirates only looked out for themselves. She moved the lid over, looking around the table.

"What do you need?" He picked up some chicken with parsnips and herbal gravy with his bare hand and popped it into his mouth.

"I think Ramble forgot to bring us spoons for the food and goblets for the wine."

"Don't need spoons," said Tristan, continuing to eat with his fingers. "Besides, they all keep getting lost so I decided we're better off without them."

"Well, what about a goblet so I can have some wine?"

He looked up, licking his fingers and handed her the bottle. She hesitated to take it.

"I told you, I don't have cooties," he told her, pushing the bottle into her hand. "Now eat up before the food gets cold. It's not often we have a hot meal."

She took the bottle and used her sleeve to wipe off the mouth of it before she took a sip. He looked up and stared at her as he continued to chew.

"What's the matter?" she asked, taking another small sip.

"Nothing." He looked down and kept eating, but she could tell something was bothering him.

"Please, tell me what troubles ye."

"I said, nothing." He didn't look at her when he spoke.

She persisted, trying to find out, but immediately wished she hadn't. "Ye can tell me."

"Dammit, Wench, you're starting to sound like that bothersome Ramble!" He pounded his fist against the table and made the dish jump. Then he stood up, wiped his hands on his tunic and pulled off his clothes, exposing his bare backside to her. In one motion, he jumped into his swinging bed.

"Are ye done eatin' already?" She looked at the plate, still full of food. "I willna eat all of this. Ye really should have some more."

"I'm going to sleep and I don't want to be bothered." He threw one arm over his face.

She let out a sigh and stood up, walking over to the side of the hanging bed. "I'm sorry if I upset ye, Tristan. Can ye tell me what I did?"

"That's enough," he muttered.

"I'm no' one of yer crew, so please stop actin' like I am. I'm yer wife now, and as yer wife, I think I deserve to ken why ye are upset."

He sat up in bed so quickly that it scared her and she gasped and jumped back.

"All right, I'll tell you. *Wife.* I'm not blind. I see the way you act when I'm around. I know you don't want me because I'm a pirate."

"What? Nay, that's no' true. After all, I married ye, didna I?"

"Hrumph," he grunted, and fell back once more on his bed. "We both made a mistake where that's concerned."

"Tristan, please," she said, not understanding why he was acting this way. "Tell me. What did I do to make ye so upset with me?"

He turned on his side and looked at her from inside the canvas bed. "You really don't know, do you?"

"Nay. Tell me."

"I was willing to put my mouth . . . well, anywhere and everywhere with you. Yet you needed to wipe off a bottle I drank from as if you were afraid of getting some sort of disease."

"Well, it was . . . dirty."

"Nay, that's not it and we both know it. It's because you think of me as naught more than a black-hearted cutthroat and a thief."

"Nairnie told ye what I said," she grumbled under her breath.

ELIZABETH ROSE

"She didn't need to. I see it in your eyes. You don't want me, and even though we're married, you never will."

"That's no' true."

"Aye, it is. You continue to push me away. Even when I try to please you, you won't let me. God's teeth, I can't even consummate our marriage. What the hell am I supposed to think?" He threw his hands up in the air.

Gavina bit the inside of her cheek, trying to keep her composure and not let him upset her. She didn't want to give him the satisfaction of seeing her vulnerable, should she start to cry. "Pirate is too guid of a word for ye!" she spat. "Ye are nothin' but a selfish cur. It is time ye realize that everythin' is no' all about ye, Tristan."

"I am not selfish." He jumped out of bed, not caring that he was naked. "All I've done is look after you since you've joined my crew."

"Joined?" She laughed at the absurdity of that, not daring to look below his waist. "Dinna ye mean since ye took me prisoner aboard the *Falcon*? It's no' like I came here of my own free will."

"You're free to go anytime you'd like. Just give me the word and I'll drop you off at the first port."

"Then do it! Drop me off on land since I ken it's what ye really want," she told him, no longer able to hold back her tears.

TRISTAN SAW his wife crying and let out a deep breath. "For God's sake, Gavina, stop crying." When she turned away from him and sobbed, he hurried over to her. Gently, he placed his hand on her shoulder.

"Dinna touch me," she said, pushing his hand away.

Tristan wasn't good at expressing his emotions or talking about them, so he didn't really know what to do. Everyone usually came to him with their problems, but now he realized he was going to have to open up to Gavina if he was ever going to get her to trust him.

"Gavina, I – I just don't know what to do to make you want me."

She sniffled and turned to face him. "What makes ye think I dinna want ye?"

"Oh, I don't know," he said, clenching his jaw and looking up at the ceiling. "Mayhap it's the way you look at me like I disgust you, or the way you talk behind my back calling me a murderer and a thief."

"Tristan, I'm married to ye now. Isna that enough proof that I do want ye?"

"Nay, it's not. I know you did it only because of some crazy reason of you wanting some of the treasure for yourself."

"Aye, that's true, but ye dinna ken anythin' about me or why I even want it. Dinna ye see that I'm all alone in this world now and that I have no one and nothin' but ye? Right now, ye're all I've got."

"So that's why you married me? So you wouldn't be alone? And you call me selfish?" He turned and headed back toward the bed. "I'll get dressed and leave. At first light, I'll take you back to shore."

He heard a rustling noise and when he looked over his shoulder, he saw his new wife standing there naked holding the torn gown in her hand. His eyes slowly traveled down her body, from her head to her feet. This was the first time he'd seen her totally naked, and it was truly breathtaking. Gavina was feminine and alluring and everything a woman should be. No more was she hidden beneath the clothes of a boy. She was baring herself to him, and all he could think about was making love to her. His manhood instantly hardened as he found himself filled with desire. He could never walk away from her now. "Gavina? What the hell are you doing?" he asked cautiously, hoping she wasn't just playing some sort of silly game.

"Ye're goin' to need to fix the gown for the next lass ye bring aboard." She tossed the gown over the trunk.

"There won't be another woman aboard," he said, turning his head away from her, biting the inside of his cheek. Damn, mayhap she wasn't looking to make love like he thought after all. He kept his focus out the open window. "You'd better hurry up and put on some clothes before someone walks in."

He heard the sound of a key turning in a lock and then the padding of her bare feet as she crossed the floor. "I've locked the door so no one will bother us," she said in a soft voice, slipping her hands around his waist from behind him.

"What are you doing?" he asked her again, trying not to throw her down and take her hard and fast, since he wanted her so bad right now.

"Ye are right. We're no' truly husband and wife until we consummate the marriage."

"What are you saying? I thought you wanted me to drop you off at shore."

"That was all yer idea. Now stop pushin' me away because I'm comin' to ye freely to consummate our marriage and make this real." He felt her hands sliding around him, and before he knew it, she had wrapped her fingers around his hardened form. Not able to hold back any longer, he turned and pulled her into his arms and kissed her hard, claiming her as his woman. When he pulled back, she was licking her lips.

"There's one thing you need to know before we couple, Gavina."

"What is it?" Her long lashes blinked more than once and he swore it was purposely and in a flirtatious manner.

"I'm a pirate, and when I want something, I take it."

"So, what is it ye want?"

"I want you."

She raised a brow. "I see. Well, I'm a pirate's wife now, and I take what I want, too."

"What is it you want?" he asked, holding his breath almost afraid to hear her answer. God, he hoped she wasn't going to say treasure right now.

"I want ye, Tristan. I want to consummate this marriage and really be yer wife."

Tristan was so filled with lust right now that he thought he was going to burst. He kissed her hard and ran his hands down the front of her, dropping to his knees. Kneeling at her feet and looking up into her innocent, blue eyes, he realized after this, she would never be a virgin again. "Spread your legs for me," he told her.

She bit her lip and nodded and did as he asked.

FILLED WITH APPREHENSION, but no longer frightened of Tristan, Gavina surrendered to what her husband was telling her to do. She wanted to learn what happened between a woman and a man, and Tristan was the one she wanted to teach her. She would do whatever he wanted, and not turn him away again. He was her husband now, and all she had. No matter how rugged and ruthless Tristan and his crew were, they were still her new family. Belonging somewhere . . . to someone . . . meant everything in the world to her. She would no longer have to feel as if she were alone.

Spreading her legs, she closed her eyes, allowing Tristan to taste her like he'd so wanted. She had never thought that once she relaxed and stopped fighting him, that it would feel as good as it did. Tristan created magic with his mouth that she never could even imagine. Her body pulsated with each flick of his tongue, and she cried out in ecstasy when his lips found their way to her hidden pearl of desire.

He continued to lick her, making her knees go weak. Trembling with elation, she reached down and grabbed his hair to keep from falling. Before she knew it, he stood up, bringing her with him as he lifted her. She wrapped her legs around his waist. With their bare bodies pressed together, she quivered with even more desire as he carried her over to the bed.

Then he threw her into the hanging bed, and jumped in after her, straddling her body with his strong legs. She looked down to see his engorged manhood, and daringly reached out, wrapping both her hands around his long shaft this time. Like silk over steel, it reminded her of running her hands over the gown.

"Aaah, lass," he said as his eyes closed when her fingers moved higher and closed around his tip. Then she started to stroke him, petting him in a way like she would a dog. "You are driving me mad!"

His hand clamped over hers and squeezed. And when she looked up into his eyes, she realized he needed to find his release.

"Let's do it," she whispered, wanting to find her release as well. He'd already brought her so close that it wouldn't take much since she was teetering on the edge.

He wedged himself between her spread legs and the next thing she knew she felt him enter her. The bed swung back and forth and the ship swayed as he thrust into her, filling her completely. She tensed at first, since it frightened her. He was so big, and she was just a virgin. But at his next words, she felt herself coming to life.

"Take me like you want me, love. Relax, and accept me for who I am. If you do, I promise you will feel what every woman wants to feel when she makes love. Let me in, and I will see to it that you will be glad you did."

It was his promise that made her relax. She trusted him now, and knew that he would never really purposely hurt her. If she listened to him, he told her she would experience feelings like never before. She believed him, since she'd already felt something when he had his head between her thighs. Releasing a breath, she relaxed. Then, like he promised, she started to feel something very enjoyable. "I – I feel somethin' happenin'," she told him in surprise as her body welcomed him and she was no longer afraid. It felt so good to have Tristan inside her. She no longer felt alone.

"Let yourself go, love," he told her, breathing heavily as they joined together, doing the dance of love. "Find the rhythm of lovemaking. It's much like the rhythm of the ship, rocking back and forth in the sea."

Sure enough, she felt the rhythm, joining him in this special union of truly becoming man and wife. Gavina felt herself climbing to heights she'd never known. When a euphoric feeling filled her being, without even realizing she did it, she screamed out in unbridled passion. Tristan grunted and then he growled, each noise getting louder with each thrust. It was followed by his release, sounding even louder than hers. The bed ropes creaked and moaned and the both of them swung back and forth. There was so much motion and swinging of the bed that she wasn't even surprised when she heard a snap of the ropes and they ended up together on the floor.

"Oomph," he said, quickly holding up his weight so as not to crush her. "Are you all right, Gavina?"

"I'm fine," she said, laughing at what happened. "I guess the bed couldna take the way a pirate makes love."

"It's not really made to hold two. I'll have to fix that now as well."

"Mayhap ye need to make a bigger hangin' bed," she laughed.

"I'm glad you're staying aboard the *Falcon*," he told her, looking down at her with his long hair encompassing them.

"So am I," she said, reaching up and kissing him once more. "I'm yer wife, Tristan, for real now. I'm here to stay."

Never again would Gavina ever have to bear the pain of being alone.

CHAPTER 12

*T*ristan pushed the needle through the material, tying a knot and breaking the thread with his teeth. He worked by candlelight, having slept only a few hours last night. After making love with his new wife, he had basked in the glory of holding her in his arms, trying to believe this was all true. His heart told him he was the luckiest man in the world to have someone like Gavina for his bride. His head only reminded him he was a pirate and that this was no life for any woman. He cursed himself inwardly, thinking he'd been the biggest fool to sail the seas. Why had he ever decided to get married?

It was almost time for his five-thirty shift. He needed to give his brothers a break. As it was, they'd stayed out of the room last night and, for that, he was grateful. Now, he just needed to take a look at the bottom of that map on Gavina's back so he could find the exact spot where the treasure was buried.

Glancing over to his wife, he saw her sleeping on her back

on the floor where his hanging bed had fallen when they'd made love. He figured it was easier this way since both of them didn't really fit in the bed anyway. He'd had plans to fix it, but mayhap he'd leave it this way for now, so he could continue sleeping with his wife pressed up against him and his arms encircling her. Gavina was snuggled up under the covers sleeping peacefully and he really didn't want to disturb her. For a girl, she was adapting quickly to life on the ship, and that made him smile. Perhaps they could make this marriage at sea work out after all.

Tristan carefully spread the gown out atop the table, and then hurriedly dressed. He looked back once more at the beautiful girl. Moonlight spilled in through the window, bathing her in a soft glow. It was as if she were an angel sent to purge him of all of his past sins. Too bad nothing could save him from his blackened heart, not even her. Nay, he was saddled with the consequences of the choices he'd made when he'd returned to piracy with his brothers. Unfortunately, Gavina was a part of those choices now, whether she liked it or not.

The girl was his wife, and he had to figure out how to move forward and make this all work. It was such an impetuous thing to do, getting married. Had he thought it over longer before saying he wanted to do it, he would have realized that this wasn't an ideal situation at all. Something in his brain made him think that if she was his wife, he'd be able to keep her safe from the rest of the crew. Mayhap so, since it was part of the pirate's code. However, what he hadn't considered was what he was going to do with her now that she was his wife and had nowhere else to go.

He couldn't keep her on the ship. Nay, she wasn't meant for the type of life he lived on the unforgiving sea. What if they ended up having children someday, like Nairnie mentioned? Bid the devil, that thought scared him more than anything because no child should be raised on a ship of pirates. Sadly, that was exactly the way this was headed.

A soft knocking noise from the cabin door took his attention. He still hadn't had a chance to look at the map on her back, but since she was sleeping so peacefully he didn't want to waken her right now. She needed to rest after all she'd been through. Blowing out the candle, Tristan headed to the door. The key was still in the lock so he turned it, opening the door to see his brothers, Mardon and Aaron, standing there. The horizon behind them started to lighten, as it was the dawn of a new day.

"It's time for your shift," Aaron announced.

"I'm ready," Tristan replied, stepping out of the room.

"Good. We stayed away as long as we could to give you two privacy, but we're beat and need some sleep." Mardon reached for the door, but Tristan quickly locked it behind him and slipped the key into his pocket.

"What the hell are you doing?" growled Mardon. "I want to go to bed. I'm tired."

"Sleep somewhere else. You two are not going in there." Tristan started to walk away.

"Tristan, I need my things," whined Aaron. "I haven't been able to get in the cabin since the girl came on board."

"To hell with your things, I need my bed," complained Mardon. "Now come on, Tristan, and open the damned door."

"Nay. I can't do that. I'm a married man now. The only one

who will share my cabin from now on is my wife." Tristan stopped only for a moment to talk to them over his shoulder. "Once she's awake, I'll let you in for your things but you'll need to be quick about it. You'll also have to sleep either in the lookout basket or with the crew on deck from now on."

"Bloody hell, we will not," growled Mardon.

"Aye. What about when it rains?" asked Aaron. "I'm not sleeping in the nest if I'm going to get wet."

"Aye, and where would I hang my bed?" Mardon waved his hands in the air and pointed up to the center mast. "From the yardarm? I hardly think so!"

"Oh, you won't have to worry about that, Mardon," said Tristan. "Since our hanging beds are too small to encompass two people, I'm giving your bed to Gavina. So you'll have to sleep on the floor, I guess."

Tristan turned and bounded up the stairs to the sterncastle, hearing both Mardon and Aaron cursing him, but he didn't listen to them at all. He had other thoughts on his mind. Thoughts that were more important than worrying about where his brothers would sleep. He decided to keep heading south since he had a general idea of where to find the treasure. After a few hours, he'd wake his wife and have a better look at her back so he'd know how to pinpoint the exact spot where the treasure was buried, and then they'd all be rich.

* * *

GAVINA WOKE to feel the warmth of the sun on her face. Opening her eyes, she saw the sunrays streaming in from the small window and realized it was already morning. But what was she doing on the ground?

She turned over, to see the bed was on the floor. Then it all came back to her. She smiled, remembering the wonderful night of lovemaking she'd shared with her husband. "Tristan?" she cooed, hoping to have a repeat of last night. "Tristan, where are ye?"

Flipping over, she scanned the room, only to see he was gone. The sun lit up the painting of the naked lady, taking her attention. Ramble told her the men snuck in there to look at it sometimes. Since she was naked, she jumped to her feet, bringing the blanket with her. No longer did she feel safe and relaxed. Had Tristan honestly just left her there like this, knowing his brothers would be back from their shifts and wanting to use their beds?

She spotted the gown laid out on the table and decided to dress. As she picked it up, she remembered Tristan had ripped it off of her last night. To her surprise, it was already repaired. She slipped it over her head and immediately felt that it was a snugger fit.

"He no' only fixed it, but he fitted it to my size," she said aloud, impressed by not only his sewing skills, but also that he knew what size to make it. She remembered him cupping her breasts and weighing them in his hands. Now she realized it wasn't just sexual foreplay but he was measuring her as well. "Ye are truly amazin', Husband," she said with a giggle.

Next, she started thinking about the map. Not once had he tried to look at it. Or at least not that she knew of, unless he did it while she slept. Then again, he'd told her he already copied it, so that must be why he hadn't even tried to see it again. He no longer needed to look at the map on her back because he had a copy of it somewhere else. Good, she decided. Then mayhap she could get a look at it as well.

Pulling on the door handle, she discovered it wouldn't open. At first she was angry that he'd locked her inside. Then she realized he must have done so to keep his brothers or any of the other men from entering while she was asleep.

With nothing to do, Gavina paced back and forth, used the chamber pot, and cleaned up the room. Then she sat down and drank some leftover wine. After a while, she started playing her flute, since her music always calmed her. Finally, she became so bored waiting for Tristan that she decided she wanted to wash up and smell good for him when he returned. Being aboard this ship made her feel dirty. This cabin, Tristan, and his brothers were somewhat clean, but the rest of ship and the men stank. The crew had filthy hands and faces, and their clothes were covered with dirt. They smelled of alcohol and sweat, plus everything on board reeked with the fishy smell of the sea.

Longing to feel clean and smell good, she headed over to the jug of water and the ewer. She managed to find a bit of soft soap and a clean rag. Digging through some trunks, she even found a bottle of rose water that must have been part of a bounty at one time. Popping open the cork she sniffed it. "Mmm," she said, closing her eyes. It reminded her of a time long ago when her mother used to wear rose water for her father. However, she only did so on special occasions since it was usually reserved for the wealthy.

"I no longer need to look or smell like a boy," she said aloud. "I'm a new woman now. A married one. I will look and smell beautiful for my new husband." She removed her gown and started to wash. Spying the platter across the room, she propped it against the wall, trying to see her reflection. When she turned and looked over her shoulder, she was able to see part of the map. It was ugly and only reminded her of that horrible man Birk and how he'd killed her father. It was time to cleanse her body and soul of anything to do with him.

Gavina wanted to truly embrace her new life. Looking over her shoulder at her reflection, she started to scrub at the map. "Oh guid, it's comin' off," she said happily, knowing it wouldn't take long to have smooth, clean skin again. When she rinsed out the rag, the water turned black from the ink. With a little more scrubbing she would be free of these horrid memories forever. Never again did she want anything to remind her of what happened back at the Crooked Crow. Eager to leave her past behind, she smiled and scrubbed some more. No longer would she have to fear that someone would abduct her just to get the treasure, because she would no longer be carrying the map on her back. Tristan had a copy of it and, by now, the entire crew must know it. This would keep her safe from the crew. It was most likely Tristan's plan.

Gavina quickly wiped off all the remnants of the map and put the empty jug back in the corner. She had just finished donning her gown again when she heard the key in the lock and spun around.

"Tristan?" Running to the door, she was ready to hug him, but stopped abruptly when she saw Nairnie.

"Are ye decent, lass?" asked the woman, sticking her head inside the room.

"Aye, I'm dressed. What are ye doin' here, Nairnie? I expected to see my husband."

"All right, boys, go on in and get yer things, but make it fast." She opened the door wider to reveal Mardon and Aaron

ELIZABETH ROSE

standing there looking madder than hell. They stomped past her, seeming like they wanted to bite off her head.

"Guid mornin', Aaron and Mardon," she said in a chipper voice. "I'm sure ye're tired and would like to get some rest. Yer beds are waitin' for ye."

"I don't have a bed anymore thanks to you," grumbled Mardon, opening a trunk and removing a few things, pushing them into a large canvas bag.

"I'll be sleeping in the rain from now on," snapped Aaron. "Thanks to you, I'll probably catch my death from the cold." Aaron picked up a bag of things and then threw his straw pallet over his shoulder.

"I dinna understand. Where are ye takin' these things?" asked Gavina.

"Tristan has thrown them out of the cabin, now that ye two are married," Nairnie answered for them.

"What? Nay. Why?" She watched as Mardon and Aaron took their belongings and trudged out the door.

"Nairnie, I didna want them to have to leave," she told the old woman. "This is their room, too."

"Well, what did ye expect?" asked the old woman. "Tristan canna let them stay in here with the two of ye. Ye're married now and need yer privacy. Especially since ye'll be wantin' to work on havin' bairns now, if ye ken what I mean."

"Bairns? Och, nay," she dismissed the thought with a nervous giggle. "I could never raise a child on a ship of pirates and neither would I want to."

"Well, mayhap ye should have thought of this earlier, lass. Ye are married now and must realize every man wants sons. It's important to them to carry on their lineage."

"Blethers, Nairnie, ye're right," she answered, suddenly

feeling confused and anxious. "Well, I'm sure Tristan will want to give up piracy now that we're married. He'll most likely want to move to land. Once we find a nice little town somewhere, we can settle down and start a family." It was just a dream and she knew it. However, by saying it aloud, she figured mayhap she'd start to believe it.

"Ye expect Tristan to give up bein' a pirate and move to the mainland?" Nairnie repeated and raised a brow. "What do ye think he'll do for income? The only thing Tristan kens is piracy. I hardly think ye are goin' to tell yer children someday that their da is out thievin' so he can fill their bellies with food so they willna starve."

Why did the old woman have to put it like that? Deep inside, Gavina knew that she was right. Piracy was Tristan's life. Would he want to give it up just for her?

"I'm sure once I talk to Tristan, we'll work this all out," she said, trying to be optimistic, but feeling deep inside that she was doomed.

"I hope ye're right," said Nairnie. "If anyone can turn Tristan away from piracy, I'm sure it's ye. After all, I would love nothin' more than to see my grandsons give up this deceitful, wretched way of life, and move back to Cornwall with their sister, Gwen, and her family. I want to live there with them and enjoy my grandchildren and great-grandchildren before I die. I'm an auld woman, Gavina. I'm afraid I'm runnin' out of time."

"Nairnie, Tristan and his brothers seem to listen to ye," said Gavina with newfound hope. "Mayhap ye can talk them into givin' up this way of livin'. If it doesna work, ye can force them into it, usin' yer ladle and iron pan."

"Hah!" she spat and cackled. "I might be able to get them to wash their hands before they eat or pick up their dirty clothes, but that's about it. No man is goin' to take orders from a lass, nor is he goin' to give up his ship and riches for her. No woman, especially no' an auld woman, is ever goin' to tell them what to do. I'm sorry, Gavina, but I'm afraid there is nothin' I can do to convince my grandsons to change. I almost didna even succeed in convincin' them to fish me out of the sea in the first place."

"Nairnie, ye were the one who told me the two ways to get a man to do what we want. I've got one of the ways down pat, but mayhap ye can teach me to cook and I can then convince Tristan."

"Nay, that willna work. No' now that ye're married. There is only one way to motivate Tristan now, and that is with treasure."

"What do ye mean?"

"The only thing a pirate truly cares about is treasure."

"Treasure?"

"Aye. The one like that map that is on yer back. The map leadin' to the king's stolen treasure. Ye hold the map so ye hold power over Tristan and the other pirates as well."

"Oh," she said, thinking of what she'd just done.

"Ye'd better protect that map on yer back, lass. With it, ye can control every man aboard this ship. But without it . . . without it, ye are naught but a worthless wench to them. Without it, ye will have lost any sort of value and they will eventually convince Tristan that ye're bad luck. Then they'll try to get rid of ye, in one way or another."

"Nay, they wouldna do that. Would they, Nairnie?" Panic started to set in.

Nairnie chuckled again. "I wouldna doubt it for a moment. Tristan is playin' with fire havin' ye on the ship in the first place, let alone marryin' ye. That map on yer back is yer ticket to safety, Gavina. Guard it well. Mayhap ye can use it to yer advantage somehow. Ye should refuse to show it to Tristan until he promises to give up piracy and move to the mainland with ye."

"Oh, Nairnie, that would never work."

"Sure, it would. Why no'?"

"Ye see, Tristan already copied down the map, so he has no need for the one on my back anymore. Besides, I scrubbed the map off my back and it's no longer there."

Nairnie's eyes opened wide, as if she'd seen something frightening. "God's teeth, please dinna tell me that is true."

"It'll be all right, Nairnie," she said, trying to calm down the old woman. "Tristan will protect me, so I'm no' worried."

"Well, ye should be. Tristan just told me that he was comin' in here in a few minutes to see the destination of the treasure. He needs to look at that map on yer back to find out exactly where the treasure is buried."

Gavina's heart jumped into her throat. "Why would he need to do that? He can just look at his copy."

"I hate to tell ye this, lass, but I dinna think he has a copy. If so, he would have already shown it to his brathairs, and they wouldna be complainin' that they havena seen a thing. Gavina, I think ye were a little hasty in gettin' rid of that map. Without it, there is no treasure. If Tristan's brathairs and crew find out what ye did, they are no' goin' to be happy about it. Each one of them is goin' to want to kill ye . . . includin' Tristan."

"No treasure?" Gavina hadn't considered this. It scared her more than thinking Tristan and the crew would be angry with her. "Nairnie, they have to find that treasure."

"I agree. It is their inheritance, so to say, and also the only thing that can turn them away from piracy. I was countin' on it. They need it."

"I need that treasure, too! I need to have my share that Tristan promised."

"I thought he changed his mind on that."

"He did, but I'm sure now that I'm his wife, I can convince him to give me a cut as well."

"Hah! I doubt it. As a matter of fact, I can guarantee ye're gettin' nothin' at all where that treasure is concerned. After all, if he did give ye a cut, the crew would probably steal it from ye and throw ye overboard."

"Nay, I'm the ship's musician now. I'm supposed to get a share as well."

"Ye might be the ship's musician, but ye are also a lassie. Do ye really think his brathairs and his crew are goin' to be all right with Tristan givin' away part of the treasure to a lass? They'll get more if ye're no' a part of it. Even if Tristan wants to give ye treasure, I'm sure it's no' in the code for a lass to have it, so ye're no' goin' to see a single coin."

"But I need that treasure to save my brathair."

"Did ye tell Tristan about it yet? What did he say?"

Her eyes dropped downward, feeling embarrassed. "I havena had a chance."

Nairnie's eyes settled on the hanging bed that had fallen and that was now on the floor.

"I see that. Well, it may no' matter anymore since ye washed off the map."

A tear dripped from her eye. "I've ruined everythin', Nairnie. I was too hasty to try to look and smell guid for my husband. Now the pirates will kill me, plus my little brathair will never come home."

"This makes me angry," spat the old woman. "What kind of man would steal children and keep them as prisoners? What is the name of this English bastard that did this to yer brathair?"

Before Gavina could answer, Ramble started shouting and ringing the ship's bell. "Fire in the galley," he called out. "Somethin' is burnin'. Fire. Fire, I say!"

"God's teeth, nay!" Nairnie spun around on her heel. "I must have left the oats cookin' on the fire and now they're burnin' since I've stayed here too long. I swore I removed them from the flame, but my memory is no' what it used to be. Tristan is goin' to kill me. I'll be lucky if he doesna throw me back into the sea and leave me there to die." She rushed off with Gavina on her heels.

TRISTAN WATCHED as smoke billowed up around the foremast. How the hell had someone been careless enough to catch the ship on fire? Crew hands rushed back and forth, lowering empty buckets attached to ropes over the side rail and hauling them back up again filled with water to put out the flames.

"Faster!" Tristan shouted to his crew. "Damn it, faster, I said!" The flames were starting to engulf the entire galley. The hanging curtain that made up Nairnie's door went up in flames. If the foremast caught a spark, it would spread quickly to the mainmast and his whole ship could go up in a matter of minutes like a torch. This was a serious, dangerous situation. He needed to act quickly. They had to put out this fire before the wind picked up or there would be no chance in hell of saving his ship, or even his crew.

"God's eyes, this can't be happening," spat Tristan, the horrors of seeing his ship burning, weighing heavy on his mind. "Stitch, take the helm," he shouted, ripping off his long coat and throwing it to the ground, rushing down the stairs to the main deck. "Fall off, Helmsman," he yelled to Stitch. "Jibe ho!" he shouted to his crew, telling them to turn the ship and get the bow upwind. It was his only chance of controlling this fire now. "I want most of you on buckets. Get that fire extinguished now!" Every second was critical and he had to make the right choices or risk losing everything.

"Aye, Cap'n," shouted Stich from the helm. Men rushed around to help him.

Aaron and some of the others helped to turn the ship out of the wind, while Mardon gathered most of the men, handing out buckets to put out the flames.

The ship slowly started to turn, taking the bow out of the direct wind. Crewmembers continued to throw down buckets of water on the flames. Tristan grabbed a bucket of water from Ramble, knocking directly into Gavina.

"Tristan!" she cried. He noticed Nairnie heading quickly toward her galley, but Goldtooth pushed her back, out of the way.

"Gavina, get up on the sterncastle with Stitch and stay there. If the fire spreads any quicker, I want you and Nairnie to get into a shuttle boat with Ramble and he'll take you to the shore."

"But I want to help."

"Nay, you'll only get in the way. I don't want to have to

worry about you. Now go!" He dumped water on the fire and shoved the bucket into a crewmember's hands, as they worked the fire line.

"Ye heard the captain, lass," said Nairnie. "Let's go."

"Ramble, grab a bucket for now, but keep an eye on the fire in case you need to get the women away from the ship," shouted Tristan.

"Aye, Cap'n," said Ramble, running to the sidewall to help the others lower the buckets.

A line of men passed buckets of water, one to the other, and the men at the end of the line threw the water onto the fire. The line continued and everyone worked hard to put out the flames. Stitch and Aaron and a few others managed to turn the ship and get the bow out of the wind. With the wind at their back now, thankfully the fire didn't spread and was soon extinguished. Feeling the sweat dripping down his face and chest, Tristan threw the last bucket of water on the smoldering fire.

"Aaron, get the crew to clean up this mess, and swab the deck," he told his brother, pulling his long hair behind his head and fastening it with a leather band.

"Aye," answered Aaron, giving instructions to the crew. Mardon inspected the damage from the fire.

"Tristan, I'm sorry," said Nairnie, hurrying back down to the deck with Gavina right behind her. She bent over and scooped up an empty bucket. "When ye asked me to check on Gavina, I didna ken I was goin' to be gone so long. I guess I must have forgotten to take the oats off the fire and they burned."

"This is because of you?" Tristan's blood boiled. "I almost

lost my ship, old woman!" he shouted angrily. "Damn it, I don't have time for distractions like this."

"It's the wenches," said Noll, glaring at Nairnie. "We never had things like this happen before they stepped foot aboard this ship."

"They're bad luck, Cap'n," agreed Wybert. "We need to get them off the ship anon."

"Both of them," added Goldtooth, nodding to Gavina who was helping Nairnie pick up buckets.

"Get to work, and I don't want to hear another word about the wenches," snapped Tristan.

The crew mumbled as they tended to their chores, not happy about having the women on board.

"They have a point, you know," said Aaron, walking over, having overhead what just transpired. "The women have brought us nothing but bad luck."

"That's right," said Mardon, joining in the conversation. "Tristan, I won't be kicked out of my own bed just so you can give it to a damned wench."

"Calm down, both of you." Tristan looked over to Nairnie who was trying her hardest to put things back together, searching through the ashes and soot, looking for something. Every time she got near one of the men, they snarled at her and walked away. They weren't looking kindly at Gavina either. He didn't like this at all. "I won't put up with any man here disrespecting my wife or Nairnie."

"What the hell's happened to you, Brother?" asked Mardon. "The men are starting to talk behind your back. You need to handle this situation before things get worse. We never should have gone against the code by allowing Gavina on the ship, let alone Nairnie."

"That's enough," said Tristan, getting right up close to his brothers to talk. He didn't want the rest of the crew starting a riot over this. "I would hope you two would support me instead of siding with the crew."

"We're all supposed to be on the same side," said Aaron. "But the way things are going, I wouldn't be surprised if the crew started turning against us soon."

"You are both overreacting," said Tristan.

"Nay, he's right," said Mardon. "First you promise a share of the treasure to Gavina and then you're giving her my bed. What's next? Making her your new quartermaster?"

"Don't tempt me!" Tristan didn't like the way his brothers were acting.

"Mayhap you should listen to the crew, Tristan," said Aaron. "As much as I'll miss grandmother's cooking, I agree that it is time the wenches go. This is no way to run a pirate ship." He shook his head in disgust.

Tristan turned to look at Mardon. Aaron always had a wild side and his thoughts were normally crazy. Mardon, on the other hand, usually had a level head and supported Tristan. "Mardon?" he asked, wanting to know how he felt.

"I'm sorry, but I have to agree with Aaron on this one," said Mardon with a shrug of his shoulders. "If the wenches stay any longer, we're all going to be taking orders from them before long. I, for one, refuse to be laughed at behind my back by the other pirate lords of the sea because of wenches. I am nobody's fool."

"Quit calling them wenches." Tristan's head buzzed and he needed a moment to rest and think. "One of these women is my wife and the other is our grandmother if I must remind you two. Yet, you both want me to drop them off at shore as if they are naught more than our trash. How the hell can you be so coldhearted?"

"We're not saying to kill them," whined Aaron. "Just get them off this ship before we go for the treasure."

"Speaking of that, I don't like the fact that you never told us the island or exact spot where the treasure is buried," said Mardon. "You're keeping things from us, Brother."

"I'm not trying to keep things from you, I just haven't seen the entire map yet, that's all," Tristan explained.

"What?" both Mardon and Aaron said together.

"Like hell, if you think we believe that." Mardon shook his head. "We all heard the moans and groans of passion coming from inside your cabin last night. You had the girl's clothes off, didn't you?"

"Of course, I did," spat Tristan. "Not that it's any of your business."

"Then, if she was naked, why didn't you take a look at the map?" Aaron picked up his bare foot and shook it off when he stepped in a puddle of sooty water.

"All right! I'll get the damned information. Aaron, get back to the crew and get this ship cleaned up. Mardon, take over the helm for Stitch. We're going to shore."

"To shore? For the treasure?" asked Mardon.

"Nay. I just told you, I still have to find out where it's buried. For now, we're going to need to make repairs to the ship and to replace our supplies. Now, both of you, leave me alone. I need to think."

"Well, think a little faster," mumbled Aaron as he and Mardon headed away.

Tristan had a bed feeling in his gut. He noticed, just like the others, that since the women came aboard they'd been having some back luck. Mayhap docking for a few hours and giving the men time to have a drink or bed a whore would get them off his back. In the meantime, he needed to get a good look at that treasure map because, right now, finding the treasure was the only thing that was going to turn their luck around.

CHAPTER 13

"Come!" commanded Tristan, grabbing Gavina by the arm and pulling her across the deck, surprising her since he was acting in such a gruff manner. He started climbing the stairs to the sterncastle much too quickly.

"Wait. Where are we goin'? I want to help clean up from the fire," she told him, hanging on to a bucket.

"Nay." Tristan grabbed the bucket from her and tossed it down the stairs.

"Who threw this bucket at me?" Peg Leg Pate stood at the bottom of the stairs rubbing his head.

"Sorry, Pate. It was me," Tristan called down to him.

"Mmmph," grumbled Pate, using his peg leg to kick the bucket. It went flying and hit Goldtooth in the head.

"Who threw this at me?" Goldtooth picked up the bucket and tossed it to the side, rubbing his mouth.

"The men are getting restless and ornery," said Tristan. I have to do something to get their minds back on track as well as get my brothers off my back. Right now, the treasure is the only thing that is going to make things right and get me out of this situation. I'm losing respect from my men quickly. If I don't gain control there might be a mutiny on my hands."

"Oh," she said. "That's no' guid."

"I need to see the map right now," he told her.

"The map?" she asked, feeling dread wash through her. "What map?"

"Don't play games, Gavina. I don't have time for this. Let me see that treasure map on your back."

"Why dinna ye just look the map ye copied?" She knew what Nairnie had told her but needed to find out for sure that it was the truth before she divulged the bad news to him.

"Nay, I don't have a copy of it. Not yet. I was going to do it earlier but you were sleeping soundly and I didn't want to disturb you."

"Tristan, why did ye tell me ye already copied the map if ye didna?" she asked.

"I . . . I don't know," he said under his breath, pulling her past Mardon and Stitch talking at the helm. "It doesn't matter. I saw most of the map but just need to see which island it's on and exactly where it is buried." He brought her to the back of the ship that was hidden from the rest of the men. "Now lower your bodice," he said, reaching for the ties.

"Tristan, nay!" She clamped her hand over his. "I dinna want anyone to see me naked."

"You won't be naked. Put your face to the wall. Only your back will be exposed and only for a minute. No one will even see." He turned her around and started pulling her gown down off her shoulders. Her heart raced. Tristan would be furious when he found out that she washed off the map. What was she going to do? She needed time to come up with a plan or he'd be leaving her on shore after all, just like his crew wanted him to do.

"Wait," she said, Nairnie's advice ringing in her ears about how to control a man. Besides through treasure, the other ways were with food, and . . .

She flipped around, exposing her bare breasts to him. "Make love to me, Husband," she blurted out, as her only way to distract him.

"Gavina, what are you doing?" His eyes flashed back and forth, looking for others watching them. "Stop this, and turn around so I can see the map."

"Kiss me," she said taking a hold of the front of his tunic and pulling him to her. She pressed her mouth hard up against his. He pushed away and eyed her curiously.

"Why are you doing this? I thought you didn't want the crew to see you."

"Well, like you said, they really can't see us back here." She smiled and whispered in his ear. "I thought it would be exciting to make love out in the open."

"Stop it, Gavina," he told her, looking like he was losing his resolve. She glanced down and noticed the bulge in his pants and smiled. Her ploy was working.

"I see ye like it, so dinna try to stop me." She grabbed his aroused form right through his clothes, causing him to gasp loudly.

"Devil take you, you have no idea the dangerous game you play," he said in sultry voice.

Her heart beat furiously when she looked up and saw the lust in his eyes. It should have scared her, but it didn't. Something odd happened instead. It aroused her. Suddenly, she forgot all about the map and also why she wanted to do this in the first place. All that mattered is that she had to know what it felt like to make love right there on the sterncastle of the ship.

"I want ye," she said, licking her lips, her only focus being on her handsome husband. When she kissed him again, she let her tongue slip into his mouth, the way he had done to her. His intriguing moan vibrated against her lips. Then he pulled her to him, this time kissing her with purpose. He pushed her bodice even lower, cupping her breasts. His mouth followed. She gasped in surprise, feeling her body coming to life as she started to climb the precipice in her mind that would lead to her release.

Her back arched and she reached out to pull his head closer, pushing her breast deeper into his mouth. Elation shot through her, only enhanced by the rocking and creaking of the ship. Her skin was kissed by the wind and her senses filled with the essence of the sea. The sun shone down on her, warming her skin and making her feel at one with nature. Joy swept through her. Freedom like she'd never felt before. She wanted this . . . needed this . . . and would make love for the first time ever out in the open on a ship and not feel guilty or embarrassed by it.

She might be wicked or acting like a strumpet, but she no longer cared. Something had changed within her now that she was a pirate's wife. It frightened her but, at the same time, excited her since it was so crazy and engaging. Gavina didn't want to hold back anymore. She wanted to live life to the fullest, not caring what others thought, and not being afraid of anything any longer. She wanted to make up for all the things she'd missed out on in life, experiencing new things she'd never even dreamed of before – like making love to her husband on the deck of a pirate ship.

Gripping at Tristan's shoulders, her body ached deliciously, longing to once again experience that wonderful feeling of coupling with him. A tingling sensation washed through her. Before she knew it, she was moaning out loud with passion and pleasure. She couldn't help herself. Her need to couple with Tristan was so strong right now, that there was nothing else in the world that mattered. Neither could she do anything to stop it.

"Damn it, Wife," he growled, pulling up her skirt next. "You don't know what you're doing." His hands slid up her bare legs, and the anticipation about drove her mad. "I'm a pirate," he reminded her through gritted teeth. "You can't play a game like this and think I'm not going to take advantage of the situation. It's in my blood to take what I want, and what I want is you right now." He squeezed her bottom end and groaned again, pushing her back up against the wall, grinding his hardened form against her.

"Then take me," she encouraged him, throwing down the challenge. "Make me scream out the way ye did last night."

Gavina's breathing deepened as she quickly unbuckled his weapon belt and dropped it to the deck with a loud clank. Her hands shook in heightened anticipation as her fingers nimbly untied the lacing on his trews, and slipped them down his legs. She was so aroused right now, that she grabbed his hardened manhood in both hands and squeezed, making him gasp once again. When she looked up and saw his eyes closed, a playful, wicked smile crossed her face. She decided to give him the same kind of pleasure that he'd given to her.

Sinking down to her knees, she daringly tried something she'd never done before, and neither was she sure how to do it. She opened her mouth and tasted him, just like he had done to her.

"Dammit, that feels . . . so . . . good," he said through ragged breathing, pushing her head further down his length. When she couldn't take all of him, she pulled back with a jerk and got to her feet. "Nay! Don't stop now," he begged her. "I have to have you."

"Then go ahead and roger me at the rail," she said, feeling naughty giving him permission to do that.

He chuckled. "Lass, you have no idea what you're asking."

"I want to experience everything aboard this ship. Now do it."

"Bid the devil, you shouldn't have said that. I'm to the point of no return." He stepped out of his trews and pulled her over to the rail of the ship, leaning her forward while he lifted her skirts and entered her from behind.

"Oh!" she gasped, not expecting that. As he thrust into her, she started to get excited, but then she saw the swirling waters of the sea far below her and she froze. "Tristan, I'm afraid," she said and he suddenly stopped his action.

He turned her around and released a deep breath, gritting his teeth and looking angry at himself.

"I'm sorry, Gavina. I never meant to frighten you. This was a bad idea."

"Nay, I enjoyed what ye were doin'," she told him. "I just can no longer look down into the water because it is fright-enin' me from this height."

"So you . . . you still want to do it?" he asked, confused.

"Aye. More than ever. Just not overlookin' the water please."

He bent down and lifted her up, spreading her legs, causing their bare skin to touch under her skirt that hung down around them. She instinctively wrapped her legs around his waist and her arms around his neck.

"Then we'll continue but over here. And this time, close your eyes."

Before she understood what he was doing, he had her back up against the bulkhead and he was making love to her standing up. She liked this exciting way of making love, impressed that he could do this while maintaining his sea legs and that they didn't fall over when the ship rocked. Her eyes closed and, once again, she forgot all about the height, the water, and even the crew. Her only focus was on enjoying the ride.

"Oh, Gavina," he all but shouted as their bodies met with no restraint, slapping up against each other. She moved in rhythm to meet his thrusts, gripping her fingers into his shoulders and squeezing her legs around his waist. His hands were on her bare bottom helping it to move as he thrust in and out. He started slow and sensuous, but as both of their passions grew, the coupling became faster and faster.

"Aaah, ahhh, oooh," she cooed, feeling herself climbing the precipice of desire. At first, she didn't want to be too loud and hid her face against his shoulder.

"Cry out, Gavina. Don't hold back."

"But what if your men hear us?"

"I hope they do. I want them all to wish they were as lucky

as me to have such an enticing wife. If I hear your cries of passion, then I'll know that I've pleased you."

Gavina's entire body was vibrating as she welcomed him in this unusual way of making love. Hearing his moans of desire only made her passion stronger. She was making love to a dark and dangerous pirate out in the open and she loved every minute of it! He asked her not to muffle her cries and, by God, she wasn't going to hold back any longer because this felt so damned good.

"Tristan . . . Tristan . . . Oooooh, Tristan!" she shouted, squealing high and loud when she found her release. As she experienced the orgasmic feeling over and over, she moaned in passion, louder and louder, until he'd found his release as well.

"Arrrrrgh! he cried out, just like a pirate.

"Arrrrgh," she shouted, mimicking him, and making them both laugh.

"What the hell is going on over there?" boomed Mardon's voice from behind them.

"Is someone hurt?" Aaron swung down from up above, landing next to Mardon.

Tristan hurriedly put Gavina back on her feet and helped her pull her bodice back into place.

"Oh!" said Aaron, seeing Tristan's bare bottom. He made a face and looked the other way.

"What the hell is the matter with you two?" Tristan hurriedly stepped into his trews and pulled them back into place. "Don't you know the sounds of two people in the midst of unbridled passion?"

Gavina turned around to see Mardon and Aaron standing there motionless with their jaws dropped open wide.

"Mayhap Nairnie needs my help in cleanin' up," said Gavina, almost laughing as she walked past the brothers.

"Get the hell back to work," grumbled Tristan, picking up his weapon belt and following her to the helm.

Gavina felt sexually satisfied and, at the same time, pleasingly smug. What started out as naught but a distraction to keep Tristan from asking about the map turned into something enjoyable for both of them. She decided they would have to do this more often. She really liked making love out in the sunshine. Taking in a deep breath of the salty sea air, she released it, starting to get used to living on the sea.

"Gavina, don't go down to the main deck right now." Tristan's hand shot out and clamped around her arm just as she was about to use the stairs.

"Why no'?" she asked. "I've got to help Nairnie clean up the mess from the fire."

"It's not safe right now."

"What do you mean? The fire is out, isna it?"

"Aye, the fire to the bow has been extinguished, but I'm afraid there is another fire raging down below that neither of us is going to be able to put out."

"Tristan, ye make no sense at all. What are ye tryin' to say?"

She turned to look down at the main deck, but he stopped her.

"Don't look," he said, turning her and pulling her against his chest. "Mardon, get us the hell to shore as fast as possible, and take some gold along to buy each man a drink and to pay for some whores. Aaron, get down there and stop them before I have to do it myself. But I swear if I do, it's not going to be a pretty sight."

"Tristan, I dinna understand," she told him. "What is it ye dinna want me to see?"

Tristan let out a sigh, shaking his head. "Well, if you're going to be the wife of a pirate, I suppose you need to know."

"Know what?" she asked, thinking her husband was acting very odd.

"Come," he told her, holding her hand. "No matter what happens, just don't let go of my hand."

CHAPTER 14

"Keep walking," Tristan told Gavina, rushing her through the randy crowd of men, headed for his cabin. "Just keep your eyes straight ahead and don't make eye contact with anyone. Don't even look at any of the crew or I promise you, you're going to see things you'll never be able to forget."

"Tristan, I'm no' a child," she told him, appreciating the fact he wanted to protect her, but not liking to be treated this way. "I'm the wife of a pirate now, and I need to ken everythin' that is goin' on aboard yer ship."

"All right, if you insist." He stopped and crossed his arms over his chest. "Go ahead and look, but don't say I didn't warn you."

When she turned to look at the crew, she realized exactly what he meant. Her eyes opened wide and she gasped when she saw what the men were all doing.

"Gavina, Gavina," one of the men moaned, undulating his hips when he spoke.

"Like what ye see, lass?" asked another, pulling his aroused manhood out of his trews and showing it to her. "Want to touch it?" As far as she could tell, all the men had their hands down their trews. And every one of them had lust in their eyes and was looking directly at her!

"Let's go!" She turned on her heel and ran to the cabin, making Tristan laugh. He entered the room behind her, closing the door.

"However bad you think a pirate is, I assure you, he's much worse," Tristan explained. "Pirates, my dear, are – and I hate to admit it – are bad to the bone. Most of them hold no respect for anyone or anything, only thinking about themselves."

"And treasure," she mumbled, but Tristan heard her. There was something about this treasure map that bothered her. He figured it was because she wanted to find the treasure for herself. Which she never would, of course. That is, not without his help.

"Come here," he said, holding out his arms. She smiled and came toward him very willingly. "I want to have a closer look at that map." She stopped in her tracks. "My crew awaits my instructions. If I'm going to keep them under control, I need to dangle it in front of their noses as motivation."

"Ye're goin' to show them . . . my back?" she asked, aghast.

"Nay, not them, just me," he chuckled, waving her over. "Come here and sit on my lap, Wife. Let me help you out of your clothes."

He picked up a bottle of whisky off the table, and straddled the barrel and sat down.

"Tristan," she said, slowly moving toward him. "There is somethin' I need to tell ye."

"We can talk later. Now come closer and turn around. I'm

anxious to see the island and the actual spot where this trea-sure is buried."

"Me, too," she said softly.

"Don't worry, I'll tell you where it is since you can't see your back."

"That's no' what I mean."

"Then what do you mean?"

"I mean . . . I mean . . . Tristan, I want to tell ye that I love bein' yer wife. I didna think I would, because ye're a pirate, but I do. I really do."

She seemed as if she were avoiding telling him something but, for the life of him, he couldn't figure out what. All he knew was that she kept talking and talking and sounding a lot like Ramble right about now.

"I'm happy being married to you, too," he told her. "Now turn around so I can see that map."

"I dinna ever want to lose ye." She reached out and squeezed his hand. A tear rolled down her cheek. "Ye're all I have and I dinna want to live my life all alone." She talked fast but by the look on her face, Tristan could tell that she meant every word of it. God's bones, he hoped she wasn't going to start crying again because he couldn't stand seeing a woman cry.

"Gavina, you're not alone," he assured her, putting the bottle on the table and reaching up to touch her on one shoul-der. "I'm your husband now, so stop worrying."

"Aye, ye're my husband but yet ye lock me in my room and get angry with me all the time," she blurted out.

"Not all the time," he corrected her. "Just sometimes. And I want you to know, I only lock you away for your own safety. Or did you forget what you saw on the way in here? Things like that, I'm sure you'll never be able to erase from your mind."

"Oh. I suppose ye are right. Well, I dinna want ye to get angry with me again."

"I'm sorry our marriage hasn't started out smoothly." He looked into her bright blue eyes, hoping she could tell he was being sincere. He was about to admit something that he probably never should because it was only going to make him vulnerable. But since she was pouring out her heart to him, he figured he'd do the same. "I . . . I sometimes can't believe I'm really married."

"Aye. Me, too." She sniffled and smiled.

"Gavina, I might sound harsh at times but it's only because I feel like . . ."

"Like what?"

"Like you deserve someone so much better than me," he said, before he could talk himself out of it.

"Ye do?" She slowly sat down on his lap and put her arm around his shoulders.

"Aye," he admitted. "I do. You see, since turning to piracy, I never thought I'd get married. This is a whole different way of life. Then when I met you, I started wondering what it would be like if I wed. I suppose having Nairnie on board and hearing about my sister being married to an ex-pirate, as well as her having a large family made me think someday it might happen to me as well."

"Well, now it has happened and ye'll have all those things." She smiled and kissed him on the cheek, sounding as if she honestly believed it.

"I'm a pirate," he reminded her in a low voice. "Sweetheart, I can never have a life like my sister's."

"Well, why dinna ye stop bein' a pirate then?" she asked, reaching out and pushing back a long strand of hair from his face.

"I don't think I can," he said in a mere whisper, taking her hand in his and gently kissing her fingers one by one. "Being a pirate is all I know. It's in my blood, and I can't change that."

"Nay, I dinna believe that at all. Ye said ye were once a fisherman along with yer faither and brathairs. Ye can go back to doin' that."

"Be a fisherman? Hah! Not likely. That's a pauper's way of life." Tristan wrinkled his nose and shook his head. "Nay. My brothers and I made a decision. We chose this life, and we can never go back. You're being naught but daft if you think we can."

"I dinna see why no'," she told him.

"Gavina." He took a deep breath and released it. There was something else he had to say and he might as well do it and get it over with. "If we even step foot on the mainland for too long, it's taking a chance that I will be killed. We're a lot safer sticking to the sea."

"I dinna understand."

"I've done a lot of things that make me a wanted man," he explained. "If a pirate is caught, it is the law that he is killed. I'd die by hanging." He reached out and stroked her cheek. "I've pillaged, plundered, and even killed to take what I wanted. I don't belong on land in a little cottage with a wife and family depending on me. The only place I belong is right here on this ship."

"What about yer family who are lookin' for ye? Dinna ye want to be with yer sister?"

"Nay," he said, shaking his head. "I've got my brothers here, and now even Nairnie, so I have family. Plus, I have my crew. Gwen is better off without my brothers and me. Trying to see her is only going to put her in danger. Especially since she is married to a man who was once a pirate as well. She has children that need to be protected. It's better this way. My home is on the sea now."

"Well, I would give anythin' to have a family that wants me," she told him. "Yet ye have a sister with a husband and children lookin' for ye but ye want nothin' to do with her at all."

He didn't know how to respond to that. Part of him did want to see Gwen again, as well as his nephews and nieces. Having his grandmother aboard was starting to rub off on him and making him feel homesick in a way, even though he'd never admit it. He actually enjoyed having his grandmother around since he never even knew she existed. Nairnie was brash and brave and he liked that about the old woman. It made him wonder how Gwen had turned out after all these years. However, even longing for all this, another part of him craved the life of a pirate and the bounties it brought him. He longed for the sea. It made him feel alive. It was an exciting life with new adventures and more riches every day. Plus, he also liked his freedom. Aboard the *Falcon*, he could go wherever he wanted and do whatever he pleased. His only responsibility was to his brothers, the crew, and the ship.

"Has your family all died then?" he asked her, changing the subject before she dragged any more emotions out of him like she had the ability to do. He'd prided himself on keeping his emotions intact and he didn't want to start looking weak in front of his men.

"Aye, almost all of them have passed on," she answered.

"Tell me about it. I want to hear all about your late father as well. He was a gambler and a drunk, right?" He lifted the whisky bottle to his mouth, but stopped in mid-motion when he saw her eyes flash over to it. He lowered it slowly without taking any.

"I dinna like it when ye call him that."

"Well, what else would you call a man who was willing to gamble away his own daughter?" The pain showed in her eyes and he started wondering if he shouldn't have said that. However, it was reality and the faster Gavina accepted the truth the better.

"He had guid reason to do it." She sounded as if she honestly believed it.

"Nay, sweetheart." Tristan took a deep draw and handed her the bottle but she refused it. "No reason is a good reason to be treating a woman like a piece of property. Especially when it's being done by the girl's own father."

"How can ye say that? After all, when ye abducted me from the Crooked Crow, that made me yer property, didna it? So ye're no better than him."

"That is different. I didn't know you were a girl. Not at first." He wasn't sure how different it really was and she did have a point. But hell, if he was going to admit it. He'd already put himself in a vulnerable position once today opening up to her, and he wasn't going to do it again.

"My faither said he was goin' to use me as part of his bet but only because he kent he was sure to win. Otherwise, I'm sure he never would have done it."

"Or mayhap he was just greedy like most men and wanted the treasure for himself, no matter what the cost."

"Nay!" she spat. "That treasure was goin' to be used to make up for his mistakes of the past."

"Some mistakes can never be fixed," he told her. "No amount of wishing can make it so."

"Well, we were goin' to make things right and I was goin' to help him."

"I don't understand. What were you going to do with the treasure? What was it that needed fixing?"

Before she could answer, there came a knock at the door.

"Who is it?" growled Tristan, not wanting to be interrupted.

"It's Ramble, Cap'n," came a voice from the other side of the door.

"Go away. I don't want to be disturbed."

"But I –"

"You heard me. Now leave. I'm busy."

He heard muffled voices that seemed to be arguing although he couldn't hear what was being said. Then the door burst open. Instead of Ramble entering like he'd expected, Nairnie pushed her way past the boy and barged into the room.

"I am no' goin' to leave because there is somethin' I need to tell ye that is of great importance."

"Nairnie? What the hell are you doing? You can't burst into my private quarters like this," complained Tristan.

"Nairnie, is somethin' wrong?" Gavina jumped up and ran over to the old woman.

"Somethin', or should I say someone, is rotten aboard this ship and I intend to get to the bottom of it and do somethin' about it."

"What the hell are you talking about?" Tristan got up and stretched.

"I'm sorry Cap'n, but I tried to tell her ye were busy and that we shouldn't disturb ye," said Ramble, still standing just outside the door. "Nairnie insisted. When she is angry, I've learned it's not a good thing to ignore her."

Ramble's continuous talking was starting to give Tristan a headache. "Well, how about I just ignore you instead?" He walked over and slammed the door in Ramble's face.

"If ye keep on doin' that, Cap'n, I am goin' to start thinkin' that ye don't like me," came Ramble's muffled voice from the other side of the door.

"All right, what is it Nairnie that has your feathers so ruffled?" asked Tristan, not really caring, but knowing the faster he calmed her down the sooner she'd leave his cabin.

"Never mind feathers, what I'm talkin' about is sabotage! Deceit, trickery, and downright dirty deeds." She ticked off a finger with each word as she listed them. "Well, I dinna like it, I tell ye. I dinna like it one bit."

"Nairnie, calm down." Tristan put his hands on her shoulders and looked into her eyes. "What in the bloody hell are you talking about?"

"I'm talkin' about the fire."

"Oh, that. Don't remind me." He released her and ran a weary hand through his long hair. "That is a real setback and something that is only going to slow us down in finding that treasure." He started to pace the floor in thought like he always did when he felt troubled.

"It wasna my fault. It seems I didna cause that fire after all," spat Nairnie.

"What?" Tristan stopped pacing and looked over his

shoulder at her. "I thought you said you left the oats on the flame too long."

"I did say that and thought that at first. Then, I remembered that when I went to talk to Gavina, I took the pot off the fire, meanin' to put it back on when I returned."

"So someone else did it, hoping to blame ye," Gavina broke in.

"Aye, that's exactly right," she answered. "I think one or more of the crew is causin' trouble and blamin' it on ye and me, Gavina."

"Why would they do that?" asked Gavina. "Dinna they like us?"

"Oh, they like you, Gavina," mumbled Tristan, thinking about the crew's actions just moments ago.

"They dinna like us on this ship, that's for sure," Nairnie told Gavina with a snort. "I'm no' blind. I see exactly what they're doin'. They are makin' it look like it's the two of us that are causin' all the bad luck."

"That's terrible," exclaimed Gavina. "Tristan, ye've got to do somethin' about this. Ye've got to help us."

"Do I?" he asked softly, not liking to be in this position. He didn't want to come between the women and his crew.

"Aye, Tristan, please," begged Gavina. "After all, Nairnie is yer grandmathair and I am yer wife."

"You don't need to remind me." His pacing continued. God, he needed a nap. All he wanted to do was rest and think things through. With these women aboard, he wasn't sure if he'd ever sleep again.

"Ye need to find the culprits and make them pay for what they've done." Nairnie wagged a finger in his face. "I'll bet it is that no-guid Noll and his crusty sidekick Wybert behind all this."

"Aye, that's who it is," agreed Gavina. "Tristan, can ye help us?"

"Now wait a minute. Both of you," said Tristan raising his hands in the air. His head spun from all the noise. Trying to handle one woman was bad enough – he didn't need two chirping in his ear day and night. "Nairnie, you are an old woman and I'm sure you forget things often."

"Are ye accusin' yer own grandmathair of lyin'?" She squinted one eye and pursed her lips. Her hands were on her hips again and he wouldn't be surprised if she started swinging at him next.

"Nay," he said with a smile, shaking his head. These women sure had a way of turning things around. "I didn't say that at all. I just meant that mayhap you . . . forgot what you did. It happens to everyone on occasion."

"Mmph," grunted Nairnie, not looking at all amused. "No' to me, it doesna happen. I remember every little thing in my life and, in the past, I have even had visions of things to come."

Now he knew she was addled. After all, nobody could see the future.

"Nairnie is the most trustworthy person on this ship," said Gavina, sticking up for the old woman. "She would never lie, Tristan. Ye have to believe her."

"I didn't say she lied," he ground out. "And I never said I didn't believe her."

"Well, ye said I'm forgetful and that I made up the whole thing." Nairnie's hands balled into fists on her hips now. This could only mean trouble for him. How the hell was he going to convince these two of anything right now? Living on a ship of men, things were cut-and-dried. If there was a problem, it was out in the open, never hidden. A man said exactly what he meant and no one ever read anything into it that wasn't there. Women, on the other hand, were always trying to twist things around and cause trouble when there was no need for it at all.

"Cap'n," called Ramble from the other side of the door, knocking again. "Cap'n, please open the door."

"Egads," Tristan spat, stomping over to the door and pulling it open. Why wouldn't everyone just leave him alone? "What is it, Ramble? And by God, this better be important or I swear I'll take off your head."

"It is important, I promise ye that. Mardon told me to let ye know we're dockin' right now. Aaron is lowerin' the flags and sails so no one realizes we're pirates. He said to tell ye that the men want to go on another raid and he agrees. After all, our supplies are low and most of what we stole from the Crooked Crow was ruined in the fire."

"Tell Mardon I don't really give a damn what he does. If he thinks we should raid the place, then go ahead and do it. He's the quartermaster and is supposed to know these things. So, stop bothering me. I'm busy."

"Aye, Cap'n."

"Oh, but tell Aaron not to drop the anchor. Come to think of it, have him keep the sails half-furled for a quick departure."

"Then everyone will know we are pirates," protested Ramble.

"I don't give a damned who knows we're coming. They'll figure it out once we raid them anyway."

"Aye, Cap'n. I'll tell them right away," said Ramble, taking off at a run.

"Tristan, ye arena really goin' to raid again so soon, are ye?" asked Gavina. "Mayhap this could just be a trip for supplies that we pay for. In an honest way."

"Don't talk to me about being honest," said Tristan, trying to stay out of this kind of conversation with these two.

"I agree with her," said Nairnie.

"I don't need women telling me what to do," he shouted. "Ramble, tell Mardon we'll take what we need and whatever the hell we want," he shouted out the door. "Then we'll go elsewhere to repair the ship's damage from the fire."

"How can ye give that order?" Nairnie glared at him now. "I canna believe my grandsons are actin' this way. Call off the pillagin' and plunderin', Tristan. Ye are no' bein' a guid example to the rest of the men."

"God's eyes, Wench! I'm a damned pirate, not a priest!"

Wanting Nairnie gone, Tristan could only think of one way to make her leave, other than him throwing her out on her arse. "Sorry, Nairnie, but the choice really lies with Mardon. He's my quartermaster and decides which ships or ports to raid. It's his job, and I back his decision. If you don't like the choice he made, then mayhap you ought to take it up with him, not me."

"Hrmph. I think I will," said Nairnie, raising her chin in the air. "I'm goin' to talk to Mardon about this right now. I'll get him to change his mind."

"You do that," said Tristan with a smile and a nod, almost feeling bad for Mardon. Then again, Mardon only had one woman to deal with while Tristan had two. He herded Nairnie out the door and quickly closed it behind her. "All right, I can no longer wait. I need to see that map right now," he told Gavina. "Now strip off your clothing."

· · ·

"TRISTAN, YE CANNA SEE THE MAP," Gavina told her husband.

"You're going to show it to me so don't even think of trying to distract me again. Aye, I know what you've been doing, just not the reason why."

"I admit I was tryin' to distract ye, Husband. However, I only didna want to disappoint ye. Ye see, I'm sorry to tell ye, but the map is no longer on my back." Gavina finally just came out and told him.

"Stop fooling around. Now let me see it." He reached out and pulled her top down off her shoulders, turning her back to him. "God's eyes, the map is gone!" she heard him gasp from behind her.

"I ken. I told ye that."

He pulled her clothes lower, down past her hips and put his hand on the small of her back. Running his fingers up and down over the top of her buttocks, he acted like he was searching for something desperately. "Nay!" he shouted. "This can't be. Where the hell is it? Why would you do such a thing?"

She stepped away from him and pulled her clothes back into place. Tying her bodice and not turning around, she spoke. "Ye told me ye made a copy of it so I didna think I needed it any longer."

"I just said that, but I didn't really do it."

"So ye lied? Like ye accused Nairnie of doin'?" She glanced at him over her shoulder.

"I didn't want to disappoint you either, Gavina, that's why I said that instead of trying to look at it when it was really what I wanted to do. And, I did not accuse Nairnie of lying! Gavina, I never even saw the bottom of the map. That's the most crucial part that shows where the treasure is buried."

She turned around to see him pacing like a caged bear. "Well, canna ye figure it out from the part ye did see?"

"Nay, I can't! I need that damned map. All of it. Why the hell did you wash it off?" he demanded to know. "What were you thinking? That was a stupid thing to do."

It angered Gavina that Tristan was acting this way. So much so, that she could no longer hold back her emotions. "I'm just as upset about losin' the map as ye are," she told him. "Tristan, ye have no right talkin' to me like that. I am yer wife."

"Stop telling me what to do." He turned around and started knocking things around. A small chest went crashing to the floor, and coins rolled out. Then he threw an empty wine bottle down and it broke, shards of glass flying everywhere. "Do you realize what you've done?"

"Aye. I've cleansed my body to look beautiful for ye," she told him in a sturdy voice. "I thought ye would like it. Now, I dinna ken why I bothered since ye didna seem to notice and neither do ye seem to care about anythin' but that stupid treasure."

He spun on his heel and stared daggers at her now. She tried to be brave, but the pirate in him was coming out and, this time, it was frightening.

"That *stupid* treasure is being anticipated by every man on this ship," he told her. "We've gone through a rough time lately and this is what we need to make things right. More than anything right now, we need this treasure. The men were counting on me. Now, when they find out I've lost the map, they are probably going to commit mutiny unless my brothers kill me first."

"It's just a map," she told him, feeling as if she weren't as important to him as that treasure. It made her heart ache. They'd spent intimate moments together, but now he seemed like a whole different person. She figured it was that pirate blood in his veins that he said he could never rid himself of.

"It's not just a map, Gavina. It's the key to our survival," he said through gritted teeth. "I should have listened to my brothers as well as my crew and never have let you and Nairnie stay on board. You've caused nothing but trouble since you've stepped foot on this ship."

"Then mayhap I'll just leave." She felt like crying, but wouldn't do it. Instead, she started to head for the door.

"You're not going anywhere," he told her, grabbing her by the arm and pulling her back, swinging her around. She stumbled and fell to the ground.

"Cap'n, everyone is waitin' for ye to disembark," came Ramble's voice from outside the door. "Cap'n, are ye in there?"

"I'm coming," he shouted and then looked back at Gavina still on the floor. "Stay here," he commanded.

"I will no'." She jumped up and ran to the door. He stopped her again. This time, his hand gripped tightly to her wrist. "Stop it, Gavina, before you force me to hurt you."

"Hurt me?" She looked up, surprised to hear him say this. "Ye would really hurt me? Ye're my husband."

"I may be your husband, but I'm also captain of this ship and you will listen to me. The same rules go for you as for any of my crew."

"Well, I'm no' yer crew. Tristan, I'm yer wife."

"Aye, and even more reason not to challenge my decisions." His eyes turned dark and dangerous, reminding her that he wasn't just her husband. Tristan was a pirate first and always would be. "I'm locking you inside the cabin until my return and I want you to know it's for your own safety. Once my men find out we have no treasure map, they'll all be ripping off your clothes looking for the map themselves."

"I willna let them," she said, rubbing her arm. "I'll go to shore and find someone to protect me."

He was walking to the door but when he heard that, he stopped in his tracks and his head snapped around. The look of disappointment filled his eyes.

"Gavina, what do you think I'm trying to do?"

"I no longer ken. I'd think if ye were really tryin' to protect me, ye'd take me with ye."

"On a raid?"

"So ye're really goin' to pillage and plunder again?"

"Well, now that I have no map, I see no other choice but to go out and do what's necessary. We're going to have to find something to replace the treasure that was so close to my grasp that I could taste it. This raid is on your head, Gavina. I didn't want to do it, but you forced my hand."

"How do I ken ye willna leave me to yer bluidy wolves after all?" she blurted out as he opened the door.

He looked down to the key in his hand when he spoke. "I guess you're just going to have to trust me."

"Trust ye? Ye want me to trust a pirate? Ha!"

His dark eyes searched out hers. Pain and sorrow filled his gaze and now she regretted saying that to him because she didn't think he'd ever forget it.

"I suppose you're right," he said softly. His eyes closed

slightly and he let out a deep breath. "Don't trust me, Gavina, because I am just a pirate." He opened the door and stuck the key in the lock.

"What do ye mean?"

"Some things were never meant to be, and I'm starting to realize our marriage is one of them. Neither of us is happy, and both of us will never change. I'm sorry, Gavina, but your life will never be the same again. Like it or not, you'll accept what goes on aboard this ship and you'll never question my decisions. You are mine now, and remember you made this choice on your own. You are naught but a wife of a pirate and don't you ever forget it again." He left, turning the key in the lock, making her his prisoner once more.

CHAPTER 15

"Everyone, listen to me," shouted Tristan, walking on deck and holding his hand in the air. "Our time here is limited, so make it a fast trip. Take extra canvas sacks and collect all the food and drink and coins that you can carry. I want those shuttle boats back to the *Falcon* before they know what hit them."

"What about wenches?" asked one of the men. "I want to find myself a girl while we're here."

"Me, too," shouted another.

"Do what you want, but stick to the whores," said Tristan. "Also, don't kill anyone unless it's in self-defense. Keep to the code."

His men hurried around the ship collecting up all the items they'd need for the raid. The sound of the pulleys filled the air as they lowered the shuttle boats into the water.

"What about the ship?" asked Peg Leg Pate, stomping over to him. "I need supplies to fix the burned deck and galley."

"Are there any holes in the hull or anything that will endanger our journey?"

"Nay, not really," answered Pate. "There is a lot of interior damage, but I suppose it could wait."

"We'll stop at the next port for supplies," Tristan promised him. "In the meantime, work on fixing that squeaky step."

"Aye, Cap'n. I'll have to rebuild it."

"Then do so. This is going to be a fast trip. Mardon, Aaron," he called out to his brothers. "Finish up and join me. I'll have Ramble prepare a boat to take us to shore."

Mardon nodded from the sterncastle while Aaron, up in the rigging, waved his hand to say he'd heard him.

"So, ye're really goin' to do it," came a voice from behind him. There stood Nairnie with her hands on her hips and glaring at him like he was the enemy.

"Nairnie, not now," he told her, not having time for this. "Why don't you keep an eye on Gavina until I return to the ship?" He slapped the key into her palm. "I told you before, if you don't like the fact we're raiding, you should take it up with Mardon."

"Yer brathair is just as stubborn of an auld goat as ye are," said Nairnie.

"Ramble, prepare a shuttle for me and my brothers," Tristan called out. "You'll come with us."

"Aye, Cap'n," Ramble responded, running to the sidewall of the ship. Tristan started collecting up extra weapons, sticking them into his waist belt.

"Ye have the map for the treasure, so why do ye need to raid another town?" asked Nairnie, following him wherever he went. He spotted some empty canvas bags and hurried over to get them, throwing them over his shoulder.

"I guess you haven't heard. My dear wife decided to wash the map off her back before I had a chance to copy it down or even see all of it. We no longer have the means of finding the king's treasure."

"I see," said Nairnie. "So ye dinna ken where to find the treasure?"

"That's right." He picked up a skein of rope, deciding to take that with him as well.

"Ye need that treasure. Ye've got to go after it."

Tristan eyed Nairnie suspiciously. "Why would you promote me to look for a buried treasure? That sounds like an odd thing for you to say."

"Why? I'd rather have ye live off buried treasure than stealin' from poor townsfolk and hurtin' them along the way."

"Really." He raised a brow. "Either way, it's stealing, so I don't see the difference."

"If ye had the map, would ye stop this raid?" asked Nairnie.

"I suppose so, but it no longer matters. I have no map and also no choice but to raid. Once the men discover the map is gone, they're going to be furious. We'll have to raid a few ships on the way to the next port just to keep them happy." He headed over to the side of the ship where Ramble was motioning him over.

"The shuttle boat is ready, Cap'n."

"Good," said Tristan walking up and looking over the side of the ship at the shuttle boat far below. "Go tell Mardon and Aaron to get a move on. Most of the men are already approaching the shore. I want as much booty as we can carry in one haul." He lifted a leg and started to climb over the side-wall, only stopping when he heard Nairnie shout out to him.

"I saw the map before Birk stole it from me. I know where to find the treasure."

Tristan stopped in mid-motion. He'd forgotten all about

this, and supposed it could be true. If the old woman truly did see the map, then he could still find the treasure and wouldn't even have to tell his men the map was gone.

He quickly jumped back to the deck, dropping the bags and rope. "Not so loud," he said, grabbing her arm, looking around to see Wybert and Noll standing nearby. They didn't seem to be paying any attention to them, but were rather lowering another shuttle into the water. He didn't think they'd even heard the old woman. He grabbed Nairnie by the arm and pulled her to the side to talk in private. "Tell me what you know, old woman."

Nairnie reached out and slapped his face. He jumped back in surprise.

"Why the hell did you do that?"

"Stop callin' me auld woman. I'm yer grandmathair, now call me that instead."

"I'm captain of the *Falcon* and not going to call any wench grandmother, no matter if it's true or not."

"Aaron calls me that."

"Aaron needs to stop that and start acting like a man."

"Real men dinna need to call a female wench or auld woman."

"Just tell me where to find the damned treasure, and do it fast."

"No' until ye call me grandmathair." She crossed her arms over her ample bosom and raised her chin.

"You're serious."

"More than I've ever been."

Tristan clenched his jaw and looked in the opposite direction. He saw Mardon and Aaron hurrying over. Most of his crew had already gone to shore. Only Peg Leg Pate was still surveying the damage of the fire. "All right," he ground out. "I'll do it once and once only. After that, I'm not saying it again, and especially not in front of my crew."

"Fair enough. Then ye'll call me Nairnie from now on, instead of auld woman or wench."

"Fine," he told her, almost choking on the word. He was bending to the will of a woman and he hated it more than anything. But right now, he was desperate and would do whatever it took to know the whereabouts of that treasure. Nairnie was the only one with the information. "Now, tell me. Where is the treasure buried?"

"Well, if I remember correctly –"

"You need to be sure. I can't be taking a crew of anxious men on a wild goose chase."

"I'm sure where the treasure is hidden," she said, giving him a nasty glare. "If ye would have let me finish, ye would have kent I was goin' to say, if I remember correctly, ye were supposed to call me grandmathair first."

"Oh, that. All right . . . *Grandmother* . . . where can I find the treasure?"

"That's better," she said with a smug smile, letting out a satisfied sigh.

"Hurry it up, will you?" He glanced around again. His brothers were approaching.

"I'm baskin' in the glory of it, since I'll never hear ye call me grandmathair again."

"You'll never hear me call you anything if you don't hurry, because I'm getting so aggravated I'm ready to forget about the treasure and dump you back into the sea to leave you for the sharks."

"Oh, stop it, Tristan. I ken ye dinna mean it."

"Want to bet?"

"All right. The treasure is on the east coast of Urchin Island, buried under two trees that form the letter T. Or is it M? Mayhap it was . . ."

"Do you mean X?"

"Aye, that's it," she said, snapping her fingers in the air.

"I know that island, it's close to Hartlepool. I've also seen those trees you mention as I sailed by."

"Tristan, there you are," said Mardon. "Come on, we're wasting time."

"Right," said Tristan, leaving Nairnie and hurrying over to his brothers. "We've got to hurry. Aaron, stay here and work with Pate and Ramble and whoever else is still on board to get the sails raised."

"Raise the sails?" Aaron exchanged glances with Mardon. "Are you feeling all right, Brother? I just got them at half-mast. Why do we want to raise them now if we're not ready to go?"

"Because Mardon and I need to stop the men from raiding."

"What?" Mardon waved a hand through the air. "You're addled, Brother. I've already given the order to the men to raid. There's nothing that will bring them back before they've claimed their booty."

"They'll return if they know how close we are to the treasure."

"Oh, so you're going to finally tell us where it is?" asked Aaron.

"What's the rush?" asked Mardon. "You've stalled this long, so why do you want to leave now?"

"I admit, I never saw the whole map, and then Gavina washed it off her back before I could see it," he explained.

"She did what?" gasped Aaron. "The crew is going to kill you."

"To hell with the crew. I'm going to kill you personally," said Mardon, stepping toward him.

"Stop it," growled Tristan. "Nairnie had the original map that Birk stole before he burned it. She looked at the map and remembered where to find the treasure. We need to go after it right away, before someone else finds it."

"Who can find it if the map is gone?" asked Aaron.

"We don't know if Birk showed the map to any of his men. If so, we might already be too late. I just hope to hell they haven't gotten to it first."

"I'll go tend to the sails," agreed Aaron.

"Let's go find the crew," said Mardon.

"Keep an eye on Gavina," Tristan told Nairnie as they walked away. "Whatever you do, don't let her out of your sight."

* * *

"LET ME OUT OF HERE," cried Gavina, pounding upon the locked door. "I'm no' a prisoner and I refuse to be treated as one. Open this door, I say."

To Gavina's surprise, she heard the sound of a key turning in the lock. She stepped back as the door opened, even more surprised to see Nairnie.

"Nairnie? What are ye doin' here?"

"Well, ye didna think I'd be out pillagin' and plunderin' with the men, did ye?"

"I suppose no'," she said with a giggle.

"Tristan sent me here to keep an eye on ye."

"No need," she said, pushing past her out the door. "I'm goin' to take a shuttle boat to shore and I'm no' comin' back."

"Ye canna mean that." Nairnie hurried after her, waddling across the deck.

"I willna be married to a pirate any longer. It was all a big mistake." She spotted Wybert and Noll loitering near the side of the ship. She could see they had lowered a shuttle into the water. "Wait!" she cried out, running to them. "Please, can I have a ride to shore in the shuttle boat with ye?"

"Gavina, nay," cried Nairnie. "Ye are supposed to stay here. I'm no' lettin' ye get into a boat with those two!"

Wybert and Noll talked in soft voices, turning their heads so the women couldn't hear them. Then they turned back around. "Sure, we'll take ye," said Noll. "Let me help ye down the ladder."

"Thank ye," said Gavina. She started down the ladder to the shuttle, hearing Nairnie arguing with the men.

"Ye're comin', too, old woman, so get in the boat," Wybert commanded.

"I willna climb over the ship's wall, and neither will I go anywhere with ye."

"I heard what ye said to the captain," Noll told her.

"Nay!" Nairnie sounded frightened. Gavina had no idea what they meant by that.

She heard them saying something in a low voice, but couldn't make out the words. Then Gavina looked up to see the two men hoisting Nairnie up and over the sidewall.

"Nay. Dinna make her come along if she doesna want to." She feared that Nairnie was going to get hurt.

"She doesn't have a choice," snapped Noll. "Come on, hurry it up before I push ye in, old woman."

"Dinna call me that!" Nairnie almost lost her hold on the ladder, and grabbed it quickly as she descended. Once the three of them were in the boat, Wybert started to row away from the ship, but not following the rest of the men.

"Where are ye goin'?" asked Gavina in confusion. "The shore is in the opposite direction."

"That would be correct, if we were goin' to shore, which we're not," said Noll.

"Where are ye takin' us?" Nairnie demanded to know.

"Let's just say, the four of us are takin' a little side trip."

"A side trip? Where?" asked Gavina, her heart pounding in her chest. She already regretted asking these two for help. She never should have done it after Nairnie told her she suspected they were the ones to start the fire.

"We're goin' to find the king's treasure," said Wybert, getting an elbow in the ribs from Noll to stay quiet.

"Well, I'm afraid we'll be of no help to ye then," Gavina told them. "Ye see, I no longer have the map on my back."

"We know," said Noll.

"Ye do? Then why are ye takin' me and Nairnie?" asked Gavina.

"We're taking ye, Wench, for insurance that yer husband won't kill us before we get the treasure."

"Well, certainly ye dinna need to abduct Nairnie. Her own grandsons nearly didna even fish her out of the sea. She's of no value to ye."

"Thanks a lot," sniffed Nairnie.

"Oh, on the contrary. Right now, she is more valuable to us than ye," said Noll with a snide chuckle.

"I dinna understand. What does that mean?"

"Do ye want to tell her?" Noll asked Nairnie.

"Och, lass, I'm afraid to say I've made a mistake," apologized Nairnie.

"Nairnie? What's goin' on?" asked Gavina.

"I told Tristan I kent the whereabouts of the treasure since I once held the map. I guess these two overhead me."

"I see," said Gavina, feeling a rush of emotions flow through her. On one hand, she was excited that they'd still be able to find the treasure and that mayhap she could use part of it to save her brother, even if Tristan said he wasn't giving her any. But on the other hand, Wybert and Noll just abducted them, and this could mean big trouble. "Well, I'm no' worried because Tristan and his crew will get there first. Ye canna think this little rowboat is goin' to be able to outrun the *Falcon*."

"Nay, of course not," said Noll. "However, I'm pretty sure the *Poseidon* can."

"The *Poseidon*? What is that?" asked Gavina.

"It's a pirate ship, lass," Nairnie told her.

"Well, how would they ken where to find the treasure?" Gavina was still confused.

"They'll know as soon as we tell them," said Noll.

"Tristan will save us long before ye can even find the *Poseidon*," said Gavina, feeling confident about this. "Then, my husband will kill ye, and the crew of the *Poseidon* will never even ken there was a treasure at all."

"Dinna be so sure of that, lass," said Nairnie, looking over Gavina's head. Nairnie's face turned white.

Gavina didn't need to turn around to know where they were headed. Still, she found herself doing so anyway, seeing a large ship sailing toward them with the name *Poseidon* painted across it and the bust of the sea god and his triton attached to the bow of the ship.

"Whose ship is that?" asked Gavina.

"It belongs to a pirate who is about to be our new captain," Wybert told her. "He's twice the pirate Tristan is, and it'll be a pleasure to serve him."

"Ye're leavin' Tristan?" she asked, getting the feeling they'd never return to the *Falcon* now.

"That's right," said Noll, laughing heartily. "Ye two are in luck. Ye're about to meet our new captain, Nereus – or as some call him, King of the Sea."

CHAPTER 16

*I*t had taken much longer to round up the crew and get them back to the ship than Tristan hoped it would. A lot of them had already started to raid. Tristan figured it best just to let them take the things back to the ship, so he didn't stop them. Some of them were also engaged with whores by the time he got to shore. That hadn't been an enjoyable task to pull them away. Especially since after hearing him and Gavina making love, they were all hot and bothered and really needed this.

There was a lot of confusion and animosity toward him right now. Tristan decided the best thing to do was to get all the men back aboard the *Falcon* and to come out and explain to them the truth about the treasure.

"Mardon," he called out to his brother after all the shuttle boats had been retrieved and they were ready to set sail. "Is everyone aboard?"

Mardon stood atop the sterncastle, looking out over the crew. "There seems to be a shuttle boat missing. Noll and Wybert aren't here so they must have taken it."

"Leave them," said Tristan, no longer caring about these two. He thought about what Nairnie had said and was almost certain they were the ones to have started the fire and blamed it on bad luck because of the women. He hadn't trusted Noll or Wybert in some time now. They were better off without them since Noll had seemed to be trying to bring about a mutiny. He honestly didn't want them along when they went for the treasure. "We can come back for them in a few days when things cool down, if I change my mind."

"Tristan, wait!" Aaron dropped down from the rigging right next to Tristan. "You can't leave yet."

"Why not?" Tristan hurried up the stairs to the helm, the stair still creaking when he walked over it. Pate could seem to fix anything on the ship, but he'd been waiting a year for him to do the step. He decided he'd just have to fix it himself when he got time.

Aaron followed Tristan. "While I was up in the rigging I'm pretty sure I saw Gavina and Nairnie leave with Noll and Wybert."

"What?" Getting to the top of the stairs, Tristan turned around and glared at his brother. "Are you pretty sure or is this for certain?"

"Well, I didn't notice them until they were already far from the ship, but . . . yeah, I'm pretty sure it was them in the boat with the men."

"Gavina wouldn't go with them. And Nairnie would never go over the side of the ship unless someone pushed her. Let's find out for sure if they're here or not." Tristan bounded down the stairs. He headed straight for his cabin. Mardon and Aaron were right behind him. When he got to the door, he realized the key was in the lock and the door was open.

"Gavina?" he called out, slamming open the door. Taking a fast scan of the cabin, it was clear she was no longer there. "Nairnie," he shouted, the name sounding foreign on his tongue since he was no longer calling her old woman or wench. He ran to the galley and the others followed. "Nairnie, where are you?" He pushed aside some burned debris and looked into the small enclosure, but no one was there.

"She's not here," said Peg Leg Pate, hobbling over the deck to meet them. "I saw her leave with yer wife. Noll and Wybert were with them."

"You saw them leave and you didn't stop them?" Tristan shouted, his temper rising.

"Was I supposed to?" Pate shrugged and glanced over at the other men crowding around them. "I thought they were going to shore like everyone else."

"To raid?" Tristan's hands shot up into the air. "God's eyes, did you really think the women would be a part of such a thing?"

"Well . . . Gavina is yer wife, Cap'n," said Pate.

"That's right," added Coop. "She's a pirate now."

"Plus, Nairnie is yer grandmother," added Stitch.

"I just figured they were family and did what the rest of us do," Pate told him.

"Well, you figured wrong. All of you. Gavina and Nairnie would rather die than raid. Damn it! We've got to find them." He raced back up to the sterncastle and looked over the side-wall, feeling bad luck encompassing them once again.

"Look!" shouted Aaron, already back climbing the rigging. He pointed out to sea. "That looks like one of our shuttles heading to that other ship."

"Whose ship is it?" asked Tristan, squinting his eyes and trying to see the sails.

"I can't tell, but I'll start heading in that direction," said Mardon.

"What is it?" Pate called out from the main deck. The rest of the men mumbled their confusion, not looking happy at all.

"It's my wife," Tristan called down to his crew. "It looks like she and Nairnie have been abducted by Noll and Wybert."

"Who cares? Let them go," called out one of his crewmen.

"You should all care, because now Noll and Wybert have the map," said Tristan.

"We've got a copy, don't we, Cap'n?" asked Goldtooth. "We'll be able to get to the treasure first."

"Aye, I know where the treasure is buried and that is why I called you all back to the *Falcon*," Tristan announced. "We're going after it right away."

Cheers went up from the men, as they were elated to know they were about to become rich.

All of a sudden, Tristan could see the sails of the ship in the distance and also the figurehead on the bow.

"Quiet down," he shouted, getting his crew's attention once again. "We've got a little problem. Noll and Wybert now know where to find the treasure, and they're headed straight for the *Poseidon*."

"The *Poseidon*?" called out Stitch. "God's eyes, I thought they were supposed to stay in the channel."

"Aye, per our agreement, they were. Yet, here they are sailing our waters," said Tristan. "Mardon get us out of here. Aaron, keep your eyes open from the lookout. We've got to catch Nereus' ship and save my wife and Nairnie. Then we've got a treasure to find before they do."

"You think we can do it?" asked Mardon, redirecting the helm.

"Well, I'd say we can either save the women or go for the treasure," Tristan told him. "But between you and me, I honestly doubt we'll be able to do both."

* * *

GAVINA NOW REGRETTED BEING SO angry with Tristan that she hadn't even taken a moment to think that Noll and Wybert weren't the best choices to ask for help. She should have heeded Nairnie's warning about them. She looked back and could barely see the *Falcon* behind them. By the time that Tristan realized they were gone and came after them, it would be too late to save them. The shuttle approached the *Poseidon*, and Noll called out, cupping his hands to his mouth.

"Nereus, we've got a present for ye."

"Who are ye scallywags?" Nereus, a large man with white hair looked over the side of the ship. He wore a tricorn hat and long coat and looked much older than Tristan.

"I'm Noll and this is Wybert."

"Ye're part of Tristan's bloody crew from the *Falcon*, aren't ye?"

"Aye, we are," admitted Wybert.

"Why the hell is that scurvy dog sendin' ye over to me?"

"He's not. We've come to join yer crew now because we no longer want to follow Tristan," Noll told him.

"Why the hell should I believe ye?" growled the man.

"Because, we brought ye Tristan's wife and grandmother, as well as the map where the king's treasure is hidden."

"Map?" That got the pirate's attention. "Let me see the

283

map." He leaned farther over the rail. "Hold it up. If it looks believable, I'll lower the ladder."

"It's right here, on this wench's back." Wybert reached out with his dagger, ripping Gavina's bodice down her back.

"Och! Nay. Leave me alone," she cried out, holding the front of her bodice to her chest as it loosened.

"Dinna hurt her, ye fool!" shouted Nairnie, walloping Wybert on the back of the head with her hand since she didn't have her ladle.

"I don't see a map," called out Nereus. "Ye're lyin'."

"Nay!" shouted Noll. "The old crone knows where to find the treasure. I heard her tell the captain myself."

"I'm no' tellin' any of ye nothin'," spat Nairnie.

Gavina was shaking her head trying to warn Nairnie not to admit it, but it was too late.

"Blethers, I shouldna have said that, should I?" Nairnie looked at Gavina apologetically and held her hand over her mouth. "I'm sorry, lass. I didna mean to," she mumbled through her fingers.

"It's all right, Nairnie." Gavina had to find a way to get out of here before it was too late. Jumping into the water would only get her drowned since it was too far to swim for shore. Besides, Nairnie would never make it. Mayhap she could knock Wybert and Noll over the head and push them into the sea. Nay, she decided. She wasn't strong enough to row fast enough before Nereus' men came after them. She only had one idea left and that was to bargain with the bloody pirate. "Nereus, we'll tell ye where to find the treasure if ye let us go," she called up to the man.

"All right," said the man, much too easily. "Drop the ladder and bring the wenches aboard."

"Nay, we'll tell ye from here," she said. But, of course, the man didn't go for it. Why did she think he would? She only hoped that she and Nairnie wouldn't be beaten or whipped or raped once aboard Nereus' ship.

"Nay, ye won't," spat the pirate. "Ye'll come aboard my ship because this is where I conduct business, not out in the water."

"Nairnie, I dinna like this," Gavina whispered as they stood up and prepared to board.

"I willna tell them a thing. I promise," Nairnie whispered back.

They got to the top of the ladder and the men pulled the women over the sidewall, throwing them to the ground. Gavina's insides shook with fear, but she tried not to act frightened.

"My husband is Tristan, Pirate Lord of the *Falcon*," she said, getting to her feet and helping Nairnie to stand. "He will hunt ye down like dogs once he discovers what happened."

"I don't care who ye are, I doubt that Tristan will come for ye at all," said Nereus with a black-toothed grin. "Ye see, I know Tristan and his bothers pretty well. If they have to choose one, they'll go after the treasure, not ye. Especially if they discover that I'm now aware of where to find the treasure, too."

"Nay, ye dinna ken him. Tristan has a side of him that no one has ever seen. He would never choose treasure over me," she cried out.

"Why no'?" asked someone from behind her. "It looks like more than just yer family will choose treasure over a wench!"

She turned around and her mouth fell open, because it was the last person she expected to see. "Birk?" she gasped, since she'd seen Tristan stab the man and leave him for dead. His body with all that blood on the floor around him was embedded in her mind. "How in heaven's name are ye still alive?"

"I had chain mail under my tunic," said the man, starting to laugh, making a face and holding his side since it seemed to hurt. "It was mostly a flesh wound that bled more than it should." When he laughed again, he ended up coughing, grimacing, and holding his side, letting out a groan. "I lived, and that is all that matters. I told Nereus how I put the map on yer back." He reached out and pulled the back of her ripped bodice down, exposing her bare back to the entire crew.

The men saw women and skin, and hurried closer.

"It's gone," said Birk. "What happened to it?"

"I scrubbed my skin until it hurt, tryin' to get rid of yer stench on it," she snarled.

"If ye want my stench on ye, then I'll give it to ye, but with ye bent over the rail this time," said Birk, reaching for her with one hand and the ties of his breeches with the other.

"Wait!" cried Nairnie, pushing her way over to Gavina. "Dinna do that."

"Why no', auld woman?" asked Birk.

"Because if anyone touches her, I'll never tell ye where to find the treasure."

"We'll beat it out of the girl then," said one of the crew.

"Nay," pleaded Nairnie. "The map was on her back but she never saw it. So right now, I'm the only one who kens where to find that treasure. If anyone so much as touches or hurts the girl or me, I swear I'll never tell ye where it is."

"Kill the girl if the old hag doesn't tell us where to find the treasure," called out one of the crew.

Gavina's knees shook nervously beneath her. The man made a good point. If Nairnie thought they were going to kill her, she would tell them what she knew to keep Gavina safe.

"My thoughts exactly," said Nereus. "Tie the girl to the center mast and we'll start by whippin' her. Then ye'll each get yer turn at the rail with her, and we'll go from there."

"Nay!" screamed Gavina, fighting frantically as the men dragged her to the center mast. As she struggled against them, her clothes started to expose more and more of her bare skin. She looked for Nairnie for help, but no longer saw her. Tears filled her eyes as they placed her hands above her head and tied her wrists to the center pole. Thoughts filled her head of Noll and how Tristan had whipped him. It was horrifying, and now it was going to happen to her! "Nairnie," she shouted. "Nairnie, help me please."

"Let her go, or I'll jump!" came Nairnie's voice.

The men parted and Gavina saw Nairnie standing on the sidewall, teetering back and forth.

"What the hell are ye doin', old woman?" asked Nereus with a chuckle. "Get off of there before ye fall."

"Fall, hah!" she spat. "By the way, dinna call me old woman because I dinna like it. Now, I'm goin' to jump unless ye promise no' to touch the lass."

The men all laughed until she wobbled again and, thankfully, managed to right herself with her arms waving around wildly for balance.

"Let her fall. We'll fish her out afterwards," said Birk.

Suddenly, Gavina knew what Nairnie was doing. She had to help her. "Nay, the fall will kill her!" shouted Gavina. "She is old and feeble and will no' survive hittin' the water from this height."

Nairnie flashed her a nasty glance. Gavina knew it was because she didn't like everyone calling her old.

"I'm the only one here who can find that treasure, because Birk saw the map but doesna remember where the treasure is," Nairnie told them.

"Is that right, Birk?" asked Nereus. "Ye told me a different story."

Birk hung his head. "Aye, I suppose it's so."

"Now promise me ye willna let anyone touch the lass and I'll tell ye where to find the treasure," Nairnie continued. "Otherwise, I'll go to my death with the knowledge and none of ye will find the treasure because my grandson, Tristan, will get to it first."

"She has a point," Birk told Nereus. "It took us this long to track them down. We dinna want to waste any more time."

"Ye're not even one of my crew, so shut yer face," commanded Nereus. "The way I see it, we'll find the treasure and then demand a ransom from Tristan if he ever wants to see his wife and grandmother again."

"Guid point," said Birk, nodding his head.

"Someone get her down from there," growled Nereus.

"Then ye agree to my terms?" asked Nairnie.

"Aye. No one will touch ye or the girl. Now, come down from there and tell me where to find my treasure."

"I'll help her," said Noll, rushing over to her side.

"Nay, dinna put yer filthy hands on me." Nairnie swiped at Noll. When she did, she lost her balance again and, this time, she fell over the side of the ship.

"Nairnie!" cried Gavina, pulling at her binds. The ropes around her wrists creaked and bit into her skin, causing her pain. She heard the old woman cry out and then the sound of her body hitting the water with a big splash.

"Damn, she must be dead," grumbled Birk.

"Well, don't just stand there," commanded Nereus. "Someone fish her out of there so we know for sure."

Gavina felt numb now, too numb to even cry. She'd made a wrong decision to leave Tristan. Now, because of it, she'd lost everyone she ever cared about in her life. It no longer mattered what happened to her because she'd rather be dead than to live the rest of her life alone or to endure what would happen to her next from this seedy-looking, motley crew.

"Tristan, I'm sorry," she whispered, closing her eyes. "I was wrong to challenge yer word and to leave ye. I love ye," she said, wishing more than ever that she were with him back on the *Falcon*, back in his protective arms, once again.

CHAPTER 17

"J see the *Poseidon* dead ahead," shouted Aaron from the lookout, causing Tristan to run to the sidewall of the sterncastle.

"Unreeve the main! Full sail ahead, we have a ship to catch," called out Tristan.

"Aye, Cap'n," several of his crew answered.

"Let's pick up the speed, Mardon," Tristan told his brother at the helm.

"We're going as fast as we can," complained Mardon.

"It's not fast enough. Give me the helm, dammit, I'll get us there faster." Tristan pushed his brother out of the way and took the helm. He wasn't going to let anyone slow him down from saving his wife as well as his grandmother. If anything happened to either of them, he'd never forgive himself. "All hands on deck," he called out. "Ready the picks, axes, and grappling hooks. Prepare for boarding. We're going to take the *Poseidon*."

"Cap'n, we can barely see the ship," yelled Stitch from the deck. "Shouldn't we wait until we're closer?"

"Nay. My wife and grandmother's lives are at stake and hell if I'm going to give Nereus any extra time to torture them or do . . . anything else. We need to be prepared." The thought horrified him of the possibilities of what Nereus and his crew could do to the women. He released a deep breath and tried to still his mind. Losing control of his emotions at a time like this was only going to cloud his thinking. He needed a clear head when they took the *Poseidon*. Nereus had been a pirate a lot longer than Tristan. Plus, he had a bigger and faster ship. Still, Tristan had a better crew. Many lives were about to be lost and he prayed it wouldn't include Gavina or Nairnie. They were family now, and he would go to his death to protect his family.

"Did you just call Nairnie grandmother?" asked Mardon with a chuckle.

"I don't know! Mayhap I did. What the hell does it matter?"

"Aaron, Tristan called Nairnie grandmother," Mardon called up to the lookout to tell his brother.

"It's about time," Aaron shouted back down. "I knew he'd cave eventually."

"Stop with all the idle chatter, you two. Mardon, get up to the bowsprit and be ready to jump aboard their ship."

"Tristan, your head isn't on straight," said Mardon. "Don't you think if we saw Nereus, he's sure to have seen us as well? He's going to be ready for us. Might not it be better if we waited until nightfall and tried to board their ship in the dark with the element of surprise?"

"Nay. I can't wait that long. By then my wife might have already been rogered at the rail, and our treasure stolen from our grasp." He gritted his teeth, feeling like killing someone right now. "God's eyes, Mardon," he said in a low voice. "If anything happens to Gavina . . ."

"Steady, Brother." Mardon laid his hand on Tristan's shoulder. "Nothing is going to happen to her. You've got me and Aaron and the whole crew behind you. Now, I know you're in love, but you've got to get a grasp on yourself, or this whole thing can go sour quickly. Once the crew sees you've lost it, they're going to be hesitant to follow you anywhere, especially onto Nereus' ship."

"In love?" Mardon's words took Tristan by surprise. He never thought about being in love with a woman. Mayhap he was in love with Gavina, and hadn't even known it. Aye, he supposed he did love her, he decided, and planned on telling her so as soon as she was back safely aboard the *Falcon* and in his arms again. "Oh, crap, Mardon, I've become soft. I've fallen in love with a woman and now I'm willing to risk my entire crew to save her."

"I'd keep that to yourself and let the crew think we're only trying to stop Nereus because we don't want him to get the treasure."

"Well, it's true. Or part of the truth, anyway."

"Keep in control," Mardon reminded him with a slight nod. "You do that, and the crew will follow you anywhere, no matter if it is to save a wench or two or not."

"Thanks, Brother," said Tristan, feeling grateful for Mardon's advice. He was right. Losing his head at a time like this could only mean trouble, and they had enough trouble lately to last a lifetime. They didn't need more.

"Don't worry about a thing," said Mardon, taking the helm from Tristan. "With Nairnie along, I'm sure not only Nereus, but his entire crew, and Noll and Wybert, too, are fearing for their lives about now. You know how she is when she gets angry. I'm sure Nairnie is angrier than a wet hornet and ready to sting."

"True," said Tristan, looking out over the water in the direction of the *Poseidon* again. "I am just thankful that Nairnie is with Gavina. If she wasn't . . . Gavina wouldn't have a chance in hell of coming out of this unscathed."

* * *

"Did ye find her yet?" Nereus called over the side of the ship as a few of his men lowered a shuttle boat to look for Nairnie once they'd doubled back to where she fell. They'd thrown items into the water for her to grab and hold on to.

"I don't see her, Cap'n," called out Rock, Nereus' first mate. "Oh wait, I see somethin' floatin' over there."

"Well, is it her?" asked Birk, hanging his head over the side as well.

"I think so," Rock called back. "Oh, we got her."

"Is she alive?" cried Gavina still tied to the center mast. "Please tell me she isna dead."

"Hush up," spat another of the crew. Gavina didn't know the man's name and neither did she care. The crew on this ship looked twice as dirty, rugged, and frightening as those on the *Falcon*.

"I'll no' be quiet when my friend might be dead," she answered boldly, pulling against the ropes that bound her hands to the mast. She would do anything to save Nairnie, and wasn't going to let a pirate intimidate her. Nairnie had been a good friend to Gavina ever since she'd stepped foot aboard the *Falcon*. She'd been there to comfort her, help her, and give her advice. She'd also scared off an entire crew of pirates with her iron skillet and oversized ladle. If Nairnie died now, Gavina would never forgive herself for putting the woman in this dangerous position in the first place.

Gavina felt horrible about all this. Why hadn't she just stayed on Tristan's ship and waited for him? Why couldn't she just have acted like the wife of a pirate . . . or had she? Mayhap a pirate's wife would have a mind of her own. She was so confused right now that she didn't know what to think or how to act anymore. All she wanted was to go back to the *Falcon* with Nairnie to be with Tristan. God willing, if that happened, she swore she would never cause trouble for Tristan again.

"If ye refuse to shut yer mouth, I'll just have to make sure ye can't talk, then." The smelly man took her chin in his rough, callused, grimy hand and pressed his mouth against hers so hard that she could barely breathe. His lips were hard and cracked, feeling like old leather. Gavina closed her eyes, wanting to be anywhere but here when he shoved his tongue into her mouth next. She was trying to bite his tongue the way she did to Tristan the first time he kissed her in this manner, when the man pulled away from her and screamed out in horror. A warm liquid splashed against her, hitting her neck. Her eyes shot open to see the man's hand lying on the ground, severed from his body. His blood soaked the front of Gavina's gown.

"Aaaaah!" she screamed in horror as the man stumbled away from her, holding his bloody stump.

"Get him off the ship. No one touches the lass. That was my deal," growled Nereus, holding his bloodied sword in his hand. "I'm not goin' to ruin the chance of gettin' that treasure because of one stupid, bilge-suckin', lustful cur."

"Nay! Don't do it, Nereus," shouted the man, bleeding everywhere. "I didn't mean anythin' by it."

"Dump him overboard," commanded Nereus.

"Aye, Cap'n," answered several of his crew. They dragged the man kicking and screaming to the side of the ship and threw him into the sea.

"Don't forget this," said Nereus, using the tip of his sword to stab the man's hand, flinging it over the side of the ship after him. "Now, someone swab this deck. I don't like the sight of blood."

Gavina's body shook. She'd never been so frightened in her life. Even while on Tristan's ship, she'd never feared him or the crew the way she did these men. What she'd just witnessed horrified her and would scar her mind for the rest of her life. The worst part was, being tied to the mast, there wasn't a thing she could do about it, not even turn away. She would give anything right now to be back in Tristan's arms. There, she always felt protected, with the man she married. Oh, why had she left the ship at all? She should have stayed locked in the cabin for her own protection, just like he'd said. Fear coursed through her. But this time, it wasn't fear of what would happen to her at the hands of Nereus. Nay, this time what frightened her the most was the thought that she might never see Tristan again.

"Some mistakes can never be fixed," she whispered, repeating Tristan's words, knowing this was one mistake that might just cost her and Nairnie their lives. Right now, she wasn't even sure if Nairnie wasn't already dead. Her eyes closed once more and only opened again when she heard the bellowing voice of the old woman.

"What the hell is the matter with ye fools? Ye almost hit me with that handless man. Look where ye're throwin' people next time, before ye toss them overboard!"

"Nairnie!" Gavina let out a sigh of relief to see that the old woman was still alive and kicking.

"I guess that bit about ye not bein' able to survive a fall from the ship wasn't accurate after all," said Nereus.

Nairnie put both feet on the deck and started to wring the water out of the bottom of her skirt. "This isna my first fall from a ship," she told him. "However, I swear it will be the last! I'm too auld for this crap."

Gavina smiled at that, since she knew that Nairnie didn't like anyone calling her old, and now she was doing it herself.

"Take her and the girl to my cabin," said Nereus. "We'll dine together." He walked over and unsheathed his dagger, making Gavina flinch when his sharp blade came near her face. She closed her eyes, somehow thinking he was going to cut off her hand or possibly cut out her tongue and throw it to the sharks next, just for fun. When she heard the snap of the ropes that held her captive, her eyes popped open to discover that he had set her free. "I don't like blood," he grumbled, looking down at his man's blood on her bodice. It seemed like an odd thing for him to say since he was the one who severed his crewmember's hand in the first place. "I also don't want the old woman drippin' water all over my deck," he told Nairnie.

"Well, excuse us, but we left in somewhat of a hurry and havena brought along a change of clothes," snapped Nairnie.

"Ye won't need them."

"W-we willna?" stuttered Gavina, half-expecting him to make them walk around naked.

"Nay. I have a trunk with women's clothes in it. Find somethin' fresh and dry to wear. Both of ye, lassies," he commanded.

"Come on, I'll take ye to the captain's cabin," said Birk, grabbing on to Gavina's elbow.

"Dinna touch me, ye filthy cur! Ye killed my faither and I'll never forgive ye." She swept his hand away.

"I'll take her," offered Noll. "Just point me in the right direction."

"Nay, ye and yer sidekick are goin' to the brig." Nereus flagged over a few of his men.

"The brig? We're part of yer crew now," complained Wybert.

"Nay, I never said that." Nereus smiled.

"B-but we brought ye the girl and also the old woman with knowledge of where to find the treasure," protested Noll.

"Aye, ye did that," said Nereus, grabbing one of his crewmembers and wiping the blood off his sword against the man's tunic. "Ye fools also brought me trouble, because now I'm goin' to have to battle with Tristan and his brothers and the entire crew of the *Falcon*."

"Nay, they don't even know where we are," protested Noll.

"Oh, they most certainly do," said Nereus. He nodded to the water. "By my calculations, they'll catch up to us in a few hours, if not sooner."

"Tristan's comin' for us!" exclaimed Gavina, relieved to hear this. It was the best news she could have asked for.

"Don't look too happy, Wench," snarled Nereus. "Whether

ye realize it or not, as soon as yer precious Tristan and his brothers step foot on this ship, they're dead."

"Nay! They're guid at fightin'. They'll kill ye," she shouted.

"Gavina, haud yer wheesht," Nairnie warned her with a scowl. "The less ye say, the better for Tristan and the others."

"Well, off ye two go," said Nereus. "Oh, wait! Tell me, old woman, where can I find this treasure?"

Nairnie hesitated. Gavina prayed she was going to tell him a lie.

"Head to Urchin Island, off the coast of Hartlepool," Nairnie told him.

Since Nairnie hadn't told Gavina where the treasure was hidden, she wasn't sure if it was the truth or not.

"All right. Then what?" he asked.

"Then, when we get there, I'll tell ye more," said Nairnie. "No' before."

"Nay! I want to know the exact place the treasure is buried and I want to know now," demanded Nereus.

"Dinna think I'm addlepated, because I'm wise to the ways of someone like ye," Nairnie answered. "If I tell ye that now, ye'll have no need for us, will ye? Nay, I'll no' have ye killin' us before we even get to the treasure. Gavina and I will be goin' along to the island and be standin' right there when the king's treasure is uncovered."

"I don't take orders from wenches!" Nereus' jaw twitched. "Besides, what makes ye think I'd ever take ye two with us once we get to the island?"

"Oh, that's right." Nairnie snapped her fingers as if she'd just remembered something. "When I said that we were goin' to be there to see the treasure unburied, I didna mean with ye. I meant after my grandsons seize yer bluidy ship and kill all ye bastards. Then, we're goin' to find the treasure with them because that is the way it should be."

"Haud yer wheesht, Nairnie," whispered Gavina, getting very frightened by the woman's bold talk. She didn't want Nairnie to anger the man and get them killed before Tristan could rescue them. She could only hope now that Tristan got there quickly, because she wasn't sure how long she and Nairnie would survive aboard the *Poseidon*.

CHAPTER 18

"*H*ave some wine," said Nereus, handing Gavina his golden chalice. She and Nairnie had changed out of their clothes and now wore gowns that looked like they were once the clothes of harlots. As much as that bothered her, it was far less upsetting than wearing a gown with a man's blood splattered on it.

Gavina didn't like the way Nereus stared down her cleavage. She only liked it when Tristan did that. Her heart ached for Tristan. Being his wife hadn't been easy, but she realized now she should have been more accepting of him. Tristan wasn't a horrible man. Not really. He'd just made bad choices and taken the wrong path. So had her father, and now so had she. She remembered her mother always telling her that there was good in everyone. But in some people, you just had to look harder to find it. She'd found the goodness in Tristan, and that is a part of him that she would never forget.

"Nay, thank ye," she answered, pushing the cup away. "It's probably poisoned."

She, Nereus, and Nairnie sat cramped at a small table in

the pirate's cabin. The room screamed of riches and wealth. Gold cups and plates and fine clothes were everywhere. Chests with coins spilling out scattered the area, and there was lots of food, wine and, of course, whisky. He even had a woven tapestry like what was found at a castle, but it covered the floor instead of the walls, and they used it to walk on.

"Now, why would I want to poison such a pretty young thing like ye?" Nereus reached out to touch her cheek and, this time, Nairnie's hand shot out and slapped his hand away.

"It seems ye're forgettin' our deal, Pirate," the old woman said, giving him the evil eye. "I willna tell ye the location if ye try to touch her again."

"My, ye're a feisty one," replied Nereus with a deep chuckle. "I can see that ye're the grandmother of Cato's sons. Actually, Cato was a lot like ye."

"Ye kent my son, Cato?" Nairnie sounded very interested.

"Aye, I've had a few run-ins with him, and we were once even friends."

"Really?" gasped Gavina.

"Aye, lass. After all, we're about the same age. We were friends until he foolishly gave up piracy to be a pitiful fisherman. Did he return to piracy again? Is he with his sons on the *Falcon*?" Nereus looked down and ran his finger along the rim of the cup as he spoke.

"My son is dead, and I never even had a chance to say guidbye to him," Nairnie told him.

"What a shame." Nereus raised the cup and drank, looking at them over the rim. "Ye know, Cato and I were supposed to find the king's treasure together, years ago. We used to be friends at one time. That map once belonged to another pirate, but we killed him. Then Cato stole the map before I ever got a good look at it. I'm genuinely surprised that he never went after the treasure. Or did he, and are ye just tryin' to fool me? Because if so, I warn ye, I am not fond of games." He picked up his eating dagger next and ran his finger along the flat end of the blade.

"Nairnie, the less ye say the better," Gavina reminded her. "He's just tryin' to get information."

"Give me yer hand, Wench," he said to Gavina, staring her in the eye.

Gavina's body shook. He still played with his dagger. She kept thinking about his crewmember that was now naught but shark bait. She didn't want to lose her hand.

"Don't worry," he said with a chuckle. "If I was goin' to cut off yer hand, lass, I'd use my sword, not my dagger. Now give me yer hand."

Gavina figured she had no choice. She started to hold out her right hand, but he stopped her.

"Nay. The other one."

She did what he asked, giving him her left hand.

"What is this?" he asked, running a finger over her amethyst ring.

"It's my weddin' ring and was once my mathair's weddin' ring as well," she told him. "Please, dinna take it from me."

"Don't be silly," he said. For a moment, she didn't think he would, but of course she was wrong. "I'm a pirate, and pirates never leave any treasure behind." He slid off the ring and held it up to inspect it. "Nice," he said in satisfaction.

"Give her the ring back," spat Nairnie. "It isna yers."

"How about if I just hold on to this for now, and ye, old woman, tell me more about Cato and that map."

Nairnie pursed her mouth and narrowed her eyes, but

talked anyway. "I dinna ken what happened with my son and the treasure, because I didna see my son since he was stolen from me by his faither when he was just a lad. It was only recently that I found the map hidden on Cato's ship. That's all I ken, and that's the truth."

"I see," said Nereus, not sounding like he believed her. He held up the ring in two fingers, angling it in different positions to watch the stone glitter in the light.

"Ye dinna believe me, do ye?" she asked.

"It's not that," he said, still playing with the ring.

"Then what is it?" she spat. "Why are ye lookin' at me like that?"

"What was yer husband's name?" he asked Nairnie.

"I wasna ever married to the man." Nairnie seemed ashamed and looked down at the table, pushing around food on her plate.

"So Cato was a bastard then," said the man, the thought seeming to amuse him.

"Dinna call my son a bastard!"

"Well, if ye never married the boy's father, that makes him a bastard. Now tell me, what was Cato's father's name?"

"Why should I tell ye? What do ye care?"

"I'm very curious," he told her. "Do tell."

"Nay!" she spat and looked the other way.

Nereus slammed his hand down on the table, with the ring in it. "I said, tell me his name."

"Nairnie, just tell him," begged Gavina, not wanting to rile the man. Nereus moved his hand and Gavina's eyes fell on the ring. She had to find a way to steal it back from him, but not now. She needed to wait until the time was right, but she would take back what was rightfully hers. However, it wouldn't be easy.

"All right, I'll tell ye, no' that it matters. His name was Robert Fisher. He was a Sassenach and a fisherman," Nairnie told him.

"Robert Fisher?" Nereus started laughing.

"What's so funny?" asked Gavina.

"I should have known," said the pirate. "Ye see, Cato stole that map from his father and we were goin' to find the treasure together."

"What do ye mean?" asked Nairnie. "Why would Robert have a treasure map in the first place?"

"Because, my dear one, Captain Bobby Bones, yer lover, was more than just a fisherman. He was a pirate!"

"What?" gasped Gavina. "Nairnie, is this true? Ye were in love with a pirate?"

"Nay!" she shouted. "He was no' a pirate. Robert was a fisherman. He told me so."

Nereus continued laughing. "That's what he wanted ye to think. The fact that he stole yer son should be proof enough that he wasn't who he said he was. Who do ye think trained Cato to be a pirate in the first place? Good ol' Bobby was wily, and very thin. Bony, ye might say. That's how he got the nickname Captain Bobby Bones." He laughed some more. "Too bad he trained his son so well, because Cato, along with me, were the ones who killed him and stole that map."

"That's enough!" spat Nairnie. "My Cato wouldna kill his own faither."

"Why no'?" asked the pirate. "He killed his own wife as well."

"He didna! And if ye continue to laugh, I swear, I'll cut out yer tongue to shut ye up. And I will never lead ye to the treasure. That treasure belongs to my grandsons, anyway, and ye have no right to it."

"Oh, my, listen to that! I see that piracy runs strong in yer family, old woman."

"Dinna call me auld!" Nairnie looked as if she would really cut out the man's tongue if he kept this up.

"Interestin' how Cato went to extremes to hide the treasure map from not only me but also his sons, yet ye are so anxious to have yer grandsons find it. Perhaps ye're more of a pirate than old Bobby Bones and Cato put together."

Nairnie slammed her hand down on the table and stood up, scaring Gavina and making her jerk backward. "Dinna continue to talk to me that way or I'll never tell ye another thing about the treasure," warned Nairnie in a threatening voice.

"Oh, on the contrary, I think ye're goin' to tell me everythin' there is to know."

He reached out and yanked Nairnie to him, placing the sharp edge of his blade against her throat. "The *Falcon* is right on our tail, but I plan on gettin' to that treasure before them. So spill yer secrets, old woman or I'm goin' to slit yer throat."

"Ye do that and ye'll never find the treasure," Nairnie answered bravely. "Go ahead, kill me. It'll be yer loss."

"Nairnie, nay!" cried Gavina.

"Dinna worry, lass. He's no' goin' to risk losin' a treasure. Ye see how he likes his riches. Just look around ye."

"Ye might be right, but consider the consequences," said Nereus. "If I kill ye, I'll do what I want to Tristan's wife, because it will no longer matter."

"Nay!" cried Gavina.

"Then when Tristan shows up, he'll tell me the where-abouts of the treasure if he wants his wife returned, as soiled and broken as she will be."

"Ye rancid cur!" said Nairnie, spitting in his eye. "Ye wouldna do that."

He jerked back, wiping his eye with the back of his hand and then moving the blade closer to her neck. "Are ye sure?" he asked with a chuckle.

"Nairnie, he cut off the hand of one of his own crewmembers and dumped him in the sea," Gavina reminded her.

"Aye, I never cared for that crewmember anyway. It was time I got rid of him," said Nereus nonchalantly.

"Nairnie, please, just tell him where to find the treasure," Gavina begged the old woman.

Nairnie looked as if she weren't going to tell him, but then at Gavina's insistence, she finally told Nereus what he wanted to know.

"It's buried on the east side of the island, under two trees that make an X," said Nairnie.

"That's more like it." Nereus released her and got to his feet. "Rock," he called for his first mate.

"Aye Cap'n," said the man, entering the room.

"Take these women to the brig while I set our new course to collect our treasure."

* * *

"It's no use, we can't catch the *Poseidon*," said Aaron, standing with Tristan and Mardon looking out to the sea as they tried to catch up to Nereus.

"Nereus had too much of a head start on us," agreed

Mardon. "If he'd stop moving, mayhap we'd have a chance. He also changed direction in the last few minutes in case you didn't notice." Mardon had the helm while Tristan looked over the sidewall, stretching his neck, trying to see Gavina. The winds changed and were holding them back. Instead of getting closer, they were moving farther apart.

"Oh, I noticed," said Tristan. "Nereus is headed for the treasure. He must have managed to get the information out of Nairnie. That's why they changed course."

"Well, I suppose that's a good thing," said Aaron. "At least now we know Nairnie is still alive. I'm sure it means Gavina is, too."

"Dammit, Aaron, I know what you're trying to do, but it doesn't comfort me at all to know that my enemy has the woman I love." Tristan ran his hand through his hair and started pacing back and forth in thought.

"Love?" asked Aaron in surprise. "Do you really love Gavina? You barely even know her."

"It doesn't matter. I know now that Gavina is the one I want to spend the rest of my life with, and I won't let Nereus have her."

"Tristan, I know you're married and all," said Aaron. "But are you really thinking you can keep a wife on board the *Falcon*? Especially if you someday have children?"

"Don't worry about it," Tristan snapped, changing positions and pacing back and forth in the other direction now.

"You're not thinking about leaving us, are you?" asked Mardon. "We made a promise to each other when we left Father that we'd always stay together, no matter what."

"That's right, Tristan, we did," agreed Aaron. "It's worked fine for us up until now."

"I don't know what I'm going to do yet," said Tristan, feeling agitated and wanting more than anything to kill Nereus right now. "All I know is that I am going to get my wife and grandmother back on the *Falcon* where they belong."

"You said grandmother again." Aaron smiled. "I knew you really cared about her. You're not as cold-hearted as you pretend."

"Shut up, Aaron, or I'll show you just how cold-hearted I can be. Now tell the crew to trim those sails. We're luffing. Nay, wait. Instead, set a new course toward the shore."

"The shore? Why?" asked Aaron.

"That will take us west instead of east and we'll never catch Nereus," Mardon pointed out.

"Aye, a different direction. However, I assure you that by doing this, we'll catch Nereus, save the women, and get our treasure, too," Tristan told them.

"Wait, I'm confused." Aaron scratched his head. "So we're not going to board the *Poseidon* to save the women now?"

"Nay," said Tristan. "The plan has changed."

"Brother, didn't you just call Nairnie your grandmother and say you loved Gavina?" asked Mardon. "Yet now you don't want to rescue them?"

"Oh, we're going to rescue them," Tristan assured his brothers. "Only, we're going to do it in a way that Nereus will never expect."

"How?" asked Mardon and Aaron at the same time.

"We're taking a little shortcut." Tristan smiled, feeling confident of this plan. "Since I know exactly where Nereus is headed, we're going to get there first. You see, we're not going after the *Poseidon* anymore, because now we have a new destination."

"What's that?" asked Mardon.

A million thoughts ran through Tristan's mind at once, but he was sure this was the right decision. "We're changing course, because now we're going after the treasure."

* * *

GAVINA HAD DOZED OFF, tied up in the hold and not able to move. She'd been dreaming of making love to Tristan when Nairnie kicked her and yanked her out of the dream.

"Wake up!" said Nairnie.

"Why did ye kick me?" Gavina couldn't believe the old woman would be acting this way. Ever since Nereus told her that Cato's father was a pirate, she'd been in a very foul mood.

"I kicked ye because my hands are tied and I couldna shake ye. Now wake up, I say."

There was only a stub of a candle stuck into the neck of a bottle that was burning, and threatening to extinguish at any time. The hold was smelly, dark, wet, and scary. An occasional rat wandered by inspecting them closely. This is the reason Gavina had closed her eyes to begin with. She didn't want to know how close the rats were to her.

Gavina heard commotion from up on the deck. At first, she thought mayhap Tristan had boarded with his crew and they were battling it out. Then she realized that the sounds weren't of battle. They were happy, joyful sounds like men laughing and celebrating. "What's goin' on?" asked Gavina.

"I'm no' sure, but I dinna like it."

The door to the hold burst opened, and Nereus' first mate staggered down the ladder. "The Cap'n wants ye two up on deck." When he reached over to cut their binds,

Gavina held her breath because the man stank so heavily from alcohol.

"What does he want with us?" asked Nairnie. "Is he goin' to kill us after all?"

"I'll let him tell ye." Rock yanked them up to a standing position and pushed them over to the stairs. When Gavina stepped out onto the deck into daylight, she blinked several times, trying to focus after having been in the dark hold. Nereus sat back on a chair that looked like a throne. He had his feet propped up on a box and he was holding something, inspecting it closely. At first Gavina thought it might be her ring.

"Go on," growled Rock, pushing the women over to Nereus.

"What is this all about?" Nairnie demanded to know.

"We're havin' a celebration and thought ye might like to join us." Nereus raised a cup to them and took a drink.

"Celebration?" asked Gavina. "Whatever for?"

"Yer lover has given up the chase and turned around." Nereus chuckled. "It seems he didn't care as much about ye as ye thought."

"Tristan's no' comin'?" asked Gavina in a panic. "Nay, that canna be true. He would never leave us here with ye."

"Oh, it seems he has and I think I know why. Ye see, once a pirate always a pirate, lassie."

"What the hell is that supposed to mean?" asked Nairnie.

"What I mean, is that even though Tristan is now married, his first love will always be treasure."

"Nay, that's no' true," said Gavina. "He wouldna choose treasure over me."

"He already has," Nereus told her with a grin. "Since he's no longer followin' us, I figure he's goin' after the treasure."

"I'm sure he kens ye're goin' after the treasure, too," said Gavina. "If so, why isna he behind us?"

"Because, my dear, yer husband doesn't know what I do. I've been to shore recently and have talked to the dockmen. I know what Tristan's tryin' to do but it won't work."

"What does that mean?" asked Nairnie.

"It seems Tristan is tryin' to get to the treasure first, usin' what he thinks is a short cut. He's headin' up the cove and approachin' the island goin' west instead, and sailin' around it. However, what he doesn't know is this last storm has made that way unpassable for now. So, he's only sabotagin' himself. He'll find out as soon as he sees all the marooned boats in the bay blockin' his way. However, by the time he figures it out and turns around, I'll have the treasure and be long gone. Oh, and did I mention that I'll also have his wife and grandmother, too?" Nereus laughed heartily.

"Nereus, are ye sure that's what they're doin'?" Birk asked from across the deck. "Those pirates seem to always have a way of kennin' where to go and how to get places quickly."

"Ye worry too much," Nereus told Birk. "I'm startin' to wonder if I did the wrong thing by pickin' ye up. After all, I don't really need ye anymore, do I?"

Birk looked worried. "Mayhap I should go to the brig and ask those crewmates of Tristan's what they ken."

"Noll and Wybert aren't in the brig," said Nereus. "I've put them to work on the ship after all. I decided to make them part of my crew now. If they knew anythin', they would have already told me. Now get yerself a drink and relax, Birk. And

prove to me ye were worth the trouble. We'll be to the island within the hour."

"What about those two?" asked Birk, nodding at the women. "Ye ken that havin' wenches on board is bad luck."

"I'll deal with that." Nereus held up something.

"My flute!" exclaimed Gavina, thinking she had lost it.

"My men found this in the shuttle boat. Do ye know how to play it?"

"Of course, I do. It's mine."

"Then play it." He tossed it to her and Gavina caught it. "I want music. Lots of it. After all, this is a celebration."

"Dinna ye think ye're celebratin' a little prematurely?" asked Nairnie.

"Not at all. There is no way that Tristan can beat me to that treasure now."

"Oh, Nairnie," whispered Gavina. "Do ye think Tristan really chose the treasure over me?"

"Dinna worry, lass." Nairnie's eyes shifted over to Nereus and then back to her. "I've had a vision, and ye and Tristan will be together again soon."

"A vision?" Gavina didn't understand what she meant.

"I sometimes have visions, my dear, and they almost always come true."

"Almost? So, they're no' always right?" asked Gavina. "So mayhap I willna be with Tristan after all?"

"The only time my visions were wrong was when I foresaw my own death, so dinna worry, lass. I have faith that Tristan will choose ye over treasure because what I saw was the two of ye in love . . . with several children."

"Oh, Nairnie, I hope ye're right," said Gavina, wanting more than anything to have a family with Tristan someday.

"Here, take this but hide it before Nereus realizes it's no longer in his cabin." Nairnie took Gavina's hand in hers, pressing something into her palm.

"My ring!" whispered Gavina, elation flowing through her to see it. "How did ye get it?"

"I've learned a few tricks bein' on a pirate ship," said Nairnie with a smile. "When I slammed my hand down on the table, I scooped up the ring and Nereus never even noticed." She chuckled softly to herself. "My grandsons would be proud of me if they kent what I did. I only hope I live long enough to see them again to tell them."

"We'll survive, Nairnie. Tristan and his brothers are comin' for us."

"Ye heard Nereus. They willna be able to make it through the pass. By the time they find out, it'll be too late. I'm afraid Nereus might have won this round."

"Nay, Tristan will save us, ye need to have faith. After all, ye just told me yer vision, so ye ken it has to be true."

"I hope so," said Nairnie.

"Play the damned flute!" yelled Nereus, causing Gavina to jump once again. As she raised the flute to her mouth, she tried to pretend she was back on the *Falcon* playing her music for Tristan instead. She prayed that Nairnie's vision was right. It was the only thing that gave her faith that they were going to get out of this with their lives.

CHAPTER 19

"Cap'n, why are we no longer chasin' after the *Poseidon?*" asked Ramble, following Tristan as he made his way back to his cabin.

"Plans changed." Tristan opened the door and walked inside. He stumbled over something and looked down to see Gavina's shoe. The one shoe she had when she first came onto his ship disguised as a boy. He picked it up, feeling a heaviness in his heart. He might never see her again, and he couldn't live with that. He had to bring her home quickly. Home. Just the word made him feel ill. While this ship and the sea were home to him, it certainly wasn't where a girl like Gavina belonged, and he knew it.

"Cap'n," said Ramble, following him into the room. "Are we not goin' to rescue yer wife and grandmother after all?"

"Of course we are." Tristan threw the shoe down, glass crunching under his boots as he crossed the floor. Thoughts of how angry he'd been and how he'd overturned and broke things in the cabin filled his head, making him wish he could go back and change the way things were because of his actions. Then he decided he couldn't be distracted by this right now. He had to push it out of his mind and stay focused. "We're going to head them off at the island since I know that's where they're going."

"Island? What island?"

"Urchin Island," he told him, digging through a trunk looking for his sharpest dagger that he kept at the bottom that his father had given him for gutting fish. "It's where the treasure is buried. We're going to get there first, dig up the treasure, and then when they come looking for it, we'll surprise them. I'll take back what is mine. Ah, here it is." He pulled out the dagger and unsheathed it, holding it up to inspect it. It had a thin blade with a very sharp edge. It could skin a fish in a matter of seconds without even nicking the flesh. He was sure it would work just as well on a man.

"Urchin Island?" asked Ramble. "Then shouldn't we be headed east instead of west?"

"Not when we're taking a shortcut around the west side of the island to get there before them. We'll catch the wind and be able to sail through the pass, making it around to the east side of the island before them." He breathed on the dagger and shined it against his sleeve. This would work well when he killed Nereus.

"Oh, I'm just surprised ye're goin' that way. I mean, since the storm and all."

"What are you rambling about now?" asked Tristan, his mind still on killing Nereus.

"Well, the pass has been blocked by a part of the cliff that broke away in the storm. All the fishin' boats that are damaged are blockin' the way. Of course, mayhap ye know somethin' I don't, but I think we're goin' to lose a lot of time if we have to turn around and head back in the original direction. Hell, by then, Nereus will have the treasure and yer wife and be gone."

Tristan wasn't really listening to Ramble, since he'd learned to block out the boy's continual chatter. However, it all suddenly registered in his brain and he realized what the boy was saying. His hand stilled and his heart lodged in his throat.

"What did you just say?" He jumped up and spun around, clutching the dagger in his hand.

"Cap'n, I'm sorry for ramblin' on. I won't do it again." The boy held out his hands and backed away. "Just don't cut out my tongue with that dagger like ye've threatened to do in the past. I'm sorry. I'll be quiet now, I swear I will." He swallowed forcefully and his hand went to his throat.

"Nay, you fool. I'm not going to hurt you." Tristan put the dagger back into the sheath and hung it from his weapon belt. "Now, tell me what you know about the pass."

"All I know is what I heard the last time we were in port. Some of the dockmen were talkin' about how the storm ruined the pass. I guess it'll be a while before they get it cleared out."

"Damn it," Tristan ground out, pushing Ramble aside and running out the door.

"What's the matter, Cap'n? Did I say somethin' wrong?" Ramble hurried after him.

"Nay, just the opposite. Thank you for that information." Tristan walked to the center of the deck and rang the ship's bell. It was nearly nighttime and some of the men had already dozed off.

"What's all the noise about? I'm tryin' to sleep," complained

Goldtooth, walking out from the hold, chewing on something.

"Trying to sleep or sneak food?" Tristan let go of the rope and hurried up the sterncastle where he met with his brothers.

"What's the matter?" asked Mardon.

"Why are you ringing the bell?" Aaron yawned, appearing from nowhere.

"There will be no sleeping tonight," Tristan announced. "Mardon turn the ship around and continue on our original course."

"Why?" grumbled Mardon. "I thought we were taking the pass to get to the treasure before Nereus."

"We were, but I just learned the pass is blocked from the last storm. We're going to have to follow the path of the *Poseidon* and hope to hell we can overtake them."

"That's impossible, Cap'n," Stitch called out from the deck. "The *Poseidon* is a faster ship. We'll never catch it."

"We will, and I don't want to hear anyone say otherwise. Now, all hands on deck because we have time to make up."

"It's goin' to be pitch dark soon," said Coop. "Can't this wait until first light when we can see where the hell we're goin'?"

"Nay. We've got a compass to guide us, and Stitch knows how to sail by the stars," said Tristan. "We're doing this and you're all going to be a part of it, like it or not."

"Just to save a few wenches?" asked one of the men.

"Nay," spat Tristan, feeling his anger growing. "They are not just a few wenches. They are my wife and grandmother. Plus, there is the king's treasure involved, unless you've already forgotten."

"Treasure," mumbled someone.

"We're with ye, Cap'n," called out another.

"Good. Then let's do this, and take back what is ours." Tristan looked up to see a few stars starting to appear in the nighttime sky, only hoping that he'd be able to stargaze with Gavina someday. Her eyes twinkled just like stars when she smiled, and he missed that. He had to save her, because without Gavina in his life, Tristan was going to feel very empty. Plus, he promised his wife he'd always be there for her and that she would never be alone. Tristan was a man who didn't like to break a promise.

* * *

GAVINA PLAYED HER FLUTE, trying to calm her own emotions, not caring about giving any enjoyment to Nereus and his crew. Nairnie sat next to her on the deck, keeping all the drunken men away from her and, for that, she was thankful.

It was dark now and Gavina was tired, yet Nereus wouldn't let her stop playing. Then, just when she thought she was going to pass out, a man called out from the lookout basket.

"Ship approaching fast," he cried, putting everyone in a frenzy.

"What the hell!" Nereus jumped up and peered over the side. "Damn yer eyes, I think it's that blasted *Falcon*."

"Tristan!" Gavina jumped up with excitement, but Nairnie grabbed her arm.

"Stay calm and stay close to me," Nairnie instructed. "I have a feelin' there is goin' to be a lot of angry men very soon."

"Rock, how close are we to the island?" Nereus called out to his man at the helm.

"We're approachin' it now, Cap'n. Do ye want to wait until first light to dock?"

"Nay, we can't wait. Prepare the shuttle boats, we're goin' to shore to get our treasure."

At hearing the word treasure, everyone stepped up the pace. It didn't take long to anchor the ship and lower the boats to take them to shore.

"Let's go, ladies," snarled Nereus, looking over to Nairnie and Gavina.

"Us?" gasped Gavina.

"We'll stay here and wait for ye," said Nairnie. "We'll only slow ye down."

"Like hell ye will. Ye're both comin' along for a little assurance that Tristan won't try to take my treasure. Birk, Rock, get the wenches into the boat."

"Aye, Cap'n," said Birk, acting now like he was part of the crew. The man disgusted Gavina. If she had a dagger on her right now, she'd stab him right through his heart, the way he did to her father. The horrible image of her father lying dead in a puddle of blood would never be erased from her mind. As far as she knew, they'd never buried him and he was still lying there. It broke her heart.

"Step it up, wenches," snapped Rock, poking her in the back. Gavina and Nairnie joined them, but against their wills. Now, the only thing that could save them is if Tristan and his brothers and the crew of the *Falcon* got there in time. That is, before Nereus found the treasure and took them back to the *Poseidon* and sailed away.

* * *

"Damn it, we're too late," spat Tristan, peering through the darkness to see the *Poseidon* already at the island when they got there. "They've already lowered the shuttle boats and are headed to the island."

"Do you see the women?" asked Mardon, steering the ship toward the *Poseidon*.

"Aye, I think so, but it's hard to tell. It almost looks like they are taking Gavina and Nairnie with them. I'm not exactly sure. Damn, why isn't there more light so I can see?"

"It's because it's nighttime, Cap'n," said Ramble, like he needed reminding.

"Lower the shuttle boats and light some torches," cried Tristan. "Bring all the weapons you can carry and don't be afraid to use them. We've got two women and a treasure to rescue."

* * *

"Is this the spot?" Nereus asked Nairnie once they'd gotten to shore and made their way to the two trees that formed a letter X. They carried torches and lanterns but it was hard to see clearly since the night was dark.

"I guess so," said Nairnie.

"Guess so? I thought ye said ye knew where the treasure was buried," fumed Nereus.

"I do! If ye would have waited until first light, it would be a hell of a lot easier to see. These old eyes are no' guid in the dark."

"Ye said it's buried beneath two leaning trees that make an X, right?"

"Are ye deaf? I told ye that already. Aye, that's the way I remember it from the map."

"Ye'd better be right because Tristan is goin' to be here any minute," warned Nereus.

"Guid!" spat Nairnie. "I canna wait for my grandsons to arrive and kick yer arse."

"Keep it down, old woman," snapped Nereus. "Birk, Rock, dig up the treasure."

They started to dig, but must have been too slow for Nereus. "Noll and Wybert, pick up a shovel and help them."

"We'd be glad to help," said Noll. "Just as long as we get our share of the treasure."

"Who said ye're gettin' anythin'?" Nereus was in a foul mood.

"We were the ones who brought the wenches to ye with the information of the treasure," Wybert complained.

"Aye, that's suspicious to begin with, and I still don't know if I can trust ye." Nereus glared at them. "Why did ye do it? Why did ye leave the *Falcon*?"

"We didn't like bein' under Tristan's command," said Wybert, starting to dig.

"Aye. Then when we heard that the old hag knew where to find the treasure, we figured we'd steal her and the girl away," explained Noll. "She had the map inked on her back. I knew ye'd be sailin' this direction since ye always do this time of year, so I was hopin' to find ye. We were lucky to notice yer ship on the water."

"Ye only found them because of me," said Birk. "If it wasna for me, none of ye would even ken there was a map."

"Shut yer mouth, Birk," Nereus warned him. "We knew about the king's treasure since it was Cato and me who found the map together years ago. That is, before he stole it from me. If he had stayed a pirate, I would have had the treasure by now. Cato hid away pretendin' to be a fisherman and stayed close to the shore from then on to save his own hide, the coward."

"My son wasna a coward!" Nairnie put her hands on her hips. "He was brave enough to leave piracy to protect his family. That's more than I can say for ye."

"Nairnie, dinna anger him," Gavina whispered, pulling the old woman back away from the men.

"Well, no matter, it all worked out, didna it?" asked Birk, sounding very proud of himself.

"We'll see. Now dig!" Nereus seemed to be losing his patience. "We need to get the treasure and get out of here before the *Falcon* gets here."

Gavina glanced nervously over her shoulder. The sky was dark but filled with beautiful, twinkling stars. The breeze was gentle and the sea calm. How she wished she were on the deck of the *Falcon* right now, enjoying this beautiful night with her husband. Then something caught her eye. She saw torches lighting up an area in the water, and they were coming from a different direction than the *Poseidon*. Her heart skipped a beat.

"Nairnie, I think Tristan is here," she whispered. Her hand went to her flute hanging at her side, gripping it for comfort. Her other hand slipped into her pocket and she pulled out her ring, slipping it onto her finger. Hopefully, at any moment, she'd be back with Tristan once again.

"All hell is about to break loose, lass," warned Nairnie.

"When the fightin' starts, be sure to stay out of the way. We dinna want to distract Tristan."

"Aye, Nairnie. I will."

One of the men's shovels hit something that sounded like wood.

"We've got it!" yelled Birk. "We found the treasure."

"Get it up here and hurry," commanded Nereus. All the men gathered around as Rock and Noll carried a large chest over to the captain.

"It's heavy," said Noll. "It must be filled with gold."

"I'll open it," Nereus told them, pushing the rest of the men back. Gavina noticed Tristan's shuttle boats landing on the beach. Nereus' men were so infatuated by the treasure that they didn't even notice.

"The lock is stuck," complained Nereus. "Rock, hit it with yer shovel."

The man did and the lock sprang open.

"I want to see how much treasure there is," said Gavina, pushing through the crowd of men, excited to be a part of this. If she could just get her hands on something, perhaps some coins, she might be able to pay off her father's gambling debts and buy back her little brother's freedom.

"Gavina, get back here." Nairnie's hand shot out but the men pushed Gavina out of her reach.

"What the hell is this?" came Nereus' boisterous voice sounding madder than hell.

Gavina peeked around the men and her jaw dropped open.

"The chest is filled with rocks," said Noll. "I don't understand."

"Well, I do. It's all been a hoax and someone is goin' to pay for this." Nereus reached for Gavina, but Nairnie shot forward and blocked her.

"Get out of the way, old woman. Or mayhap I should kill ye first." Nereus yanked his dagger from his belt.

"Look!" said Nairnie, pointing at the chest. "I see somethin' under the rocks. It looks like a rolled-up parchment."

"What?" Nereus turned back to the treasure. "Move the torch closer," he commanded his men. Gavina looked down to see that what Nairnie said was true. There really was a parchment inside the chest of rocks. "Give that to me," commanded Nereus.

Rock pulled it out and handed it to his captain.

"What does it say?" asked Wybert, pushing his way closer.

"This is not where the treasure is buried," Nereus read aloud. "Follow the next clue to find it."

"What clue?" asked Noll.

"Is there a clue?" Birk wondered.

"I don't see one." Nereus' finger ran down the parchment, reading the words again. "What kind of an ill jest is this?"

"Let me see that." Nairnie snatched the parchment out of his hand. Gavina watched the old woman turn it over. Her eyes opened wide and she flipped it back quickly. "This must have been Cato's idea of a guid jest. Too bad there isna a treasure." She stuck the parchment under her arm. "Gavina, let's go." Nairnie turned Gavina around, but before they could leave, a voice called out.

"Get away from the women and hand over the treasure."

It was Tristan, approaching with his brothers and his crew. They were right behind them and all held weapons, ready to fight.

The sound of clashing swords filled the night air. Men

pushed, and torches were dropped, making it hard to tell who was fighting whom. Gavina got separated from Nairnie and couldn't find her.

"Nairnie!" she cried.

"Run and hide," Nairnie called out to her as men fell all around her. Gavina started to run, but stopped in her tracks when a man fell dead at her feet. She screamed, and looked down to see Birk's lifeless body on the ground with his eyes bulging out. When she looked up, Tristan was pulling his sword out of the man's chest.

"That's for killing Gavina's father," spat Tristan. "Now stay dead this time!" Just to be sure, he stabbed him again, right in front of her.

"Stop it!" she cried, holding her hand to her mouth. Feeling like she was about to retch, she couldn't watch anyone else be killed.

"Gavina, sweetheart," said Tristan, taking her by the arm and pulling her behind him. "Stay behind me, and keep away from everyone."

"I want to leave, Tristan," she said, tears streaming down her cheeks. She'd never been in the midst of a battle like this, and certainly not with pirates. She stared in shock as she watched Mardon slit a man's throat that was part of Nereus' crew. He threw the man to the ground as if it meant nothing to him at all.

"Mardon, duck," yelled Aaron, flinging a battleaxe through the air. Mardon ducked and the axe struck into a pirate's head, right between his eyes. Another of Nereus' crew fell dead to the ground.

Gavina screamed again. This was the most frightening

thing she'd ever experienced in her life and she wanted it all to be over.

"Stop!" shouted Nereus. "Stop right now, or I'll kill her, I swear I will."

TRISTAN LOOKED up to see Nereus with the edge of his dagger pressed to Nairnie's throat. The man held her hands behind her, and under his arm he held a rolled-up parchment.

"Men, hold up," said Tristan, but his crew didn't want to stop fighting.

"They've got our treasure, and we're not givin' it up," shouted Goldtooth, taking down another man.

"There is no treasure here," called out Nairnie. "It's a trunk full of rocks."

"What?" asked Tristan, not able to believe his ears. His eyes shot over to the chest to see that what she said was true. Sure enough, the chest was open and there was no treasure. It was filled with worthless rocks.

"Since there is no treasure, I see no point in continuin' this fight," said Nereus. "And unless ye want to watch as I slit yer grandmother's throat, call off yer men and let us pass."

"Nay, never!" shouted Coop.

"They took the women, Tristan. Don't let them get away with that," called out Stitch.

"Nairnie!" yelled Gavina. "Tristan, ye have to save her."

"Nay, let them kill me," said Nairnie. "I'm an auld woman and it doesna matter. Just take care of Gavina, Tristan. Keep her safe."

"Nay, Nairnie, ye canna die," cried Gavina.

"If I die, I die happy," Nairnie told her. "At least I've had the chance to spend time with the grandsons I never even kent I had."

"Lower yer weapons and let them pass," Tristan shouted to his crew.

"Cap'n, ye're just goin' to let them leave?" asked Ramble.

"Like Nereus said, since there is no treasure, there is no need to fight. Nairnie is my grandmother and I will not let her die," said Tristan. "Now do as I say."

"You heard him," Mardon called out to the others. "Follow your captain's orders."

"We're not letting our grandmother die," agreed Aaron.

The men begrudgingly did as they were told.

"Get to the shuttles, men. Quickly," Nereus commanded. "Make yer way back to the *Poseidon*. We leave anon."

"Traitors. We should kill you two for what you did," said Mardon, grabbing Noll by the tunic as he and Wybert passed by.

"Let them go," said Tristan, maintaining control. "They're part of Nereus' crew now, and he can have them."

"But they betrayed us," said Aaron.

"Aye, and if they want to answer to Nereus now, then so be it."

"That's right. We've got a new captain now," said Wybert. "A better one."

"If either of you ever cross our paths again, I give my men permission to kill you without even batting an eye," said Tristan. "Now get the hell out of my sight."

Noll pulled out of Mardon's grip and the two of them took off at a near run for the water.

"Nereus, wait! Release Nairnie," commanded Tristan.

"Not until we're safely out of here." Nereus pulled her with him to the shuttle boats.

"Should we head them off at the shore?" asked Aaron, as his brothers came to his side.

"Nay. Let them go." Tristan wasn't worried.

"They've got Nairnie," Mardon reminded them.

"They'll release her once they're safely to their ship." Tristan had no doubt about this.

"How do ye ken that?" asked Gavina. "They might take her with them."

"Nay, not Nairnie." Tristan smiled and shook his head. "Believe me, they won't want her along because they'll think she's bad luck."

"True," added Mardon. "Even if they try to take her back onto their ship, she'll probably fight them off single-handedly."

"Aye, they'll wish they left her with us," said Aaron with a chuckle.

"I hope ye're right," said Gavina. "Oh, Tristan, I've missed ye."

"I've missed you, too, Wife." Tristan pulled Gavina into his arms and kissed her deeply. "Did he . . . did he touch you?" he asked, wanting to know more than that but not wanting to come out and ask her.

"Nay, we werena hurt, and he didna touch me in that manner," she assured him. She stood on her tiptoes and whispered into his ear. "Ye're still the only man who has ever rogered me at the rail, Tristan." She flashed him a small smile and, with that, he felt relieved.

"Bury our dead before we go," Tristan commanded, looking around to see that they only lost a few men, but the losses for Nereus' crew were more than twice as many. "Then hurry back to the ship."

Tristan took Gavina to the shuttles and loaded her in a boat along with Ramble and his brothers. Ramble rowed toward the *Falcon*.

"Look, they're at the *Poseidon*," said Gavina, pointing in that direction. "They still havena released Nairnie."

"Ramble, take us over there," ordered Tristan.

"Aye, Cap'n," said Ramble.

"Are ye goin' to fight them to save Nairnie?" asked Gavina.

"We won't have to. Look. Just as I thought."

Gavina looked over to see Nereus' men dumping Nairnie over the side of the shuttle into the sea. They continued on to their ship, while Nairnie splashed around in the water.

"Hold on, Nairnie, we're coming," shouted Tristan, but the woman was struggling and it was taking them too long to get to her. "Ramble, row faster."

"I'm sorry, Cap'n, but I'm goin' as fast as I can." Ramble wasn't the strongest since he was still a young man and didn't have the muscles like the rest of the men.

"Out of the way. Let me row." Mardon switched spots and took the oars. He was able to row much faster, but Nairnie went under, and came back up sputtering. With nothing to hold on to, the old woman wasn't going to be able to stay afloat for long.

Tristan stood up and removed his weapon belt, coat and boots.

"Tristan? What are ye doin'?" asked Gavina.

"Saving my grandmother before she drowns." He dove into the water and swam as hard as he could, getting to Nairnie just as she looked like she was going under for the last time.

With one arm around her, he tried to hold her and swim back to the shuttle. Nairnie seemed panicked and kept squirming, her desperate actions about to make them both drown.

"Stop your struggling old woman or we'll both die."

"Dinna – call me an – auld woman." She wasn't making this easy. Her panic had overtaken her and Tristan had to do something to give the shuttle time to get to him or he was going to lose his grip and she was going to drown.

"Forgive me for this, but it's the only way, Grandmother." He reached out with his other fist and hit her hard in the head. Her eyes rolled back and she stopped struggling. Her body went limp in his arms. "That'll do it."

"Is she alive?" Gavina called out as the shuttle boat finally got there.

"Aye. I just knocked her out to shut her up." Tristan pushed her while his brothers pulled her into the boat, almost capsizing them all. Then Tristan flopped into the shuttle as well, seeing the *Poseidon* sailing away.

"Worried that we shouldn't have let them go?" asked Mardon, taking the oars again.

Tristan looked back at Nairnie who was starting to come to. "Not as worried as I am about Nairnie's wrath. God's toes, I'm never going to hear the end of this one, am I?"

CHAPTER 20

*L*ater that morning, the *Falcon* headed in the direction that the *Poseidon* had taken, heading south away from Hartlepool. Tristan and his brothers sat on the deck around the main mast drinking whisky, passing around the bottle while Stitch manned the helm. They'd buried their dead but they'd also ended up with nothing to show for the lost lives. They still had no treasure. The crew was in bad spirits, so Tristan had broken out the whisky he'd hidden, letting them drink their fill.

"I still dinna understand why ye had to hit me, Tristan. There is no excuse for hurtin' yer own grandmathair." Nairnie scowled at Tristan as Gavina dabbed at the cut above her eye. "Och!" she cried out in pain, her hand touching her eye. "I'm lucky ye didna try to break my neck while ye were at it just to shut me up."

Gavina's eyes shot over to Tristan.

"You told her what I said?" he asked.

"Well . . . I guess I did," said Gavina. "Sorry."

"Nairnie, I only hit you to save your life," explained Tristan. "How many times do I have to tell you I'm sorry I hurt you?"

"Hrmph. Once more," Nairnie retorted. "But this time call me grandmathair, no' Nairnie, or auld woman, or anythin' else."

Gavina saw Tristan look around to see who was watching. "Mardon doesn't call you grandmother," said Tristan.

"He will. In time." Nairnie gently pushed Gavina's hand away. "I'm waitin', Tristan."

"Will you stop bothering me about this and swear to never mention it again if I do?"

"Well . . . all right," she agreed.

"I'm sorry . . . Grandmother," he said, lifting the bottle high and nodding. He sounded to Gavina as if he had drunk too much whisky.

"That'll do. Thank ye," she said, squeezing the remaining water out of her wet gown. "I wish I had somethin' hot to serve ye." She glanced over at the galley that was still black with soot from the fire.

"Don't even think about starting a fire to cook on the ship," Mardon warned her. "We're going back to cold meals again. It's not as dangerous."

"I agree," said Tristan.

"Well, I don't," complained Aaron. "I really liked those hot buttered biscuits."

"I'm tellin' ye, it wasna me, but those two traitors, Noll and Wybert, who did it," Nairnie said in her defense. "Ye'll see now that they're gone that Gavina and I are no' bad luck at all."

"I believe you," said Tristan. "Still, no more fires on board. We'll get our hot meals on shore from now on. We're going to dock somewhere so Peg Leg Pate can get materials to make the repairs. Here, have yourself a good swig of whisky. It'll help your eye feel better." He handed Nairnie the bottle.

"Well, why the hell no'?" she asked, surprising Gavina when she took a huge swig. Lowering the bottle she smacked her lips in satisfaction. "Blethers, ye're right, Tristan. My eye already feels better." She started to lift the bottle to her lips again, but Gavina pulled it away.

"Perhaps, ye should give someone else a turn."

"Go ahead, Wife," said Tristan with a grin. "Try some. You'll see why we like it so much."

"Have you ever had whisky before?" Aaron asked her.

"Well, nay, I dinna think so." Gavina looked down to the bottle in her hand.

"Take a sip," Tristan coaxed her. "Unless you want me to wipe it off first."

"No need. I like puttin' my mouth where yers was," she said, lifting the bottle and taking a big swallow the way she saw Nairnie do. She immediately felt the burning in her throat and felt as if she couldn't breathe. The whisky was too strong for her.

"That's enough." Tristan took the bottle from her and handed it to Aaron.

"I still dinna understand why there was no treasure," said Gavina as soon as she could talk.

"It was our father's idea of a cruel jest," said Aaron, sounding disgusted.

"Losh me, I almost forgot!" Nairnie patted herself, then reached into her bodice and pulled out a torn piece of parchment.

"What's that?" asked Tristan, as Nairnie held it up to the sun to dry it.

"It's part of the parchment with a clue we found instead of treasure. Nereus has the rest of it, but I was able to rip off a piece first right before they dumped me in the water."

"I don't even want to think about the king's treasure anymore," mumbled Tristan.

"Father must have found it years ago," said Mardon.

"I wonder what he did with it?" asked Aaron.

"He hid it and left clues," said Nairnie, holding up the piece of parchment. "On the back of the parchment are clues tellin' where to find the real treasure."

The crew heard this and they all perked up.

"Let me see that," said Ramble taking it from her.

"So there is a treasure after all?" asked Gavina.

"It looks like it," said Nairnie. "Ye lads just havena found it yet."

"Give me that, Ramble." Tristan took the piece of parchment away from him. "This is only part of something," said Tristan. "It makes no sense at all."

"Well, at least Nereus only has part of it, too, so we'll have just as much of a chance of findin' it as he does," said Nairnie with a smile. "We just need to figure out the rest of the clue."

"The sooner the better," Mardon chimed in. "The longer we wait, the more chance Nereus is going to get there before us."

"The women are not going after any treasure," said Tristan.

"Tristan, I have to," exclaimed Gavina.

"Why?" he asked. "You never did explain to me why this treasure was so important to you."

"It's to pay off her faither's debt and buy back the freedom of her little brathair," said Nairnie. "Tristan, ye are her husband. Ye should ken this."

"Aye, I suppose I should," he said. "So your brother is someone's prisoner?" he asked. "Who? Where?"

"An English lord raided our Scottish town because my faither was supposed to collect protection money for him from the border villages where we used to live."

"Let me guess," said Tristan. "Your father gambled it all away."

"Aye," she admitted. "He had a habit of makin' bad choices. When the lord discovered the money was gone, he wanted revenge. In return, our town was attacked, and my mathair and older brathair died in the battle. We were no' warriors or knights and were no match for them. Some of the children of our village were taken by the English as servants, includin' my little brathair. My faither was told that they would no' be returned until he paid back all the money he lost. That is why we wanted to find that treasure. It would buy back no' only my brathair's freedom, but also the freedom of the other four children that were taken. It would right the wrongs of my faither."

"That's awful. What kind of man would take children as prisoners?" asked Tristan.

"Aye, who was this man, Gavina?" asked Nairnie. "Ye never told me."

"He is called the Beast of Ravenscar," she said, noticing the way Nairnie's eyes popped open.

"How old was yer brathair?" asked Nairnie.

"He would be seven now," she told her.

"Och, lass! Is his name Rab by any chance?"

"Aye, it's Rab. How did ye ken that?" asked Gavina.

"I have met him as well as the rest of the orphan children."

"Where? I dinna remember ever meetin' ye in Scotland."

"Nay, lass, it wasna in Scotland. It was in England. In Ravenscar to be exact. Ye see, I ken Lord Ravenscar, because I raised him as my own son."

"Ravenscar? Are ye sure?" she asked. "How could ye? He wasna a young man."

"Och, ye're talkin' about the black-hearted Beast of Ravenscar who served as lord before my Benedict took his place. Benedict is Lord of Ravenscar now."

"So . . . then the man who took my brathair is dead? Are ye sure?" asked Gavina.

"Dead and long gone."

"Was Rab set free?"

"Benedict married Autumn, one of the sisters of the Legendary Bastards of the Crown," Nairnie explained. "I was close to all of the girls – Autumn, Spring, Summer and Winter."

"Are you talking about Rowen the Restless' sister?" asked Mardon. "He was one hell of a pirate."

"Was," Nairnie stressed the word. "He gave up piracy and now pays fealty to King Edward, his faither."

"Wait, the Demon Thief who used to raid the king is now on his side?" asked Aaron.

"Aye, Rowen and also his brathairs, Rook and Reed. Well, Reed no' so much, but that's no' important right now. What I mean to say is that Benedict and Autumn have taken a likin' to the children and are raisin' them as their own. They thought they were all orphans."

"They all are. Except my brathair, Rab," Gavina explained.

"Rab, that little rascal is the one they like the best," said Nairnie. "They'll be sorry to see him go. But dinna worry, I'll talk to them. Ye'll get yer brathair back, I promise."

"Then I willna even need to find a treasure?"

"Nay," said Nairnie. "Benedict is no' that kind of man. Plus, if he even thinks about askin' ye to pay back any debts, I'll box his ears."

Gavina, as well as the others all laughed. "Oh, Nairnie, thank ye," said Gavina, hugging the old woman.

"Watch the eye." Nairnie's eye was swollen and she looked even scarier now when she gave the boys the evil eye.

"Stitch, how close are we to Ravenscar?" Tristan called out.

"We're just approachin' the shores of Ravenscar now, Cap'n. Why do ye ask?"

"We're going to dock there."

"Aye, Cap'n," Stitch answered.

"Why are we going there?" asked Mardon.

"Because we're dropping off the women on shore," Tristan told him. "They will not be going along to find any more treasures."

"Ye're goin' to leave me there?" asked Gavina, her heart aching. "Please, Tristan. Change yer mind. Let me stay on the *Falcon* with ye."

"Nay, I can't do that."

"Why no'? I dinna want to be apart from ye. Ye are my husband. I am yer wife!"

"Aye, that's true," he responded. "That is also why I'm going to stay with you in Ravenscar."

"What?" both Mardon and Aaron asked together.

"Does that mean ye're no' goin' out to look for more treasure?" asked Nairnie.

"It means, I'm going to settle down and, hopefully, raise a family with my wonderful wife." Tristan held out his arms and Gavina ran to him, hugging him, never wanting to let him go.

"Oh, Tristan, I am so happy," she said, her cheek pressed up against his chest. "Now, I will never be alone. I'll have the family I always wanted. I'll be happy after all. I canna wait."

TRISTAN HUGGED HIS WIFE, feeling her excited heart beating rapidly against his chest. He kissed her atop the head. After the scare he'd had concerning Nereus, he decided he never wanted to be apart from his wife again.

"Tristan, what the hell are you saying?" Mardon stared daggers at him. "You're the captain of this ship."

"Aye," said Aaron. "So how can you be staying there?"

"Not anymore, I'm not," he answered. "I'm relinquishing the position of captain to you, Mardon."

"You're jesting with us. Right?" Aaron's eyes went back and forth. "He can't mean he's giving up piracy. It was his idea in the first place. We made a promise to each other!"

"Aye, that's true, Aaron. However, I made a promise to Gavina as well when I married her." Tristan pulled Gavina closer to him, wrapping his arms around her. "I love Gavina, and I don't want to ever take the chance again that I might lose her. A pirate ship is no place for a woman, and certainly not where I want to raise my children."

"We'll make Ravenscar our new home," said Gavina excitedly. "Now that I ken the true Beast of Ravenscar is dead, we can stay there."

"Och, I'm sure Autumn and Benedict would love that," said Nairnie. "Autumn will be so excited to have ye around, Gavina. Did ye ken her sister, Spring, is Scottish? Actually, Autumn and all her sisters are half-Scottish."

"How excitin'," said Gavina, smiling more than Tristan had ever seen. "I canna wait to meet her."

Nairnie and Gavina talked more than Ramble, making Tristan's head spin with all the noise. Still, he loved every minute of it and wouldn't trade it for anything. It felt right. It felt like he'd made the correct choice, and he was happy with that. However, things weren't going to be easy.

"Tristan, what's the matter?" asked Gavina, realizing he was in deep thought.

"It will not be all that easy for me to live on land," he told her.

"Is that all?" she asked with a giggle. "If I can learn to live on a ship, ye can get used to land."

"That's not what I mean, sweetheart."

"He's a pirate," Aaron told her.

"Nay. No' anymore he's no'." Gavina shook her head. "He said he's givin' up piracy."

"I am, Gavina, however there are consequences I'll have to endure," he told her, wishing that it wasn't so.

"What kind of consequences?"

"If our brother stays on land too long, they're going to hang him," said Mardon.

"Aye, all pirates that get caught get hanged," Aaron told her. "That's why we live on a ship at sea. It's safer that way."

"Nay," said Gavina. "Please, there must be a way to stop this."

"It's true," he told her. "I'll always be looking over my shoulder and I'll always be on the run. I made a choice to be a pirate and now I'll pay for it the rest of my life. It will only be a matter of time before they catch me and condemn me to death."

"Nay," she cried. "Nairnie said Brody was a pirate and he has a family. They didna kill him."

"That's because he's been pardoned," Nairnie explained.

"How did he do that?" asked Aaron.

"Aye. It's highly unlikely," added Mardon.

"True, it usually is, but ye're all forgettin' that Brody was once Rowen's first mate," Nairnie explained. "Rowen is a Legendary Bastard of the Crown. The king is the man's faither."

"Then Rowen was able to get King Edward to pardon Brody?" asked Gavina.

"Aye." Nairnie reached up and touched her eye and winced. "I'm sure if I tell Autumn yer story, Tristan, she'll get a hold of Rowen and he'll talk to his faither for ye. If anyone can get ye a pardon from the king, it's Rowen and his brathairs, Rook and Reed."

"Do you really think so?" asked Tristan, not allowing himself to get too excited about this in case Rowen couldn't pull it off.

"I ken he can do it. However, it might take a while, so ye might have to keep a low profile until it happens. I'm sure there is no need to worry because my Benedict will hide ye if need be. He's like a son to me and will do what I ask. He took the place of yer faither once my poor Cato was stolen from me."

"What do ye think, Tristan?" asked Gavina with hope in her eyes.

"Well, I like the idea, but I'm sure my brothers aren't going to accept it." Tristan dared to look over to his brothers. They were both scowling at him.

"We made a promise to each other," snapped Mardon.

"You can't go back on it, Tristan. Not over a wench. We're brothers." Aaron glared at him.

"That's true," he said, feeling awful to leave them in this position. "So, mayhap it's time that the two of you give up piracy and settle down to raise families as well."

"Never," snapped Aaron.

"Are you daft?" Mardon growled. "If you want to spend your life as a pauper, then do it. But I'm going after that treasure. All we have to do is figure out what the rest of the clue said, and we'll find it before Nereus does." He got up and started up the stairs to the sterncastle.

"I'm with him." Aaron shook his head and followed Mardon.

"Tristan, I'm sorry," said Gavina. "I never meant to put ye in such a position with yer brathairs."

"They'll get over it. In time. I hope." Tristan's heart broke as he watched his brothers talking to the other pirates. They all shunned him now for his decision. He was giving up much to be with Gavina, but it was all worth it. "I just wonder why our father is playing games with us from the grave."

"What do ye mean?" asked Gavina. "Because there was no treasure?"

"Aye. Why did he move it and just leave a note?"

"Mayhap yer faither did it as a precaution," said Nairnie.

"How's that?" asked Tristan.

"Ye said he didna want ye boys to turn back to piracy."

"Aye, that's true."

"Then mayhap he figured if ye ever found the map, he was goin' to make it hard for ye and then mayhap ye'd give up the hunt for guid."

"I doubt it. Our father wasn't that clever of a man. It's

more likely that he just kept changing his mind where he wanted to hide it."

"We're approachin' Ravenscar, Cap'n," called out Stitch.

"Good. They've got a deep dock, so take us right in." Tristan stood up, bringing his wife with him.

"He was talking to me, not you, Tristan." Mardon looked down at him from the sterncastle. Aaron was at his side. Tristan felt as if he were deserting his brothers. It wasn't a good feeling. He started to question his decision in his mind, and was ready to start pacing again. But when he felt the gentle touch of Gavina's hand on his arm and saw the love shining in her bright blue eyes, all doubts left him and he knew he'd made the right choice for the first time in his life.

"Aye, you're not the captain anymore, or have you already forgotten?" Aaron called down to him.

"Nay. I haven't forgotten," said Tristan, releasing a deep sigh. Damn, he was really going to miss his brothers.

CHAPTER 21

PIRATE
LORDS

*T*he next day, Tristan stood on the dock with his arm around Gavina, watching his ship and his brothers sail away. Gavina carried her little brother, Rab, in her arms, attached to her hip. She was so happy to have found him that she'd yet to let him go.

"We're glad to have you here," said Autumn, a pretty woman with bright red hair.

"Aye, and we're happy you decided to stay in Ravenscar, since we'd miss Rab too much if you took him from us." Her husband, Benedict Ravenscar, was once known as the Beast of Ravenscar, but only because he took the identity of a truly evil man. Gavina and Tristan hadn't been there long, but it was enough time for Nairnie to explain things and for the crew to get the supplies they needed to repair the ship. Tristan also told Gavina that he'd paid someone to bury her father and give him a headstone and that they could visit his grave soon.

Benedict had agreed to let them stay in his castle for now. Once Autumn talked to Rowen and the king pardoned Tristan, things might be different. Gavina and Tristan might find a new place to settle down, and even go back to visit Tristan's sister, Gwen. For now, they had to wait, so Ravenscar was their new home.

"I can't wait for you to get to know all of our children," said Autumn. "I think you two will be very happy here."

"Thank ye for yer kindness," said Gavina. "And thank ye for takin' guid care of my wee brathair, Rab. I only wish my faither was still alive to see Rab again." She hugged her brother and gave him a kiss on the head.

"Gavina, can I go play with the other children now? We're takin' the dogs to the garden to play ball."

"Oh, so ye have a dog? How nice." Gavina put her brother down.

"We have a few more dogs than just one," said Autumn.

"Really? How many?"

Rab ran off and joined a group of children. To Tristan's surprise, about a dozen dogs ran after them. He started laughing.

"This is going to be even more interesting than sailing with Nairnie," he told his wife.

"Speaking of Nairnie, where is she?" Gavina looked around. "I thought she'd be here to watch the *Falcon* leave."

"Mayhap she couldn't stand pirate life anymore," said Tristan with a chuckle. As he watched his ship sail away with his crew and brothers, he saw something else that he never expected to see. "Then again, mayhap she likes it more than we know."

"What do ye mean?" asked Gavina.

"Look." He pointed to the bow of the ship where the galley used to be. There at the rail was someone waving at them.

"Is that . . . Nairnie on the ship?" asked Gavina.

"It sure is," he answered. "Nairnie, what are you doing? Get down here at once," Tristan shouted.

Nairnie held her finger to her lips, telling him to be quiet. Then, she threw them a kiss and her head disappeared from the rail as she ducked down on the ship.

"I'm surprised to see her there," said Gavina.

"Not as surprised as my brothers are going to be once they find out." Tristan laughed heartily, pulling Gavina into his arms.

"Thank ye, Husband, for givin' up piracy to stay with me," said Gavina with a twinkle in her eyes. "I hope ye can get used to this kind of life, Cap'n."

"Not captain, not anymore," he corrected her, taking one last look as his ship sailed away without him. Part of his heart went with them, and he would always miss his brothers, his ship, his crew, and most of all, Nairnie. Piracy had been his life, and it didn't feel right to break a promise to his brothers. He could only hope that they'd find women to love as well, and realize they no longer needed to be pirates. Tristan had a woman he loved now, and a new life awaiting him, as soon as he got that pardon. New promises for happiness were on the horizon, and that is one ship he couldn't let sail away without him.

Gavina was his world now, and their love for each other would lead to better choices . . . a better life than piracy could ever give him.

"Tristan, what are ye thinkin' about?" asked Gavina, snuggling up closer to him. "Are ye going to miss the *Falcon* and life on the sea, Cap'n?"

He smiled, pulling her closer and kissing her gently on the

ELIZABETH ROSE

lips. "Don't call me Cap'n, anymore," he told her. "That's no longer who I am. From this day on, just call me *Tristan*."

FROM THE AUTHOR

As the story closes, we see Tristan leaving piracy, and his brothers behind. However, life is all about choices and, this time, he's made the right one. Love is always the answer. Now he'll have a new life with his wife, Gavina.

If you're wondering if Tristan ever met up with his sister, Gwen, and her husband, Brody, you'll have to wait a little longer to find out. While Tristan's story ends, I hope you will embark on the next journey to find out more about his brothers, the treasure and, of course, the antics of his meddlesome, boisterous, but loving grandmother, Nairnie.

The journey continues in *Mardon – Book 2* of the **Pirate Lords Series**, so be sure to jump on board.

If you'd like to read about Rowen the Restless, you can find him as well as his first mate, Brody, in *Restless Sea Lord – Book 1* of my **Legendary Bastards of the Crown Series.** You'll also read about his brothers, Rook and Reed. This is one of my favorite series.

Brody ends up with his own story in *Pirate in the Mist, Book 1* of my **Second in Command Series**.

Autumn, the sister of the Legendary Bastards, and her husband, The Beast of Ravenscar, as well as Gavina's little brother, Rab, are all in *Autumn's Touch – Book 3* of the **Seasons of Fortitude Series**. Here is where you will also find out more of Nairnie's backstory. Nairnie is a main character in each of the books of this series.

All of these books are stand-alones and can be read in any order, and without prior knowledge of any of the others. However, if you are someone who likes to read the books in chronological order, I am including a list of these series in order for you.

The books in the Legendary Bastards of the Crown series are:
    Destiny's Kiss – Series Prequel
    Restless Sea Lord – Book 1 (Rowen): *Reviewer's Choice, Books and Benches*
    Ruthless Knight – Book 2 (Rook)
    Reckless Highlander – Book 3 (Reed)

This is followed by the Seasons of Fortitude Series:
    Highland Spring – Book 1 *International Digital Awards Finalist*
    Summer's Reign – Book 2 *RONE Award Finalist*
    Autumn's Touch – Book 3
    Winter's Flame – Book 4

Second in Command Series:

Pirate in the Mist – Book 1 (Brody)

Secrets of the Heart Series:

Highland Secrets – Book 1 (Fia – Reed's daughter): *RONE Award Finalist, Raven Awards Runner Up, Wishing Shelf Award Finalist*

Seductive Secrets – Book 2 (Willow – Rook's daughter): *RONE Award Finalist*

Rebellious Secrets – Book 3 (Maira – Rowen's daughter)

Forgotten Secrets – Book 4 (Morag – Reed's daughter): *RONE Award Finalist*

Thank you, and please feel free to leave a review for Tristan on Amazon if you get the chance.

Elizabeth

ABOUT ELIZABETH

Elizabeth Rose is a multi-published, bestselling author, writing medieval, historical, contemporary, paranormal, and western romance. Her books are available as EBooks, paperbacks, and audiobooks as well.

Her favorite characters in her works include dark, dangerous and tortured heroes, and feisty, independent heroines who know how to wield a sword. She loves writing 14th century medieval novels, and is well-known for her many series.

Her twelve-book small town contemporary series, Tarnished Saints, was inspired by incidents in her own life.

After being traditionally published, she started self-publishing, creating her own covers and book trailers on a dare from her two sons.

Elizabeth loves the outdoors. In the summertime, you can find her in her secret garden with her laptop, swinging in her hammock working on her next book. Elizabeth is a born storyteller and passionate about sharing her works with her readers.

Please visit her website at **Elizabethrosenovels.com** to read excerpts from any of her novels and get sneak peeks at covers of upcoming books. You can follow her on **Twitter, Facebook**, **Goodreads** or **BookBub.** Be sure to sign up for her

newsletter so you don't miss out on new releases or upcoming events.

ALSO BY ELIZABETH ROSE

Medieval

Legendary Bastards of the Crown Series

Seasons of Fortitude Series

Secrets of the Heart Series

Legacy of the Blade Series

Daughters of the Dagger Series

MadMan MacKeefe Series

Barons of the Cinque Ports Series

Second in Command Series

Holiday Knights Series

Highland Chronicles Series

Pirate Lords Series

Medieval/Paranormal

Elemental Magick Series

Greek Myth Fantasy Series

Tangled Tales Series

Contemporary

Tarnished Saints Series

Working Man Series

Western

Cowboys of the Old West Series

And more!

Please visit http://elizabethrosenovels.com

Elizabeth Rose

Made in the USA
Middletown, DE
30 January 2021